Praise for Georg...

'Brava to this new, engaging vo... ...ren Odden,
author of *A Lady in the Smoke*

'A gripping page-turner with a sassy and fabulously original
heroine in the form of Lizzie Hardwicke – I loved it!'
– **Annie Lyons, bestselling author of**
The Brilliant Life of Eudora Honeysett

'Razor sharp and brilliantly original' – **Joe Heap,**
author of *The Rules of Seeing*

'Sparkling and twisty' – **Celia Anderson, author of**
59 Memory Lane

'A truly gripping story that is full of historical atmosphere and
a devilish plot... Full of pace from beginning to end. I can't
recommend this book highly enough' – **Peter Donnelly,**
The Reading Desk

'Irresistible' – **5-star Reader Review**

'The author has razor-sharp wit and knows how to use it...
An absolute delight' – **5-star Reader Review**

Also by Georgina Clarke

Death and the Harlot
The Corpse Played Dead

THE
DAZZLE
OF THE
LIGHT

GEORGINA CLARKE

VERVE BOOKS

First published in 2022 by VERVE Books,
an imprint of The Crime & Mystery Club Ltd,
Harpenden, UK

vervebooks.co.uk
@VERVE_Books

A CIP catalogue record for this book is available from the British Library.

ISBN
978-0-85730-830-6 (print)
978-0-85730-831-3 (epub)

2 4 6 8 10 9 7 5 3 1

Typeset in 11 on 12.75pt Minion Pro
by Avocet Typeset, Bideford, Devon, EX39 2BP
Printed and bound by CPI Group (UK) Ltd, Croydon, CR0 4YY

For Faith Claringbull and Jane Tillier.
My soul sisters and partners in crime.

1

Ruby Mills runs her knuckles along the mink collar, enjoying the softness of the fur. The coat is perfect. She will look like a queen.

'I'll try this one.' The words are addressed to the shop assistant, but she talks to the coat.

She doesn't need to see the girl. She's already noted everything about her: lank hair, too many teeth and a badly picked spot on her chin. Trussed up in soulless navy – the uniform of one of London's smartest stores. Ruby is indifferent to her. But if she bothered to turn her attention from the coat, she would observe the assistant staring, open-mouthed, at the shiny black bobbed hair, the powdered face, the deep red stain on the lips.

Ruby Mills, although barely older than the girl at the counter, could be a film star.

Ruby knows the shop assistant will be staring. She is used to the stares. It's part of it. Part of the fun. She swings around now to repeat her demand, adding a hint of impatience.

'This one?'

The girl starts out of her daydream, snaps her mouth shut and hurries from behind the wide mahogany counter to remove the coat from the hanger. She helps Ruby put it on, taking her own surreptitious stroke of the fur as she smooths the shoulders and breathes in the waft of expensive French scent.

Ruby admires her reflection in the full-length gilt mirror. Yes, this will be the one.

She frowns.

'No. There's something not quite right.' She keeps her words crisp and clipped – a world away from the Cockney drawl she ordinarily uses. 'It needs... It needs...?' There's a querying lilt in her tone now as she draws the girl into the game, stretching her neck to reveal a triangle of bare flesh at her throat.

'A scarf of some sort, madam?' The girl ventures. 'We have silk...'

Ruby tilts her head, considering. It's quiet in this corner of the store. She can take her time. Just the two of them in the side room and all these beautiful things laid out on the table and counter for her to look at. Scarves, gloves of buttoned silk, a chinchilla stole with light brown ribbons.

'Yes... I think you might be right, you clever thing. Something in scarlet, perhaps.'

'Scarlet silk?' The girl repeats, more earnest now, wanting to get it right. Her manager will be most impressed. She imagines the commission.

Scarlet is a daring shade for a store like this, and, although they sell them, Ruby knows that there is no scarlet silk scarf on open display. The girl will need to go to the back room to fetch one.

She pulls a face, turning this way and that to examine how the coat hangs.

'I have the perfect thing next door, madam, if you don't mind waiting.'

Ruby smiles now at the reflection of the girl standing next to her. It's her signature, her trick, the smile. Conspiratorial. She smiles as though she is sharing a secret.

'I really mustn't delay. My husband is expecting me home soon. Do you think you can find it quickly?' She touches the curl of hair behind her ear with her ungloved left hand, making sure that the girl sees the size of the diamonds on the ring she's borrowed.

The girl grins, delighted to be sharing the confidence. Her teeth are like disorganised tombstones.

'You won't know I'm gone.'

She scurries back behind the enormous counter and disappears through the door.

Ruby Mills pulls five pairs of silk stockings from the countertop and pushes them into the cotton bag that is secreted under her skirts. She folds her old coat and loops it through the thick belt she is wearing along with the chinchilla stole from the table. She grabs a handful of the silk scarves that are on display – not scarlet, but greens and blues, and someone will want them – and shoves them up the sleeves of her new full-length mink.

She buttons up the coat, pausing for a fraction of a second before sliding several brooches from the countertop into the pockets.

She reaches for a fur muff on the table. She has one at home, but this is sable and too tempting. It's also useful. She presses three pairs of kid gloves into the hand space. She acts quickly, in one easy, fluid movement, with the poise of a dancer.

She takes a last look at herself in the mirror, wrinkling her nose at the bulkiness that she's added; it's spoiling the line of the coat. Then she shrugs, checks her wristwatch, and makes her way from this section of the department store towards the impressively gilded doors that will lead her to the street. She glides through them, safe in the knowledge that no one will stop her while she's dressed like this. She doesn't look like a thief.

Just beyond the doorway, another woman is waiting for her on the pavement. She nods to Ruby and tucks an arm through hers, squeezing her, and starts to walk immediately.

'Nice coat, Ruby.'

Ruby smirks. 'Thought I needed a new one.'

'Why not?' the woman says. 'A girl deserves a treat now and again, don't she?'

They merge with the crowds on the pavement, walking briskly east, towards Knightsbridge, but not so fast as to attract attention.

'What else you get? You didn't just pull the coat, did you?'

'Course not. The pockets are enormous. I've got silk scarves, stockings, brooches – paste, but good. A fur stole. And there's this.' She lifts the sable muff.

'Quality.'

'Handy, too. I've got three pairs of gloves shoved in here. How about you, Maggs?' Ruby tips back her head, to get a better view from under the rim of her hat. Maggs pulls her along, almost imperceptibly increasing the pace, staring only ahead, eyes fixed on the street and the direction they are heading.

'Blouses. Silk underthings. They're in my skirts. And there's more than one hatpin holding down this hat. It's like a pincushion right now.'

Maggs always does this: keeps her face rigid while trying to make Ruby laugh.

'Shame it's not windy at all, then,' Ruby says.

'I could do with a pin in my bloody knickers,' Maggs grunts. 'One of the blouses is slipping. Might have to stop and hitch it up before we reach the river.'

'Are we doing anywhere else? It's not afternoon yet.'

Maggs shakes her head. 'Not today. We've done well enough between us, but word'll soon be out that we're in town and there's no point risking getting caught. We'll get these goods over to the warehouse for Grace to sort. And then I think we might deserve a trip to the pictures.'

'Smashing.' Ruby loves the picture house. She knows all the film stars. '*Passion's Playground* is showing. Norman Kerry *and* Rudolph Valentino! And Katherine MacDonald – she was so good in *Turning Point*…'

Maggs lets her prattle on but ignores her. Ruby's a dreamer, and someone has to stay alert. They turn the corner and she slackens her walk, her arm still linked through Ruby's. Buckingham Palace is not far now.

Ahead of them, two women push through the doors of another store. One of them glances down the street and catches sight of Maggs and Ruby, but she makes no sign that she knows them. Instead, she nods to her friend and the pair set off towards the bridge. Neither Maggs nor Ruby passes comment as they follow at a distance.

They won't acknowledge one another until they've crossed the river into Lambeth and they know they're nearly home. That's how it's done. They all know the game. Hoisting. Lifting. They've been playing it since they were children, one way or another. Say nothing until you're safe.

Ruby can see that Alice Dunning is limping. Her hip is causing her pain again and slowing her down. She says she fell off a ladder and injured herself trying to climb into someone's house, or climb out of it. She laughs it off and says she can't remember which way around it was, and anyway, everyone knows that's not the truth.

On her own, Alice looks like any other smartly dressed woman browsing the shops. Apart from the broken nose that makes her face look squashed. But next to Edith, she is clumsy, lumbering along.

Edith Lennox is wearing her new coat. It's been specially made, lined with small pockets, so that she doesn't have to push anything into her skirts. She's not going to make herself uncomfortable. She'll only have hoisted one or two items. Ruby watches Edith's feet criss-cross as she walks. This makes her body sway, and the coat skimming her dainty frame swings at just the right length to show off her ankles. Edith is as vain as she is lazy.

Maggs is watching Edith, too, as she tries to hold the blouse between her thighs. She lets go of Ruby's arm and clutches her skirt to keep the silk garments in place. It doesn't matter, though. The bridge is in sight, and they are a long way from the store now.

The lank-haired shop girl emerges from the storeroom, holding up the red silk scarf in triumph: a tribute for the goddess of the silver screen. Her arm falls as she surveys the disruption of her station. The goddess, along with the mink coat and several items from her counter and carefully arranged table, have disappeared into thin air.

Later, wiping her nose on the stiff cuff of her sleeve, she will try to remember exactly what the customer had looked like and tell her story to her manager and several policemen. Over her head, the inspector will confirm to the manager that his store has been raided by a gang from Southwark. It will matter little to her that this gang is notorious – 'the Forty Thieves', they call themselves – she has never heard of them until now. A serious-faced young woman will record her words in a tiny black notebook, offering no words of sympathy as the shop girl gestures vaguely, red-eyed and sniffing, speaking of diamonds and film-star looks. The woman will lower her brows in a frown, tuck the notebook and pencil into her handbag and re-pin her hat. As she leaves, she will give the girl half a crown for her words – small compensation for the loss of her job. She will also give her, as an afterthought, a folded handkerchief which, by its very plainness, will seem so much at odds with the luxury on display.

2

Ruby makes her way along Borough High Street as darkness falls. She passes the old timber-framed shops, set with angled lanterns that lean precariously from their fittings. The shops are crowded together, almost one on top of the other, as they have been since the days of Charles II, selling everything a person should want or need – sometimes in the same shop, according to the signs. She could, should she wish, buy a pint of tea for a penny at Shuttleworth's, inspect the umbrella warehouse and then find elastic stockings at Chaplin's.

None of these places sells the sort of goods she hankers after. Only Solly Palmer's jewellery shop – where she lives and allegedly works – sells the stuff that sparkles, and for silks, satins and furs, she must visit a warehouse or travel over the river.

Behind the High Street lies a maze of streets and courtyards. The wall of the nearby lumber yard is so high that, even in the daytime, the sun fails to touch the melancholy, dark-bricked homes, and on a starless night, this part of the Borough is impenetrable to anyone who does not live here. The dwellings are flimsy and run-down but crammed so hard against one another that they have never yet collapsed. These tenements are stacked not with fancy goods, but with hundreds of dirty-faced children. They are nests and nurseries of criminality – although Ruby knows that even the children can be bought and sold as easily as a bag of trotters or a barrel of beer.

She walks without considering her surroundings. This is where she lives – where she's always lived. But she's imagining herself in a casino in Monte Carlo where everyone drinks champagne, just like in the pictures.

She stops outside a public house at the corner of the street. Through the frosted glass, the lights are bright and inviting. She pushes open the door, a broad smile fixed on her face, ready to greet those already inside.

The Crown is certainly busy tonight. It's noisy, too, heaving with people having a good time. There is always a party when the Forty Thieves have returned from a raid up west, and the laughter is raucous. The scarves and gloves that were, this morning, tucked inside Ruby's coat and skirts, have already gone to Grace Bartlett's warehouse. By tomorrow, they'll have been separated and sold through one of half a dozen shops between London and Kent that do business with the Forties. The paste brooches and the muff will have gone too. Ruby begged Maggs to let her keep the coat. It's against the rules to keep your own steals. Unwise, too, to be caught wearing something you never paid for. But she told Maggs it was her birthday, and Maggs pretended she didn't know otherwise, so she's wearing it just for tonight.

Ruby eases herself into the wooden settle next to Maggs and takes a deep breath. The familiar mingled smell of beer, cigarette smoke and perfume hits the back of her throat, sharp and warm, and she snuggles into the fur collar.

Through the fog of tobacco, she watches Billy Walsh trying to talk his way into Daisy Gould's knickers. He fancies himself a smooth talker, does Billy. He's not tried it on with Daisy before, but her old man's just been sent down for five years hard labour, so he'll imagine he's in with a chance tonight. He hasn't a hope: Daisy's pining for Harry, everyone knows that.

She presses a fingertip to the rough chip in the rim of her gin glass, remembering the last time she wrapped her own legs around his waist. Billy Walsh has been a rite of passage for several of the Forties, and she'd be happy enough to repeat the experience. A successful day's hoisting, outrunning the coppers and not getting caught, always gives her the itch.

The women are sitting in their usual corner, set apart from the men. Maggs is deep in conversation with Edith, Alice and Grace. Ruby pulls her thoughts away from Billy Walsh and back to the table.

Margaret Wilson, also known as Maggs, Peg, Polly or Dolly – depending on which copper she's talking to or which court she's in – is a hard-eyed woman of around thirty. To Ruby, she's like a mother – her own one long buried – but to most people, she's more terrifying than a Zeppelin raid and about as lethal. Ruby once watched Maggs kick a man over and over, leaving him groaning in agony on the ground, before walking away to talk to Grace about a trip to the pictures, as if nothing had happened. Ruby never found out why she gave him a kicking. Perhaps he'd said something to upset Grace.

Grace Bartlett owns a clothing and fancy goods warehouse out towards London Bridge, which is well located for storing and re-selling anything the Forties have hoisted over the other side of the river. Her husband died some years ago, before the war. She never liked him much and only married because she was pregnant. She's never bothered to find another husband. Her son's old enough to be helpful now, and business is thriving and she prefers to remain in charge of her own life.

'You're getting slow, Alice,' Edith says in her mean voice, taking a draw on her cigarette and blowing smoke into the air while she watches Daisy giggling at something Billy has said. 'I can't pull you along, you know. You're too heavy for that.'

'It's my hip.' Alice rubs the offending joint, laughing away the insult. 'It'll right itself soon enough. And I still lift more than you, you lazy cow.'

'Neither of you lifted half as much as young Ruby,' says Maggs, throwing an arm over Ruby's shoulders and pulling her close. 'You could both do with taking a lesson from her.'

Edith levels her gaze at Ruby, saying nothing for a second. Then she forces her mouth into a smile. 'Yeah. Ruby's our best now, we all know that.'

'Cheers, Ede.' Ruby raises her glass, returning the cold smile with an empty expression of her own.

The men jostle one another around the bar, beer glasses in their hands. From the gestures and jeers, Ruby knows they'll be talking about sport – boxing, probably. There's a big match coming up next week. Watching someone else fight makes a change from fighting yourself, they tell her. They're always fighting. They call themselves the Elephant Boys – a nod to the Elephant and Castle at the end of the High Street, the southern tip of their territory. They fought the Germans alongside other local gangs, joining men from Clerkenwell, Bermondsey, Bethnal Green, and the

Titanic Boys from Hackney, but, now they're back home, the usual hostilities have resumed. The forthcoming match is focusing their attention. It'll be a night out and an opportunity to settle some scores with the men of Clerkenwell. Few of them will come home without bruises.

Charlie Wagstaff, a mountain of a man with a shock of ginger hair, is talking loudly about the betting on the match. He's the bookmaker, on the side, when he's not working for the brewery – the occupation he always gives to the coppers.

A woman, known to everyone as Doll, sits peeling her potatoes a few seats away from Ruby. A sliver of dirty peel falls to the floor, and she reaches down to gather it up, mouthing a curse and then laughing. She blows off the sawdust and drops the curl into the pile that's gathering on the sheet of newspaper spread over the table. She puts the naked potato into the pocket of her apron before taking another mouthful of her brown stout. She'll make it last, that single pint, before making her way back to the chaotic crowd of children in her house. Not all of them are hers. She minds the babies for the women who travel over the river to char and launder. She's always tired, is Doll. Not far past twenty-five, but she looks nearer forty. The old woman who lives in a shoe – like in the nursery rhyme.

A cheer rises from the other side of the saloon; men's voices, nearer the door to begin with, but then the women join in. They're chanting and clapping as a small crowd of people enters the pub. Everyone has been waiting for them. Ruby sets her glass down and claps along with the rising rhythm. Grace bangs the table, her rings smacking so hard on the wood that Ruby hears the *crack, crack, crack* above everything else. Maggs starts a low cheer. Ruby strains for a glimpse of the woman who will emerge through the crowd at any moment.

The chant grows louder, faster. 'A-nnie, A-nnie, A-nnie!' Even Billy Walsh is joining in. He's given up on Daisy and is standing with the men, elbowing and shoving, laughing as he spills his beer over a nearby table.

The cluster of women in the centre of the saloon breaks apart, and one woman makes her way through them towards the bar. A drink has already been poured for her – a glass of stout, as always.

She takes it, raises it in a toast to the company, and the company responds with a roar.

Annie Richmond has arrived. The Queen of the Forty Thieves.

Ruby's heart beats faster. She loves this. Loves the thrill of it. Loves to imagine that, one day, it'll be her name that's chanted and her drink that's waiting on the bar. When she's the Queen and famous throughout London. One day. One day... *Ru-by, Ru-by*.

The public house settles into a hum of conversation and laughter as the party continues. Someone starts playing the piano, a crazy tune, a regular old favourite, and several men start to sing along with loud, tuneless voices. There are many who will have sore heads on Sunday morning at the rate they're drinking.

Clara Hibbert, Billy Walsh's sister, winds her way through the group and wipes a cloth over the table that is now dripping with her brother's beer. She pauses when she returns to the bar and touches a finger to the picture that hangs on the wall, mouthing a prayer for reassurance. It is a photograph of Tommy Hibbert, her husband, looking proud of himself in his uniform. He used to be the king of the Crown: handsome, fearless and always laughing. The stories of his courage, and the medals he won, are no comfort to Clara. There are three smaller pictures next to Tommy: two other Walsh brothers and Tommy's little sister, Ada, who ran away one day and never came back.

Annie Richmond catches hold of Billy's arm. He turns away from his conversation with another man and bends his head to her, almost bowing as she speaks to him. He looks over towards the table as he listens, nodding, a wolfish smile growing slowly at the words spoken into his ear.

Ruby takes a breath when she sees it, but it is Edith who sighs.

Leaving Billy, Annie elbows her way to the Forties' table, shadowed by two men. None of this family is blessed with fine features or delicate bones. Annie is tall, taller than Maggs, and broad across the shoulders, terrifying in her manner and majestic in her full-length fur coat. Albert and Ronald are several inches taller and wider. Ronald's eyes flick about the room, as if he's searching for trouble even among friends and associates. Albert has a thin scar on his face that runs from his left eyebrow to his chin. He never smiles. Rarely speaks since he came home from France. When he walks down the street, the coppers touch their hats and stand back in respect. Or fear. Like he's a bomb that might explode at any moment.

The boys have returned from the war with an impressive set of medals between them, and stories of mud and death. The youngest brother, Stanley, never so lucky, was caught by a German bullet and lies buried in France, his absence noted in the black ribbons that are still pinned to their coat sleeves. But even without Stanley, the Richmonds carry authority in the Borough – Annie most of all.

She puts down her glass and plants both her hands on the table, fingers spread wide. Rings adorn every digit, many of them set with jewels. Diamond Annie, the coppers call her, although she goes by several other names whenever she's appearing in court.

Her voice is low, grown cracked and husky from the Woodbines. She leans in and speaks like a thief: always quiet, never wanting to be overheard.

'Maggs.' She gives her old associate an easy smile. They go way back – as far as the gutter they were born in, they both say. Annie might be Queen, but Maggs is the general of her thieving army. Annie turns to survey the rest of her troops. 'Ladies.'

Daisy slips into the seat next to Ruby. There are dark circles under her eyes and her cheeks are pale. Beneath the table, Ruby reaches out a hand and squeezes Daisy's fingers.

'Sit down, Annie.' Maggs drags a chair over from a neighbouring table, wiping her hand over the seat to make sure it's clean and dry. 'Join us.' The look she gives to Ronald and Albert makes it clear that the invitation is not extended to them, and they fall back, blending into the crowd of dark-suited men, happier to down pints with their friends than stand guard over their sister. She needs no guarding.

'Pay day,' says Annie, lifting a large cream handbag onto her lap. 'I hear your cell did well this morning, Maggs.'

The Forties are split into cells. There are six of them in Maggs's cell: five who go out hoisting and Grace, who is too old to run from the coppers these days, but who takes care of whatever they bring back. They all know that Annie will have gone over the accounts with Grace at the warehouse. Nothing will have been written down – nothing is ever written down if it's not legitimately supposed to be there – but Annie will have a note of the merchandise, the figures, the designated outlets, all in her head. She will know what each item was worth and how much to expect for it.

'We did alright.' Maggs picks up her glass and swills down her stout. 'No trouble. It worked well for us to split into two pairs.'

Daisy tenses her shoulders.

'How are you doing, Daisy?' Annie looks at the crumpled woman. 'You look like you need some cheering up, some new clothes, a pretty hat and a decent meal.'

'I'm a'right.' Daisy's voice is small, but she's proud. 'Managing.'

'Well, we'll look after you, like we always do. You won't go short while Harry's away.'

'I know. Thanks, Annie.' Her eyes redden and tears begin to form. 'I'm strong. I can work. It's only that… I'll miss him.'

She presses her face into Ruby's shoulder.

Grace gives her a fond look. 'Bless you, darling. What it must be to have a man worth missing.'

'And you'll be back out with the girls when you're ready,' says Annie.

'Next time,' the muffled voice agrees.

'Did you say something about pay, or did I mishear you?' Maggs is keen to see her money. She always is.

Annie cackles and reaches into the handbag to find several small envelopes. Each is marked, not named – nothing is ever named. She hands them out. 'Here you are. Try not to spend it all at once,' she rasps. She reaches into her bag again, pulls out her cigarettes and lights up, leaning back in her seat.

'Here you are, Daisy.' Edith pushes a small coin across the table. 'A bit extra.' Edith likes everyone to think she's generous.

Ruby scowls at the display. She doesn't want to part with her cash – not when she's brought back the largest share of the goods for the second time in a row, and not when she's cleaned out her purse for silk stockings and tickets to the picture house – but when Maggs, Grace and Alice all push a few coins towards Daisy she feels obliged to do the same. Daisy needs cheering up – a night out, not extra pennies.

'Your hip's still slowing you down, I hear,' Annie says, nodding at Alice.

'I'm alright.' Alice never wants to be thought weak or unfit.

'All the same, I can't afford to lose another girl since Mabel went inside. Perhaps you should wait until you can run again. You should rest her,' she says to Maggs, who is counting her money.

Maggs says nothing. She knows Alice is a risk to the cell, but Alice is her neighbour and her friend, and she needs to be out of the house.

'Besides, there's other ways to raise funds,' Annie says, tapping ash into a cracked china dish on the table. 'It's time we made more of little Ruby.'

Ruby has pushed her envelope into her handbag and is watching the bar. Billy is standing with his back to her, a beer in one hand, talking with a couple of the men. She has no idea what they are talking about, but his shirt sleeves are rolled up and she can see the muscles in his forearm contracting as he clenches a fist in his pocket.

She is alert and immediately attentive to the mention of her name.

'There's a jeweller's shop, South Ken, Gloucester Road,' Annie is saying. 'I've just heard about it. Small place, but very upmarket. Enderby's. There's only the old man running it, and his daughter. It'll be easy to pick it.'

'Sounds interesting,' Maggs says.

'Are we going to have a look?' Alice leans forward.

'Like I said, I thought we might send Ruby,' Annie says. 'She's done well with the stores recently.'

Ruby sits up very straight. This is it. This is her moment. She's started to lift jewels on the quiet, for herself, but this is the first time Annie has asked her to do a job for the group alone. It's an art, and she, Ruby Mills, is an artist – not a common thief. She's ready.

'I'm not so sure, Annie,' Maggs says, shaking her head. 'I don't know…'

'I'll do it,' Ruby says, before Maggs sways Annie's mind. 'I can do it. You've taught me enough, Maggs. I couldn't have had a better teacher.'

'It's different,' Maggs grumbles into her drink. 'You've got to play the part, make them give you the items rather than just grab and run –'

'That's what I did today,' Ruby says. 'I pretended like I was a movie star, and the shop girl just wrapped the coat around me.'

She strokes the mink collar and then regrets the slip she's just made. Annie hasn't noticed it, though. She's too focused on the jeweller.

'I think she's ready, Maggs. She's not been inside. She isn't known to anyone. And this is a new location for us to try. Besides' – she winks at Ruby – 'I've asked Billy Walsh to go with her. He'll keep her in line. And Ron'll drive them away when they're done.'

Ruby's heart begins to pound again.

'I'm ready, Annie,' she says, her eyes glittering, ignoring Edith, whose face has suddenly taken on a pinched expression. 'Just tell me when.'

Annie finishes her stout and raises a hand to her mouth to stifle the belch. 'You can go on Wednesday,' she says. 'Late morning, near lunchtime. Half-day closing on Wednesdays, so it'll be quiet. And you'll have a few days to sort your story out with Billy.' Annie stands up, her business concluded. She cranes her neck towards the bar, looking for someone. 'We'll go out again as a group soon, too. Next week.'

She nods to Maggs and then leans forward and crooks a finger under Ruby's chin. 'Make sure Grace takes that mink off your hands, Ruby Mills,' she says. 'You know the rules, sweetheart. Don't break them.'

Ruby says nothing. It's not a good idea to argue with the Queen.

Annie leaves them and finds her man, Frederick Moss, standing with her brothers. Freddy Moss, the King of the Elephant Boys, smokes quietly, while the others talk. He's always quiet and watchful, always thinking and planning. In a gang known across London for their muscle, Moss stands apart for his cool intelligence. That doesn't mean he's afraid to dirty his knuckles in a fight, although he prefers to run a razor blade across someone's throat – a quicker and more precise way of dealing with trouble than slugging it out on a street. He has a scar of his own, a memento from an encounter last year, stitched small and neat, just under his right eye. The man who gave it to him spent several hours bleeding slowly until he died. No one crosses Freddy Moss.

Annie slips her arm through Freddy's, and he smiles fondly at her. The men shuffle to make room for her to stand in the group.

Ruby catches Billy's eye as he drags on his cigarette and blows a whirl of smoke to the ceiling. She can anticipate the night ahead, and even the thought of it sends a sensation rushing down her body that makes her shift in her seat.

3

Saturday, early evening

In the reporters' hall of the *Kensington Gazette*, Harriet Littlemore rubs her right eyebrow and reads over the words one more time. She tugs the sheet of paper from the black Remington typewriter and lays it over another immaculately typed page on the table. She might be thought a slow worker, but she can, she knows, reliably type a clean page. She takes a sip of her tea and straightens her aching back. From somewhere down the street, far beyond the grimy windows, a clock chimes five.

Unusually, the room is quiet enough to enable her to hear the clock. It is Saturday, and the reporters – the men whose raucous voices normally fill this space – have already disappeared to the public house next door. Their words have been slotted into the lead columns of the linotype machines that live under the building and are even now being disgorged onto vast rolls of paper. The noise of the printing room will be deafening – she knows because she was once allowed to see it – but here, two floors above, it is only a distant rumble, and she is barely disturbed. The *Gazette*, an evening newspaper, will be landing on doormats in Kensington and Chelsea within the hour. The reporters have nothing to do, apart from gather stories, until Monday. And no one wants to gather stories on Saturday evening when there is beer to be drunk.

Harriet is alone, hunched over her cramped desk, typing up her copy. It is not, of course, *her* desk. It is James Curran's desk and is still always referred to as such. But James Curran no longer has need of it; he lies scattered in a thousand pieces somewhere over the Belgian countryside.

She takes another mouthful of tea, replaces her cup on the saucer and flips open her notebook to make sure that she hasn't missed anything, gently massaging her left shoulder. Three and half hours ago, she had been in Hartleys department store on the High Street, listening to a shop assistant explaining how a young woman had walked away with a mink coat, a sable muff, a chinchilla stole, some jewellery and several silk scarves. Elsewhere, another woman had lifted blouses. Hartleys, she thinks, will need to employ someone to watch the store, just as some of the larger establishments, like Whiteleys and Selfridges, have done. She had only gone in at lunchtime to inspect the new hats but had caught wind of the thefts. The shop girl, a plain-looking creature with terrible teeth, her face blotchy from crying, had been persuaded to tell Harriet what had happened. She'd blurted out rather a lot for half a crown.

Harriet runs a finger over her scribbled words.

On the small side, young, probably eighteen or thereabouts, dark-haired. Black hair. Jet black and cut short. Like she'd just stepped out of a moving picture.

She should go home. Ralph is coming for dinner, and her mother will expect her to take the time to look presentable, but this is the most exciting thing she has written since she began at the *Gazette* some months ago, and she is loath to leave it. All she has been asked to write so far are frivolous articles about hats and handbags. This is her own piece, written because she used her instincts and initiative and grasped the story when it presented itself. It has taken over two hours to get the phrasing just right, and she is on the verge of a headache. She pushes her fingers into the knot of hair at the back of her head, loosening it a little.

'Are you still here, Miss Littlemore? I have a teacup that needs rinsing.'

A man's voice calls out from the doorway at the far end of the reporters' hall.

This is her opportunity to put the piece in front of him.

Harriet puts down her notebook and picks up the two sheets of paper that are lying next to the typewriter. She walks to the other end of the room and places the papers on the edge of the man's cluttered desk.

'I wondered whether you might look at this, Mr Pickford.'

Robert Pickford, editor of the *Kensington Gazette*, is lounging in the chair behind his desk, reading a newspaper that has been folded over several times, making it small enough to be held in one hand. The other hand is tapping ash from the end of a cigarette into a saucer that is chipped almost all the way around the edge. She can see that he's smoked four in the last hour. A teacup, also chipped, stands independently on a pile of papers, on top of which is a first edition of this evening's *Gazette*. Now that his own paper has gone to bed, he can afford to relax. He will wander to the public house shortly to join the men.

'What is it?'

'Something I wrote this afternoon. There was a theft at Hartleys at lunchtime. Shoplifters. I interviewed the shop assistant and spoke to the police.'

He stubs out the fifth cigarette, hands her the saucer and reaches for the cup, still half-full, which he pushes into her other hand. Cold tea slops about.

She takes both items from him, trying to keep her thumb out of the ash.

He lays down his copy of the *Times* and pulls her report across the table. He sighs, picks up his blue pencil and begins to correct her copy at speed as she stands, chewing her lip, in front of his desk. Three carefully structured paragraphs are dismissed in a single stroke. He scratches his thinning hair with the end of the pencil, cocks his head then scrubs out another sentence. A little man, who has never become anything more than the editor of a small newspaper, and still he does not appreciate her writing.

'Good.'

The comment is unexpected.

'Good?'

'It's what we want. The feminine angle. Lose the sermonising. No one wants to know what you think about these women – why they steal, what might be done about the' – he peers at the paper – '"virulent spread of crime in the capital". You're writing the women's section in a local newspaper, not the editorial of the *Daily Express*.' He stares up at her. 'Stick with the film-star looks and describe the goods she's taken. That's all the female readers want to know about.' He shoves the paper across the desk and gives her a half-hearted smile before returning to his *Times*. 'Rewrite it on Monday morning.'

'Yes, Mr Pickford.' She sets down the saucer and pinches the sheets of paper between her third and fourth fingers before collecting the saucer again.

He waves a hand, dismissing her.

She lingers, clutching the saucer. He looks up.

'Is there anything else, Miss Littlemore?'

'Well…' She hesitates. 'These shoplifters. The women. I understand they call themselves the "Forty Thieves". These women at Hartleys could well have been –'

'I know. I have heard of them.'

'I spoke with the policemen, as I said. The inspector from Scotland Yard is a friend of my father's, and he told me –'

Pickford gives her a weary look. 'We have men in the magistrates' courts, writing our trial reports whenever they catch one of them. They will have all the information.'

She says nothing.

The greying moustache twitches a fraction. 'Go home, Miss Littlemore. Go and enjoy your evening. I'll print your piece.'

He doesn't have to print anything she writes, she reminds herself, as she scrubs at the teacups and saucers that have piled up next to the sink in the dank washroom along the corridor. The women's section is a new feature in the *Gazette*. Not even a whole page. It only appears twice a week, and never with her name. She tips the cigarette ends into a wastepaper basket.

She can write. She will write. Once Mr Pickford puts his shabby chauvinism aside and lets her. She was the editor of her school newspaper. She submitted several articles to suffragette journals – one of which was printed. She rinses a cup and leaves it to drain with the others, shaking water from her fingers. There is no tea towel.

At her desk, she folds the edited pages into her handbag, shrugs on her coat and fixes her hat.

Only when she is through the front door and on the pavement does she reach into her coat pocket to extract the ring that is carefully secreted in a folded handkerchief. A large lozenge of a diamond surrounded by twelve smaller ones. She slips the ring onto her left hand. It still feels heavy and new, but she assumes she will grow used to it.

She walks quickly, pulling on her gloves as she goes. The evening is drawing in and the air is damp and chilly. She has no reason to fear the dark and does not have far to walk, but her parents will be waiting.

Nearing home, she pauses outside a jeweller's shop on Gloucester Road. The jeweller is tidying away the trays of rings and necklaces that he was laying out when she passed this morning. He catches her eye and nods a greeting. She nods in return. Mr Enderby did not go off to France or Belgium like Ralph and the rest, being an older man, but he lost all three sons, and his eyes are still dark with grief. There is no one left to take over this small family business now except his daughter. Cecily Enderby is a nervous, twitchy creature, and Harriet does not suppose that she would have the least notion of how to run a business. The best Mr Enderby can hope for is that she marries a man who knows a sapphire from an emerald.

Harriet clenches her left hand inside her glove to feel the solidity of the diamonds on it. She is one of the lucky ones. She must always remember that.

She reaches the front door of her parents' house – a fine town house in one of South Kensington's grander squares – and checks her wristwatch by the light of the lamp. Her journey has been swift, and she does not need to rehearse an excuse. She puts a hand to one of the thick columns that supports the portico and turns to gaze out over the dark gated garden that graces the square. She has many reasons to be thankful for her lot.

4

Saturday evening

Isabel Littlemore is in the hallway when Harriet pushes open the door. One of the blocks of the parquet floor is loose and makes a heavy *clack-clack* sound as she walks over it. She frowns as she hears it. The uneven floor might irritate her more than Harriet's arrival, but when she sees her daughter dressed in her office clothes – with a hemline far too short for decency – and catches the miasma of cigarette smoke that follows her into the house, she is reminded of her customary cause for dismay.

'You're late, Harriet.'

'Good evening, Mummy.' Harriet knows that she is not late, but to enter into an argument on the threshold of the house would be unwise.

'Ralph will be here very soon. You'll need to change for dinner.' The words are issued as a command.

Harriet smiles brightly as she pulls off her gloves and unbuttons her coat. 'Of course. I stink of the office.' She knows that easy compliance is almost as much of a provocation to her mother as contention. She hands her coat and hat to the waiting maid and kisses her mother lightly on the cheek before making her way upstairs.

Isabel's lips tighten as she stares at her daughter's ankles.

'Put that out to air somewhere,' she snaps at the maid, who is clutching the coat.

The loose wooden block *clacks* again as the girl leaves.

Isabel needs to speak to Gerald but doesn't know whether he is downstairs yet; he may still be dressing. She needs to talk to him about Harriet. The wedding will take place this summer, but Harriet shows no signs of urgency whenever Isabel attempts to discuss the arrangements with her, and really, plans need to be made if this is to be the sort of event to draw admiration from everyone in London. Gerald is far too indulgent of his daughter, of course. Perhaps Ralph's visit this evening will encourage her to greater enthusiasm.

Isabel smooths her skirt at her hip – a habit born years ago – and takes a steadying breath. The silk velvet of her old evening gown reassures her. Although forty-seven, she is still considered a handsome woman, and this particular gown suits her figure well. She straightens her back and walks towards the drawing room. The dreadful smell of stale cigarettes has been carried away and replaced by the more pleasing odours of dinner coming from the kitchen.

Roast beef, because dear Ralph is coming.

Harriet changes into a dark blue dress, something more suited to an evening than the utilitarian grey flannel skirt of the office. She washes her hands and face and unpins her hair.

She doesn't smoke at work. The men don't offer, and she has never asked, so it seems unfair that her clothes should smell so terribly.

She could do with a cigarette now.

She opens her silk-lined jewellery box and picks out a favourite pair of earrings and a necklace.

The diamonds on her finger sparkle in the light. The central diamond is a substantial stone, and she knows that the ring cost the earth. Ralph proposed to her not long after her twenty-first birthday, and she had felt so very grown up when he put the ring on her finger. He told her that she could look at it whenever they were apart and know that something of him was with her. 'Almost all my wordly goods you're wearing,' he had joked, 'but not quite.' And then he had kissed her rather fulsomely, as if he had been trying to possess her.

She dabs herself with a light perfume and rakes her fingers through her hair. She lifts it up under her chin, considering herself in the mirror, before tidying it into a suitable style for the evening. A strand of hair becomes caught under one of the diamond's claws and is torn from her scalp.

'Do you think I should cut my hair?'

Gerald Littlemore is pouring sherry. He turns to regard his

daughter, pausing briefly, decanter in hand, before filling her glass.

'It's perfectly acceptable as it is,' he says, handing over the drink. 'Why on earth would you want to cut it?' He rubs a finger over his thick moustache, perplexed by her question.

'I was asking Ralph, I think, Daddy.'

Ralph Christie has made himself comfortable in the armchair. He is a comfortable sort of man, confident in his skin, with a profile that announces his impeccable lineage. He is already part of the family, at ease with her parents in a way that she has never managed to be since she began voicing her own 'radical' opinions. He talks affably with her father about politics, the party, the club; he was once thought of as Gerald's protégé, but recently he has caught the eye of even more significant players, and now, after a by-election and a safe seat, there is talk of a position for him within the next government – Westminster's rising star. He teases Isabel, gently, but in such a way that makes her simper like a debutante.

'I'm minded to agree with your father,' he says, taking a sip of his whisky. Isabel has made sure that the best-cut glasses have been put out. 'I like it already. Don't let my opinion hold you back if you wish to ape the fashions' – he laughs into the glass – 'but I'm quite sure that you won't.'

A small mouthful of sherry makes its glowing journey down Harriet's throat, and she doesn't respond. The drawing room has been lit softly, the lamps turned down low, setting everyone at their best advantage. The thick green velvet curtains have shut out the February night and their neighbours on the square, cocooning them together. It is too warm. It is always too warm in this room.

'But I really ought to have asked: how was your day, Harriet?' The thorny issue of hairstyles has reached a diplomatic conclusion, as far as Ralph is concerned. 'How is life at the *Kensington Gazette*? Any exclusive headlines for us?'

He smiles at her over his drink – the studied, conspiratorial smile of their alliance against the older generation. He would never dream of revealing it to his fiancée, but he knows, of course, how Harriet has come by her job at the *Gazette*. Gerald let it slip one evening at the club. Harriet had begun to read literature from the suffrage movement – radical pamphlets written by the Pankhursts and their followers from before the war, and such like. Worse, she started spouting their opinions. She had declared that she wanted to have her own career. Gerald had decided that the wisest course of action was to set her up at the fusty old *Gazette*, which offered little more than local gossip dressed up as news, rather than to continue to see her head turned by those lunatic women. He had had a quiet word with the proprietor of the *Gazette* and a small job had been found. Unusually for Gerald, he had acted without consulting his wife on the matter. Isabel disapproves of Harriet going out to work. Even now, at the mention of the newspaper, she is all angles, fingers curled tight around her sherry glass, lips puckering.

Ralph, who had made up his mind to marry Harriet by then, saw no reason to object to the scheme. She is not the cleverest woman of his acquaintance, rather young and impressionable, but this job will be harmless enough: just a little pastime that will come to a natural end when they marry, something to exorcise those more outrageous ideas. He has no quarrel with Gerald's handling of the matter. He would even go so far as to claim in public that he is proud to have a modern working woman as his fiancée. And privately, he imagines that the insight into the world of journalism, even at a local rag like the *Gazette*, will enable her to assist him in his own political ambitions. She might even see to his letters and speeches, and save him the bother of retaining a typist.

'Mr Pickford is publishing one of my pieces in Monday's edition,' she says. 'You'll see it then. Rather different from my usual.'

'Really, darling? How thrilling!' He beams at her. 'What's it about? Won't you tell us now?'

'Alright, I shall. There was a shoplifting incident at Hartleys, on Kensington High Street.'

'Hartleys?' Isabel is shocked by the information. 'But Hartleys is a respectable store. Who would steal from Hartleys?'

'Women,' Harriet says, before taking a larger mouthful of sherry, relishing it almost as much as she relishes the horror on her mother's face. She catches Ralph's eye. 'Young women. Two of them. They lifted a mink coat, some blouses, scarves, gloves and paste jewellery. That's why it's my piece – it's news, but I'm using it for the women's section of the paper.'

'"Lifted" – what a dreadful expression!' Isabel says. 'Poor Mr Hartley.'

'And a sable muff.'

'Young, you say?' Gerald enquires from the second armchair. 'Did they catch them?'

Harriet shakes her head. 'No. I went to look at the hats in my lunch hour – you should go, Mummy, they have some very lovely creations – but one of the shop girls was in floods of tears. They'd taken the goods from her station, you see. I think she may have lost her job. But I gave her half a crown and she told me everything about the thief.'

'Half a crown?' Ralph chuckles. 'Is that what information is worth, I wonder?'

'Well, I had the story,' Harriet says, flushing. 'And a full description of one of the thieves. Like a film star, the girl said. Short black hair and painted red lips. Around eighteen years old, she thought. And a pretty thing, on her account.'

'Well, now I *am* interested,' says Ralph.

'Oh, it defies belief,' Isabel says. 'Why must they steal? And from a lovely place like Hartleys?'

Harriet shrugs. 'I understand this one is part of a gang, a group of women who call themselves the Forty Thieves. Inspector MacKenzie was there, Daddy. They're notorious, he said.'

'They are,' Ralph agrees. 'And they're becoming a menace. Larger stores are having to hire store walkers, women trained to wander around looking out for thieves, like policemen.'

'I'm sure that Arthur MacKenzie will be doing his utmost to keep them in check,' Gerald says. 'We should have the MacKenzies round for dinner again, Isabel…'

'I think they sound rather daring,' says Harriet. 'It takes some bravado to walk into a shop and walk out again with a mink coat. I should like to meet them.'

'Oh, Harriet,' Isabel says with exasperation. 'Don't be ridiculous.'

'Well, I should.'

'Ralph, talk some sense into her, would you?'

'Your mother's right, I'm afraid, Harriet,' Ralph interjects, seeing his hostess begin to bristle. 'These are hard, criminal women you're talking about, certainly not the sort you should be meeting. They live like sewer rats in Southwark and then come swarming over the river to raid shops like Hartleys.'

'Do rats swarm, Ralph?' Gerald asks, absently, lifting his glass to his lips. 'I thought that was bees…'

The butler taps the door to announce that dinner is ready to be served and the question of how rats and bees travel in number is left unanswered. Harriet gives her hand to Ralph as they follow her parents.

'I wonder, shall I have the opportunity to steal *you* for a few moments tonight, darling Harriet? Just the two of us?' He murmurs softly into her ear as they walk. 'I've been thinking of you all day.'

'We can try and escape,' she whispers back, flattered by the knowledge that he has been thinking of her and warmed by the prospect of being held in his embrace, even for a few minutes. 'The garden, perhaps, but you'd better put on a good show for them first. Mummy's always desperate to impress you, so try to make the right noises. And please don't fall into discussing the Irish Question with Daddy over the brandy, or you'll be there all night and I shall have to retire to bed.'

He lifts her hand and smiles as he kisses his diamonds. 'Well now, there's a thought.'

She feels heat rising at the back of her neck.

5

Wednesday morning

Ruby fights to control her excitement as they walk along the street. She's like a boxer, preparing for a fight – or, no, she's a racehorse, jumping in the line-up before the starter drops the flag. She's ready: keen to be at the jewellers, itching to get her hands on the goods. She shivers a little and squeezes Billy's arm.

'Easy, Ruby,' he says, as surely and as quietly as he'd talk to a horse while he was stroking its neck. 'Don't want you giving yourself away, do we?' He doesn't look at her; he keeps his eyes on the road. He's watching the pavements, scouring them for trouble. There won't be any. This is Kensington. The only trouble around here will be the two of them.

She glances up at him from under her hat. She's never seen him looking so good. A new brown suit, a crisp white shirt and a tie that he's spent time folding just right. He smells good, too, clean and sharp, like he's just come from the barbers – which he has. Billy always says he's got a lucky face, by which he means that, unlike some others – Ronald and Albert, for instance – he's not been marked in a fight or in the trenches. He carries no scar or gouged flesh, and both his ears are neat and intact. That's why he's sent on jobs like this. He looks like the man he's about to become: Mr Warner, the film producer.

It was Billy's idea, the story they'll spin. He knows Ruby loves the movies so he's suggested that she's a girl on the brink of becoming a star. She's Ruby Wilder, soon to be appearing in movie theatres across the world. Mr Warner is not only her producer, but her lover who wants to shower her with diamonds.

They've spent the last three days rehearsing their story. When they've not been rolling around Billy's bed, in the room above the Crown, they've been planning the details: which rings they'll ask to see; how they'll separate the old man who owns the shop from the girl who works with him; how they'll bide their time if they see other customers; and where Ron will be waiting with the car. He's dropped them off two streets away, but he'll be just outside when they're done. Which is a good thing, because Ruby's wearing new shoes and they are already pinching a little. She won't want to run too far or too fast in these heels – jewels or no jewels.

The street is quiet, and the jeweller's shop is empty, save for the owner, who is bent over a table with a cylindrical eyeglass stuck into one eye socket, examining a ring, a pair of tweezers in one hand. As Annie has told them, he closes at midday on Wednesdays, and it's gone half past eleven. He's not expecting any more customers.

The bell on the door gives a bright jangle as Billy pushes it and the old man looks up. His expression changes from surprise to delight as he takes in the vision of a wealthy young couple, and he scrambles down from his stool, pulling the glass from his eye.

Billy removes his hat and greets him, and the game begins.

'I'm looking for something special for the lady,' Billy says. His voice has altered: gone is the rough growl of the Borough dog. He's purring softly in an imitation American drawl – an accent he picked up from soldiers he encountered in France. Ruby turns away to hide the twitch on her lips. She affects nonchalance, as though every day rich American men buy her diamonds. She finds a hand mirror on the counter, picks it up and smooths the black curl that's peeping out from the underside of her close-fitting hat. She's more interested in her own appearance, Ruby Wilder, the movie star, at least until the jeweller can show her something worth looking at. She's wearing a coat she took from Grace Bartlett's warehouse. It's a gorgeous shade of blue and Grace said it came from Paris.

'Very special,' Billy continues, leaning closer to the man, allowing him to notice the cut and quality of his suit. It's a good suit, one that Billy had made somewhere in Piccadilly, albeit with the cash he'd taken from an envelope addressed to someone else. But the man won't know that. He'll only see the tailoring, smell the scent of wealth. Billy is oozing new money – the sort of money made off the back of the war, but money all the same. He wants the man to smell it, sense it, so that he relaxes and brings out all the goods. 'I need the whole world to see what this little lady means to me.'

At this, Ruby turns and gives Billy an adoring smile.

'You've seen Miss Wilder, I assume?' Billy asks. 'Ruby Wilder? The movie star? She's gonna be bigger than Mary Pickford, you mark my words.'

Ruby simpers just a little, and the man, keen to oblige, nods. 'I'm not really one for the moving pictures,' he says. 'But my daughter's very keen. It's a pity that she's out at the moment.' He wheezes as he speaks. He has some sort of weakness with his lungs. He won't be giving them much of a chase. Annie Richmond has chosen this place very carefully.

'Then you'll know what I'm looking for,' Billy says. 'Something that sparkles even more than she does – if such a thing exists. Diamonds and – hell, why not – how about a ruby?'

'Oh, Mr Warner, you're such a darling,' Ruby is interested now, laying down the mirror and moving to his arm. 'A ruby for a Ruby.'

'But diamonds, too, sweetheart, to match the fire in those eyes.'

The jeweller ignores their cooing. He scrambles for the trays of diamond rings, necklaces and earrings. There's a pad of brooches, some nearly as big as Ruby's fist. He lays them all out on the counter. There's one shaped like a crescent moon and encrusted with diamonds that catches Ruby's eye. She reaches out a gloved hand and strokes it.

'This is very pretty.' It's very large. Just what they're looking for. Solly Palmer will pull it apart for them, sell off the stones in Amsterdam and make twice whatever this jeweller wants for it.

'I'd give you the moon if I could,' Billy says, laying a hand over hers. 'Perhaps this one will have to do for now. May we take a closer look?' he asks the jeweller.

'Certainly, sir.' The old man is willing to become more obsequious towards the rich young American now there might be a purchase. He pulls the brooch from the pad and hands it to Ruby, who holds it against her coat. Billy reaches for the little mirror and lifts it up for her to inspect herself.

It's a shame it'll go to Solly. She pouts a little at the thought of parting with it.

'You wear it very well, miss,' the jeweller says. 'Perhaps on an evening gown…'

She flashes him a smile. 'Oh, yes!' Her voice is breathy with excitement. 'I have just the gown for it – in midnight blue.' The gown exists in her imagination.

'I know the one,' says Billy. 'You're right. You can wear it for Mr Chaplin's party.'

The jeweller's face lights up. He might not be as committed to the moving pictures as his daughter, but he's heard of Charlie Chaplin. Billy ignores the man's sudden interest and focuses on the jewellery.

'You have some fine rings.'

Ruby giggles and lays the diamond crescent brooch on the

counter. 'You going to buy me a ring, Billy?' She nudges him, sharing a private joke, forgetting for a moment that she should not be using his name.

He gives a short laugh. 'Not that sort of ring, sweetheart. My wife won't share me, and I can't afford the divorce. But yeah, I'll buy you something you can wear every day, not just on a party gown.'

The jeweller checks his disapproval. No one can afford morality these days. He needs the money too much.

'What about this one?' Billy points to a neat ruby ring.

'An excellent choice, sir,' the man interjects, before Ruby grumbles about the smallness of it. 'Or perhaps the lady would like something…' He doesn't say 'larger', but simply points to a more substantial gem.

Ruby gives him her most radiant smile as he pulls it from the tray. She tugs off her glove and drops it over the brooch on the counter before slipping the ring onto her finger. It fits very well. She admires it, stretching out her hand for the men to see.

'I adore it. I truly adore it,' she says to them both. She means it.

'You can't wear it yet, baby,' Billy chides her, as if she's a child. 'Your birthday isn't until tomorrow.'

'Oh, but I want to wear it now!'

'No, I want to give it you tomorrow morning, when it's just the two of us…' He leans in towards her and whispers something into her ear, making her giggle.

The jeweller looks uneasy again but offers his suggestion of a compromise as he coughs and looks away. 'I have a small box for it,' he says. 'You should have a box for it anyway, miss, to keep it safe and clean. Let me find it.'

This is it. This is the moment.

The old man turns away to look for the ring box in a drawer behind him.

Ruby scoops up the brooch with her discarded glove and shoves it into her coat pocket as Billy stacks three trays on top of one another in a single swift movement. Then she runs to the door and pulls it open – just as a sad-faced young woman in a dowdy coat enters the shop.

'Good morning.' The girl's face brightens a little as she sees the customers, and her sloping shoulders lift. Her frame is fragile, like a child's. She is in the doorway, blocking their exit. The jeweller turns, hearing her voice.

'Where are you going with my rings?' he asks in surprise, noticing what Billy's carrying.

'Excuse me, we're just leaving,' Ruby says to the girl, the politeness of her expression at odds with the hard look in her eye.

The girl doesn't move; she stands rigid, fixed to the spot, her mouth gaping. Ruby doesn't know if she's terrified or just stupid.

'Move!'

The girl doesn't respond. The jeweller runs around his counter and grasps at the ring trays in Billy's hands.

This is not how it was supposed to be.

Billy keeps one hand firmly on the trays and shoves the man away with the other. The jeweller clatters back towards his counter and lands heavily.

'Pa!' the girl cries out to him. But rather than running inside, she steps back, out of the doorway and onto the pavement, and begins shrieking for help. She's surprisingly loud for one so tiny, and a few people across the street turn their heads to see what is happening.

'Go!' Billy calls to Ruby, and without a second thought, she runs out to the road, with Billy following right behind her.

The girl is still screeching.

As he runs from the shop, Billy charges her with his shoulder, jewellery trays still in his hands. He is much larger than she is, and she is knocked to the ground. A woman, turning the corner, freezes in mute shock, trying to make sense of what's happening, before rushing to the girl's aid.

'Ron's here,' Billy shouts.

The car is waiting for them across the street, as planned. Ronald's enormous car – the one he bought from an officer in the war.

'Stop, thief! I've been robbed!' The jeweller is out of the door, pointing at them, shouting as loud as he can to the whole street. 'Thief!'

The woman on the pavement with the terrified girl looks up, and her eyes find Ruby's.

Ruby stares back at her for a spilt second before running to the car door. Billy sprints around to the other side and Ronald pulls away as he climbs in.

'Let's go,' is all he says, as his foot slams the pedal.

Ruby watches from the rear window as the car accelerates. In one glance, she takes it all in, exulting in the scene as if she's watching it in the picture house: the man standing in the doorway of his shop, one hand on the doorframe, bent and panting; the stricken girl on the ground, who was too stupid to move and is now wailing loudly; and the woman, wrapped in a beautiful honey-coloured coat, crouching to hold her.

The woman does not take her eyes off Ruby.

The car turns the corner at the end of the street. Ruby leans back into her seat. The image of the woman staring at her, shocked and amazed, burns into her mind. She has been seen. A thrill runs through her body – a surge of something like electricity.

Harriet watches the car drive away. The vehicle is substantial enough to tell her it might have been used in the war. A Vauxhall. It has a London registration plate. She commits the details to memory, even as she tries to calm little Cecily Enderby.

She has witnessed a crime.

Cecily is not really hurt, but she's shocked and frightened. Mr Enderby leans on the doorframe of his shop, wheezing, trying to catch a breath.

Cecily's cries have brought further interested onlookers and local shopkeepers, and a crowd of Good Samaritans gathers around the fragile girl, who has recovered enough to tell the story over and over: the man pushing her to the ground and the woman laughing as they ran to the car. Cecily Enderby has never received this much attention in her life and is now revelling in it – the tragic heroine in her very own melodrama.

Harriet does not recall the woman laughing. She had looked… What was it? There had been something vital about her.

One of the more useful bystanders has taken it upon himself to locate a police officer in a neighbouring street and the local constable, whose face is familiar to Harriet, is quick to recognise the heart of the matter. He makes kind noises towards the wilting

Cecily, before making his way to Mr Enderby. He touches his hat to Harriet and encourages the jeweller inside.

Harriet was supposed to be posting a letter for her father. He has been composing it for most of the morning and will be annoyed at her for failing him in this one simple task, but she has seen the young couple make their escape – she has a clear recollection of them and is, therefore, a witness. She has a duty to speak to the policeman. She is also a reporter for the *Kensington Gazette*. She had not wanted to work today and had decided to take the day off, but she is not going to miss out on this story.

She stands, helps Cecily into the shop and then gazes out at the street for a moment. She watches the greengrocer opposite, who has returned to hauling crates of vegetables into his shop, closing up for the afternoon.

It was the same woman that the shop girl at Hartleys had described to her, she is sure of it. Not that she was wearing mink today. A beautiful coat of mid-blue wool – a copy of a Poiret by the look of it, probably stolen – and a matching cloche hat. She was holding a cream-coloured glove in one hand. Dark hair, black, cut short, and red lips. Young. It had to be the same person.

Again, she sees the girl's face, staring at her from the car, daring her to stare back.

She had looked exhilarated by it all.

When had she, Harriet, last felt *exhilarated* by life? When Mr Pickford agreed to take her on at the *Gazette*? When Ralph proposed to her? When the war ended? She cannot now recall a single moment that would cause her face to look like that.

It would be wonderful to feel something. To feel alive.

She reaches inside her handbag for her notebook and enters Mr Enderby's shop.

6

Harriet does not wait for the porter to open the doors to the newspaper office. She pushes her shoulder against the door herself and hurries into the foyer. The doorman apologises, but she waves away his concern as she hurries up the wide marble stairs to the reporters' hall.

She nearly crashes into Jimmy Cartwright, one of Mr Pickford's favoured news gatherers.

'What's the hurry?' He pretends to dust himself down.

Jimmy is one of the few reporters who will pass the time of day with her – unless he has his head bent to the typewriter or is running out to pick up a story. Like most of the younger men, he has lately returned from France. He bears no obvious physical injury that she can see, but she has learned that this means very little. For some, the scars are hidden or embedded deep inside their heads.

'I have a story, Jimmy. A good one. I've just witnessed a theft, no, a *robbery*, at a jewellery store. Quite violent. I need to tell Mr Pickford.'

'Hey, slow down,' he laughs. 'Good for you. The old man's in his office.' He checks the clock on the wall. 'He's just returned from lunch. Meeting with the subeditor in half an hour.'

'Come with me?' she asks. 'Please? He likes you. If he thinks you're involved, he'll listen. Otherwise, he'll just ignore me.'

Harriet is already halfway across the room to the editor's office. It is as noisy as usual in the hall as the men smoke and talk loudly, even as they type. None of them takes any notice of her.

She taps on Mr Pickford's door and pushes it open. The room is even thicker with smoke than the hall. She presses a gloved hand to her nose. He is standing, hands on hips, cigarette in his mouth, staring down at some papers on his desk.

'Mr Pickford, I have a story.'

'How decent of you to show up, Miss Littlemore. I assumed you weren't coming in today. What are you doing here?' He barely raises his eyes from the desk.

'It sounds interesting to me, sir,' Jimmy says at her shoulder. 'Perhaps you should let her tell you about it.' He closes the door behind them.

Pickford lifts a hand, and she supposes this means she should speak. Still, he stares at the papers in front of him.

She opens her handbag and removes her notebook, talking as she does so, before he changes his mind. 'Mr Enderby, he owns a jewellery shop on Gloucester Road, he lost three sons in the war. I watched a couple – a young woman and a man – run off with trays of jewellery. They had a motorcar pick them up. A Vauxhall it was. She was wearing a lovely coat, it looked like Poiret, or possibly –'

Now he lifts his head to stare at her.

'Would you slow down, Miss Littlemore?'

'I'm sorry, Mr Pickford. It's just that this is so very important.'

'Important to you, yes, I can see that. But if you can be more precise in your retelling, then I can judge whether it will also be important to our readers.'

Harriet takes a breath and begins to explain what happened, as carefully and as slowly as she can. She tells him not only what she saw, but what Mr Enderby has told the police. Mr Pickford does, to his credit, pay attention.

'And I think this was the same girl who stole the mink coat from Hartleys,' she finishes. 'One of the Forty Thieves.'

'Perhaps we should let the police decide,' Pickford says, stubbing out his cigarette and reaching for another.

'They are becoming a menace,' she says, gazing at her notes. 'I understand larger stores are employing store walkers to watch out for thieves. They swarm over the river from Southwark, like rats.'

Pickford catches Jimmy's eye.

'Well, I don't think that two thieves can be classed as a swarm, Harriet,' Jimmy says. 'Although Mr Enderby is lucky not to have been hurt.'

'He was hurt,' she says. 'He's not a well man. And his daughter will have nightmares, I just know it.'

'Possibly,' he says, turning away and opening the door to the hall. 'But our job is reporting, not speculating. Concentrate on the facts for a news piece.' He wanders back to his desk, threading his way between the other reporters, collects his notebook and pencil and then slips out.

Harriet bites her lip. Jimmy knows what he is talking about when it comes to writing the news, of course, but she has a story to tell. She was *there*.

'May I write something about it, Mr Pickford?'

'Be my guest. If I like it, I'll print it. Not today, though.' He gestures to the reports in front of him. 'Tomorrow.'

'Thank you.'

He has returned to the work on his desk and has already forgotten that she is in the room.

She will go home and consider her words carefully and write out some phrases. Then she will submit her typed copy first thing tomorrow morning. She wants to ponder how best to frame the horror and the drama. And to recall the wildness of that girl whose eyes had gleamed with such excitement.

7

Wednesday afternoon

Solly Palmer takes the trays of jewels from Billy and lays them out on his counter.

'Lock the door, Ruby, there's a good girl,' he says in his gravel voice, without looking up.

Ruby draws the bolt across the top of the door. She used to have to stand on tiptoe to reach it, but not these days. She turns the sign to *closed*, pulls down the flimsy blind and keeps guard.

Solomon Palmer is a respectable jeweller in one of the smarter streets south of the river. He's been operating here for years. The people who buy his goods are hardworking folk looking for their own work of art – something classy, but without the West End price attached, no questions asked. Everyone knows that Solly will do you a good deal: help you pay for your wedding ring over a couple of months, that sort of thing. He has a reputation for honesty – useful for a fence – that he is keen to protect, especially whenever the police come to sniff around. He looks the part in a well-cut grey suit and waistcoat, clean shirt and silk tie, carefully knotted and sitting straight.

In Solly's shop there are glass display cases on every wall, containing the better items: necklaces dangling from hooks and stands, rings stacked in blue velvet trays and bracelets laid out to show off every gemstone and every gilded link. For those on slender means, there is a wooden box on a table by the window, full of brass wedding rings – any size you want – and paste brooches, popular with the factory girls with big dreams and no money. The shop is like a miniature palace, glittering and twinkling with gold and jewels reflected in fancy mirrors.

He straightens each of the newly delivered rings carefully and examines them under the lamp, his glass held right up to his eye.

Billy peers into the cabinets, hands in pockets, restless.

'You've done well here,' Solly says after a while, dropping the eyeglass to the counter. 'This is quality merchandise.' He tilts his balding head to and fro and scratches a neatly manicured fingernail on his upper lip, visibly calculating the potential value of it all in his head.

None of the merchandise will be sold in his shop. The goods will fetch a better price once they're split up and sent to different parts of the country or overseas. Besides, they're hot.

'So how about you give me something for my trouble?' Billy says, from the other side of the shop.

'Something for your trouble?'

'Yeah, that's right.' Billy crosses to the counter and smiles benignly. 'It's what Annie would tell you, were she here.'

'Annie never said anything about paying you.' Solly slides an emerald ring back into the cushioned tray. 'This is Forties' business, not mine.'

'Open your strongbox, old man,' Billy growls at him. 'I could find myself back in the Scrubs for what I did this morning. Show some respect.'

Solly looks up at the glowering, broad-shouldered young man

who is leaning on the counter and considers him for a moment. He then turns to the cash register behind his counter, shaking his head. He removes a wad of bank notes and counts out a couple onto the counter as Billy watches, swearing softly when he is encouraged to put down two more.

Billy collects the notes, folds them then shoves them inside his coat, favouring Solly with one of his winning smiles.

Solly turns away, flustered, and replaces the remaining notes in the till. He calls to Ruby across the shop. 'And what have you brought for me, Magpie?'

Ruby has left the doorway and is running her fingers over the paste brooches on the table, her back to the men. She presses gently on one or two of them to see how well the glass catches the light. Solly has called her Magpie ever since he found her, a dirty six-year-old skeleton in rags, pressing her nose against the grime of his window, peering in at the trays of rings, more interested in jewels than food. She is just like the birds, he tells her – attracted to anything that sparkles.

She waves at the trays on the counter. 'That's it. I was with Billy – we were working as a team.'

Solly frowns at her and holds out his hand. He knows her too well. She's the same thieving wretch she always was.

'Give it up, Ruby, whatever it is.'

'No.'

'You know the rules. It belongs to the Forties, for a start. And if the police find you with it, you'll be getting comfortable in a prison cell before you know it.'

'You lifted the brooch, Ruby,' Billy says. 'The big one, moon-shaped – I saw you drop your glove over it. Like Solly says, give it up.'

She flashes her eyes at him. 'I don't want to give it up. I shan't wear it. I just want to keep it. I don't see why I can't.'

'Don't give me that face. There'll be trouble if you don't hand it over. Solly's right. If the coppers don't have you for it, then Maggs and Annie certainly will. Annie'll beat you black and blue.'

'They'll only know if you tell 'em, Billy Walsh, and you wouldn't do that, would you?' She smiles and flutters her lashes.

'No, but I will,' says Solly, firmly. 'Come on.'

The tone of his voice persuades Ruby. She might be able to wind Billy around her little finger, but not Solly.

She pulls the crescent brooch from her pocket, scowling at the two of them. She turns it over in her hand and enjoys the weight of it, this solid, glittering object. The light catches the diamonds, and she is transported to the world of her dreams.

'I wanted to wear this on a dress made of midnight blue satin,' she says, placing it carefully on the counter, not quite letting go of it. 'At Charlie Chaplin's party.'

'Another time, Magpie.' Solly prises it from under her fingers. 'Another party. This piece has got to go elsewhere.' He examines it with his eyeglass and whistles. 'You've a good eye, my girl, if you picked this one. Someone trained you well, eh? Very nice. Some good stones in this. I can split them and sell them very easily. New contact in Amsterdam.'

'Well, you'd better hand over some notes to me then as well as Billy,' Ruby pouts. 'You owe me, Solly.'

He gives a short, cackling laugh. 'You'll get your share from Annie.'

'That's not fair. You've given Billy something. I took this brooch, not him.'

Billy laughs, too, but his voice is gruff – a warning to the jeweller. 'She's right, Sol. Give her a little something. Pay up. You know she wanted the piece herself.'

Solly mutters under his breath as he opens the cash register again and lays three notes on the counter; he hesitates, then lays a fourth. 'That's it. The pair of you will make an end of me. I'll be out of business.'

Ruby scoops up the notes, folds them over and over again into a tight roll and pushes them into her handbag, right down, below her purse and handkerchief. You can't be too careful with so many thieves about. 'True, Solly. That's why you've got a new suit and a new car. You do so badly out of us.'

He chuckles. 'Little Magpie. Go and play with Billy Boy and leave me in peace. I have work to do. Coppers'll be here very soon, as you know, wanting to search my books, turn over my display cases, examine my storeroom... I need to squirrel these away.'

'I'll help,' says Ruby. 'I know all your hiding places.'

Billy tugs her hand. 'Come on, Ruby, leave the old man to his stones. Let's go and play, like he says –'

'Later, Billy.' She shakes his hand away. 'I'll come over to the Crown in a bit. Solly'll be faster if I help. Go on, go and have a pint.' She fingers the lapel of his jacket. She knows he's desperate. He was all over her in the car. It won't hurt to keep him waiting. 'I'll see you later, lover.'

He kisses her. 'Alright. Good job I know you're staying here to fiddle with the display cases and not with Solly, or I'd break his legs.'

'I've only got eyes for you, Billy Walsh.'

'You've only got eyes for diamonds, Ruby Mills.' He kisses her again before unlocking the door. 'I know you.'

She sees him out, locks the door again and pulls down the blinds at the doorway and windows.

They work quickly, practised in their movements, communicating without speaking, like two people who understand one another more intimately than lovers. Solly has never been her lover; he is more likely to be interested in Billy than her, she knows, and he's the age she imagines her grandfather would be, if she'd ever known one. He taught her to survive long before she met Maggs and Annie: how to slip unnoticed into a crowd and pick a pocket, how to use distractions and diversions, how to have a simple excuse or lie ready on your tongue if you're stopped by the coppers. He imparted other valuable knowledge too – like how to calculate odds on betting slips and how to tell the worth of a diamond by its cut. She could do all of this before she turned eight. He's been far more useful than her brief spell at school ever was. Everything else, she's caught from the Forty Thieves or the moving pictures. Or, lately, from Billy Walsh.

If her mother hadn't died, if she'd gone to school regularly, if she'd hung around with decent children who had honest, God-fearing parents, then she'd have been sent out west in service to some fancy house, or be working as an assistant in a store, or be spending hours earning a pittance at the leather factory in Bermondsey. Solly took her in, gave her a home and fed her because there was no one else. A kindness, perhaps, but she has proved useful to him. She always had an eye for jewels and a quick hand.

Ruby Mills was born to be a thief.

In no time at all, Solly is satisfied that when the coppers call – and they will at any moment – nothing will connect him to the robbery in Kensington. Nothing except the presence of Ruby in his shop. Now he must send her away. He lets her out and locks the door behind her. It is half-day closing – as he will tell the police.

He has not yet noticed that the crescent moon is missing.

8

Wednesday, early evening

Ruby runs her hand over Billy's scalp as he kisses her. His hair's cut short at the back, shaved with a razor down to the nape, like a lot of the Elephant Boys. She likes it short; she can see the scars on his head, feel them under her fingers. The wounds read like stories of his life – the battles he's survived, here and in France. He's proud of them, and the close crop displays them to anyone who sees him bareheaded. They serve as a warning that he's a fighter. He fights hard, like there's a storm crammed inside him. He swears he'd never hit her, but Ruby knows better than to believe any man who tells her that.

The scars on his back tell different stories; she's familiar with these, too, absorbing his history through the sweat of his skin. Stories of young Billy, on the wrong end of his father's drunken rages and belt buckle, and on the wrong end of the birch during his first spell in prison. His only spell, as it happens. He's never been caught since then. And three years with the infantry kept him mostly out of trouble.

He rounds his back as she touches him, kisses her again, groaning into her mouth as he pushes into her. She lifts her knees higher, needing more of him, matching his rhythms, urging him harder, deeper, feeling the mattress give under their bodies, until he suddenly shudders and cries out and then is still.

He rolls off her.

'Christ, Ruby, I'll have spent all Solly Palmer's cash on rubbers by next week at this rate.' He wraps the soiled item in a piece of torn newspaper and then reaches for his cigarettes. 'Not that I'm complaining, course.'

Ruby tucks an arm behind her head, watching him light up. He's not managed to satisfy her this time, and her thoughts skip quickly elsewhere.

'It was good, wasn't it?'

'You're always good for me, baby.' He grins at her, cigarette between his teeth.

'No, not that – I mean the raid. It went well. We did well.'

'What? Yeah, it went well. Solly was pleased enough. Annie'll be happy, too, once the money comes in.'

'I loved it, Billy. The look on that girl's face when we told her to move, and that feeling when the car took off down the street. It was amazing.'

He leans over and kisses her before handing over the cigarette. 'You're a natural.'

'I am. I dunno why Annie Richmond doesn't send me out for jewellery more often. The diamonds stick to my fingers. I'm born to sparkle.'

He laughs.

'I mean it, Billy.' She draws on the cigarette and passes it back, propping herself on an elbow. 'Why am I pocketing paste brooches and shoving cheap blouses into my skirts when I could be lifting pearls and diamonds? She doesn't see my talent like you do.'

'She does see it. That's why she sent you out with me. But she's running a long campaign. You're more use to her and to the Forties out on the street than you are in Holloway. She's protecting you.'

Ruby snorts. 'I'm more likely to be picked up by the coppers when I'm standing waiting for Maggs and Alice.'

'That's true. Alice is hobbling about like an old woman lately.'

'It's not her fault.' Ruby gives a short sigh and picks at the bedsheet. 'She's hurt her hip. Bastard husband threw her down the stairs. She's telling everyone that she fell off a ladder, but all her neighbours know what happened.'

Alice lives next door to Maggs. It's hard not to know about George Dunning's filthy temper when the walls are as thin as paper. It was Maggs who picked Alice up from the floor, once she knew that George had gone out to the Crown.

'She's always been slow, though. Maggs tells me I'm a daydreamer, but Alice is always just standing there, staring into space. She's Maggs's oldest friend besides Annie, of course, so she comes out with us. And we can keep an eye on her, keep her away from George when we're out.'

Billy lies back, smoking. He won't pass any criticism. George is a respectable ironmonger on the High Street and a respected burglar everywhere else. He is also one of the Elephant Boys, and loyalty is loyalty.

'We should go downstairs,' he says, handing back the cigarette. 'We'll be expected.' He swings his legs off the bed, rubs a hand over his chin and stands up.

News of their raid will have gone around the Forties and the Elephants. Ruby wriggles her toes and listens to the sounds of the pub below, watching him shave. Billy's room is small. He keeps it neat – three years with the army means he's used to everything being tidy and within easy reach. He cleans everything obsessively, like he's still trying to get rid of the French mud. He's always picking dirt from under his fingernails, and he shaves his face dangerously close, happier to nick his chin with the razor than to let the stubble grow.

It's already dark beyond the window, and Ruby imagines the street outside: the children playing marbles with stones; the women calling them in for something to eat; the working men on their way home from the brewery, the sawmill or the tannery, stopping off at the pub for a pint and a bet; the bookies' runners lurking in the alleyway. There's a good chance the coppers will be around this evening because there's been a jewellery raid. Billy's right – she'd better get up, get dressed and look as though nothing has happened. She stretches, stubs out the cigarette and sits up, planting her stockingless feet on the threadbare rug.

She thinks about the crescent moon in her handbag. She wants to take it out and look at it, cradle it in her hands and watch the light dance over the stones. She'd also like to wear it, to show it off and have everyone admire it – and admire her skill – but she can't.

All the proceeds of a job are shared. And the Forties do not wear what they steal. She knows the rules.

But she hates the rules sometimes.

She's been a member of the Forties for as long as she can remember, and she's growing tired of being ordered around by Annie and Maggs, sent out only when they say so and going only where she's told. It's the excitement of raiding that fires her up. The rush of energy she feels when she leaves a store with something special hidden inside her coat. She wants more of it – and she wants to choose and keep her steals.

'We should go out on our own more often, Billy. Just you and me,' she says, rolling on her stockings. She stands to smooth down her dress and slips her right foot into its shoe while hunting under the bed for the left one.

'Out on our own?' He's flipping one end of his tie over the other, studying himself in the mirror. 'What do you mean?'

'We should start our own operations out west, just the two of us and a few friendly fences. Lift some stuff we could keep or sell for ourselves. We could be famous throughout London.'

He eyes her through the mirror.

'I've got plenty of my own business to take care of, without you hanging around with me.'

'What business? You never said. I can come with you.'

'It's Elephant business,' he says, gruffly, staring back at himself. 'We're expanding our operations. Freddy Moss thinks we should be moving west. I don't want you involved with it. Besides, you do alright here, working with the others. The Forties provide security, and you never go short of clothes and money for the pictures, do you? You don't want to be out lifting without the girls watching your back.'

'You'd watch my back,' she says, raking fingers through her hair. 'I could help you, whatever the business is. Imagine: just the two of us, away from Annie Richmond's rules, nicking stuff for ourselves. We'd make a mint. And I'd be even bigger than the Queen of the Forties.'

He glances behind, scowling. 'That's not the way, Ruby. You've had a good day, but don't get cocky about it. We all have good days – and days when we're a gnat's whisker from gaol. Besides, you'll do as Annie tells you, if you know what's good for you.'

The finality of his tone tells her that there is little point in arguing now. She'll try again later.

'Yeah, maybe you're right,' she wraps her arms around him and nuzzles into his back, hiding her annoyance for a moment before turning him to face her. 'Here, let me sort your tie out. It's crooked. You can't walk into the Crown like that.'

She repositions the knot to her liking, waiting for his frown to disappear.

The saloon is filling up. It's only Wednesday so there's no rowdy party, just people coming in to meet, drink and converse. Mostly men. The honest women are in their houses, trying to create miracles with scrag ends of meat and yesterday's cabbage, but a few of the Forties are here. Billy swaggers in as though it's he who owns the place, not his sister. He pauses at the bar to collect a gin for Ruby and a pint for himself and exchanges a few words with Clara before hailing his business partner, Charlie Wagstaff. Charlie and Billy run the betting from the Crown. Charlie, the more fastidious of the two, is sitting at a table, hunching his burly shoulders over a copy of *Sporting Life*, with several sheets of notepaper also spread out in front of him and his pencil scratching a scab on his ginger scalp. Charlie has a head for figures and a stomach for beer, counting up and down in multiples faster than most people can blink even when he can barely stand upright. Billy's nearly as quick, but no one can sort the odds faster than Charlie.

'Billy.' Charlie raises his chin and shifts his chair to make room.

Billy hands Ruby her gin, plants his glass on the table, reaches for his cigarettes and then the two men immediately turn to studying the papers, heads together, locked in joint concentration over the odds.

Ruby wanders over to Maggs, who is sitting with Grace and Edith. Alice hasn't come out tonight. Daisy neither. She pauses, watching them before she joins them. They're old, Maggs and Grace. Past their best. And sour-faced Edith isn't as pretty as she thinks she is. Ruby stands a little taller in her heels, pulls off her hat and shakes out her hair. Solly Palmer is as precise with scissors as he is with gemstones, and he trimmed her bobbed cut this morning, before the raid. She knows that more than one pair of eyes is on her – even if Billy now only has eyes for the *Sporting Life*. These are her people. Her family. Everyone knows her here. One day, they will look up to her.

A small queue forms by Billy, men shuffling in the sawdust on the floor, as he and Charlie gather up bets – small folded notes bearing the names of horses and race times, together with the coins. Each slip, Ruby knows, will also carry the gambler's nickname – never their real name – so that they can be identified by Billy and Charlie alone. In the world of illegal betting, no one wants their name to fall into the hands of the coppers.

She could be so much more than a small-time player in a scrubby little place like this.

'Evening, Ruby.' Maggs indicates a space at the table.

Ruby eases herself in and nods to the others.

Clara's told them that Ruby and Billy have spent most of the afternoon in bed, and they know the jewellery raid was successful, but they want to hear the details from her – about the raid, not about Billy Walsh. Edith, at least, is familiar enough with Billy.

Ruby tells them about the jewels they've taken to Solly, not mentioning the crescent brooch that she's pinned on the underside of her dress, out of sight and high up near her thigh, in a place where no one is going to notice. She tells them about the old jeweller and his screeching daughter and an open-mouthed woman who stared after her when Ron picked them up in the car.

Ruby sips her gin, recalling the woman and her astonished expression. And her coat. The sort of coat that you can only wear if you have money. Dark beige, it was. The colour of warm honey. She had almost glowed with wealth.

Ruby lifts her head, her eyes closed, imagining what that would feel like.

A boy, barely more than seven years old, pops his head around the pub's door and asks loudly if there's a Mr Bull in this evening. Ruby's eyes flick open.

Faster than lightning, Billy and Charlie roll up their papers and scoop the betting slips into their pockets. The gamblers disperse as swiftly back to their tables. And within ten seconds, all evidence of gambling has vanished into thin air. The patrons of the Crown are enjoying a quiet evening drink; there's forced laughter from one of the tables, and someone has started to play the piano. This is the sight that greets Inspector MacKenzie from Scotland Yard and two other men in dark suits as they push open the door. It is the sight that Inspector MacKenzie expects to see – he is not stupid and, although he heard no whistle or shout, he knows his arrival will have been announced in some way.

'Evening, gentlemen. What are you having?' Clara greets the newcomers as old friends. In many ways, they are. The coppers are always welcome in her pub, and they are always happy to drop by. There's an easy rapport between the police and the Elephants. Each views the other with contempt, but they are, usually, cordial.

MacKenzie is a proud man. He lives over the river, in a comfortable corner of Kensington, but he's confident in his ability to move among the gangs of south London without fear. He is too old to have been in France – this slight against his manhood is marked only by a permanent frown – but young enough to believe himself to be a match against any of the Elephants on their own. He carries a gun, after all, and would use it if he had to.

He despises them all. Not for their brutality, but because they are so sly and slippery. Hard to catch. There's not an honest one among them. Not like in the old days.

The policemen stand and chat with Clara for a while, affable enough, drinking the pints she pours for them. They make easy conversation with the men who are leaning against the counter. They all know one another.

The young boy who asked for Mr Bull – Clara's son, Alfie – winds his way between the men and disappears back behind the bar long before any of them will notice their pockets have been picked.

Inspector MacKenzie makes his way to Billy and stands, pint in hand, saying nothing for a moment. Just watching intently.

Billy and Charlie appear to be reminiscing about a pal from the trenches; Ruby catches a name she's heard before – someone who kept them entertained in the slow hours.

'Billy Walsh, can you tell me where you were this morning, around half past eleven?'

'Evening to you, too, Inspector MacKenzie,' Billy nods a friendly greeting. 'Where am I supposed to have been?'

'A jeweller's store on Gloucester Road was raided late this morning. One of the thieves sounded very much like you, so I thought I'd ask, while I'm here.'

Ruby squeezes her thighs together. If the copper has a description of Billy, he'll also have one of her. She's glad he's gone to Billy first. He has nothing on Billy, of course. The evidence of the robbery has all gone to Solly's, where he'll never find it.

'Can't have been me, inspector,' Billy sips his beer. 'I've been in bed most of the day. Not long got up.' He grins and rolls his shoulders.

'Anyone vouch for you?'

'I expect my sister will confirm it; she called me an idle shit and a no-good toerag about an hour ago.'

'You spend all day banging Ruby upstairs instead of helping me behind the bar, what else am I going to call you?' Clara snaps from the counter. She's used to this game, too. 'Oh no, I tell a lie, inspector. He did get up. I forgot. He managed briefly to drag himself away from his little tart to ask me for his dinner.'

'Watch your mouth, Clara,' Billy growls back. His sister's barbed comment is unnecessary.

Ruby's stomach tightens as MacKenzie turns to the group of women at the table. He narrows his eyes as he looks them over. He's arrested Maggs before and is familiar enough with the others, but he's never had dealings with Ruby. So far, she has escaped his notice; now, she commands his full attention. She bats her darkened eyelashes at him.

'And you, I think, must be Ruby. The other thief in the jeweller's was a woman calling herself Ruby Wilder, answering your description.'

'Lots of women look like me,' says Ruby nonchalantly, knowing very well that they do not. 'Could have been anyone. And as Billy says, I've been occupied for most of the day. Had my hands full.' She lifts her hands to demonstrate that they are empty before miming a gesture that makes the copper's eyes widen. She sniggers as he turns away in disgust.

'Oh dear, inspector,' says Billy. 'Don't you like my Ruby? Not your type? I can assure you, she's the only jewel I'm interested in.'

MacKenzie's hand tightens on the handle of his glass. 'So, if I brought Mr Enderby, the old jeweller with a bad heart whom you terrorised today, into this pub, or his young daughter who's a jumping bag of nerves after what you did, they wouldn't pick you two out of everyone here?'

Billy reaches for the fag packet and matches in his jacket pocket, lights a cigarette and considers the three policemen, a polite smile playing on his lips. 'I really have no idea who this Mr Enderby would point to in a pub full of villains like us, even if you did have the guts to bring him here. But what I do know is this: you have nothing to prove I was anywhere except upstairs all day – the word of a man with a dodgy heart, perhaps, at most. And his eyesight is bound to be poor. You can search this establishment from top to bottom and you won't find a ring or a brooch that hasn't been properly paid for by any member of my family.' He pauses, as if turning something over in his mind. 'We've probably still got the receipts.'

Ruby can feel the crescent brooch hard against her skin. The diamonds are sticking into her flesh.

The door swings open to admit Annie Richmond on the arm of Frederick Moss. Ronald and Albert are a pace behind them. Annie doesn't even check her step as she takes in the scene. It is familiar enough. She knows Inspector MacKenzie, as do Moss and her brothers.

'Miss Richmond; good evening.' The inspector is scrupulously polite, respectful, even. He nods to the men. 'How's that car of yours, Ronnie?'

Ronald looks puzzled for a moment. He's not known for the speed of his wits. Ruby chews her lip.

'My car? What do you want to know about my car for?' Ronald scratches his ear and frowns. 'Bloody thing's useless. I should never have had it. Crankshaft's gone again. Been talking with a man who might be able to fix it, but he's had it these past two days, so I dunno...' He shrugs.

Perhaps he's not as stupid as he looks. Ruby chews harder on her lip to stop herself laughing. Annie was clever to use him. She normally prefers her black Chrysler for a swift escape but sending Ronald with his own car was a smart move.

The inspector finishes his pint and lays the glass down on the counter before turning back to Billy. 'Mr Enderby is a sick man, Mr Walsh, a sick and old man, who lost all his sons in the war. If he dies as a result of the shock he's had, as a result of an aggressive robbery, then you'll be responsible for more than the theft of a few stones. I know you did it – you and your charming lady love over there – and you know I know. I can find a way to make it stick on you. Robbery with violence.'

Billy holds his gaze and shakes his head very gently. 'I don't think so, inspector. You're fishing, and you're not catching anything but tin cans. You've got no evidence – nothing that would stand up in court. My lawyer would make light work of you very quickly.' His eyes harden, even as he smiles. 'You're disturbing my evening. Why don't you go somewhere else, before I decide to disturb yours?'

'Is that a threat?'

'Certainly not. When I threaten you, you'll know about it. Call it a friendly suggestion.'

The inspector stands, resolute, staring at Billy for what seems like a long time, his frown deepening and his face etched with revulsion, as though the scent from the nearby tanneries has reached his nostrils. 'We'll see.' He turns to the door and walks out, nodding to Annie and Clara on the way. The two coppers stride after him, trying to maintain their confident swagger as they pass the Richmonds and Frederick Moss.

Moss, with Ronald and Albert, makes his way over to Charlie to discuss yesterday's races at Kempton, aware that the coppers might still be outside. Annie takes the seat next to Maggs.

'Well done,' she nods to Ruby, voice low and rasping. 'You did well, with Billy and with the coppers.'

Ruby feels a flush of pride. Belonging, even. This is what they all strive for: a word of congratulation from the Queen of the Thieves. She soaks up the acclamation. Billy is looking over, too, his face beaming. She's stood her ground with MacKenzie for the first time. She is strong.

The sense of elation lasts only for a moment.

'I've been over to Solly's,' Annie says, tapping her fingertips gently on the table, as if beating to music no one else can hear, making her rings jangle. She'll reach for a cigarette any minute. She's edgy. 'Told me what you and Billy brought in. Sounds like a good amount. He'll sell it on over the next few weeks, in dribs and drabs; it won't be noticed.'

Maggs grins at Ruby. 'Good news,' she says. 'The shares'll be appreciated by the girls when Solly pays out.'

'They will,' says Annie. 'We'll all enjoy the proceeds. Which is why' – she gives Ruby a hard stare – 'I'd like to know what happened to the brooch.'

'What brooch?' Ruby will brazen it out.

Annie shakes her head gently. The tapping fingers lie still. 'Solly said there was a diamond brooch, shaped like a crescent moon. He said it was worth a small fortune; he was going to pick out the stones and send them to Amsterdam and put glass and paste in their place. That way, he can sell the knock-off in his shop and get a good deal on the real diamonds. Except, he can no longer find it.'

'He's probably hidden it too well,' Maggs scoffs. 'You know what he's like. That place is like Aladdin's cave.'

'No, Maggs. Solly says that it stuck to Ruby's fingers as she was helping him hide the goods. He says she didn't want to give it up in the first place. And that she's a thieving bloody magpie – his exact words to me.' She is still staring at Ruby, waiting for her to respond.

Ruby shrugs. 'He always says that. That's what he calls me. Like Maggs says, he'll have forgotten where he's put it. I bet if I were to go home, I could find it in five minutes.'

Annie keeps staring. She says nothing for a moment. Then she sniffs and reaches into her handbag for her cigarettes. 'Alright,' she says, fiddling for a smoke. 'Have it your way. You go home to Solly's, and you go right now, and you find that brooch in five minutes, like you say, and give it to the old man. Or I swear, Ruby Mills, I'll shake you so hard you'll be shitting diamonds all week.'

Ruby does not blink. She does not move.

'Go on, fuck off.' Annie lights up and rests back in her chair.

'And don't ever forget who you work for – and what you owe to us.'

Ruby drains her glass, as slowly as she dares, before standing up and pulling on her coat. The crescent moon is weighing heavier on the inside of her dress, and she wonders briefly if any of the women will notice the altered line of her clothes or hear it, if it knocks against the table. She eases herself carefully away from them, the fury growing in her chest.

She doesn't look at Billy as she walks across the saloon to the door. He will know, he will guess, what has happened. And he won't be happy.

9

Thursday morning

In a back street near the Haymarket, early in the grey morning, Ruby scrapes dog shit from the underside of her shoe on the edge of the pavement. It's only an ordinary shoe but it doesn't deserve to stink. She finds a small puddle and taps the ball of her foot into the muddy water, shakes the shoe, then lifts her heel up to inspect the damage. The sticky mess is all gone, but she'll smell it for the rest of the day unless she can distract herself.

She leans against a lamppost for a moment and watches a drayman rolling barrels into the cellar of a small public house. She has no desire to rush on with her errand. The iron hoops land hard against the cellar floor with a metallic clang and men's shouts reverberate from below the ground. The noise fills the street.

Easing herself from the lamppost, Ruby turns and pushes on the door of an unprepossessing jeweller's shop. The sign announces that it is closed, but she knows that the door will be unlocked.

Raymond Calladine is the owner of this particular emporium. To most of the world, he is a respectable jeweller, but to those in the know, he is a fence, just like Solly. He takes and sells on some of Solly's better goods, after they've been lying in Solly's secret hideaways for a while and are no longer missed by their original owners. Ruby has known Ray for years. Solly first sent her to him when she was little more than a child – before the war began. She had carried a small bag over her shoulder, innocent enough to anyone who saw her, even though she knew, aged twelve, that the bag was full of stolen watches.

Ray looks up and smiles when he sees her arrive. He has a face like a rat: small eyes and protruding teeth.

'Good morning, Ruby.' He greets her as an old friend. 'Come in, come in out of the chill.'

She edges inside and her body tenses instinctively as he bustles about, shutting and locking the door behind her, lowering the blinds, making jokes about the weather.

The deal will happen as quickly as she can manage it and then she'll escape back to the street and lose herself in a crowd. She lifts her handbag onto the counter, pulls off her gloves and begins to lay out what she's brought.

'How's my friend Solly today?' Ray stands so close to her that she can hear him breathing.

'Grumbling about everything, you know how he is. Prices rising, people unwilling to pay, too many thieves about, not enough decent stuff to sell. Same as always.' She drapes a gold bracelet next to a fine lady's wristwatch, aligning them carefully.

'And how about you, little Ruby? How are you?'

'You know me, Ray' she says, edging away. 'Always looking out for the sparkles.'

'This is a nice piece, isn't it?' He runs the nail of his forefinger down the bracelet. The nail is a little too long and lightly stained with tobacco at the tip. It needs clipping. 'The wristwatch, too. I know just the right sort of buyer. Knew it as soon as I saw it over at Solly's place.'

She can smell the scent of the pomade he wears on his hair. It is oily and sweet, and it sticks in the back of her throat, making her want to gag.

'Good. Solly's written his prices down for you. He says there's no arguing or haggling. I'm to leave and flog them elsewhere if you won't pay.'

He chuckles. 'I know, I know. He doesn't trust me any more than I trust him – but he's got a good eye and he knows what sells. Tell him I'll call again next week. Business is beginning to pick up again. People around here have money and they like to spend it. As long as they don't recognise any of these as goods they might have mislaid a year ago, we're all laughing, aren't we?'

He reaches into his jacket, pulls out a pile of notes, folded, and places it on the counter.

'And what about you? How do you fancy earning a spot of commission, while the doors are still closed?'

This was how it started with Ray, years ago. A few coins for a kiss and a hand down his trousers, and not a word to Solly. She doesn't need his money these days. She doesn't want it.

'Thanks Ray, not today. I've got places to be.'

'Ah, c'mon, sweetheart.' He wraps an arm around her and his hand strokes the side of her waist. 'I was thinking about you all night.' His thumb begins to rub to a faster rhythm. 'We're so good together, me and my little girl.' He leans in and kisses her ear, wetly, generating old sensations of repugnance.

'Fuck off, Ray. Not now. I've told you: I have places to be.' She pushes him away and gathers up the cash. 'People to see.'

'Billy Walsh, you mean?' There's a sneer on his face.

'I'm only here for Solly today. And for his money. So, now we're done, I'll be on my way.'

'Steer clear of Billy. He's no good for you.'

She rolls her eyes, tucks her handbag back under her arm, heads for the door and turns the key. 'Goodbye, Ray.'

She steps on to the pavement and takes a deep breath of the air. She can still smell the shit.

She has little else to do before meeting Maggs later as planned, so decides to wander through St James's Park and along the wide roads until she finds herself on a smart street in Kensington. She likes this part of London. There could be rich pickings here, if she were not having to dance to Annie Richmond's tune and hand over her steals all the time. The rules will be different when she's in charge. Billy might think she's growing cocky, but she can take anything she wants, if she puts her mind to it.

She shoves her hands into her pockets, cursing herself for

leaving her gloves on Ray's counter. Cursing Ray. She checks her reflection in a shop window. She's not wearing much make-up. She doesn't look like a film star, but she's dressed herself carefully for the day and her hat is smart enough. She tilts her head, beginning to imagine her story. Today, she decides, she is a well-connected young woman who has lost her purse and needs assistance. It's an old trick she's played a few times – although never in this part of town.

She could be an actress, if she wanted. Play in the movies.

She sees her mark long before he notices her. Of course, he will notice her. She will make certain of it. He is old, well over fifty, possibly sixty, and immaculately attired in a grey suit and dark overcoat. His hat is placed with care on his head, so he's either very precise or else has a servant to check his appearance before he leaves the house. Even at a distance, she can see that his shoes have been polished.

He has just left the bank on the corner, which is a good sign.

He reaches inside his coat and pulls out a pocket watch. The gold shines, even on this dank morning. He's a man of character and distinction. She likes him already.

She begins before he catches sight of her, rubbing her eyes hard to make them red. Then she walks towards him: a young woman, down on her luck, miserable about something that has devastated her world. He sees her, of course. She is fragile, beautiful and tragic. She pretends not to notice him, but then accidentally jolts his shoulder as she walks into him.

'Oh, I am so sorry,' she begins, her voice weak and faltering. 'I wasn't looking where I was going. I'm so *very* sorry.'

'Not at all, don't worry about it.' He lifts his hat politely and peers down at her.

Ruby peeps up with shy eyes, like a startled animal, and gives him a watery smile. 'Thank you.'

She makes as though to walk away, but, as she anticipated, he catches her arm and gives her an enquiring look.

'If you don't mind my saying so, you look quite out of sorts, miss. Is there anything wrong?'

A tear forms in Ruby's right eye, and then another in the left. Two perfect globes of water begin to make their way down her cheeks. She can cry on demand – it is a trick she has practised for many hours in front of a mirror.

She begins to pour her story out with the tears: a failed love affair, a violent lover, the need to leave his house quickly – so quickly that she has forgotten her purse. She sobs out her desire to return to her parents' home in Surrey and reconcile with her aging father. She is a miserable and penitent daughter, now without the means to journey home.

There is something sweet about the old man. Perhaps he has a daughter of a similar age. A daughter who is a little wilful sometimes, but dearly loved. Or perhaps he is charmed by the story of a reformed sinner with its hint of promiscuity and corrupted innocence? It matters not to Ruby as he lays an arm around her shoulder and conducts her to the shelter of a shop doorway.

He must help her. He will certainly help her. Where are her parents? She names a large town in Surrey, accessible by train, confident that it is a place he will know, but populous enough that he won't press her for more detail. She has been foolish in her decision to come to London. She bitterly regrets wasting her life and her money on such a callous and unfeeling young man. Oh, what will her parents think – and however will she return home?

The tears fall much faster now. He is soon reaching into his coat for bank notes, pressing them on her and insisting she takes enough for a train journey, some food and a little more for any emergency that might arise along the way.

'Oh, you are too kind, dear sir,' Ruby eventually takes the notes from him. 'How shall I repay you? Please do give me your name and address, and my father will, I know, make sure to send you what I owe.'

He will hear none of this. Ruby is grateful to hear that he does, indeed, have a daughter, not much older than her, who once foolishly threatened to throw her life away on a wastrel but was persuaded against this. He is still so thankful that her virtue was not compromised that he is glad to restore Ruby to her parents, who must, he is sure, be worried sick.

Ruby is glad that he's decent. He's not after anything more. She's not really in the mood for a lecher.

Instead, she sniffs back her tears, dries her eyes with a handkerchief and bids him farewell. She only quickens her pace once she's turned the corner of the street. Then she makes two further swift turns, to take herself completely away from him.

He was a dear – and far too easy.

She grins. She has reason to be cocky, and she now has money in her handbag, hidden carefully in the secret pocket of the lining. She won't hand it over to Annie. She stands still for a moment, wondering what she might do with it.

She begins walking again, thoughts racing. He gave her a lot of money. Real cash – not something she has to pawn. She can spend it however she likes. She passes dressmakers, milliners, glove shops and florists. She moves lightly, her body humming with excitement at the possibilities. For a couple of hours, she can be whoever she wants to be – an heiress, a starlet, an exotic dancer or a high-stakes gambler from Monte Carlo waiting for Rudolph Valentino. She pulls the man's gold watch from her pocket. It is half past nine. She has plenty of time to wander about the shops, trying on endless identities as she tries on hats, before joining up with Maggs and the others at Earl's Court. She will certainly buy a new pair of gloves. She might even slip her hand into a few pockets, like she used to when she was younger. She should probably move to a different area, or at least a different street, though, just in case that dear gentleman realises he's been picked. She thinks for a moment, then turns left, towards Chelsea.

10

Thursday, late morning

Harriet stands, arms folded, watching Robert Pickford. Her editor is in the reporters' hall, in deep discussion with his chief news writer, Jimmy Cartwright, about his story. She is furious. The fury is so intense that she dares not speak, for fear of losing her temper, her job and the slim respect she's earned at the *Gazette* in the last few months.

But it was her story. It was *her* story.

Pickford doesn't look up. He doesn't see anything except the words on Jimmy's sheet of paper.

She can't hear what they're saying; the noise in the hall is as loud as ever. Their conversation is lost beneath the rattle of keys and impenetrable hum of voices as the roomful of men talk, share information and hammer out copy on their typewriters. But she knows that Pickford is asking for details from Jimmy. Details that she knows and he does not, because she was there when it happened.

News of yesterday's raid at Mr Enderby's jewellery shop will be all over Kensington and Chelsea by this evening – with Jimmy's name attached to it.

Pickford wanders back to his office, talking to one or two of the other men as he goes.

Harriet waits, growing steadily angrier, until she sees Jimmy Cartwright making his way over to her.

He runs a hand through his hair and grins. The war did not dint his confidence in his ability to charm any woman. But he is not, Harriet knows, an innocent. There is a hard, ambitious side to Jimmy, underneath the boyish friendliness. She has not yet worked out whether he is angling for Pickford's job or whether he sees himself as serving his apprenticeship at the *Gazette* before making his way into one of the national papers. Whichever it is, as long as he is here, Jimmy is Pickford's ace. His golden boy.

But he has also stolen her story.

As she had agonised over the framing of sentences and tried to capture the essence of the raid in her own words, the vivid brilliance of that girl, Jimmy had slipped out to interview Mr Enderby, returned with the story and tapped out his report in swift staccato. It had been too late for yesterday's edition – but even so, Pickford had chosen his piece over hers. He wrote it faster and more efficiently than she did. And, in truth, it is this realisation that has stung her. He is by far the better writer.

'The old boy's in a good mood.' He jerks his head towards Pickford's office. 'Asked me to tell you that he'd like you to write a piece on jewellery for the women's section. Who's buying what now the war's over. How about that?'

'I'd rather write the report on the raid at Mr Enderby's,' she says, trying not to sound petulant. 'I was there, after all. It was my story, Jimmy.'

'And it was a great story,' he says, dropping the foolish smile and looking serious. 'Not quite what Pickford was after, but it's all in the writing, not the newsgathering. You're a natural at finding the story.'

She will not let him flatter her. It is just a trick.

'It was my story,' she says again, more firmly. 'I wanted to write it, and you took it from me. You stole it.'

He frowns at this.

'If I hear of a raid, I'm going to run out for the story, Harriet. That's how it works. Don't accuse me of stealing something when I'm doing my job. You should pay more attention to your own work if you want to get on around here.' He pauses for a moment before adopting a less snappish tone. 'Come on, don't be angry with me, eh? I can help you, if that's what you want – show you how to write the sort of copy Pickford loves?'

In a matter of months, once she marries Ralph, her time at the *Gazette* will be over. She is determined to finish with her words on the news pages – and with a byline – if it kills her. She swallows her pride. Jimmy is the star reporter. She could learn from him.

'I'm sorry. Yes, I would like that, I would like some help. It's kind of you to offer.'

The smile returns, along with the softer gleam in his eye.

'Happy to help. Once you've written your piece about the jewellery habits in Chelsea and Kensington, I'll take a look at it. Make some comments and help you craft it.'

He turns to walk away but stops and turns back to her, head cocked to one side.

'By the way, the car they used, to escape from Enderby's, what model did you say it was?'

It was a Vauxhall. She gave the details – including the registration number – to the police officer. She didn't think to mention it in her piece for Mr Pickford.

'I don't know. It looked like any other motor car to me.' She is still too cross with him to share the information.

He stares at her for a moment, unblinking. Then he smiles again. 'That's a shame. It doesn't matter.' He walks away.

Harriet takes a deep breath, picks up her handbag and hat and reaches for the coat she has folded over the back of her chair. She says nothing to any of the men as she leaves the room and makes no comment to the porter in the reception hall as he holds open the front door.

It is only when she reaches the pavement that she exhales.

It was a white lie – an omission – but she is unused to lying.

And she did it out of spite.

She paces the streets for ten minutes, walking briskly away from the newspaper offices, stamping out her annoyance with Jimmy – and her frustration with herself. The morning air is still damp. It might rain again before the day is over. Her umbrella is propped up next to her desk, but she will not return for it.

The sensation of being squeezed, crushed about the ribs, begins to subside as she paces, until she finally feels ready to return to the typewriter and consider a piece about jewellery fashions. She knows the sort of thing Pickford will expect: 'Engagement Rings for the New Decade'; why London jewellers are following Paris; the influence of American film stars on the choices women make. Light, frothy stuff. Nothing to upset or tax the minds of the Kensington and Chelsea ladies – people like her mother.

She really should not think about her mother. She turns down another street, travelling further away from the office again, stamping harder.

There are women, heroic women, writing serious articles for newspapers far superior to the *Kensington Gazette*. Women write about war, prison conditions and starving children in blockaded Europe. They have been foreign correspondents and literary reviewers. There is even a society for women journalists. If she could only push a foot through a door, the right door, she could…

She could what?

She rubs a thumb over her naked fourth finger. She has a marriage to look forward to.

She loves Ralph. Of course, she loves him. She has committed herself to him and, come summer, she will be liberated from her parents' suffocating hold. Ralph is a modern man, and their marriage will be the adventure she longs for. Besides, she won't need to report the news when Ralph will be making it, when he is in government. And she will be there to influence his politics, support his campaigns against injustice and corruption. They will stand, side by side, for dignity and decency, and build a new post-war world fit for women as well as men. And in a few years, once she turns thirty, she will be proud to vote for him herself.

She stops still and tries to shake away the wounded pride. Jimmy Cartwright was only doing his job. He is bloody good at it. And he needs the job far more than she does.

Harriet turns around and heads back towards the office.

'Hurry up,' Maggs grumbles when Ruby meets her on the agreed street corner. Albert Richmond and her own husband, Alf, are in tow. 'We've got work to do. Where've you been?'

'Out and about,' Ruby says. 'Nowhere in particular.' She hasn't bought anything. She's spent the last couple of hours just looking, dreaming, trying to decide what to buy. She didn't even buy a new pair of gloves. She remembered that she was working with Maggs and didn't want to arrive with armfuls of goods. But she has seen plenty of lovely things and will enjoy spending her money another day.

Maggs narrows her eyes. 'You never go nowhere in particular.' She tears Ruby's handbag from her shoulder. 'Where was this nowhere, exactly?'

The men walk ahead, leaving Maggs to her business.

Maggs jostles Ruby away from her as she rummages in the handbag.

'Aw, Maggs, leave it out,' she whines.

'You're a filthy liar, Ruby. What's this?'

'It's Solly's money. I've been at Ray Calladine's this morning, on Solly's business. That's his money.'

Maggs grunts but continues to rifle through the bag. She finds the secret pocket in the lining and tugs out the notes from the old gentleman and the few extra coins she's lifted on her way here. 'How about this, then? There's more than a score here. Twenty quid.'

'It's mine,' Ruby says. 'I'm saving it.' She has already spent it, in her head.

Maggs takes the notes and coins and pushes them into her coat pocket. 'Not yours. This is money for the girls. You've worked with the Forties long enough to know the rules. You were keeping this for yourself.' Maggs is angry. She's looked after Ruby for several years, and still the girl insists on operating on her own. 'Where did you have it from?'

Ruby pulls a sulky face.

'Picked a pocket a few streets away on my way here. Rich gent. He wasn't looking where he was going so I bumped into him. It's mine, Maggs. My money.'

She takes a sharp breath as Maggs grabs her arm and twists it. No one will notice. To passers-by, they will look like two friends, arm in arm. But Maggs could dislocate her shoulder with one movement. It hurts enough even now.

Maggs remains silent as they march along the street, following the men. She does not need to say anything. Ruby is very aware that she is in trouble.

They turn into a quiet crescent just beyond Earl's Court station. She's not really noticed where they are because she's so concentrated on fighting against the pain in her arm. There's another of the Elephant Boys ahead, leaning against a wall.

'The houses are chalked,' he says, casually, when they reach him. 'We've got four of them. One of the lads was watching earlier.'

They are letter-raiding. The postman has made his deliveries. He won't have known it, but he was carefully observed. In this street, the houses are set back a little, offering privacy to home-owners – and to thieves. On the pavement, in four places, one of the Elephants has scratched a short double line, not with chalk, but with a stone, marking out those places where no one is at home. No innocent passer-by will notice the marks – no innocent passer-by will be looking for them.

'That one.' Alf jerks his head to Maggs, who is still twisting Ruby's arm. 'Take her to that one.'

Maggs drops her arm, causing more pain than when she twisted it. Ruby does not cry out but curses, silently, violently.

The two women make their way up the path to the front door.

Maggs nods to Ruby, her lips still fixed in a hard and angry line. She doesn't need to tell her what to do – Ruby has done this hundreds of times. The letterbox is set low in the door, barely above ankle height. She kneels on the step, her face only inches away from Maggs's boots, and pushes it open. She slides her hand through the gap and reaches inside for the letters on the hallway floor, then brings her hand back slowly through the letterbox, trying not to scrape her skin. There are four letters. She silently hands them to Maggs and stands up.

They repeat this activity twice more, working swiftly, but make no attempt on the fourth property when they hear a low whistle of warning from one of the men.

Three out of four is not bad. The letters may contain money, cheques that can be altered and cashed or information that may be useful to housebreakers. Ruby, with her slender arms and hands, will be paid for her work. This thought almost makes up for the ache in her shoulder blade.

Once they are safely away from the street and have separated from the men, Maggs becomes her usual self, laughing about something or other. Ruby's attempt to keep her own cash – and the vicious twisting of her arm – are forgotten. By Maggs, at least. Maggs always forgets about that sort of thing. Instead, she loops her arm through Ruby's and drags her to meet up with other members of the Forties on Oxford Street for an afternoon of hoisting, promising a pot of tea and a plate of cakes at Maison Lyons on the way.

11

Thursday afternoon

They walk in pairs down Oxford Street, keeping at a distance from one another. Ruby is full of cream buns and has her arm threaded through Edith's. She enjoyed the buns so much that she's even feeling kindly disposed to Edith, whose shoes are pinching. Edith is bellyaching about her blisters. It serves her right; the shoes are new. They're smart, so Ruby can't help but admire them. Perhaps she can persuade Edith to let her have them – once she's worn them in and softened up the leather. It wouldn't be the first time she's benefitted from Edith's cast-offs.

Ahead are Maggs and Alice, followed by Daisy and little Florrie. Florrie is thirteen and already an experienced lifter in the smaller shops. This is her first outing with Maggs's cell in a large department store and, even from several paces behind, Ruby can hear that she's twittering like a canary. Daisy is allowing her to chirrup on, making occasional noises so that Florrie won't think her rude. Ruby can remember what it was like, going out hoisting with the older women for the first time. Daisy will remember, too, and she won't want to dampen Florrie's excitement. Even so, she is quieter than usual and her shoulders are sagging. Maggs will be annoyed if she turns around and sees it.

The Forties make a habit of entering places like Selfridges or Debenham and Freebody as though they own the place. *Dress to the nines and look like you have money to spend,* Maggs always says, *and no one will suspect that you're there to do anything else.* Ruby knows this is true. If you shuffle in looking like a pauper, then everyone's watching, wondering why someone like you would be in the store, knowing that you can't afford the goods on sale. Daisy is still mooning over Harry. No good will come of that – he's banged up for five years – and she needs to walk tall and look like a lady. Especially in the store they're raiding.

Pair by pair they turn into Wigmore Street and prepare to enter the vast white building that is Debenham and Freebody. Ruby gives a little shiver of excitement as she stares up at five gleaming floors of wonder. Windows glint in the dull afternoon, shimmering with light from inside. There must be hundreds of windows across the front of this building, all scrubbed and polished and showing none of the dust and dirt that has covered the whole of London during the war. Sculpted cherubs appear to fly about the portico, and above the grand doorway with its lacquered wooden doors stand two giant green-marbled columns. They are entering a temple, a hallowed place.

Florrie stifles a gasp as she tips her hat back to look up. Everyone looks up. Everyone's heart beats a little faster the first time they come here. It's not as exciting as Selfridges, of course, but it is beautiful and majestic.

It is one of Ruby's favourite haunts, mostly because it is quieter than Selfridges. She's even been known to pay for goods here. But not today.

They know what to do. They've had instructions from Maggs. They will remain in their pairs and operate on different floors, as usual. That way, if anyone is caught, the others can make their escape. Ruby gives Daisy a sharp poke between the shoulders as she passes, reminding her to stand up straight, before she and Edith saunter through the marble-clad entrance hall, still arm in arm, like two well-to-do young women out for a shopping expedition. They inhale the luxurious perfumes of Guerlain, Coty and Poiret that waft through the archway leading to the ground floor. They chatter about the cinema, about the picture they saw last week, as they ascend the wide staircase to the third floor, ostensibly to look at coats. The words are meaningless nonsense; they are communicating more by gesture and instinct, as only the Forties can.

A stand of umbrellas, brightly coloured, catches Ruby's eye as they arrive at their floor. The stand is unattended, so she picks one up as she passes and hooks it over her arm. The blue matches the colour of her best French coat. The colour of a cloudless sky when you walk through a park on a summer's day. She bought it the other day, she decides. Monday, or was it last week? She can't recall now and she's lost the receipt.

They make their way to the main room. The area is busy, but the atmosphere is hushed and reverent. Women of all ages mill around touching the coats, stroking them, bowing to inspect the quality of the cuffs and buttons, squeezing the shoulders before asking to try them on. This is why stores like Debenham and Freebody are so successful: they allow a customer to decide what she wants to examine, what she wants to wear. They give her choice and credit her with intelligence and discernment.

They also enable someone to lift with relative ease.

Ruby strokes a fur wrap. Silver fox, lined with grey silk. Not her personal style, and they are not in the store to take coats or wraps today.

'What do you think?' she asks Edith, who is admiring the fur collar on a long coat of the finest black wool. 'A bit old-fashioned?'

Edith plays the game. 'You'll look like my grandmother.'

'Shame. It feels lovely and soft.'

The conversation causes another woman to turn her head. She is wearing a dull grey coat and a very ordinary, wide-brimmed navy blue felt hat that doesn't fit very well. She is middle-aged, but not old. She is trailing a hand rather listlessly down the arm of a garment that she is unlikely to buy – the sort of coat one might wear out in a motor car. She doesn't seem like the adventurous, driving-out-for-the-day sort.

Ruby smiles at her and leans into Edith.

'Come on,' she says. 'I'm done with this, let's go elsewhere.'

She squeezes Edith's wrist twice, quickly and sharply, and Edith nods. She will leave now that she's been given the agreed signal, and the two of them glide away, out of the main room and back to the store's central staircase.

'They're using detectives now?' Edith mutters, limping down the stairs, heels clacking on the marble. She scowls at Ruby, her feet feeling the blisters.

Ruby checks the stairs behind her, making sure that they are not being followed.

'She looked like one. The woman with the navy blue hat. Didn't you see her? There was just something about her.'

'No, I didn't see her.' Edith takes a surreptitious glance over her shoulder. 'More places are using them now; I suppose we should have expected it.'

'We should warn the others.'

Edith pulls a face. 'Maybe. If there's a woman with the coats, there'll definitely be someone by the smaller goods – they're easier to lift.' Edith stops at the entrance to the first floor. 'I'll look for Daisy and Florrie. You go down to Maggs and Alice. If Maggs wants to move on to another store, come and find us. Otherwise, go to the second floor, not back to the third, and pick up the gloves as planned. Do you understand?'

Edith likes giving orders. She's ready to lead a cell of her own. She's said so to Annie more than once.

Ruby gives the smallest nod and continues down the stairs. She would not be in Edith's cell even if she were paid her own weight in diamonds.

She spots Maggs easily enough, next to a counter selling boxes of Coty talcum powder. She won't stand anywhere near her, but hovers several yards away, waiting for her to look up. Maggs, who can always sense when she is being watched, lifts her head and sees Ruby. She does not look directly at her. She doesn't know her as long as they are in the same store.

Ruby makes a small gesture, confident Maggs is watching even as she pretends to browse the goods. The men have their secret codes for betting; the Forties have developed their own for hoisting.

Maggs nods almost imperceptibly and turns away to look for Alice, who is browsing the perfume bottles that are arranged on top of several glass-fronted cabinets. The nod means Maggs is wary and on her guard, but that there's no need to leave the store. They just have to be careful.

Ruby trails back to the stairs and climbs up a storey to make sure that Edith has given the signal to the others. Edith jerks her head, and the two of them head up to the second floor, leaving Daisy and Florrie studying blouses and dresses, now alert to the danger.

The pockets of their coats have been specially adapted. Gertrude Squires is a seamstress with her own shop on Borough High Street. She's an established businesswoman with a respectable trade, but she grew up next door to Maggs and is an old friend of the Forties. Long beyond the age for running wild in department stores, Gert maintains her allegiance by fashioning the specialist clothing they all wear when they're out hoisting. There's not a dress or a coat that she can't adapt with deep pockets and folds. Ruby knows that she can fit at least a dozen pairs of gloves into the plain brown coat she's wearing today and no one will be the wiser.

But it is Edith who will be lifting today. She's decided to change the plan, worrying about the woman Ruby has seen, the store's eyes on the third floor.

'You'll do as I say,' she hisses when Ruby begins to argue. 'Maggs told me you'd hidden a score in your handbag earlier, trying to keep it for yourself. You're too much, Ruby Mills. You think you're the best of us, just because you're with Billy now, but you don't work on your own, remember? You're nothing without the Forties. Nothing.'

'Oh, Billy Boy,' Ruby croons, eyeing up the gloves as Edith looks about nervously. 'Quite a lover, ain't he…?'

Edith gives her a look that would freeze hell, but Ruby has already turned her back and started to walk away. She's not going to trade barbed words with Edith – she can do that later – not when she's seen what she is looking for.

A young woman, of a similar age to her, is inspecting a collection of kid leather gloves. These are the items that Edith intends to lift. Ruby wanders over and stands next to the woman, casually picking up a pair to examine the lines of stitching. They are pretty, set with neat, pearly buttons.

'Dear me,' she says, weakly, to no one in particular. 'I feel rather faint. Is it me, or is it unbearably hot in here?'

The woman turns at her words, about to say that she feels perfectly cool, when Ruby grips her arm and falls into a slump, dragging the woman down as she collapses to the floor.

'Somebody, help us!' The woman calls out to anyone who might assist. A shop assistant scurries over, and another woman who, Ruby can see through half-closed eyes, had also been masquerading as a real customer. Another store walker.

'She just fell. Fainted, I think,' the young woman says, disentangling herself from Ruby and standing upright. 'She said something about feeling hot and then… She just sank down.'

The store walker chafes her hands in front of Ruby's face.

'Should we take her hat off? Loosen her coat a little?' the woman asks. 'Help her cool down, perhaps?'

'Let's remove her to a chair,' the shop assistant decides. 'Will you help me?' she asks the store walker. 'Put a hand under her armpit and lift her up. I'm sure we can carry her between us. She's quite small.'

The two shop workers, along with the young woman, bundle Ruby to a chair at the side of the room.

A small crowd gathers to fuss over her. Through her lashes, she sees Edith at the glove table picking out half a dozen pairs. She pushes them down into her long outer coat pockets and then moves quickly and quietly to the other side of room. She scoops up some fur-edged gloves and winds several scarves into a tight ball, shoving them into the inside coat pockets. Her blisters are obviously stinging her heels and she's had enough already. As a parting thought, she picks up a pretty brooch from a display of glittering silver marcasite jewellery before disappearing from Ruby's squinted eyeline to the staircase and down, out of the store through the solid wooden doors. There, Ruby knows, the doorman will usher her onto the street with a smile and a slight bow. Edith will thank him graciously enough, but in a suitably haughty tone. Being too familiar with men like that only leads them to pass comment. Besides, if she is not careful, he will try to engage her in conversation – and she needs to be away.

Ruby opens her eyes wide and expresses some dismay at having caused a scene. She reassures everyone that she is quite well but accepts the glass of water that has been brought for her with a weak smile. Perhaps she might try to stand? Her legs wobble, and she sits down for a moment before attempting again. She will go home straight away, she agrees. She'll catch the omnibus directly and have a lie down for the remainder of the afternoon. She acquiesces as the shop assistant makes suggestions, offers diagnoses. Yes, Ruby decides, recognising her means of escape, it probably is the monthly curse. She should have realised because it always makes her light-headed. She really ought to be on her way, to take care of herself.

At this, the small crowd predictably parts and drifts away. The women are sympathetic, but there is nothing more that they can do except encourage her to stay warm and go to bed.

Ruby moves slowly, carefully, as one who might be unwell or at least in discomfort. She makes use of her new umbrella, leaning on it as if it is a walking stick as she takes the first couple of steps. Then, gingerly, she crosses the floor to the stairwell, growing stronger with every yard she takes. If it were not for the fact that she is almost certain she is being watched, she would pick up a few items on the way out.

Instead, she contents herself with the umbrella – at least on this floor.

She trots down the stairs to the ground floor, where she might find a few things to take with her. She has, she reflects, already contributed an unintended twenty pounds to the Forties today, so she's not done badly – but a compact mirror, a few lipsticks or a pot of rouge might please Annie Richmond more than an umbrella.

When she reaches the archway to the ground floor, she freezes.

Standing in her eyeline is the girl from Hartleys, the one with the spots and the teeth, the one who knows that she lifted a mink coat. Ruby cannot reach the main door without passing her, and the girl might recognise her.

She ducks her head, grateful that she has noticed the girl first. She's not in her Hartleys uniform and she looks even more dowdy than before. Perhaps she comes here on her half-day to look at goods she can't afford on her wages.

Ruby watches as the girl peeps around then stretches a hand across the counter to pick up a pot of Pond's face cream. She looks about her again and then, to Ruby's amused astonishment, slips it into her pocket. Well, well.

Ruby is about to approach the door when the large-shouldered woman in the grey coat and navy hat, who had earlier been on the third floor, pushes past her, jolting her shoulder, and grabs the Hartleys girl. The girl calls out in shock, fright, panic. She is not a thief. She is not a thief. She only put it in her pocket to take it to the counter. She is not a thief.

Another woman emerges from out of nowhere, red-faced and flustered.

'There are others in the store. They've taken gloves – a pile of kid gloves – and several silk blouses.' There is a howl rising in her voice, and she announces to the whole floor: 'There are thieves in this store!'

Ruby presses herself against a solid white pillar, trying to melt into it. Daisy and Florrie will have left the store by now, surely. Edith will be long gone – which is a good thing because she can't run in those shoes.

Maggs is near the door. She hears the commotion and her chin rises as she tries to see what is happening. It is time to leave.

Alice is still at the other side of the large ground-floor room, cut off from Maggs by counters, tables and stacked displays. She panics, recognising that something has happened. Who has been caught? She drops the manicure set she was holding and lurches away from the table. She stumbles heavily and bumps into a man who is craning his neck to see what the fuss is about.

Twenty or so handkerchiefs, tucked too hastily inside her skirt, slip to the floor by her feet.

'Another one!' The man shouts excitedly and waves a hand high in the air as though he has just won the Derby. He reaches for Alice, but she staggers past him, pushing him roughly, and begins to run for the door, desperately clutching her thigh. She cannot run far – not without leaping over the counters, and not with customers in the way. She would not make it to the door even without a sore hip.

The grey-coated store detective meets her halfway and the two of them jostle one another in the centre of the floor, to the fascination of everyone who stands watching. Alice is wrestled to the ground and the woman sits on her. She starts shrieking and swearing – the woman is on her bad hip, pressing it into the hard floor. People are shocked that a well-dressed woman might know such words, let alone use them at volume.

Someone has called the police. They push their way through the customers to reach Alice. One of them appears to recognise her and greets her like an old friend: he tells her to calm down and shut up before hauling her up from the floor. The man who had been next to the handkerchiefs has scooped them up from where they fell and has brought them to the police. He offers to tell them what he saw. Says that she thumped him in the chest.

The store walker opens Alice's coat and, like a magician plucking rabbits from a hat, pulls out bottles of perfume, swansdown powder puffs, packets of hairnets and several boxes of assorted cosmetics. The goods keep emerging, to the entertainment of the gathering crowd.

Ruby groans and rolls herself away from the pillar. She slinks away like a cat, unseen by the police, the store detective or the girl from Hartleys, and leaves quietly through the main door.

Poor Alice.

At least if she ends up in Holloway, she'll have some time away from George.

That thought cheers Ruby. She pushes open her new sky blue umbrella to keep the drizzle from her hat.

12

Thursday evening

Maggs nurses her pint of brown stout, trying to cup it in hands that won't keep still. Alice was her friend, as well as a member of her cell. She won't say it, but she feels responsible for her arrest.

They sit around a table in the Crown and talk about nothing in particular. No one wants to speak about Alice; no one wants to upset Maggs.

'It's quiet in here tonight.' Grace Bartlett picks at a blister in the varnish of the tabletop as she surveys the saloon. 'Not many of the men about.'

'There won't be.' Maggs looks up from her drink, her eyes heavy and red-rimmed. 'Alf told me they're going to the fight. They're getting themselves ready.'

The boxing match that they have been talking about for days is taking place tonight. Ruby knows that the Elephants will be arming themselves for the inevitable skirmish. Maggs knows it, too, but for a woman who has no problem with fighting – as long as she's the one throwing the punches, twisting the arms and causing the actual bodily harm – Maggs is surprisingly protective of her husband. It's not only the loss of Alice that's playing on her mind.

Ruby says nothing. Billy is standing at the bar, talking with Clara, downing a pint. He doesn't look like he's going out in search of trouble: he's wearing a decent suit and his favourite tie.

'What's this about a fight?' Edith leans into Maggs. 'You mean the boxing match?'

'I mean the fight after the match. I saw him packing a knife and his razor blades,' says Maggs, pushing her away with a scowl.

'Could be worse; he's got a gun he keeps in a drawer he doesn't think I know about. It's still there. I checked.'

Alf had spent most of the war as a prisoner in Belgium. He was fed and watered and missed most of the action. Like many of the Elephants, he'd brought a gun home and failed to hand it into the authorities. There are plenty such weapons around London.

'They're going over to Clerkenwell,' Maggs continues. 'Boxing match at the back of Frank Parsons' billiards hall, but there's going to be trouble.'

'What's new? There's always trouble after a match,' Grace rolls her eyes. 'Or during.'

Grace views all men with a degree of disdain. They fight too readily when they've had a beer, and they're haphazard about it, not being as organised as the Forties.

'This is different. Planned.'

Edith gives a little shiver. 'Why? Why are they fighting?'

Edith detests fighting. Every man she's stepped out with has had to put up with her whining about it. She was sweet on Billy for a while when he returned from the war, but she clung to him like a barnacle, trying to suppress his natural instincts for brawling with a combination of neediness and over-protection. Billy chose to move on, preferring to cling instead to an uncomplicated blonde with enormous breasts two streets away. And, lately, to Ruby.

'Alf said that someone took all the flowers off our roll of honour,' Maggs says. 'Couple of MacCarthy's boys, he says. Clerkenwell gang.'

Grace spits on the ground. 'The bastards. Why on earth would anyone do that? I hope they chop their hands off.'

The roll of honour began as a sheet of paper during the war, updated weekly and hung on a board on the railings of St Mary's Church. The vicar had started it. He had been a lively young man, desperate to volunteer for the war himself. He had written down the names of any lad in the parish who had signed up, so everyone could see them and pray for them. Then a second sheet had begun, noting those who had died or were missing in action. The vicar had gone out to France as a chaplain, and his parishioners had added to the list by themselves while he was away and laid piles of flowers on the pavement underneath the names. The vicar had returned, sombre, paler. The inked sheets of paper had been removed and a painted board had been put up in its place, with containers for the flowers either side. He had paid for it himself. The board was always covered with flowers, and everyone who passed it whispered the names they knew, touched their hats or pressed a hand to their heart.

'How do they know it was the MacCarthys?' Edith asks.

'It wouldn't be anyone from around here, would it?' Maggs growls. 'People here have more respect.'

Most of them do. Some people will nick anything that isn't nailed down, but no one steals from their own. And no one from the Borough would disturb so sacred a site.

Gertrude Squires, the seamstress, wanders over, a dainty glass of sherry in her hand.

'We're talking about the fight, Gert,' Edith says, pushing out a seat for her. She raises her voice a little because Gert is hard of hearing. She spent too much time in the mills, years ago, surrounded by the noise of the machines. 'Not the boxing match, the other fight.'

'I heard about the match,' Gert says, sitting down and making room for herself. 'Mad MacCarthy's fighting – he's one of their own, so all the Clerkenwell boys will be there. Ronnie and Bert Richmond have gathered our lads together to go and sort them out. Teach them a lesson.' She takes a sip of her sherry and shrugs. 'He's a good fighter, Mad MacCarthy. I've seen him myself once or twice. I hope the Richmonds let him go a few rounds before they start…'

'The coppers'll be all over it, if they get wind of it,' Grace says wryly.

They will. The combination of an illegal boxing match, betting and a fight between two notorious London gangs will be too much to resist, and the police will probably stir up extra trouble so they can make a few arrests.

A draught whistles across the pub floor as the door opens. Annie Richmond marches in, shaking the evening's rain from her shoulders.

Maggs stiffens as she approaches. Annie hasn't even bothered to stop and collect a stout on her way to their table.

'I heard about Alice.' Annie won't worry about upsetting Maggs.

Maggs's shoulders droop. 'That bad hip was slowing her down. She was unlucky, though. Tripped over and dropped half her goods on the floor.'

'Shame to lose a good hoister like Alice,' Annie says, sitting down in the gap on the bench that Ruby and Edith have made for her. She sniffs and reaches into her handbag for her cigarettes. 'She's been solid for years. Loyal. Reliable.' She moves small bundles of bank notes around to find the smokes. She is carrying a lot of cash in her bag, but no one will touch her so it's all safe. 'I said you should have rested her. You should have listened to me.'

The cigarettes are right at the bottom.

'Where are the others?' She looks around as she lays the packet on the table and rummages again for matches. 'Daisy, Florrie? Don't tell me you lost them as well, Maggs.'

Maggs bristles. 'I can manage my cell, Annie,' she says tersely. 'You know that. Florrie's home with her ma and Daisy's home on her own, as far as I know.'

'Alright. Alright. We'll keep quiet for a day or two. I can't afford to lose any more girls after Mabel, and now Alice.'

They are all quiet. No one says anything while Annie lights up.

Little Alfie, Clara's boy, arrives at the table with her drink. He ducks away when she ruffles his hair and runs back to the bar.

Billy is standing at the counter, draining his pint and talking to his sister. As Alfie crashes into him, he cuffs the boy on the head and looks over to where the Forties are sitting. His face is expressionless, but Ruby takes this as enough of an excuse to leave the tense atmosphere of the table, her gin half-finished, and wanders over.

'I hear there's a boxing match at Frank Parsons' tonight,' she says, running her fingers down the lapels of Billy's jacket. 'You'll take care of yourself, yeah?' She slides her hands inside, trying to find whatever it is he is carrying. Her hand nudges the gun that's strapped under his left armpit. 'Yeah?'

He pulls away. 'Course I will.'

There's uncertainty in his voice. She squints at him and again wonders why he is wearing his best suit. He smells good, too. Something's not right.

'The other men have gone already. Where are you going? What's going on?'

'I'm going to Frank's, like the others.' He hands his beer glass to his sister.

'You're too smart for a fight. It's not like you to ruin a good jacket.'

'I've got some business to attend to first.' He picks at a well-scrubbed fingernail, running another nail under it to clean out imagined grime.

'What business? Can I come?'

'No. I told you, this has nothing to do with you.'

'Where are you going?'

'Leave it, Ruby.' He gives his sister a curt nod before walking off, out of the pub.

Clara watches him disappear through the door, wearing the strained expression of a woman who has lost too many men to violence.

'Where's he going, Clara?' Ruby asks. 'He won't say.'

Clara shakes her head. 'He wouldn't tell me either.' She wipes the bar with a damp cloth. 'I expect he's acting for Freddy Moss.'

Ruby returns to her abandoned glass and sits considering its contents as the conversation grows more light-hearted again. Annie, like Ruby, has decided that Alice will, at least, have some peace in Holloway. She's been there before, so she might find herself inside for four or five months. But she will be away from George.

'Food's not so bad, as I recall,' Maggs agrees. 'She won't starve. And she can pick up some useful information while she's there.'

The floor is sticky under Ruby's feet.

She could spend her whole life sitting in the Crown, waiting for Billy or waiting for Annie Richmond to tell her what to do and where to go. She could spend the rest of her days living in her small room at Solly's, tidying up his shop, hiding his stolen goods and shipping them to Ray. Eventually, the coppers will catch up with her and she'll take her turn in Holloway for a month or two, just like Alice.

The future, like the gin, is beginning to sour. Her shoulder still aches from where Maggs wrenched it earlier.

She closes her eyes, listening to the Forties chatting and cackling, trying to lose herself in her dreams, in a world where she is living on her wits, picking up jewels, dazzling with life.

She opens her eyes and makes a point of yawning.

'I'd better go back to Solly,' she says. 'Help him close up. I could do with an early night.'

Maggs nods her approval. 'Goodnight, Ruby. You did well today, with the letters and with the cash you lifted. Pay day on Saturday, don't forget.'

'I never forget pay day.'

Annie pats her handbag. She doesn't believe in banks. She doesn't leave the money in her house either. No one on her street would ever take it, but her brothers would happily borrow from the Forties' fund if they could get their hands on it, so Ruby imagines Annie takes the bag to bed with her and uses it as a pillow.

'It's all here,' Annie says. 'Even the score that Maggs prised out of you.'

Ruby stands, pretending not to have heard. Annie reaches out and grabs her hand, squeezing it so tightly that her rings press hard on Ruby's fingers, crushing them between the bands of metal.

'I don't want to have to remind you again, Ruby. We share everything in the Forties. We don't keep money back for ourselves – or diamond brooches.'

She drops the hand.

There is no answer to this except grovelling agreement, so Ruby makes none. Instead, she drains the gin, holding the glass as if her fingers are not pulsing with pain. The filthy liquor swills against the back of her mouth.

'Goodnight, Annie.'

She picks up her old brown coat and her new umbrella and walks home to Solly's.

She'll hand the umbrella over to Grace Bartlett eventually.

13

When she returns to the shop, Solly is packing away trays of jewellery. She doesn't say much, but stands in her coat, touching a pair of earrings in a box. He's left them on the counter. Neat, square-cut emeralds surrounded by small diamonds. The sort of thing a proper lady would wear. That honey-coloured woman outside Enderby's on Gloucester Road, maybe. She would wear something like these. She picks one of them up and holds it to the gas lamp, observing it sparkle in the soft glow. It's a good piece.

'Are you running off with both of them or just the one?' Solly is wiping down the shelves and the cash register, like he always does before he goes upstairs. He'll have wiped them already when he closed the door for the evening, but it's a habit to do it again. Ruby thinks that he's only making sure she hasn't nicked anything – not without reason.

She drops the earring back into the box with its twin.

'Neither, Solly. These ain't my style. A bit too ladylike for me.'

He chuckles at this and takes the box from her hand, just to be certain.

'Why are you home so early? You don't normally come back until I've finished packing everything away.'

Ruby pulls a face. 'Not in the mood, really. We lost Alice today. She was caught red-handed in the store we were doing over, and the coppers came and took her away. I saw them arrive. And besides, it's quiet at the Crown. The boys have gone to a boxing match at Frank Parsons'. There's going to be trouble.'

'Poor Alice. No wonder you're out of sorts. That's bad news.' He rubs a hand over his thinning scalp. 'You didn't get caught, though. Did you find anything pretty, Magpie?'

She shrugs and turns away. 'Nah. Edith Lennox is still giving me a hard time about Billy. She decided it was my turn to cause the diversion while she swiped the gloves. She didn't take as many as I would have. I found an umbrella, that's all.' She won't tell him about the gentleman in Kensington or about the other pockets she picked. She doesn't trust him any more than he trusts her. 'Are you on your way upstairs?'

'Just about to lock up for the night. I'll make us both a cup of tea, and you can tell old Solly what happened to Alice. And you have my money from Raymond Calladine? I ain't seen you since this morning.' It's typical of Solly. Even when he's being considerate, he still won't forget that she'll have his money. He knows she'll try and keep it for herself if she can get away with it. It wouldn't be the first time.

They sit above the shop together, like they have done for years, in the little kitchen at the back. Ruby perches on a stool, while Solly has the chair with the wobbly leg.

'You should fix that,' she says, nodding at the chair leg, beginning a familiar thread of conversation.

'When I get a spare moment,' he says, smiling as he sets the kettle to boil on the range and pokes the fire underneath. This is his customary reply. 'Tell me about your day, then.'

She talks about Ray – and hands over his money. She tells him about the letter raiding, feeding him the sort of detail he loves, watching him cackle away over his teacup at her impressions of Maggs. Finally, she tells him what she saw at the store – Alice, sat on by the store superintendent, and the police arriving and finding her coat full of perfume bottles and powder puffs.

'I'd miss you, you know,' he says, with a sniff, suddenly serious. 'If you got nicked. Is that what's bothering you? Something is, and it ain't just Alice.'

She scoffs at the idea. 'I won't get nicked, Solly. I'm too good. Too quick. And nothing's bothering me.'

She would miss her easy conversations with Solly if she *was* ever caught and sent to Holloway. Of all the men she's known in her life, he's the only one who has looked out for her.

Perhaps she's tired, she tells him. She'll have an early night. It's been a busy day. She drifts from the kitchen to the tiny bedroom that she has called her own for twelve years.

She's not tired at all. She is restless.

She opens the small tea caddy on the table that serves as her jewellery box and plucks out her treasures. These are hers – really hers – items that she has paid for or stolen for herself, rather than borrowed from Solly or Maggs for a job. She lays out a pearl necklace, three pairs of earrings and two brooches on her pillow and contemplates them for a moment in the waning light of the gas lamp. She then drops them back into the tin. She lifts the mattress and stretches her arm to find the roll of bank notes, counting them out twice before re-rolling them and shoving them back as far as she can reach. Money that she keeps, just in case.

She is twenty quid lighter than she should have been. She scowls, remembering the way Annie Richmond patted that bloody handbag.

Bang, bang, bang. The sudden loud noise makes her jump.

Downstairs, round the back of the shop. Someone is in the yard, knocking at the back door, furiously, as if they're going to break it down. She rushes into the kitchen, crashing into Solly, clad in his ancient night shirt.

'What in the name of God...?'

Solly hauls up the window. Ruby rushes to his side, grabbing the thick stick they keep for protection. If someone is trying to raid the shop, it's better if two of them are there, and she will be better at wielding the stick than Solly.

It's nearly pitch-black darkness, drizzling with rain, almost too impenetrable to see anything, but they make out the shape of a man standing in the yard. Even if it were impossible to see him, they could still hear him – he is continuously banging the palms of his hands on the back door. He stares up at the window, the clouds part, and they catch a glimpse of his face in the thin moonlight.

'Billy!'

'Let me in, would you? Quick. It's pissing down out here.'

Ruby scrambles away from the window and runs down the stairs to let him in.

She has barely opened the door for him before he slams it shut again and bolts it, familiar enough with the mechanism of the lock. He grabs her hand and pulls her into the shop, away from the door.

'Billy, what's going on?' Ruby can feel the energy fizzing in him, the throb of violence, fear and aggression in the wet clasp of his hand.

He doesn't answer; he's still breathing hard. He propels her back the way she's come, up the stairs to the flat, until the two of them tumble into the kitchen.

'Away from that window,' Billy gasps at Solly. 'Pull the curtain as well.'

They never pull the curtain. Solly fumbles with the fabric.

Ruby stands, hands on her hips, examining Billy. He's wet through to the skin. There's a cut over his right eyebrow that's leaked blood down his cheek. His eye socket is swollen already, and there's a filthy-looking bruise on his head just above the right ear, where he's clearly been hit with something sharp and heavy. A belt buckle, probably. They always pull their belts off and fight with them.

'You've come from Frank Parsons', yeah? The fight? Who was there?'

'Never mind that, Ruby.' Solly is filling a bowl with tepid water from the kettle and adding a splash of brandy. 'Sort this fire. The man's soaking wet and injured. Come on, Billy boy, let's have a look at it. Take your coat off and sit near the warmth.' He presses Billy to sit on the stool next to the range while he soaks a cloth in the water and begins to clean the wounds. 'Is this it? Any more gashes or bruises on you? Take your shirt off.'

Billy shakes his head and throws his jacket on the table. The shirt, although damp, is not torn or bloodied. 'Nah. I'm good. Apart from the black eye that's coming and the bash on the head. Jesus, Sol–' He pulls away as the cloth touches his head. 'That fuckin' hurts more than the buckle did.'

'Keep still, you fool,' Solly chides him. 'Or I'll let Ruby do it.'

'Oi, what are you saying?' Ruby laughs, poking vigorously at the glowing embers, sending up sparks of fire.

'That you're more interested in finding out what happened in a fight than tending to a boy's injuries,' Solly says. 'And I've got the gentler touch. Years of practice setting stones.'

Ruby snorts. 'Listen to you. La-di-da. I know Billy – he'll want a drink and a smoke and a chance to tell us what's happened.'

'I want both,' Billy cuts in, still wincing at Solly's ministrations. 'You're no match for Sol as a nurse, but you've got your uses, sweetheart. Pour me a drink, eh?'

She opens the cupboard to find Solly's whisky and pours several fingers of liquor into a glass. Billy knocks it back and hands her the glass again, wanting another. Ruby pours obligingly.

'Hey, this had better be a good story,' Solly says, rinsing the bloody cloth in the bowl. 'That's my only bottle.'

Billy gulps half of the second glass and hisses through his teeth. 'Alright.' His voice is rough with whisky, pain and running. 'There was a match at Frank Parsons' place, Solly. Boxing. Ruby knew of it. The Clerkenwell boys were there, MacCarthy's lot. Mad MacCarthy was fighting. But we heard that some of their lads had destroyed our honour board, so decided we should sort them out.'

'You went up against the Clerkenwell boys on their own turf?'

'That's right. They've had it coming for a while.'

The Elephant Boys and the Clerkenwell gang have been edging towards another big fight for months. The honour roll was an excuse.

Ruby sits on the floor and hugs her knees. 'How did we do? What happened?'

'We were doing fine when Moss and I arrived. A few bumps' – he gestures to his head – 'but nothing bad. There were guns, but I didn't hear any go off, and then the coppers arrived.'

'Many of them?'

'Plenty. Too many. And they'd come ready to fight. They brought coshes, so someone had told them we would be there. One of the MacCarthys, probably. MacKenzie was with them.'

'I've never liked him,' Solly says. 'He came sniffing around here the other day, after you and Ruby had brought back the pretties from South Ken –'

'He was sniffing around the Crown, too.' Ruby interrupts, keen to hear more. 'What happened, though? Did they arrest people or knock them out with the coshes?'

'Both. I ran before they could do either to me.' Billy grins, and then winces at the pain in his eye.

Solly rinses the cloth again and pours the bloodied water

away. Billy and Ruby sit in silence as they watch him.

'Why are you here, Billy?' Solly asks as he wipes his hands on a dry towel. He hands the towel to Billy. 'Why aren't you at the Crown? You'll bring the coppers here.'

'Nah. They'll go to the Crown first, if they saw me at Parsons'. I didn't want to take trouble to Clara. She doesn't need that.'

Solly grunts. 'So, you're staying the night, then?'

Billy rubs his chin with the towel and catches Ruby's eye.

'If that's alright by you, Solly. I'll be gone first thing.'

Solly removes the damp jacket from his table and lays it over the back of the wobbly chair, smoothing the shoulders. 'Make sure you are,' is all he says as he leaves the kitchen. 'Clara's not the only one who doesn't need trouble.'

They are silent for a moment, listening to Solly grumble to himself as he goes back to his bedroom and shuts the door.

Billy knocks back the remainder of the whisky.

'You'll need somewhere to sleep, then,' says Ruby, climbing up from the floor. 'You can't sleep on that stool.'

He catches her hand and pulls her close, drawing her head down to his and kissing her. His own hands are still dirty and red, his fingernails black, but he doesn't seem to care. He reeks of scotch, sweat, smoke and the metallic scent of blood. She can taste the fight on his tongue. It excites her so much she can barely stand.

We were doing fine when Moss and I arrived. The words drift through her head even as she feels herself spinning. He was late to the fight. He had been somewhere else first.

She wants to ask him about it, but he's already unbuttoned her blouse. He yanks the chemise up from her skirt's waistband and begins to run his bloodied hands over her stomach and breasts, thumbing her nipples and making her gasp, and the thought vanishes in her violent surge of arousal.

'I don't want to sleep, Ruby.' He leans in and kisses the skin of her belly, the kisses not soft, but rough, urgent. 'Why d'you think I'm here?'

She can feel the energy humming through his body. She wants more of it. Wants him.

She tugs him up from the stool and towards her room.

14

'Has he gone?' Solly is frying eggs when Ruby staggers into the kitchen the next morning. The sky is dank and grey, and the back of the flat is still dark, but the little clock over the fireplace tells her it is half past eight.

'Got any bacon, Solly?' She touches the teapot with the back of her hand to see if it's still warm and then pours herself a cup.

He clicks his tongue. 'You can go elsewhere if you want bacon, Magpie. Is Billy still here?'

'No. He left early. Said he was going over the river. I've got a message for Clara.'

Billy doesn't want his sister to worry. She won't fuss, but if there's been a fight – and arrests – she'll be glad to know he's safe. He still won't say where he's going or what he's up to with Freddy Moss. He wasn't at Frank Parsons' place in time for the match. He didn't even know who had won when she asked, he just made some vague comment and changed the subject.

'Hmm.' Solly stares at the egg as it starts to splutter. He shakes the pan before sliding the egg onto a plate and then presses a slice of bread into the dripping so that it hisses. 'You want this?' he gestures to the egg.

Ruby beams at him and sits on the stool. 'I'd love it. I'm starving.'

'I'm not surprised.' Solly flips the bread and continues to cook. Ruby's stomach aches at the smell. He cuts the piece in half and piles the two crisp golden slices on the plate next to the egg.

'Is he going to marry you, Ruby, or is he just screwing you until the next girl comes along?' He places the plate on the table in front of her along with a knife and fork and watches her attack it.

Solomon Palmer is the closest thing Ruby has to a father. He's not protective, but he's trained her, taught her, given her a roof over her head and never asked too many questions. He has never married. He says he never had time for a wife. But Ruby has seen him watching the men – watching them like she watches them. She doesn't ask too many questions, either. Not even all those years ago, when she was small, when he would slip out at night and return the next morning smelling of someone else.

Ruby doesn't answer immediately. The fried bread is too good. She cuts neat portions and dips them in the gleaming yolk.

'He's not going to marry me, Solly, because I'm not the marrying kind, am I? He'll want someone like his sister, at home, minding the pub, having his babies. Edith Lennox, probably. I'm the one he goes raiding with. I'm more of a smash-and-grab sort.'

'And this doesn't bother you?'

She shakes her head.

He pulls the chair closer to the table, sits down and tries to gauge the reality. 'You don't worry about what that makes you? What people will say about you?'

Ruby lays down her fork.

'I've never worried about what people say about me, Solly. I've only worried about being stuck in prison or stuck in a bad marriage. I can see too many of those around here.' She jerks her head towards the shared backyard. 'Women squashed into tiny houses with hundreds of kids, married to a man who spends his money on the horses and his winnings on beer and thumps his wife if she complains. Pretty much like prison, if you ask me. That's not what I want.'

'What do you want?'

He's always assumed that she will fall into the same life as every other woman in the Forty Thieves: that she'll stick with one of the Elephant Boys, marry and raise a family. It's not the life he chose for himself, but they both know it's the usual pattern, what's expected. The younger women do most of the hoisting then, when they're older and saddled with kids, they help with the distribution and sorting of goods. Or, like Maggs, they train up the younger girls and oversee operations. Annie Richmond is different. She's well over twenty-five, and although she's been stepping out with Frederick Moss for a while, she's in no hurry to marry. She's too busy being Queen of the Thieves to settle into the usual life. It's what Ruby most admires in her. But it also means that Annie won't give up her crown to Ruby just yet – if ever.

'I don't know.' She mops up the yolk with the bread.

'No plans?'

'No.'

She does have plans. Such big plans. But she does not know how to share them with Solly. She does not know how to articulate them even to herself. How can she find the words to tell him that she wants so much more than *this*? How can she tell him that she dreams of being someone, something, special, when she is only alive at all because of him?

The clock ticks in the silence as she eats, solemnly considering her plate.

'I need to open up the shop, Ruby,' he says eventually, standing.

'I'll be down soon.'

She sits in the kitchen for a while, listening to Solly rattling around downstairs and watching the clouds through the window as they race hard across the pale grey sky, before reaching into the pocket of her skirt and pulling out a single card, three inches by two. She had found it when she went through Billy's jacket – as she does habitually. She flicks the business card over and over in her fingers. It carries the name of a Soho nightclub – the Angel – and is decorated with a feminine figure, her wings outstretched in an ecstasy that looks more sensual than religious.

On the back of the card, someone has written a date and time: Tuesday's date, seven o'clock. Four days from now.

The handwriting is not Billy's. It might be Moss's.

Billy has not said anything about the Angel or what he's up to – and he's up to something.

She turns the card again and stares at the angel.

Something flickers deep inside her.

15

Another theft at a department store. Hoisters. Lifters. An arrest this time.

Harriet listens to the men discussing yesterday's incident at Debenham and Freebody. She sets down the tea tray and pours out cups for Jimmy Cartwright and Michael Pickard – another of the *Gazette*'s reporters.

'Sugar?'

Michael only nods and continues to share the story with Jimmy. Jimmy takes the second cup from Harriet.

'You'll be interested in this,' he says. 'It's your thieves again.'

Something in his eyes suggests that, despite what he told her yesterday, he is a little ashamed of taking her story about Enderby's.

'It was her, do you think? Ruby Wilder? The so-called film star with the black bobbed hair?' She is interested.

'No, not this time. This one's name is Alice Dunning, but she's another of the Forty Thieves. She's been in court before, Michael says.'

'I reported on it.' Michael gulps down his tea and reaches for his notebook. 'I expect I'll cover this trial as well.' He spends a lot of his time at the magistrates' court.

'You're going there now?'

'Yes, but not for Alice Dunning. She'll be in Holloway. Won't be tried yet, but she'll end up back there – it's hardly worth the expense of bringing in the magistrate. Caught red-handed with half of the Coty counter, from what I've heard.'

'What's she like, can you recall her?'

'Alice? Well, she was no film star, that's for sure. Quite a plain-looking woman. Broken nose, I think. Hard as nails, too, like all of them.' He picks up the coat slung over the back of his chair. 'I should go. I'll see you later.'

'I suppose they would have to be hard as nails, if they're criminals,' Harriet says to Jimmy. 'But fancy choosing to break the law for the sake of some frippery from a perfume counter.' She watches Michael, speaking with one of the other men on the way out. 'To end up in prison for some talcum powder.'

'Not everyone can afford the prices in Debenham and Freebody, even if they might like the fripperies,' Jimmy says, lowering his teacup. 'Besides, she wouldn't have kept any of it for herself. She would have sold the goods on. That's how they work.'

'They don't keep what they steal, the Forty Thieves?'

'No.' He takes a large mouthful of tea, draining the cup and shakes his head as he replaces it on the saucer. 'Goods go to a fence who sells them on at a more affordable price and Alice takes a cut. It's money she wants, not talcum powder. She's probably not going hungry – the Forty Thieves look after their own better than a trade union would – but she'll need to pay her rent and she might like a new hat occasionally.'

'You sound as though you sympathise.'

'Not with the law-breaking. But I can understand hardship well enough.'

She can understand, too. She has read Charles Dickens and Victor Hugo and attended political meetings. She has listened to Ralph talking about how best to lift the poor from poverty. Jimmy, though, speaks about it in a way that is quite different. Passionate. Almost aggressive. Her father's words of caution against associating with 'hotheads' spring to mind. She can certainly remember his anxiety about Mrs Pankhurst and the ever-present danger of 'Reds' from Russia.

'Are you a Bolshevik, Jimmy?'

'No,' he laughs. 'Certainly not. I'm just a reporter. I try to look under the surface of what other people see rather than jump to easy conclusions.' He picks up his notebook. 'Thanks for the tea.'

She takes the tray out to the washroom and tries to shake her irritation at Jimmy's condescending manner as she washes up.

Alice Dunning steals because she needs the money. The same might be true of Ruby Wilder. Did she risk prison simply to pay her rent – or even to have money for food – like Alice?

Alice Dunning. She repeats the name to herself. Alice Dunning. Alice Dunning, one of the Forty Thieves, is in Holloway.

It might be possible to interview her if she has not been tried yet. She does not know how, but there must be a way. What a scoop that would be! It would be pleasing to put Jimmy's nose out of joint and have her words on the main news page, certainly. She might find out more about the Forty Thieves and their circumstances. And the wild girl she saw in the back of the motor car.

Harriet unloads the milk jug and sugar bowl onto the shelf and returns to her desk. The women's section article that Mr Pickford has asked for – 'What the discerning fiancée looks for in an engagement ring' – is almost written. And it can wait.

She places her hands flat on the desk and thinks hard. A newspaper reporter like Jimmy – or even a polite female one – surely wouldn't be allowed into the prison. But a well-spoken woman of the right sort *ought* to be able to visit any prisoner. One of her mother's friends visits such unfortunates. She takes them Bible tracts and improving literature. She once attempted to encourage Isabel to visit with her, on behalf of the church, and was disappointed by Isabel's frosty refusal.

Dare she?

Perhaps she might make use of her own knowledge and family connections and do as Jimmy would do – look under the surface of what other people see.

She collects her handbag and coat, walks down to the front hall and asks the doorman to hail her a taxicab.

She steps out of the cab on Camden Road less than half an hour later and instructs the driver to wait for her, swallowing down her nervousness as she gazes up at the thick walls and imposing turrets of the prison. It looks like a fortress, a fantastical castle built to contain monsters rather than women who steal a few silk blouses, like Alice Dunning. She knows that the driver is watching as she makes her way carefully down the driveway to the gatehouse, feigning boldness.

Just inside the main gate, she finds a porter's lodge that is only a little less austere. The man standing behind the desk is sturdy, with a greying moustache and a head of hair that is balding at the peaks. He is neatly dressed in police uniform. He raises his eyebrows as she approaches.

'May I be of assistance, madam?' The tone of his enquiry suggests that she has wandered in by accident, lost her Pekinese or mislaid her umbrella. She is out of place.

'*Miss* Harriet Littlemore,' she says, extending a gloved hand. 'From St Saviour's Christian Mission.'

He does not shake her hand, barely able to hide his disdain. He knows this type of woman, all mannish pretensions and strong opinions on the incarceration of women. He watched dozens of well-meaning, well-bred young ladies like this one brought through the gates before the war – Mrs Pankhurst and her crowd. And he has seen plenty of women broken by Holloway. This one wouldn't last five minutes.

'I understand that you have Alice Dunning here.' She peers out across the open courtyard, towards the inner gate of the prison. She can see two griffins, carved from stone, standing guard on either side of a great wooden door. The presence of these oversized mythical creatures, their eyes glaring, their talons clutching iron bars and a key, only serves to compound her sense that she should not have come.

'Alice Dunning?' The amusement in his voice irritates her and jolts her back into life.

'Alice Dunning,' she repeats the name as if he is simple. 'The shoplifter? One of the Forty Thieves?'

'I know who she is, *Miss* Littlemore. Question is, what business might you have with her?'

'I heard that she's just been brought in and that she's awaiting trial. I've come to offer solace in her hour of need and to encourage her to repent.' This is the sort of thing her mother's friend would say. Isabel does not believe in offering solace to wrongdoers.

He raises his brows. 'Solace? To Alice Dunning?'

'On behalf of the parish, yes.'

He does not hide the chuckle. 'Hard labour is what she needs, not God.'

It was a mistake to come here. He will not let her pass and she is making a fool of herself. She ought to leave the investigating to Jimmy Cartwright.

He reaches wearily for his helmet and gestures towards the courtyard. 'Ah, I suppose it'll be in order. You can give her some hellfire, if you like. We're quiet today.'

It takes Harriet another half an hour to be admitted into the inner prison. There is another brief conversation to be had with the warder in charge, where she has to repeat her request. She is required to sign her name and tries to ignore her worries about what her parents will say if they discover she has visited a prison. Then she is forced to abandon her handbag on a small shelf. No one searches her intimately or intrusively, but she is asked to turn out her pockets, and an unsmiling female warder runs her hands over her blouse and skirt to make sure that she is not carrying any means of escape for Alice, nor anything that might be used as a weapon. By the end of it all, she feels like a criminal herself. Looking up at the high walls, set with many tiny windows, each one suggesting a cramped cell, Harriet can only fancy that the inmates would long to escape such a place – but she cannot conceive of how it would ever be done.

But then, even this morning, she would never have imagined that she would be standing inside Holloway prison at all. A thrill of excitement pulses through her body. She has never done anything quite so daring.

The female warder leads her under a high-roofed tunnel and into a second, much larger courtyard surrounded by walls that reach to the sky. The courtyard stands empty, save for a few women dressed in dark blue uniforms, similar to the one this warder is wearing. These must be prison staff rather than inmates.

Harriet follows meekly, clutching the notebook and pencil that she has been allowed to bring, as the warder crosses the yard towards a door in the corner. A voice yells something incoherent from one of the high windows. Her presence has caught someone's attention. Another shout echoes over the yard, and then a third. Harriet cannot hear what they are shouting, but it is aimed at her. Her heart begins to beat harder, and she is aware of a rising terror that's making every step more difficult.

The warder unlocks the door and ushers her in.

'They're edgy,' she says, rolling her eyes. 'It's nearly time for their exercise, and some of them are ready to get out. Ignore them.'

They walk in silence down a narrow corridor. It's gloomy in here – no wonder the women want to be in the open air. There is a sour smell of unwashed bodies and poor drainage that makes Harriet's stomach lurch.

They pass ten doors along the corridor before the warder stops and bangs on the eleventh. She slides a small metal trap open, disclosing a window into a cell, and peers through.

'Dunning, someone to see you.'

'Who is it? I'm not expecting visitors.'

'It's the Church, Dunning. This young lady here's come to save your soul.'

The warder opens the door and Harriet comes face to face with the thief.

'Thank you for your assistance,' Harriet says quickly to the warder. 'I don't think I need you with me while I pray.'

She licks her drying lips. She is not afraid of Alice Dunning. She cannot be. After all, she is not the one locked in the cell. But something about her makes Harriet nervous. She strides through the door and reaches a hand to Alice, affecting confidence. Like horses, she tells herself. You have to show such people that you are not afraid.

'Harriet Littlemore, from St Saviour's Christian Mission. I've come to read some Bible verses and talk to you about Jesus Christ.'

Alice's expression moves swiftly from puzzlement to suspicion, and then to interest. She has no idea what this woman wants, but she is sufficiently intrigued to take Harriet's hand and shake it.

'Pleased to meet you, miss, I'm sure.'

'I'll be outside,' the warder says to Harriet. 'You can have fifteen minutes. Bang on the door if you want to leave sooner. Don't let her fox you.'

The room is small. Alice is sitting on a narrow bed. Above her – above head height – is an arched window set with metal bars. There is a table, devoid even of personal effects, and a chair. Harriet pulls out the chair and sits down. Her knuckles are white as she grasps her notebook.

Plain, Michael Pickard had called her. Alice Dunning has the sort of face that would be lost in a crowd. It probably helps if you're shoplifting.

'Alice. May I call you Alice? Will you tell me what happened at Debenham and Freebody yesterday afternoon?'

Alice is already in prison clothes, Harriet notes. The cloth is poor quality, but clean. Alice looks almost at ease, content to be here. But then, she has been in prison before.

Alice gives her a lazy look. 'I don't know what you're talking about. I don't know anything about Debenham and Freebody.'

Of course, she knows nothing about it. Harriet scolds herself silently for asking such a foolish question. The woman is not going to tell her anything that will compromise the defence in her trial. They continue to face one another. Alice shifts awkwardly on the bed and her face spasms in pain.

'You're injured. Have you had an accident?'

Alice shrugs. 'Fell down the stairs. Stupid really. Still, I'll have chance to heal nicely while I'm here, won't I?'

'You think you'll be here for a while?'

'Four months. Five, maybe. Depends.'

'It depends on what?'

Alice smiles but says nothing.

'Where do you come from? Are you married?'

Alice's expression changes, only a fraction, but Harriet sees it. 'Did he die? In the war? Your husband, I mean?'

'No. All the men we cried over, and George Dunning was the one sod who had to come home.' She shifts again, obviously in discomfort.

'A shame,' says Harriet, staring at her leg. 'A shame that you fell down the stairs. I imagine it affects your mobility, your movement.'

'Bloody hurts, that's what it does.'

'You should ask someone to look at it, while you're here.'

Alice grunts. 'And what are you here for, miss whoever-you-are? Apart from worrying about my hip. You ain't Church, I know that. You haven't started spouting about Jesus yet.'

Alice Dunning is a square-jawed girl not much older than herself. Twenty-four or twenty-five, perhaps. She has a frizz of mid-brown hair around her face, cut in no particular style. Her eyes have dark grey moons underneath them and her skin is unwashed, the colour of watery milk. She clearly hasn't had much sleep for a while, and it isn't prison that has wearied her. She steals, Harriet hears Jimmy's voice in her head, because she needs the money.

Her nose is an odd shape. Michael had said it was broken. In a fight, perhaps. Harriet thinks of little Cecily Enderby, entirely innocent, shoved to the ground by another woman like this one – another woman as used to giving out violence as to being on the receiving end of it. She sits up straighter. She will most definitely not be 'foxed'.

'Information.'

'What information?'

'About the Forty Thieves. I'm a reporter, at a newspaper. I should like to know about the Forty Thieves – who they are, where they live, how they operate.'

A sneer forms on Alice's lips. 'Well, aren't you a clever girl, getting past the warders?' She folds her arms. 'I have nothing to say about the Forty Thieves. I don't know them.'

Harriet finds the ten-shilling note that is carefully secreted between the leaves of her notebook and lays it on the brown blanket, before smiling brightly at the young woman on the bed, who is now watching her with wary eyes. 'I'm prepared to pay, and I'll be very discreet. No one will know you've said anything.'

Alice runs a tongue around her gums and considers the note. It wouldn't hurt to have money in a place like this. Could be useful.

'The whole of Holloway knows you're here,' she says. 'One word about the Forties appears in the newspapers and I'm dead.'

Harriet puts the pencil tip to the paper and does not look up. 'The whole of Holloway thinks I'm praying for your soul and urging you to repent of your sins.'

Alice touches the edge of the note gently, considering it. She draws it towards her.

'What do you want to know?'

16

Tuesday evening

The Angel club is in Soho, tucked away down Gerrard Street. It has an unprepossessing door which makes it appear like an office; a solicitor might operate from such a building. The bland entrance gives no hint of the interior. There is not even a door plate, giving the name of the place. Ruby only knows that this is the correct address by the faded number over the lintel and the presence of a burly man, leaning against the wall, opening the door to guests.

She pulls the little card from her coat pocket and checks it again. Tuesday, seven o'clock.

She takes a deep breath, trying to suppress the nervous excitement. She flashes the card and gives her name to the doorman. He looks her up and down, as if the decision to admit her depends on her vital statistics. It probably does. In places like this, the men will pay to become temporary members in order to skirt around the liquor licensing laws and drink all night, but the women, if they're the right sort, will enter for free. She tells him she's with Billy Walsh, and his eyes widen a fraction, confirming that Billy is known here. He gives her a curt nod and opens the door, saying nothing.

Another man stands at cloakroom, ready to relieve her of her coat. This one is extremely tall and shaped like a thin stick of willow, flexible and graceful. His face looks like a girl's, and Ruby is certain that he is wearing kohl around his eyes and possibly rouge. His eyelashes are long and fluttering. He greets her in a gentle sing-song voice that is both unnerving and strangely alluring. She would bet all the money in her handbag that this one wouldn't try to push his hands up her dress. She gives him her coat and hat. It's not her best coat tonight – not her French one – but it's another favourite from Grace Bartlett's warehouse. The dark green matches her eyes and the wool, although not of the best quality, is still fine.

'Lovely colour,' he murmurs, stroking a hand over the sleeve. 'It suits you.'

'Thank you. I like it. Tell me' – she smiles back at him – 'is Billy Walsh here tonight?'

He steps back, a thoughtful expression on his face. 'Yes, he's here. He's busy, I think.'

'I expect he is,' she says lightly. 'He told me he would be.'

She makes her way through another door, down a flight of stairs and into the cavernous heart of the club and its deep, insistent throb of music. She stands listening for a moment, watching the small orchestra of dark-skinned men on a raised platform. The pianist, cigarette hanging from his lips, plays for a clarinet, banjo and drum. They are good. She recognises the tune and hums along. 'Hindustan'; she likes this one.

She pulls a mirror from her handbag and checks her make-up, applying a fresh layer of lipstick and pinching her cheeks before shaking out her hair so that it falls into its perfect, precise bob. She enjoys the way the music makes her hips sway of their own accord. It's not busy yet – it's far too early – but, even in the dim light and the fog of cigarette smoke, she can see that there are men and women drinking and talking, heads bent together, bodies close – some very close. There are tables and seats, in modern, uncomfortable-looking designs, near to the dancefloor. Against the walls, she can see alcoves set with low sofas, hiding their occupants from prying eyes. Languid women carry trays of drinks from the bar to the tables, each of them walking in the same stylised, effortless manner.

She lifts her chest, standing taller, and scans the room, but there is no sign of Billy.

'Hello, pretty lady.' A man snakes his arm around her waist. 'I've not seen you here before. You're all alone. Have you come to party?'

He's wearing a well-cut suit and smells expensive. Ruby breathes in deeply and smiles up at him, taking in everything. There are flecks of silver hair at his temples. Wallet on the inside-left pocket, she guesses, a game she always plays. No gun or knife. He's right-handed. The watch on his wrist is elegant rather than flashy – Cartier, she thinks, without examining it closely – and there's a discreet ring on his right hand that looks like the sort that has been passed down through his family. The gold is old. She wouldn't mind a closer look at it.

'Perhaps I have,' she says. 'I'm expecting to see a friend of mine, but I could murder a drink while I'm waiting for him.'

She scans the room again, but Billy is still nowhere to be seen.

He still has a hand on her. 'I'll be your friend, if you like. Let me find you that drink to murder. Champagne? You look like a girl who drinks champagne.'

She laughs and pulls away from him. 'Alright.'

He reaches out a hand and a waitress, hovering only a few feet away, moves gracefully towards him. He speaks quietly into her ear; she nods, deferential, and glides away.

'Who are you looking for? This friend of yours, who is he?'

'Billy Walsh. Do you know him?'

He does not respond immediately but stands listening to the orchestra reach the end of their piece before applauding them softly. Ruby does the same.

'I know him. I know him well. He's in the club this evening, I think, but busy at the moment.'

'He's here on business, I know.'

The waitress arrives with the drinks on a tray. He takes both glasses and nods to a plush sofa, tucked away in a shadowy corner. There is no alternative but to slide in next to him. She's passed the time with worse company, and it might be worth her while sitting with him, while she waits for Billy. It won't be too difficult to reach into his pocket.

'Here you are,' he says, placing her drink on the table in front of her.

'Cheers, mister…'

'Lazenby,' he says, touching his glass to hers. 'Peter Lazenby. And you are?'

'Ruby Mills.'

'Is that your real name or just the one you're wearing tonight?' He doesn't so much speak as allow words to seep from his lips like honey. She's met his sort from time to time – wealthy, confident in his own opinions – but she can see from his eyes that he is no fool. She remains on her guard.

'Ha. You're sharp, Mr Peter Lazenby. But, yes, it's my real name.'

'Then I'm honoured you've chosen to share it with me. I, by the way, always go by my real name. It's the only one I've ever needed.'

'And what are you doing here, Mr Lazenby? Are you here on business, like my friend?'

'I own the club, so that means I don't ever do very much except watch people spending money at the bar and drink with the clientele. That is my business. And it's Peter, if I buy you a drink.'

'If you own the club, then you don't have to buy the drinks, do you?' Ruby smiles, putting the glass to her lips. 'You can just help yourself to whatever you fancy, Peter.'

She is enjoying the flirtation, especially as he is doing most of the work.

'I do just that. And you, Ruby, are, I think…' He squints at her and rubs a thumb across his lower lip. 'Either an actress or a dancer, or perhaps… A thief.'

'Or all of the above,' she says.

'I thought so. I've been around enough of them. I noticed the way you were looking at my jacket, working out where my wallet was.'

'You've a nice watch, too,' she says.

He extends his arm to display it. 'Ah, but not even the best of London's pickpockets can take this. The clasp is too good. Cartier.'

'Well, the best sort of thief would wait until you left it on your bedside table,' she says, giving him a knowing look before taking another mouthful of the champagne.

He smiles at this. 'I'm growing to like you, Ruby Mills. You're my kind of thief.'

He's not bad-looking for an older man; he's rich, charming and he's offering champagne. It's sliding down very easily and she's drinking on an empty stomach. Too much more of it and she'll be developing a close acquaintance with his bedside table, she knows.

'I like you, too, Peter Lazenby. And I'd like to stay here, enjoying your company, but…' Her eye is caught by the sight of

Billy, emerging from a door in the far corner, his arm wrapped around a girl she doesn't know. 'I came to meet Billy Walsh, so I'd better go and meet him. Thanks for the drink.'

He stands to let her pass, touching a hand to the small of her back in just the right place to send a spark of fire through her. 'Come and find me later then. Come and have another glass with me.'

She steps away. 'Perhaps I will.'

The prickling sensation of arousal quickly disappears as she threads her way through the tables and chairs. Billy hasn't noticed her; he's too entranced by the girl he's with. He's laughing at something she's saying – that exaggerated sort of laugh he does when he's turning on the charm. Like you're the most fascinating girl in the whole of London. This creature is blonde, with fluffy, wispy hair that surrounds her face, like a dandelion clock you'd find in the dirt down by the canal. She seems bored or half-asleep. Perhaps that's the attraction: she's ready for bed already. She's barely more than a child – an unusual choice for Billy.

'Billy Walsh, I want to talk to you.' There's a lull in the music as the small orchestra swaps over with another, and her voice carries across the floor, shriller than she would like. A screech from south of the river. Billy hears her, certainly. He stands still and stares across at her, a guilty expression on his face, as though he's been caught with his hand in the biscuit tin, or up someone's blouse.

The woman stiffens, sensing a rival. Ruby dismisses her as offering little threat. She has none of the power in her shoulders or hands that Maggs does, or even Edith. Ruby could knock her over with a swing of a handbag.

'Billy. A word. Just a word. Then you can carry on enjoying yourself.' Whatever business he's planning to conduct tonight, Ruby knows exactly what sort of business has been going on already. She can see it in his face. She can smell it.

He unwraps himself from the girl and pushes her gently towards the bar, promising her a drink later.

'I need a little bit of something else, lover. Something to pick me up.' She talks in a squeaky, babyish voice.

He reaches into his pocket and pulls out a note. She heads for a doorway in the far wall rather than the bar. That's where she'll find the cocaine dealer, Ruby assumes. This sort of club will have at least one.

'I'll have her drink, if your tart's gone to powder her nose,' she says sharply.

Billy chooses not to rise to this comment and instead gestures her over to the counter. 'What would you like to drink, Ruby? Gin?'

She moves to stand beside him at the bar. 'A kind gentleman took pity on me, here on my own, and bought me champagne just now, so I'll have another of those.'

'Who bought you champagne?' He stares around the room. The bruise on his cheek has turned yellow and purple.

The barman pops open a fresh bottle and pours her a glass. It's a sound that always makes her smile.

'Peter Lazenby. He owns this place. He was very charming.'

'He would be.' He hands her the glass, frowning. 'Watch him, Ruby. Keep away from him. He's trouble.'

She takes the champagne and waits for him to down his whisky and ask the barman for another, like he always does.

'What are you doing here anyway?' He sips this second one.

'I came to find you.' She plucks the card from her skirt and holds it up to his nose.

He sucks his teeth. 'I thought I'd lost that. You took it from my jacket, didn't you? That's how you knew I'd be here. What do you want?'

'I want to know what you're up to. Why have you been so secretive lately? You've got something going on, some sort of deal, and you're not cutting me in. I can't believe you'd do that, after I said I wanted us to work together.'

'For the last time, Ruby, we are not working together. Keep your damned nose out of my business. Go home.' He growls the words through his teeth before gulping another mouthful of whisky. 'Christ almighty, Annie Richmond should keep you on a leash. Go back to the Borough where you belong.'

'Don't you tell me where I belong. I belong wherever I want. And right now, I want to know what you're up to. I want you to cut me in.'

'Alright,' he says, wearily. He will always give in to her eventually. And she knows he's weak when he's only recently rebuttoned his trousers. 'Alright, I'll tell you. Just to keep you quiet. But I'm not cutting you in. The boys want me to make enquiries into some business arrangements this side of the river. That's all it is.'

'What sort of business?'

'Buying and selling, this and that. Whisky, mostly. The sort that's not been past the tax man. Cigarettes. That sort of thing.'

'Don't the Elephants do that already? Buy stuff, or nick stuff, and sell it on?'

'The business opportunities are bigger this side of the river and we want to be part of them. Moss wants us to be part of them. The Richmonds have been talking about working with Billy Kimber, but Moss thinks we should move in with Lazenby and his friends.'

'Billy Kimber? The man from Birmingham? I've heard of him.'

'Of course you have. The whole world has heard of his Brummagem gang. Kimber's already running the bookmaking at most of the racecourses, and now he wants to move into Soho. There are rich pickings to be had this side of the river, especially in places like this. But Moss thinks Kimber's overreaching himself. He wants us to be better connected. And Lazenby is very well connected.' He stares over her head towards the entrance to the club. 'There's a man I'm meeting – the meeting you know about – he's going to sit down with me and discuss some terms for our arrangement.'

'This one isn't from Birmingham?'

'No. He's from London. Moss has decided we should play quietly, like gentlemen. He thinks we should leave the noise to Kimber and the other ruffs. Plenty of the old gangs are scrapping over the racecourses and dog tracks, attracting attention, getting rounded up by the coppers, you know that. Moss says we should make ourselves useful to a better class of businessman. Which is why I'm here tonight.'

'Why you? Why not one of the others?'

He grins over his glass. ''Cause even with a black eye, I look the part. Ronnie and Bert look like barrow boys or cats' meat sellers. I look like a man who can do business in Soho.'

There's more to the choice of Billy Walsh than just his looks. She shakes her head.

'Pull the other leg, Billy. What's the real story? Why you?'

He drains his glass and places it on the counter, waving the barman away, not wanting another. He doesn't look directly at her. 'They're men we met in France, Ruby – me and Moss. People we know already. That's why I'm here.'

'I thought you were fighting the Germans in France, collecting medals and all that.'

'We were. Some of the time. But there's a lot of hanging around in war, much more than you'd think. You meet people. You get talking. They introduce you to other people and it goes on. Word went around very quickly that the Elephants were fighting for King and Country, and we fought proudly, but we were making plans as well, on the quiet, for when we came home – for those of us that came home. These men we met were officers, but when you're stuck in a field of mud it doesn't matter whether you were born rich or poor. We made connections.'

Ruby laughs. She might have known it. A thief is a thief wherever he lands, so of course alliances between crooks had been made across boundaries and borders hundreds of miles away, where there were no coppers around. Those sorts of conferences were never mentioned in the newspaper dispatches, but Ruby can see now exactly how they would have happened.

'So, the man you're meeting tonight, you knew him in France?'

'That's right.'

'And the girl? Did you meet her in France as well?'

'Don't be like that, Ruby. She's nothing. Just a bit of fun.'

'She's a child, Billy.'

'So are you,' he grins at her.

The orchestra starts to play again, a livelier tempo, and a few people appear nearby, dancing.

'You're going back to Solly's now?' He's trying to get rid of her – and not because of the dandelion-headed girl. His eyes search the shadowy corners of the club. He's looking for his new associate and doesn't want to be seen with her. Behind him, Ruby sees the blonde reappear, her eyes brighter and more awake than before.

At least she's wiped the powder from her nostrils. She hangs back, leaning against the bar, talking to one of the waitresses.

'Not sure I am. I might stay, find someone to dance with, have a drink with. Perhaps I can do business here as well. You're not the only one who can look the part.'

'Go home, sweetheart.' He speaks through his teeth and takes the empty glass from her hand. 'You're in the way.'

'Is everything alright, Mr Walsh?' There's a man behind her, at her shoulder. She spins around, unnerved. She hadn't heard him arrive. 'No trouble here, is there?'

'None at all, General.' Billy nods to Ruby as he lays the champagne glass on the counter. 'As it happens, the lady was just about to leave.'

This man looks like a soldier, an officer. Smart suit, standing straight, with broad shoulders, a soft plummy voice and a hard expression. Someone used to dishing out orders, although not old enough to be a real general. A man who moves silently. A better class of businessman, Billy said.

He studies Ruby for a moment, unspeaking. Billy makes no move to introduce her.

'Is she part of your operation?'

'No.' Billy is quick to respond. 'She's nothing to do with it.'

'I could be,' she says. 'I'm Ruby Mills.'

'Miss Mills.' He nods his head. He's more polite than Billy.

'She's nothing to do with it,' Billy repeats and glares at her. 'Just a girl from the Borough with ideas above her station. And she's going home.'

'I'll go home when I want.'

'Well, I don't have time to deal in petty domestic disagreements, Mr Walsh. I'm a busy man.' He is amused, rather than irritated. 'And we still have arrangements to make. One or two details to look over. I suggest we use the back office, once you've finished here.'

'I'll come now.'

The man stands aside as Billy grabs Ruby's arm – roughly – and leans his face into hers, dropping his voice to little more than a whisper.

'I won't tell you again, Ruby. You're out of your depth here. Go home.' He plants a kiss on her lips, but shakes her arm, just to make sure she's understood.

Just a girl from the Borough. The fury flashes through her. His words are more of an insult than the shake. Or the kiss. She swings a fist up at his face, but he knows her too well and catches her wrist and squeezes it hard, squashing bone against bone, making her cry out – in frustration more than pain. She wrenches herself free.

'I'll kill you, Billy Walsh, one of these days, you see if I don't.'

She turns her back on Billy and walks to the stairs with as much dignity as she can muster, becoming angrier with every step as she hears him laughing. She could have forgiven him for the other woman – she knows that women flock around Billy – but that he has cast her aside now a business opportunity has arisen is, to her, inexcusable.

She needs to clear her head. Not that she's drunk. Barely tipsy. A glass or two of champagne.

The same gentle-eyed attendant greets her at the cloakroom.

'What's the matter?' he asks. 'Didn't you like the music?'

'Music's good,' Ruby replies tersely. 'It's the company that's full of shit.'

'Sorry to hear that, sweetheart. Come again on another evening? Or later tonight? When there's more of the dancing and less of the shit.'

'You're leaving us so soon?'

Ruby turns to see Peter Lazenby in the foyer, glass in hand. She wonders whether he followed her up the stairs, whether he saw her rowing with Billy.

'Other places to see, Peter. People to meet.'

'And the company is shit here.'

'Not you,' she laughs. 'You were a perfect gentleman.'

'Not a view shared by everyone, eh, Daniel?' he laughs back.

The young man shrinks a little and chooses not to answer, instead turning to find Ruby her hat and coat.

'So where are you visiting now, Miss Ruby Mills?' Peter asks. 'Which other clubs are going to enjoy your charms, if not mine? Or are you going home for an early night, tucked up in your bed all alone?'

'I might do that. Have a quiet evening. Just me and my cocoa.'

'That would be a pity,' he says, moving closer to her. She catches a hint of his scent again. 'Pity for a lovely girl like you to be on her own. I'll be glad to buy you another drink. Or, should I say, I'll ask a waitress to bring you one? I don't, as you pointed out, need to *buy* my drinks. I can have *whatever* I fancy.'

He takes her hand and makes as if to kiss her knuckle. Instead, he turns it over and raises her wrist to his mouth, right where Billy crushed it. His lips are soft, and they graze her skin briefly before they press in a warm kiss. Ruby shivers.

Why not? Why not let this man try it on with her? Her anger at Billy's response – his insistence that she should go back to Annie, back to being just a small-time, bit-part player in the Forties, rather than sharing a new adventure with him – is making her reckless. And this man is making her hot.

She revels in the sensation of lust, intoxicated by the possibilities of her own potency.

'Well, perhaps one more won't kill me. But we might take a quiet corner. There's someone I don't want to be looking at right now.'

'Your friend Billy Walsh?'

'He's not my friend.'

'You don't have to look at him if you don't want to. I have some matters to attend to later tonight, but I have a small flat, just upstairs. We could enjoy our drinks there, in private. Do you know, I have a refrigerator? I keep it just for the champagne. And you' – he touches her chin – 'are welcome stay until the morning, if you've nowhere better to go. You have nowhere, do you, in truth?'

Ruby and the truth parted company years ago. And now she recognises that there is potential in this evening after all. She doesn't need Billy Walsh. She sighs.

'No. You're right. I have nowhere to go tonight, and no money – even for a taxicab to nowhere.'

'Then your luck has just changed. Mine certainly has.'

He takes the coat and hat from the attendant and tucks Ruby's arm under his, steering her not to the door that leads downstairs, but to another, marked 'Private'.

17

'I meant what I said. You're welcome to stay for the night.' Peter Lazenby fastens the cufflink at his wrist. 'I need to be downstairs in the club – I have business to deal with – but please, do stay. I'd like you to stay. Drink your way through the refrigerator if you wish, while you wait for me. There's also some food in the kitchen, I believe.'

He unwinds the silk tie from the brass rail above her head and knots it around his neck, nodding at himself in the mirror. Ruby sits up in the bed, pulling the sheet against her warm skin, and watches him.

'You're taking a risk, leaving a thief alone in your house. I might walk off with the teaspoons.'

'I'll be disappointed if you don't. Consider it a tip.'

He's already left a pile of bank notes on the bedside table. A generous amount.

He sits on the bed and strokes her hair. 'You know, if you're in the mire, financially, there's work here for a girl like you – and there are men downstairs who'll pay far more than I have for a bit of fun. You could be sporting diamonds every night.'

Or feeding a cocaine habit like the dead-eyed, fluffy-headed creature she saw with Billy.

'Think about it,' he says again, tugging the sheet away from her chest and gazing down at her. 'And maybe I'll find you here waiting for me when I come home, eh? Ready to play some more?'

'What time will that be?'

'Around dawn.' He checks his watch and smiles at her, taking her enquiry as agreement. 'I'll be imagining you in my bed while I'm away.'

She waits for him to leave and then cocoons herself in the sheets. The money is useful, but she has no intention of tying herself to a pimp; however charming he might be, she knows that's what he is.

He won't be charming forever – not once he's passed her around his friends for a 'bit of fun', and for a little less cash each time.

It will do her no harm to close her eyes for a while, but she'll be gone long before dawn. And he might find his flat is missing more than a few silver teaspoons.

She wakes with a start. She had been on the edge of a dream – one that she cannot now recall – and aware of noises that were not part of it. Animals of some kind, screeching, whinnying, barking. And then a loud *crack*. She lies still, her heart racing.

She strains her ears. She can hear the dull thump of music in the club two floors below and some street sounds – men wandering home drunk as lords – but nothing more, nothing sinister or unusual. Just Soho noises.

She listens to the sound of her own breathing for a while and then switches on the lamp and swings herself out of bed, reaching for her handbag and her watch. It is ten past three – a long way off dawn, but time to be moving on. She presses the money he's left into her bag and finds her clothes and shoes.

She tiptoes around the flat, examining Peter's possessions. She's not looking for silver teaspoons. Or cash. He's flash, but he's got class. The whole place is decorated in the latest style, but that's just to impress whoever he brings here. He's old money. He reeks of it. There will be something here, something small and discreet, that will be worth finding, like the watch he's taken with him. She's not just a thief: she's been trained by Solly Palmer and she knows the sort of things she's looking for.

There is a heavy-framed painting on the wall of the main room. It's hard to tell in the dark, but it might be worth a fortune. It looks like the pictures Solly showed her when she was still a child, in the galleries. It is too big for her to lift. A small bronze statue on the mantelpiece might be better, but that is also too heavy, and she is not certain of its value.

She wanders back into the bedroom. She investigates the small table and opens the drawers in the tallboy. Under the socks she discovers a gun, wrapped in a handkerchief. Billy keeps his gun with his socks, too, when it's not strapped to his body.

She can feel something else: a box. She pulls it out and opens it. She smiles at what she sees. This is what she was looking for: another watch, but old-fashioned – a pocket watch. It has a bulbous shape and feels heavy in her hand. Solid silver. The case is set with jewels that wink at her even in the dim light of the lamp. The back opens to reveal a delicate mechanism and a tiny engraving that she can't quite read in the lamplight. This is real workmanship. It's old, perhaps even a couple of hundred years old. And worth a packet. That's what she calls a tip. She slips it into her handbag and replaces the empty box where she found it.

It's time to go.

She leaves without being seen, back down the stairs and through the main entrance of the club. It's busy, even at this time of night, and people are coming and going. They're dressed up, still ready for a good time, she can see. Men who are worse for drink stand smoking in the doorway as she slips past, clouding the clear night air with their tobacco and alcoholic breath. One of them squeezes her arse and asks her if she's looking for his company. She assures him that she is not, puts her head down, clamps her handbag under her arm and hurries away.

She would like to find a taxicab, if it's possible at this time of night, and walks swiftly, hoping to catch sight of one.

18

Wednesday morning

'The Forty Thieves?'
'Yes. I'm writing a piece about them. They intrigue me.' Harriet spoons sugar into her teacup at the breakfast table.

Isabel frowns – at the sugar and at the reminder of her daughter's desire to work in a newspaper office. 'I don't see why a group of criminal women would be of any interest to anybody. And they really should not be written about.'

'Why not? It would make a good article for the *Gazette*. I've decided to write a feature about them, their lives, why they steal –'

'They shouldn't be given any attention. They should be in prison. Or at home, looking after their children. Not so much sugar, Harriet. You're getting married in a few months and Ralph won't want you spilling out of your dress.'

Harriet bites her lip. She rather imagines that Ralph would be delighted if she spilled out of her dress, but her mother doesn't need to hear that.

'They are real women, Mummy. Some of them do have children, but they all look after one another, better than a trade union, even.'

'Nonsense,' Gerald grunts from behind the newspaper. 'Don't make them out to be saintly matrons. Those who aren't thieving themselves are living off the criminal activity of the men they associate with.'

'Well, none of them has much money, Daddy.' She takes a careful sip of her tea. 'They don't steal because they want the items *per se*, they sell them on, so that they can eat and pay the rent. They are desperate people, some of them.'

Gerald groans, lowering the newspaper. 'Dear God, must I be lectured over the breakfast table? This is nearly as bad as when you were fired up by the Pankhurst women.'

'I'm not lecturing. I am simply saying that we should ask *why* the women steal in the first place –'

'They steal because they want to have the sort of fancy goods you or I might have, without bothering to purchase them,' Isabel snaps. 'It has nothing to do with paying the rent.'

'By the way, I ought to have asked before, is Robert Pickford content for you to continue at the *Gazette*?' Gerald lays down his newspaper and reaches for the marmalade jar. 'Knowing that you'll be married soon? You're sitting waving that enormous diamond around.'

'Quite content.' Harriet returns to her tea, avoiding her father's eye. 'But I won't let the Forty Thieves go, you know,' she says finally, with quiet conviction. 'I'm going into the office this morning to write about them.'

Gerald shakes his head and begins to spread marmalade on thin slices of white toast.

'But your dress, Harriet, your wedding dress.' Isabel taps a finger on the table, wanting to talk of something other than the *Kensington Gazette* and the Forty Thieves. 'The dressmaker is expecting us at half past ten, and you don't need to go into the newspaper office. I booked the appointment for today.'

Harriet had planned to spend the morning reading copies of old newspapers in the office, to glean more information about the women from Southwark to add to what she's learned from Alice Dunning. She has even decided how she will frame the piece, having coaxed from Alice the name of the thief she saw.

Not Ruby Wilder, but Ruby Mills. Ruby Mills, with her film-star looks and fondness for diamonds and mink. She will write about her. The girl whose face she can see when she closes her eyes.

She had also already agreed to meet Ralph for lunch in town, after a short morning in the office. Now, it appears her mother has other plans.

'You need, at least, to begin to put your mind to the wedding day,' Isabel continues. 'It will only be for an hour or two.' She reaches out to take her daughter's hand. 'It'll be pleasurable. Dressing up, choosing the fabric, and the dressmaker is very keen to begin.' Isabel's tone is superficially cordial but admits no argument.

'You ought to listen your mother, Harrio,' Gerald says, cutting the toast into triangles. 'It's always for the best, you know. To listen. She has our best interests at heart.'

Harriet catches the meaning, and her heart sinks a little. Isabel has been discussing the wedding plans with Gerald. Everything will have been decided by her mother and has now been approved by her father. She might as well try to hold back the tide like King Canute. It is always easier to give in.

'Alright, Mummy. The Forty Thieves can wait, I'm sure. And the office. And, yes, I'll admit, I am looking forward to wearing something lovely.' She squeezes her mother's hand. There will be further arguments. She knows that she and Isabel will have different ideas about what a wedding dress should look like and hopes that the dressmaker they are visiting will know about modern cuts and styles. She will submit to her mother's wishes only so far.

'But I am meeting Ralph for lunch,' she says, giving her mother a warm smile and playing with the string of pearls at her throat. 'So we mustn't spend too long with the satin.'

The lobes of Isabel's ears turn pink. 'Of course, darling. We won't keep you from your fiancé, even if the morning is being spent for his benefit.'

The morning is being spent for Isabel's benefit. It is she who wants to visit the dressmaker. She is determined to control and organise the wedding, to ensure that it is the society event of the year. Ralph, who will undoubtedly be content to let his future mother-in-law have her way in this regard, has only a passing interest in fashion. He likes Harriet to look well turned out, but not what he calls 'overdone', by which, she assumes, he means heavy-eyed with make-up and covered in jewellery. But even he, Harriet ruefully admits, will expect her to look her best on her wedding day.

July. Less than five months away.

In less than five months, she will breathe the fresher air of a different house. She will look up from her breakfast and see Ralph's handsome, smiling face rather than her father, pushing toast under his grey moustache, into his mouth. Ralph will read out snippets from the newspaper rather than huff and mutter to himself, and she will no longer have to endure her father's opinions on the shortcomings of Lloyd George's government or her mother's constant sniping. Together, she and Ralph will change the world.

'I can't wait,' she says aloud.

'Well.' Isabel sits up and smooths her palms over her skirts. 'I am pleased to hear it.'

'Tell him I need a word, when you see him,' Gerald says, still chewing. 'Ralph. Haven't seen him at the club for a while.' He picks up his newspaper and shakes it out to resume his reading. He will not emerge from it again until the maid comes in to clear the table.

Harriet dabs a napkin to her lips and lays it on the tablecloth.

'I shall do that. But now, I ought to change my outfit. Mummy won't approve of me dressing like a typist when we're visiting a fashion house.'

'Certainly not. Try to look a little more refined than you usually do. And do something with your hair. It looks like a bird's nest.'

Harriet bends down and plants a kiss on her mother's cheek. 'Thank goodness Ralph likes me as I am.'

'You can be sure that he will like you even more if you make an effort. You know so little of what men want, darling.' She pats her daughter's hand. 'Change your shoes as well, please. Those look dreadfully scuffed and in need of a good polish. Leave them out for Hanson.'

Harriet leaves her parents to their own company, her mother picking at a boiled egg and her father chewing steadily from behind the newspaper.

It is half past twelve when Harriet arrives, exhausted and jittery, at Claridge's, where Ralph is waiting for her. He kisses her swiftly on the cheek and ushers her through the foyer and into the dining room. Even though the day is bright, the chandeliers are sparkling with electric lights, making the white stuccoed arches gleam. The room hums with quiet, convivial conversation.

'Am I late?' Harriet catches sight of herself in one of the large mirrors on the wall. She has, since parting from her mother, applied a slick of lipstick and pressed a touch of powder to her nose and chin. Nothing too daring or 'fast', as Isabel would say, but enough to help her feel a little special.

'No, not at all. I don't think so.'

'Thank goodness. Mummy has had me draped in ivory satin for what seemed like hours.'

'Sounds horrifying.'

'It was. And it's all for your benefit, she says, so that you're met by a vision of loveliness on our wedding day and not the despicable drab you'll have to put up with thereafter.'

The waiter pulls the seat for her, and she sits down.

'You're hardly a drab, my darling. I wouldn't be marrying you if you were.' He sits and takes the menu from the waiter, nodding the man away.

'Thank you. That's what I told her.'

'Intelligence and beauty; it's a rare combination,' he says, gazing idly down at the menu rather than at his bride. 'Is it too early for champagne, do you suppose?'

It seems like only yesterday that they were emerging from the privations of war: meatless Tuesdays, endless dreary vegetables and unrefined flour in their bread. They had learned remarkably quickly how to be adventurous and indulgent again.

'No, champagne would be wonderful.'

Ralph orders them both a meal of consommé, sole in cream, followed by stuffed veal breast with potatoes. Harriet talks of the dressmaker, and of her mother's fussing. Ralph is amused.

'I think Isabel intends for us to rival the King and Queen.'

'She will make certain of it, and my life will be unbearable unless I fall into line.'

He raises his glass to her. 'I suspect that even the great Gerald Littlemore trembles behind closed doors.'

'I suspect you're right,' she laughs, enjoying the champagne and relaxing. 'Not that you'd know it from the way she defers in public.'

The potatoes arrive served a la crème.

Harriet sighs as she inspects them. 'Oh dear, I'm supposed to be slimming. And here you are, fattening me up like the prize heifer with all this cream.'

'Why are you slimming?'

'Mummy thinks I'm growing fat.'

'Well, please don't starve yourself on my account.' He smiles, reaching out to squeeze her hand. He pats it as he releases it. 'Besides,' he continues, helping himself to another spoon of carrots. 'Most men prefer a little flesh.'

It must be the champagne; something in his tone, the dark suggestiveness of it, thrills Harriet. She wonders what it will be like when he comes to explore her flesh more intimately. He has behaved impeccably towards her so far, of course, though she can't help but imagine the two of them entwined together, away from parents, propriety, other people's expectations. How it will feel to be alone, naked, with him –

'Christie? Fancy finding you here. No, no, don't get up.'

Her brief drunken reverie is interrupted. Ralph is being hailed by an impressive man in a smart overcoat. Not much older than Ralph, he is probably a politician or a banker, if he knows her fiancé.

Harriet feels her cheeks reddening with embarrassment, as though the lascivious thoughts she had been entertaining had been spoken aloud to this stranger.

'We were only talking of you the other day.'

'All good, I hope.' Ralph leans back in his seat, concerned now with neither his fiancée's figure nor her flesh. The affable club man again, and fully at ease.

'What else?'

'This is my fiancée, Harriet Littlemore. You'll know her father, Gerald, of course.'

The man nods to Harriet. 'I do know your father. Charles Haversham, by the way.'

Harriet is used to men knowing her father. She smiles, automatically. 'How do you do?'

'You're having lunch. I shouldn't interrupt, Ralph, but I'm glad to have spotted you. Will you be at the House later? I wouldn't mind a word. I have some news on that venture we spoke of. Some interesting developments.'

Ralph pulls a watch from his pocket. He's not yet taken to wearing a wristwatch – he is convinced they are only for women. This one is gold. A Christie heirloom. He clicks open the case and consults it before glancing up at Harriet. She knows before he opens his mouth, from his expression, what he is likely to say. The soft glow of passion that had been stirring inside her moments ago has already been dampened.

'I might wander over in an hour or two. Shall I find you in the bar?'

'Only if I can steal you from your lovely fiancée? I'd hate to be the third wheel...'

'Not at all. Harriet and I are enjoying a quiet moment of liberation from her parents, but' – he looks again at Harriet, hesitating, trying to judge her mood – 'we've nearly finished our lunch, and then I'll need to return her safely to the front door. Mustn't find myself on the wrong side of my future father-in-law.' He winks at Harriet. 'Or my mother-in-law.'

She smiles brightly, masking her disappointment. 'That would not be a good idea.'

'Later, then.' Ralph stands, shakes hands with Charles

Haversham and shares some final pleasantries before sitting to resume his meal.

'A useful man to know, Haversham,' he tells Harriet, spearing a slice of potato. 'Good contacts.'

They return to Onslow Square not long after, strolling through Hyde Park, arm in arm. They talk of the restaurant, how they enjoyed the veal especially. Ralph jokes about the cream and her anxiety about gaining weight, but the delicious possibilities of carnality have vanished from Harriet's thoughts now that she is sober, and she really does think that perhaps she ought to lose a few pounds. They talk of the wedding, of needing to decorate Ralph's house in Mayfair before Harriet moves in. Anyone listening to the conversation would assume from the animated way they speak that they were a couple wildly in love, planning their future with good sense and careful thought.

That is exactly what we are, Harriet tells herself. But as they embrace on the steps of her parents' house – before greeting Gerald and Isabel formally and properly – she feels a little flat. As though something is missing.

19

Wednesday morning

'This ain't no ordinary piece, Magpie.'

Solly sits in the kitchen above the shop, his eyeglass pressed into his socket, a cigarette dangling from his lower lip. He is examining Peter Lazenby's pocket watch. The tiny stones on the case glisten in the morning light. Solly presses the catch, and the case opens. Ruby hears him murmur an appreciative curse under his breath. She has already seen it – the exquisite movement, so delicate and precise – and knows why he is swearing. It mesmerised her for a long time. He's right: it isn't ordinary. How long will it be before Peter realises it is missing? How often does he open the box that is lying among his socks and check that his family heirloom is still there? How often does he entertain thieves in his bedroom?

'Where did you find it?' He closes it and lays it on the table. The initials engraved into the back of the casing stare up at her, accusing her now that she can read them. *P.F.G.L.* They've been added recently, by the look of them, by the sort of man who might want to mark his property. Perhaps it wasn't an heirloom, after all. Just something else he fancied.

Ruby stands, her back leaning against the sink, chewing her lip.

'Fell into my hand. You know how it is.'

He drops the eyeglass onto the table and stares at her. 'Come off it. What's the story? I'm not an expert when it comes to watches, but it's old and made by someone who knew what he was doing. Where did you find it?'

'Alright. Man in Soho. Gentleman. Owns a nightclub in Gerrard Street. It's his watch.'

Solly wipes a hand over his scalp and frowns. 'If he's rich enough to own something like this, and he runs a club in Soho, then he's a crook. A real one. You know that as well as I do.'

'Yeah, he's a crook. Billy Walsh was at the club. He's doing some business there for the Elephants. That's how I met this man, Peter Lazenby.'

He sucks his teeth and runs a thumb over the initials. '*P.F.G.L.* You should know better than to take something from a man like that. Someone with contacts. He'll have people looking for it, as soon as he knows it's gone.'

'You'll have to get rid of it then. Strip it down, sell off the parts, like you usually do.'

Solly shakes his head. 'I'm not keeping it. The Richmonds offer me protection, but if the Elephants are looking to do business over in Soho, then it sounds as though they wouldn't stand in the way if this Lazenby came calling. You'll have to lose it.'

'I'm not losing it. It's worth something.'

'It's worth a lot. But it's difficult to sell when it's got someone's initials on it.'

'You won't take it apart?' She leans over the table, inspecting it. 'It's got diamonds in it.'

He picks it up and cradles it, turning it this way and that. 'Breaking a watch like this would be criminal, Magpie. It's a work of art.'

She sighs and snatches it up. 'It's a watch, Solly. It's money. You never worry about picking jewellery apart. You're getting sentimental in your old age.' She feels the weight of it, the coolness of the silver heavy in the hollow of her palm.

'And you're getting greedy. And foolish. You'll slip up, if you carry on like this. Find yourself in Holloway with Alice.'

She rolls her eyes and wanders out of kitchen.

She fights the sense of loathing, shakes herself as she walks, and makes her way back over the river to see Raymond Calladine. He doesn't normally deal with men's pocket watches, but he'll know where to sell it. Or at least he'll look after it, while she decides what to do with it. She can persuade him. She always can.

There's a couple in the shop browsing when she enters. She recognises, from the way that Ray is speaking to them, that they are not going to spend a lot of money. He's rushing them into a sale – the best he can hope for is that they will choose a slightly better cut of diamond solitaire, for which he will charge them accordingly. The woman's skirt is trailing the hem at the back, and the man appears as though he's still in France in his head – he has that nervous, jumpy look about him, as if he expects someone to shout or point a bayonet at him at any moment.

Ray nods a greeting to her but continues to push his sale.

The woman turns frightened eyes to Ruby. She's anxious about something – probably the expense of the ring. Too many people are worried about money, even as others are flashing it about.

Ruby looks at the meagre fare they are contemplating. Tiny diamonds are not worth the effort as far as she is concerned, but then she's never had a poor soldier ask her to marry him. She frowns as she thinks of Billy. She needs this couple to hurry up and leave.

'That one.' She points to a ring at the edge of the cushion. 'Try that one.'

The woman gives a nervous laugh. 'It looks too expensive.'

Ruby shakes her head. 'Nah. It's the way it's cut. Makes it look bigger, more impressive. And the shape of the shoulders on the mount make it stand out. But the stone isn't as big as that one, in reality.' She gestures to the one Ray is holding. 'So, it'll be cheaper.'

Ray scowls at Ruby but pulls out the ring for the woman to try. It fits her finger, and she extends her arm to inspect it. Ruby catches the look in her eye – the smallest gleam of joy and relief.

'Is this one *really* less expensive?' The panic returns swiftly. 'When it's so much prettier?'

Ray beams at her. He may be gritting his teeth at losing a few pounds, but at least he is nearer to a sale than he was a moment ago. He offers the price to the young man, who glances warily at his girl to make sure that she doesn't mind wearing a lesser jewel. He is shaking. When he turns around, Ruby sees that his jacket dangles limply from the shoulder. He's lost an arm.

It takes only a moment for Ray to nestle the ring in a box and relieve the young man of his money.

This is what love is then, Ruby thinks. Or this is what it comes down to. Being willing to settle for second best rather than holding out for something more. Or perhaps that's just marriage.

'You should come and work for me, not Solly Palmer,' Ray says to Ruby, once the couple is through the door. 'I thought I was never going to make a sale there. Hardly got tuppence between them, the poor bastards.'

She shrugs. 'Close the shop, Ray. I've brought you something.'

'What?'

'Well, I'm not going to show you unless you lock the door.' She swings her handbag back and forth, knowing that he won't be able to resist.

He draws the bolt, turns the sign to 'closed' and lowers the blinds.

'There's not enough light in here,' he says. 'We'll go out the back.'

She hesitates for only a fraction of a second before following him into the back office. The light is hardly better here, but he turns on a lamp and there's a high window that gives a reasonable amount of daylight from the backyard.

He's offhand with her, barely acknowledging her, twitchy.

Usually by now he would have touched her, pressed against her or suggested some sort of liaison. She's not expected here today. Solly hasn't sent her, and this is not arranged. He was not anticipating a thief in his shop, and it has made him ill at ease. Still, he wants to know what she has brought.

She pulls the watch from her bag and lays it, with care, on the table. He says nothing. He never reacts when Solly places pieces in front of him either – never gives away his interest. He remains silent as he reaches for his eyeglass to take a better look, opening the back to examine the mechanism. She watches his expression keenly. It barely alters, but she can hear that he is breathing a little faster.

He licks his lower lip and takes the glass from his eye.

'Where did you get this?' He runs his fingers across the back of the case, across the engraved initials.

'It fell into my hand.' The same line she gave Solly.

He doesn't buy it either. 'This is the sort of watch that belongs in a museum, not the sort that falls into your grubby paws. Eighteenth-century, solid silver, made by a master of his craft and worth an absolute mint, despite this later engraving.'

'Can you sell it for me? I'll take a share of the profit.'

He raises his eyebrows.

'You think it'll be easy to sell a piece like this? Even if I can rub out these initials, the only sort of person who'll be interested in buying will be a serious collector – and that sort will want to know where it comes from. How hot is it? When did you lift it?'

'Last night.'

He takes a sharp breath. 'Jesus Christ, Ruby.'

'Solly won't touch it.'

'I'm not surprised. Look –' He blinks at Ruby. His lips slide into something resembling a smile. 'Tell you what, I'll keep it here, save you carrying it about. As a favour to my best girl.'

She can sense what's coming.

'Thanks.'

'I'll ask around, see if anyone might be after a piece like this. I've contacts across London. I know people. It's almost unsellable, but I'll see if I can get rid of it, just for you. I'll see what I can do.'

'I appreciate it, Ray.'

He pulls his own watch from the pocket in his waistcoat, glances at it, then sighs. He needs to open the shop again.

He stands up, wraps the silver watch in his silk handkerchief and lays it in his desk drawer.

'I'll have customers queuing if I don't return to the shop.'

'I should go, too.'

He pauses, so close to her that the smell of his pomade hits the back of her throat. She tries not to breathe as he touches her, caresses her face. He drags a fingernail down her cheek and over her mouth.

'We'll have to discuss terms, percentages of the sale and such like, another time.' The long nail grazes her lower lip. 'I'll look forward to that.'

'Yeah, of course, Ray…' She puts a hand on his chest. She can't afford to push him away but wants to keep him at a distance. It's a good thing that she chose a busy time to visit.

20

Saturday evening

The Borough stinks tonight. The light easterly wind carries the rancid stench of the Bermondsey tanneries to Ruby's nostrils. It layers the scent of rotting excrement and the pungent, sulphurous smell of a brewery's wastewater that blow down the High Street whatever the wind direction.

She tries to remember the rich fragrance that pervades the ground floor of Debenham and Freebody or Selfridges, and the bottles of French perfume that one might sniff and dab on one's skin. Or the warm smell of the fur coats she has wrapped around her shoulders in those stores while pretending that she has means to purchase such luxuries.

Someone is cooking smoked haddock and cabbage. The whole street is eating fish tonight.

She has spent the day wandering the stores over the river, venturing into places she doesn't usually go hoisting, buying a few items – a handbag, some cosmetics, perfume, silk underwear – and stopping to have lunch. Now she is cleaned out of cash again.

There has been no word from Raymond Calladine. He hasn't sent a message to say that he has sold her watch. It's Saturday. He's only had the piece since Wednesday, but she'd hoped that he might have found someone. She wants the money – even if it means she will have to go to bed with him. The prospect of it makes her feel sick, but she knows that's the price he'll demand, as well as his share of the sale, the vile bastard.

She pushes on the heavy door of the Crown and surveys the saloon. Billy is sitting with Charlie Wagstaff, in deep discussion about something. Horses, probably. Charlie is sporting a black eye. It's worse than Billy's. Looks like he might have broken his nose, too. She scowls at them both when Billy raises his head and makes her way over to the far end of the room, where some of the Forties have gathered, collecting a gin on the way. It's a far cry from the champagne she drank with Peter Lazenby.

Edith shuffles along to create a small amount of room for her on the settle.

'What's wrong with your face?' she asks. 'You look miserable. It's Saturday. Party night. And pay day.'

Ruby takes a sip of her drink and opens her handbag, hunting for cigarettes.

'Good job. I need the cash.'

The rest of the Forties drift in slowly, mostly in pairs. There will be as many women here tonight as men, because it's Saturday. Doll sits in the corner, talking to herself, cutting up a cabbage on the table with a large knife and tipping the slices into a saucepan. Her pint of brown stout is half-drunk already. The men are fewer in number than usual – some of them were arrested at the fight in Clerkenwell last week and are awaiting trial. The ones who have turned up, like Charlie Wagstaff, are still wearing bruises and battle scars as proudly as they wear their war medals.

Annie Richmond enters the saloon, arm in arm with Maggs. They pause at the bar to talk with Clara, and Ronald buys them both a drink. Albert is one of those in a police cell. Edith tells Ruby that Ron left him at the fight and drove off in his car. Bert is furious. Howling curses from behind bars. She heard this from Maggs.

Maggs looks to be in a cheerful mood.

'And George was arrested by the police, like Bert.' Edith has all the news. She's talking to Ruby without worrying whether Ruby is listening. She's been working in Grace's warehouse today, helping to sort clothes. She's been picking over the best of them for herself. She always does. She has picked up all the gossip as well.

'George?'

'George Dunning. Alf told Maggs that he went for a copper with a knife – we all know what he's like when he's fired up. It's serious this time. He'll be inside for a lot longer than Alice. When she gets out of Holloway, she'll have the house to herself.'

Finally, Ruby breaks into a chuckle. 'Lucky old Alice. We'll have the party at her house when she comes out.'

'We'll throw out all his clothes and stuff, and he can find himself a new home when he's served his time.'

'We should try and get word to her. She'd love to hear it.'

'If we can't reach her before the trial, Annie'll shout it across the court to her.' Edith laughs. 'There'll be a fuss in the gallery if she does, but Annie won't mind, and I doubt the judge will trouble himself over it.'

'Daisy!' Ruby, now more animated by the gin and the good news about Alice's husband, spots Daisy Gould enter the saloon by herself. Without Harry, she looks lost, thinner. Her weary eyes catch Ruby waving to her, and her mouth curls into a half-hearted smile.

'Daisy looks rough,' Ruby mutters. 'She's taking it really hard, Harry being inside.'

'I never fancied Harry much myself, but she really loves him.' Edith is philosophical about other people's problems. 'Five years is forever as far as she's concerned.'

They shuffle up to make room for her.

'How are you, Daisy?' Ruby asks.

'Not so bad, I'spose. I had a letter from Harry yesterday. He's well, he says. Been smashing up rocks and hurt his hand, but he's coping. It's not the first time he's been inside.'

Harry and Daisy had lived well enough between them. Harry

had worked in a local brewery, delivering barrels to the few public houses that took the beer. It was not well-paid work, but it was honest. The burglaries, the fights, the betting and the casual pilfering were what he did after hours. Daisy went out with the Forties and helped sometimes with the brewery – more so when the men were away at war, less when they came home on leave. They never starved. Harry returned from France with ambitions for a better life for himself and his new wife from the brewery, and the money came in. Daisy started walking around in prettier hats, a smarter coat. Harry was talking about a car. He was not earning enough at the brewery to buy a car, but the money miraculously appeared, and a car was purchased. They talked about moving house and living somewhere better.

And then Harry overreached himself. He travelled out west to ransack a house on his own and was caught by the householder. He might have run away, slipped into the night and been lost to the police, except he decided to attack the man, tried to cut his throat. The man's housemaid had raised the alarm, running shrieking into the street and finding two constables right outside the house as if they had been waiting there. And Harry had gone to Pentonville.

It might not be the first time Harry Gould has been in prison, but thieving from a store and burgling a house are crimes of a different order, especially if you also try to murder the house's occupier. He will have plenty of time to grow used to his incarceration.

'And you?' Ruby can see Daisy's eyes are still dark. She's twitchy, too. 'How are you? Really?'

'I'm managing. Just about. I need a job – not just with the Forties, I mean. A regular job. Something to keep me going while Harry's inside. I really need the cash. Trouble is, everyone in the Borough knows where he is and what he's done, and I can't find any straight work. No one wants me.'

Jobs are scarce. The men who returned from the war have moved back into the factories and shops and offices and reclaimed their jobs. The women who kept those jobs warm for them have returned to laundering, serving in small shops and crossing the river at dawn to char in homes and offices in the City. Women like Daisy, suddenly in need of work, are discovering that many jobs are taken. And employers don't want to hire a woman whose husband is a burglar with a knife. Who knows what she would make off with? They certainly won't hire her if they know of her association with the Forties. She is tainted, as well as penniless.

'I thought I'd ask Grace if there's any work at the warehouse.'

Edith says nothing. She knows that Grace will be reluctant to take on another worker, even out of charity. And she won't give up her own place, not even for Daisy.

The Crown continues to fill with people. Men wearing their better suits for party night mill around, still discussing the boxing match and the fight that came after it. Snatches of conversation rise and fall – talk of the coppers and their coshes, who is in the cells and, most importantly of all, how the Clerkenwell lads received the thrashing they deserved. The Elephants might be depleted in number, by one or two, but they have restored the honour of the Borough and their reputation among the London gangs. There are cheers, roars, laughs swirling into the air with the tobacco smoke.

Ruby knows that this world is fading. The people here cling onto a past that has slipped away with the war. Twenty, thirty years ago, the Elephants were mighty in this part of London. Now, they are scrappy thieves and crooked bookmakers. They run the betting at the racetrack and the dog track, but others like Billy Kimber and the men from Birmingham are moving in, and the real money – the real influence – is to be had where the rich men play.

She looks over at Billy, joshing and joking with the others. This is what he's doing – he and Frederick Moss are trying to lead the others into modernity. Dragging them by the nose. Moss and Billy are forging alliances with bigger players, elbowing aside Kimber's Brummagems, building up the Elephants' reputation in new ways. Moss is shrewd – almost as shrewd as Annie Richmond. He knows that the men who operate in Peter Lazenby's circle will be far better protected than those working with the gang leaders like Kimber, for all their knife-wielding bravado. Billy Walsh has been sent in to deal and negotiate because he's fought alongside these men in France, and he's earned their respect.

Ruby can admire them for it, even if she's annoyed that Billy won't let her be part of the business. It's not unknown for the Forties and Elephants to work side by side, and he knows it. He is deliberately keeping her out of it. Keeping her small and in her place.

The Forties are adapting, too. The larger department stores have grown wise to their ways, and it is not only Debenham and Freebody who are employing superintendents to walk and watch the customers. Even Gert's ingenious clothing has had its day – with the changing fashions, it is becoming increasingly difficult to shove stolen goods up your skirts without spoiling the line of your outfit and standing out like a sore thumb. Annie has noticed this in the London stores and is already exploring the possibilities of taking the girls raiding around the country, in places where they won't be expected nor noticed. She pores over the train timetables, like Charlie Wagstaff pores over the *Sporting Life*. And because the odds of being caught in the capital are increasing, she is planning more raids with motorcars, so that the Forties can escape at speed, driving faster than a policeman can run or cycle.

Maggs, Grace and Gert weave their way to where Ruby, Daisy and Edith are sitting. They part, like ladies in waiting, and the Queen of the Thieves passes through, making her stately progress to the table.

'Ladies.' Annie smiles affably as she sits, a glass of stout in her hand, rings glittering over her fingers. 'Pay day today, as I'm sure you're all aware.'

She opens her handbag and pulls out several envelopes. 'We did well this week, despite losing Alice.' Annie hands out the envelopes. 'Try not to spend it all at once, girls,' she cackles, pulling cigarettes out of the bag as well. 'But if you need to lose it, I've got a good tip on a horse running at Newmarket next week – and I know a bookie offering very reasonable odds.'

They all laugh at this.

Ruby opens her envelope and skims a thumb across the thin bundle of notes. She could have more for herself if she worked on her own. The others don't even check their earnings; they shove the packet into their pockets or bags and carry on the conversation.

'Never mind Newmarket, I've heard that Whiteleys is having a sale next week,' Maggs says, leaning in. 'We should go. I love a good sale.'

They all love a sale. Hundreds of hands will be grasping, rummaging, sifting, pawing at the goods, making it all too easy for the Forties to slip in, hoist and escape unseen.

Annie considers it. 'We could pull a couple of the cells together,' she says, puffing on her smoke. 'Make up the numbers. Your girls, Maggs, and Scotch Mary's. That'll take us to eight girls. We'll put six hoisters in the store – no one will notice you among the crowds. You can jostle and hustle and pack half the store into your coats. Gert, we'll need some new expandable bags to fit inside blouses and under skirts. There'll be a lot of merchandise.'

Gert nods. 'I can do that.'

'There's Scotch Mary.' Grace waves and a tall woman with a halo of bright red hair wanders over. She's not Scottish, nor is her name always Mary.

'We're discussing Whiteleys, Scotch,' Maggs says, pulling out a seat. 'Annie thinks we should put our girls together next week. They've got a sale on.'

Mary's eyes light up. She places her whisky on the table and eases her lanky body into the chair. 'Sounds good to me. I can bring my three.'

'We'll put six inside and keep two bolsters on Queen's Road, ready to catch the goods that are in hand and run for the cars,' says Annie. 'I'll bring the Chrysler and Ronnie'll be around, too. Ruby, you're nippy, so you can bolster, and we'll put little Florrie outside as well.'

'I want to be inside,' says Ruby. 'I can pack a pile inside my coat.' She hates standing on the street, turning blue in the cold, waiting to take the goods from the others and quickly carry them away. She prefers to be part of the crush inside when there's a sale. You can swipe a lot in a crowd.

Annie shakes her head. 'You'll do as I say and stay outside. You're too small for this kind of operation. You'll be better suited to receiving anything brought out and bolstering it to the cars.'

Ruby chews her lip, saying nothing. It's Annie's quiet way of keeping her down. She's stepped out of line once or twice recently, so now she's being given a lower responsibility – relegated to the same role as Florrie, who is only thirteen and still learning.

The chatter continues over Ruby's head. Outwardly, she laughs and jokes, but she's still seething at Annie's insult. She, Ruby Mills, can pick up priceless watches, go to bed with nightclub owners, find diamonds and pearls that others would miss. And Annie won't let her inside Whiteleys during a sale.

After a while, Annie, Grace and Maggs leave the table to talk to some of the other Forties. Scotch Mary goes with them. Edith grabs Daisy's hand and drags her over to the piano, determined to raise her spirits. The man who is sitting on the stool happily bangs out the song she requests, and half of the saloon joins in singing. Even Doll puts down her knife to hum and tap along, before finishing the last inch of her pint and reluctantly standing to go home. Ruby sits, observing, no longer in the mood for their company.

Annie has left her handbag open on her seat.

Ruby checks the room. No one is looking in her direction; they are too busy singing. Quietly, she moves to sit next to the bag and feels around inside it. There are several tightly rolled wads of notes among the envelopes. She squeezes them, assessing how much there is. It would be easy enough to lift one, to pull her hand out slowly as if she were raiding a letterbox. It's tempting.

She withdraws her hand quickly – empty. Annie is as sharp as a knife. She will have counted the notes and she will know exactly where and with whom she left her bag. Even if she only suspected Ruby of stealing, Annie would maim her for life, or worse, throw her out of the Forties and turn everyone against her.

Ruby stands and drains her gin, eyes scanning the room. No one has seen her hand in Annie's bag, she's sure of it.

She hitches her coat over her shoulders and walks to the door. She gives Maggs's arm a pat as she passes, claiming a headache that requires an early night, and nods goodnight to Annie, fire burning inside her chest.

One day, she will be better than all of them. One day, she will be Queen.

21

Monday afternoon

Y ou've sold it?' Ruby stands in Ray's back office, hands on hips. 'You never sent word. You said selling it would be difficult – impossible except to a collector.'

He sits behind his desk, relishing her agitation.

'It was mine, you bastard. You had no right to sell it without telling me first. You said we'd sort the terms. Who bought it? How much did you make from it? Where's it gone?'

He leans back in the chair. 'You overreached yourself with this one, Ruby. I knew you'd be in trouble over it. Knew you'd come crawling back.'

'Fuck yourself, Ray. I'm not crawling. I just want my cut.'

He reaches into his jacket pocket and takes out his cigarette case, opens it and finds a smoke, addressing her without looking up. 'Pass me the matches, Ruby, there's a good girl. They're on the shelf behind you.'

She knows where the matches are. Where they always are. She grinds her teeth as she throws the box to him.

He lights up and settles further into his seat, drawing on the cigarette. She hates it when he's like this. He knows she's desperate. She can see the glint of triumph in his face and despises him for it. She tries to keep still, but her body fidgets with mounting impatience.

He blows smoke into the air.

'I want my cut, Ray. My money. That was my watch. You said we'd discuss the terms, so let's discuss them.'

He sits, smoking, staring at her thoughtfully, as if he's giving their business arrangement serious consideration. He's making her wait. Even this is beginning to annoy her, but she bites down her frustration.

The clock on the wall ticks heavily. It's louder than usual.

He takes a final draw on the cigarette, stubs it out in a thick glass ashtray and smiles.

'I'd better close up for the afternoon, then, hadn't I?'

He eases himself out of his seat and makes his way to the front door of the shop to lock up, brushing past her as he goes.

His heavy, sweet scent thickens in her throat.

Perhaps she could kill him – once he's given her the money.

Harriet types up her notes steadily. The reporters' hall is noisy, clattering, shouty. Someone makes a loud comment about needing a cup of tea, but she ignores it, shuts it out of her mind, keeps her head down. Alice Dunning had been helpful enough, and along with the comments from the girl at Hartleys and her own recollections from the theft at Mr Enderby's jewellery shop, she will soon have a decent piece to take to Mr Pickford. She has given him what he asked for already. The copy about engagement rings was declared 'charming', though it led to an awkward exchange when he enquired about whether she had a young man and if she was expecting to become engaged in the near future. She had glanced, anxiously, at her left hand, worrying that she had forgotten to remove her diamond ring.

According to Alice Dunning, Ruby Mills had been in Debenham and Freebody with her, but on a different floor. She had not been looking at talcum powder or perfume – she had been elsewhere. It was gloves, possibly, or scarfs, that she had lifted. Harriet imagines Ruby's lithe figure wrapped in bright silk. Or a daring evening gown with sheer fabric that skims one's skin. Ruby Mills would be the sort of girl to dare, she is certain.

She frowns at her typewriter, willing herself to concentrate on the last sentences, before finally tugging the paper from it and advancing towards Pickford's office.

'Make us a cup of tea, Harriet,' one of the reporters wails plaintively. 'A man could die of thirst here.'

'In a minute,' she says, clutching the paper. 'I need to speak with Mr Pickford first.'

She taps on his door and stands at the threshold. He is with one of the subeditors, discussing the layout of a page. She waits, listening to the details of their conversation, fascinated as always with the mechanics of creating a newspaper, until the subeditor is sent away.

'I have something,' she says. 'Would you read it?'

'I'm busy, Miss Littlemore. What is it?'

He runs a hand over his scalp and gestures for her to show him the page. He may be busy, but he is always interested.

He picks up his pencil and sits down to read, silently. Only once does he mark the page, striking out a word – a tautology – before he lays the sheet on his desk. He stares at the paper, then speaks quietly.

'Where did you get this?'

She has done something wrong, and she does not know what it is. 'I don't understand, Mr Pickford.'

'Where did you find this information?'

Harriet decided to shape her piece around Ruby Mills and her life as a thief. She spent the whole weekend thinking about it and planning it. It's short, snappy and written in a lively style, better suited to the *Daily Sketch* than the *Kensington Gazette*.

She flusters. 'Well, I went to visit one of the Forty Thieves in Holloway, a young woman called Alice Dunning – the one caught red-handed in Debenham and Freebody – and she gave me some of it. She gave me a lot about the Thieves and how they operate.'

'I won't ask how you got into Holloway. And the rest?'

'I was the one who saw the girl – Ruby Mills – I saw her raid Mr Enderby's jewellery shop,' she says, standing taller. 'You gave the piece to Jimmy, to Mr Cartwright, but I was an eyewitness. I saw her.'

'And from that, you've conjured' – he taps the paper – 'this. "The Jewel of the Borough".'

She feels her body sinking into the floor. 'Yes,' she says, meekly. 'It's nothing, really, I know. I just thought –'

'It's good,' he says, sounding surprised. 'Sensational writing, and not our usual style, but it's a new angle on the Forty Thieves – to focus on this one girl, Ruby Mills, and make it more personal. You've already whetted the readers' appetite with your Hartleys piece. What was it? The film-star looks and the mink? Now, this.'

He pushes the piece of paper back across his desk.

'You'll print it?'

'Yes, I'll print it. In tomorrow's edition – I've got enough for today. We'll put it on one of the news pages. You can remember what this girl looked like?'

The face, staring out from the motor car. Those wild eyes, full of life.

'I can remember.'

'Good. Go and find Tuft and ask him to draw her for you, so that the readers have a better idea.' Sam Tuft is the artist for the *Gazette*. He creates line drawings when they cannot find a photograph or when they have spent too much money on real images and need only a suggestion of a picture.

'Thank you, Mr Pickford.'

Harriet struggles to contain the thrill that now ripples within her. She trots with a new lightness to James Curran's desk. Perhaps it is finally her desk after all.

'Did you say you were making the tea, Harriet?' Another man, incapable of finding the kettle by himself, passes her before she can even sit down, nudging her arm. 'Put the pot on, love.'

'I was just on my way,' she says, smiling. 'It appears that several of you are so parched you're about to wilt. If you come with me, I'll show you where to find the kettle.'

He laughs and walks off.

This does not irritate her. Nothing can overshadow the shine of Mr Pickford's praise. *It's good*.

It is good.

She wants to run from the building and tell someone that she wrote something she is proud of. Something that the editor likes. Her parents will not share her enthusiasm for a female criminal, but she would like to find Ralph, to read him her piece and hear him say that it was wonderful. He would put his arms around her, kiss her lovingly and tell her that he was proud of her. Yes, she would share this moment with Ralph. Indeed, she will enjoy sharing it.

She fills the kettle with water and sets it to boil, thinking about Ralph and anticipating what he will say.

But the face at the forefront of her mind is not Ralph's.

The one person Harriet truly hopes will read this piece is the subject of it. The girl whose image Sam Tuft will spend the afternoon creating. Of course, she never will. She might not be able to read, Harriet thinks, and besides, the *Kensington Gazette* is not read in Southwark.

Harriet sets the cups on the tray.

'Peter Lazenby?' Ruby snatches up her dress and throws it over her head. 'You sold the watch to Peter *fucking* Lazenby?' She is hopping with fury, incredulous at what Ray the Rat has just told her. 'When did he come here? How did he know about it?'

Ray leans back on his pillow, his arms folded over his head, watching her with a contented sneer on his face.

'You want more answers, you'd better come back to bed, you little firecracker.'

'No. Fuck off. You've had what you wanted. How did he know about the watch?' She buttons up the neck of her dress, hating him, hating everything about him and everything she's done with him. 'Oh… No… I know what you did, you slimy old bastard. You told him about it, didn't you? You went to him.'

He laughs. 'He's a collector. A toff. He's loaded with money. I know him. I recognised his initials on the watch as soon as I saw them and sent a message to him. He's had it for days.'

'So, you sold him his own watch?' She tugs on her stockings as fast as she can without snagging them, spittle flying out of her mouth. 'Where's my cut, then?'

'You don't get a cut, little Ruby. It wasn't a sale. I told you, this is a top-class, top-quality establishment – not like Solly's backstreet hovel. I told him that it had come into my possession and that I was returning it. He gave me a very healthy reward for its safe recovery, no questions asked, and I maintain my reputation as an honest man of business.'

'Honest man of business? You? You're just an old fence in a cheap suit, Ray.'

'And what are you, do you think, eh?' He cackles at her. 'A film star, picking out your diamonds? Or a grubby little tart from the

Borough who had my cock in her mouth half an hour ago? You're just the girl you always were, and there's no amount of diamonds or fancy clothes that can hide that.'

'Fuck you, Ray.'

'Well, you just did, didn't you, sweetheart?'

She picks up an ashtray from the windowsill and hurls it at him with a howl, scattering its stinking contents all over the pillows. He continues to laugh.

She cannot bear to be in the room any longer. She grabs her coat, hat and bag and rushes out, forcing a heel into a shoe as she goes, knowing, at least, that he won't be following her when he's undressed.

Out on the street, she shakes as she puts on her coat and presses her hat to her head.

She is going to be sick.

'Are you alright, miss?' A young man, a soldier, still in uniform, stops, a worried expression on his brow.

'Thank you. I'm well,' she answers in a clipped, controlled voice. 'Just feeling a little dizzy. I'll be fine in a moment.'

'If you're sure…' He touches his hat and walks away. She blinks back her rage as she watches him striding down the pavement like he's on parade.

22

Friday evening

Isabel Littlemore presses the satin at her thigh, smoothing out an imagined crease in her gown. It is new and she is not at all certain about it, but after the deprivations of recent years she has taken to treating herself now and again. Not that the Littlemores had needed to draw in their belts too tightly during the war, but it had not seemed *right* to run about buying fripperies when so many were apparently going short. She licks the corner of her mouth and touches her knuckle to her lip. They will be here soon. She resists the urge to stand up and pace about; she sits, straight-backed, on the edge of her chair in the receiving room.

It will be easier once they arrive. It is always easier once the conversation is flowing and Gerald is holding court at the table. She will enjoy watching him take the lead and rely on him to decide the subjects they will discuss, knowing that her own duties will have been discharged.

She has already reprimanded the cook. When she peered into the kitchen an hour ago, she found the staff idling. There was, cook had said, nothing at that precise moment that needed doing. Everything was under control. But they *should* have been doing something. A frenzy of activity would have reassured her far more than the shrug of *laissez-faire* she encountered. At least the dining table is gleaming. Hanson has spent the afternoon polishing the silver and added extra candles.

She did not dare look in at Harriet's room, for fear of causing an attack of nerves. Harriet will not be dressed, even now. She will be gazing out of her window or fiddling with something at her dressing table.

Gerald is relaxed. He is always relaxed – even when wearing his stiffest evening collar. He has not overseen any of the dining arrangements and is unperturbed by his daughter's tardiness. He strokes the leather arm of the chair and gazes benignly at his wife, confident that she will have everything under control. Besides, the MacKenzies are friends – not the sort to stand on ceremony. He is looking forward to a simple evening of good company and honest food.

Isabel twitches when the doorbell rings. They are early and Harriet has still not appeared downstairs.

She hears Hanson opening the door and greeting the first guest. Ralph's rich baritone reaches her ears as he exchanges a few words with their butler. Then he laughs – a solid, hearty sound – and her nerves melt away.

'Darling, you look wonderful. Yes, I love it.'

Harriet.

Isabel sits a little straighter and smooths her skirt once more, waiting for Hanson to announce Ralph.

Gerald is hosting the evening, but it is Ralph who will fill the room with effortless charisma. He may well become prime minister one day, Isabel realises. Her stomach somersaults at the prospect, and her heart bursts with pride even now, before it has happened. She tries to contain her excitement and smiles up at her daughter's fiancé. Ralph, charming as always, bends down to greet her by kissing her hand and remarks on the elegance of her gown.

'Something new, Isabel, yes? That colour suits you perfectly. Salmon, does one call it? Apricot?' He does not pause long enough to allow her to respond, but turns to Gerald. 'Now, tell me, have I beaten Scotland Yard this evening?' He pulls out his pocket watch in a theatrical fashion and consults it. 'I shall enjoy teasing the inspector about his timekeeping.'

Harriet, at his side, laughs heartily, sharing some sort of private joke to which Isabel is not party. Isabel stares at her, a frown deepening on her forehead.

The doorbell rings again.

'It sounds as though the inspector is only a little way behind you, Ralph,' Gerald says. 'And perfectly on time, given that you were early. You're growing far too familiar.' Gerald is enjoying the joke, even if Isabel is struggling to understand what is quite so amusing. She continues to stare at her daughter, who has joined Ralph and Gerald in welcoming the MacKenzies.

Harriet's dress is made of a lightweight turquoise fabric that shimmers and clings to the curves of her body. It is so sheer that Isabel can discern every part of her and – Dear God – she is revealing her ankles in an evening gown. No wonder she didn't appear downstairs before the guests arrived; Isabel would have instructed her to return to her room and change. Indeed, she would not have allowed her daughter to buy such a vulgar creation in the first place. Ralph has an arm around Harriet's waist, his hand resting lightly on her hip. Isabel turns away as she notices and makes a point of asking Hanson to pour drinks before moving to greet Mary MacKenzie. Thank goodness they will be sitting down at the table soon and the outfit will be mostly hidden.

Arthur MacKenzie is similar in age to Gerald, although his wife is several years younger. The MacKenzies have dined with them before, but Isabel never knows quite how to speak to Mary.

She worries that she is too condescending, or else too familiar, and it is so difficult to find the right pitch and tone with someone with whom one has little in common. But their husbands are on good terms, so she makes the effort, putting to one side her own discomfort in order to be hospitable. She has taken care with the menu – nothing too fancy or challenging – but is now bothered about her choices. Fish, because it's Friday and old habits die hard. It had seemed a good idea two days ago. She has no idea how the men came to know one another initially. Gerald's club, probably. Or the party. Arthur MacKenzie is the sort of man who *aspires* to make something of himself – so the Tory party is a natural home. Gerald and Ralph, of course, are party men by blood, even more so than by temperament or inclination.

Ralph loosens his arm from Harriet's waist to engage Arthur MacKenzie in further conversation, leaving her with her mother and poor little Mary. Not that Mary *is* poor, exactly. She is, Isabel has been given to understand, from rather a smart family. The MacKenzies are comfortable enough and live in one of the smaller houses just around the corner – not on the square, but only a little way off it – but Mary has the dowdy and provincial appearance of a woman raised in a northern part of England that Isabel has never visited and never desires to know. She is a quiet woman, not given to expressions of strong opinion – she leaves those to her husband, who has enough for the two of them. She has raised three sons, none of whom was old enough to join the army before the war ended. Indeed, the eldest is still only sixteen. Mary says that he wishes he had been older. Arthur would have been proud to send his son to France and she agrees, in public, that she would have joined him in this sentiment. But privately, she is happier that her boy always looked immature and that, at thirteen, keen to join up, he was told to return to the schoolyard by the laughing recruiting officer. Isabel, for all she despairs of her daughter, is glad that she did not have to send a son to war, although she declares that she would have been honoured to do so, the cause being so just. There had been a boy, their lovely David, but he had died when he was two. The pain of it still tugs at her belly every so often. And then she remembers to thank God that he died in her arms, sweaty and pale and docile, rather than in the cold foreign mud, alone and unmothered. Isabel and Mary have much that might draw them deeply together into friendship, if they could bring themselves to speak openly. Instead, they make the customary light-but-desultory conversation of polite women – the weather being the easiest and safest entrée – before Mary admires Harriet's gown.

'I found it in Hartleys, would you believe? I bought it on a whim.' Harriet swings her hips a little. She knows it is the sort of gown her mother will disapprove of – far too daring in its cut and the sheerness of its fabric. 'Even Hartleys is following the more modern fashions.' Hartleys is one of her mother's favourite stores. She catches Isabel's eye and decides to moderate her jocularity, changing the subject. 'I must tell you, Mrs MacKenzie, Mummy and I spent a very happy time with Mrs Spencer the other day. She's making my wedding gown and I do declare that it's going to be rather lovely. I shall be quite the most ravishing bride London has ever seen – all thanks to her handiwork.'

Isabel smiles, although her eyes are still cold with disapproval. 'The dress will certainly be beautiful, Harriet. And *modest*.' She emphasises the word.

'Every bride should feel beautiful on her wedding day,' Mary MacKenzie adds in her flat tone. 'When are you marrying? Is it soon?'

'July. Although the exact day hasn't been decided. Ralph says he will be taking care of the formalities very soon, Mummy. The church and everything.' She fiddles with the diamond necklace at her throat, so that the largest stone hangs more in the centre.

'Good,' says Isabel. 'And then we shall have a date at last.'

'Do you have somewhere to live, or shall you reside here?' Mrs MacKenzie asks.

'No!' Harriet laughs away such a dreadful thought. 'Ralph has a house in Mayfair.'

Hanson emerges in the doorway and gives one of his discreet nods, indicating that dinner is ready.

'Oh, yes,' Mrs MacKenzie says. 'I'd forgotten that he was so well set up. You've done very well for yourself, Harriet.'

*

Ruby stares into her glass. She picks it up and lets a large swig of gin wash around her mouth before swallowing it. She still cannot believe that Ray Calladine gave the watch back to Peter Lazenby and denied her the cash for it. For five days she has been fuming. At least it will be Saturday tomorrow – pay day.

'You alright, Ruby?' Maggs stands with one hand on her hip and the other clutching the handle of her pint glass. 'You look like you're carrying the weight of the world on your shoulders.'

'Nah. Just thinking about something. Nothing really. Do you want a seat?'

She shifts along the settle to make room for her old friend.

The Crown is not especially busy. Clara is standing chatting to a group of men at the bar in a rare moment of idleness. She looks tired, washed out. She could be a good-looking woman with a decent night's sleep and a bit of fun. But she won't give herself the night off. She says she can't trust her staff to run the place properly, but Ruby knows that she can't bear to enjoy herself while she's still thinking of Tommy. So, Clara continues to work herself into an early grave. She picks up a greying cloth and wipes the counter.

'She could do with Billy to help her out,' Maggs says, seeing where Ruby is looking. 'He should look after the bar for a night or two. Where is he?'

'How should I know?' Ruby sniffs. 'He's not my business.'

'I thought you were walking out with him.' Maggs reaches into her handbag for her cigarettes and offers one to Ruby. 'After you did that jewellery job together in Kensington. Aren't you?'

'Not sure.'

'That'll account for the long face,' Maggs says, knowingly. 'At least you're not crying over him all the time, like Edith Lennox.'

Ruby pulls a face. 'That's because I've never expected him to stay put. And I never wanted to marry him or anything like that. Edith had visions of hundreds of little Billys running around her skirts.'

Maggs chuckles, cigarette in her teeth.

'I found out he was involved in something up west – Soho – and I went to see what it was. He told me that Freddy Moss is looking to expand the Elephants' business across the river. He's speaking with people over there because he has the right sort of face, he says, the right manner.'

Maggs shrugs. 'Sounds reasonable. They all know that's where the money is. There's nothing around here anymore.'

'I thought he might ask me to be a part of it. I don't want to have his babies, Maggs, but if there are rich pickings to be had, I would have thought he would want to share them with me. I thought we were a team.'

Maggs says nothing.

'He didn't want to know me. He was draped over some tart, a cocaine-sniffer, by the look of her. And then he told me to go away, like I was a child.'

'Why do you want to work with Billy? You work with me.'

The cigarette touches Ruby's lips, but she pauses for a fraction of a second before lighting up. It was foolish to tell Maggs about Billy. She should have made something up. She strikes the match and draws quickly on the smoke.

'I know. It was just an idea. Just me chasing after Billy. Bastard isn't worth my time.'

Maggs's opinions on Billy, and on Ruby's involvement in Soho, go unheard as Annie and Grace arrive at their table.

Annie is in a bad mood; Ruby can sense it. She's learned to read all the Forties over the years. Tonight, there's something in the way Annie drops her handbag on the table – heavily, rather than carefully. Ruby nods to her and greets Grace, who is as affable as always.

'You won't believe the pantomime we went through!' Grace is laughing before she has even begun telling them what's happened. 'You should have seen us, Maggs. It took me back to the old days, when we were kids, pinching pies from the shop over the bridge – do you remember?'

'Pattersons? I remember. Patterson and his meat pies. Why, what were you doing? Pinching pies?' Maggs asks.

Annie is scowling now. Her hand curls around her glass of stout and her diamond rings stand proud like knuckledusters.

Ruby sees it: Grace is enjoying a joke at Annie's expense. This is why she's so sullen. It will do Annie good, Ruby thinks – she's always too serious, too impressed by her own importance.

Grace reaches inside her own handbag as she sits down and pulls out a parcel of newspaper, wrapped in string.

'What you got there?' Maggs asks. Her eyes are shining with mischief. She's known Annie since they were babies and, although she's loyal to the Queen of the Thieves, like Grace, she's ready to tease.

Annie growls. 'The most expensive fucking vegetables in the whole world, that's what.'

Edith has joined them. She stands, peering over the parcel. They all stare at it.

'Vegetables?' Maggs is trying to keep the laughter from her voice. 'What vegetables?'

'We were over the river,' Grace says. 'We were shopping, really shopping, not hoisting. Two old friends checking the shops to see what they have. Saving the information, of course, for a later date. And then Annie decided she wanted to look in a greengrocer's.'

'What?'

'I just thought I'd look,' says Annie, now beginning to see the funny side of Grace's story. 'You know, like ladies do. They don't just visit department stores. They peruse the vegetables.'

Edith starts to giggle. '*Peruse...*'

'We were *perusing* the vegetables,' Grace continues, 'when who should walk in but a copper we know.'

'He was never going to believe we were there on innocent business,' Annie says. 'He stood in the shop, just watching us.'

'Watching you?' Maggs asks in disbelief.

'He stood there, hands behind his back, watching us discuss the leeks and cabbages. So we had to buy something.'

They are all laughing now.

'What was he expecting you to do?' Ruby says. 'Push pea pods into your pocket?'

'Carrots under your hat?' Maggs roars. 'A cabbage in your drawers?'

'We ended up buying half a dozen leeks,' says Annie. 'I don't even like 'em.'

'The most expensive leeks in London, too,' Grace adds. 'You could buy a shop full of 'em for the price he charged, but 'cos the copper was there, watching us like a hawk, we had to bloody well pay up.'

'Let's see them, then!' Maggs is crying now, tears running down her cheeks. She brushes them away with the back of her hand. 'These expensive leeks bought by a woman who doesn't even like them. I want to see if they're coated in gold.'

Grace is already untying the neatly knotted string and opening out the newspaper.

'Here you go, ladies, these are what they're eating in Kensington this evening. No finer vegetables to be had in the whole of London, if the price Annie paid is anything to go by.'

'You should offer one to Doll,' Ruby says. 'The poor cow sits here shelling peas for her kids. Just think what a fancy leek would mean to her.'

'I don't think Doll's ever seen a leek,' Grace says, stroking them. 'She wouldn't know what to do with it.'

'What's to do except chop it up and stick it in the pot?'

'What's that?' Edith peers over the leeks.

'It's leeks, Edith, *leeks*.' Maggs is still having trouble breathing as she speaks; she's laughing and crying at the same time.

'Not the bloody leeks, Maggs!' Edith pushes the vegetables to one side, shunting them off the newspaper. 'That.' She jabs a finger at a line drawing of a young woman in a cloche hat. 'That looks like Ruby.'

'What?' Ruby leans over, pushing Edith's head out of the way. 'What looks like me?'

She shoves the rest of the leeks from the newspaper, ignoring Grace's protests, and turns the image around to face her. Her own face stares up at her – or near enough. It's as though she has sat for a portrait. But she doesn't ever remember anyone drawing her picture.

She presses out the crease where the greengrocer has folded the *Kensington Gazette* and, bending over the table, sees not only her face, but her name and a description of her. 'A notorious thief'. The report is about her, and the Forties. Mostly about her.

An odd sensation creeps around the back of her legs. Crawls up to her thighs. Fear.

'"All the secrets of the Forty Thieves,"' Edith reads aloud over her shoulder. 'What have you been telling the newspapers, Ruby? Or "the Jewel of the Borough", I should say. Is that what you're calling yourself now?'

Perhaps, if she can keep very quiet and still – if she doesn't even breathe – then no one will see her. She might just disappear into thin air, like a whisp of smoke.

A hand thrusts its way into her collar and drags her away from the table.

'What's this, Ruby?' Annie Richmond's voice is soft. Dangerous.

'I dunno, Annie. First I've seen of it –' Her throat constricts as Annie's fingers tightly twist the neck of her dress. Annie holds her like this as she reads the article in its entirety, drawing the newspaper close to her nose for inspection.

A single leek rolls off the table.

'Hey!' Grace bends to collect it. 'You paid more for that leek than for any hat.' She blows the sawdust from it and wipes it with her cuff.

Annie ignores her, still reading the newspaper, her lips moving slightly, her scowl growing heavier, her fist clenching tighter and tighter on the back of Ruby's collar.

Finally, she releases her grip and presses the article to Ruby's face, so close that she can almost smell the ink. She can certainly smell the leeks.

'Who've you been talking to, Ruby Mills?' Annie's voice is still worryingly quiet. The low snarl a dog makes before it attacks a rat.

'I ain't talked to no one.'

Edith takes a step back, sensing trouble. She never likes to be in the middle of it, although she is content to watch from the sidelines since Ruby is involved.

The saloon has fallen silent.

'There's information in here about the Forties,' Annie continues. 'The sort of information that only we know. How would a reporter have found out you were stepping out with Billy Walsh unless you told them?'

'I'm not stepping out with Billy Walsh, so it wasn't me.'

'Just lying on your back for him, then,' Edith mutters, ducking her head when Ruby glares at her.

'But how would a reporter in Kensington know that? And all this other stuff about Debenham and Freebody – which floor you were working when Alice was arrested, and how you distract the shop girls?'

'How the hell do I know?'

Annie drops the paper and grabs Ruby by the back of the neck again, twisting her fingers into the hair at the nape before pulling Ruby close and hissing into her ear.

'You were already in for a hiding, Ruby. You're forever trying to keep your steals, you greedy little bitch. But now this? No one shares secrets about the Forties. Not with the coppers and not with the newspapers, do you hear me? I don't know who you think you are, Ruby Mills, with your "film-star face" and your "modern style", but here in the Borough, you're one of my girls.' Annie's voice begins to rise in pitch and volume. Everyone in the Crown is listening now as the rasp becomes a bark and spittle flies from her lips onto Ruby's cheek. 'We work as a group; we don't try to set ourselves apart. We're loyal. We don't thieve from each other. And we never, *never* talk about what we do and how we do it.' She gives Ruby's hair another yank – just to make certain she's understood the magnitude of what's happened. 'You made out you were someone special. And you talked.'

'I never. I *never!*'

Annie releases her, but as Ruby turns to plead, she slaps her hard across the face. The thick diamond rings meet her cheek and eyebrow and send her juddering into the table. Annie hauls her up roughly by the hair and then strikes her again and again, harder, palm and fist, palm and fist, until her face is a ball of pain and blood.

'Go home, Ruby. Get out of my sight. I don't want to look at you right now. Piss off back to Solly's. Better still, piss off out of the Borough.' She commands the whole room. 'And no one, *no one* is to speak to this ungrateful little squealer unless I say so.'

Ruby puts one hand to her face, pressing an injured cheek, and another to the back of her neck, to check that she still has hair.

She won't cry. She never cries. She clamps her teeth together only to stop herself from shouting back at Annie, screaming the Crown down. No good would come of that.

She can taste the blood in her mouth. Surely a bone in her face is broken. At least one.

She says nothing as she picks up her handbag. Maggs, troubled, steps aside to let her leave.

Ruby shoves the half a dozen leeks off the table and walks out as best she can, staggering only a little, her wounded head high. The men at the bar part, contempt on their faces, to let her pass. Even without turning back to see, she knows that Grace will be on her hands and knees, gathering up the vegetables.

23

Friday evening, later

Harriet has never found Arthur MacKenzie an easy man to converse with. He is not as old as her father, but nevertheless speaks to her in paternal tones, explaining everything as if he imagines her barely out of the schoolroom. It irritates her. Most especially when she is required to be polite over the dinner table.

This is a simple dinner – although the cook has found turbot from heaven knows where – and the couples are familiar enough with one another. Gerald, at the head of the table, directs the conversation and the evening passes as such affairs always do. He talks politics, mostly, because that is the world he inhabits. He proffers the insights of a man who devours the *Times* through the morning, lunches with politicians and other men of influence most days and sits in his club almost every afternoon. His thoughts are the thoughts of every sensible man in England – at least, they are the thoughts of those he believes ought to be running the country. He waxes about the potential for the economy, the need to cut public spending to pay off the war debt and ways to ensure employment. He voices bellicose opinions about Germany, Russia, the trade unions, radicals and anyone else who might 'upset the natural order', by which he means his own comfortable place in it.

Inspector MacKenzie, who spends his days enforcing the laws that Ralph and her father's associates are making, agrees with almost all of Gerald's opinions. When the conversation turns to law and lawlessness – another of Gerald's favourite topics – he adds the earthier stories, the real-life examples that support the abstract theory. For every concern Gerald expresses about the increase in criminality, MacKenzie can supply the anecdote, the description, the name, even, of the pickpocket, burglar or beggar that best exemplifies it. His fingers clench when he talks of them, his whole hand bulging with power and fury, as if he would rather be landing his fist into someone's face at the dog track than sitting buttoned up in an evening suit, contained by politeness, at this Kensington dining table. His own face is currently carrying a bruise, just around his left eyebrow, suggesting he might have been caught up in the sort of violent affray that he claims the gangs engage in.

Ralph is mostly quiet as they eat, listening to the older men, nodding occasionally, adding his voice for a 'modern' or 'youthful' perspective but saying little to counter them explicitly. However, Harriet is certain he disagrees with much of their thinking. He is always far more progressive when he is discussing matters with her. He sits next to Isabel, opposite Harriet, so she can see, through the candelabra on the dining table, that his brow furrows now and then as he weighs how far to correct or contend. He, after all, is the politician at the beginning of his career, with the sense to recognise that he still needs the support of men like Gerald and Arthur MacKenzie – even if their world and their pre-war sentiments are ebbing away, to be replaced by the incoming tide of the future.

Neither Isabel nor Mary raises her voice, except to murmur general agreement. Isabel, at least, shares her husband's views on most subjects; indeed, Gerald's loud public opinions are but an echo of everything she has said more than once to him in private. She won't express strong sentiments in front of the MacKenzies, of course, being the model of a dutiful and loyal political wife, and would, if asked, declare herself quite content for her husband to speak on behalf of the whole household. Mary certainly prefers to let Arthur speak for the two of them. Harriet, on the other hand, sits in discomfort, trying not to grind her teeth, concentrating on her plate, knowing that if she opens her mouth, she will be in danger of giving way to precisely the sort of passion and emotion that Arthur MacKenzie and her parents believe disqualifies her from exercising any opinion at all.

Once the usual political topics have been covered, the conversation lulls, allowing consideration of matters closer to home.

'I'm not sure that I've congratulated you on your engagement yet, Christie,' MacKenzie says, nodding to Ralph. 'Good for you. Harriet's a lovely young lady.'

Ralph glances apologetically across the table before murmuring his thanks and his ready agreement that Harriet is, indeed, lovely.

Harriet reminds herself not to respond, except to tilt her head graciously at the dinner guest seated next to her while poking at a slice of leek on her plate.

'You'll be an asset, I'm sure, as Ralph makes his way up the ranks of government,' MacKenzie says, reaching for his glass of wine and deigning to address Harriet now. 'We all have such high hopes for him.'

'Of course,' Harriet says, unclenching her jaw and laying down her knife. She gives her attention to Ralph, preferring to keep her eyes on him rather than the inspector. 'I can hardly wait. We'll make such a magnificent team.'

'We shall indeed,' Ralph raises his glass in a private toast to her. 'With Harriet by my side, and good men behind me, I can hardly fail, can I?'

'Dinners in Downing Street before the end of the decade,' says Isabel, to the murmured approval of the company.

'Steady on,' Ralph coughs. 'It's one thing to have the support of the party, Isabel, but one needs the support of the country – and that's always more problematic.'

'Well, as long as someone unseats that dreadful Welshman, I suppose I shall be happy for now,' Isabel counters.

They all agree to that. Even Harriet thinks that Lloyd George is insufferable.

'I'll miss your articles, Harriet,' Mary says, not looking up from her plate as she gingerly attempts to extract a bone from the turbot. 'In the *Kensington Gazette*, I mean. Of course, you'll stop writing when you marry, but it's a pity, because I always guess when it's you writing the women's page, and I like to say that I know you. You have a certain turn of phrase. It's different, I think, from the way the men write.' She speaks in one long, flat-vowelled breath. 'They really should put your name above your articles, though, I think.'

'You read my pieces?' Harriet stares at her.

'Why yes, I do.' Mary presses the deboned piece of fish against her fork with her knife and looks up. 'I rather enjoy the *Gazette*. I find it more straightforward than the *Times*, and it has local news, of course. You wrote about the girl thief, the other day, didn't you? Tuesday's edition, I believe it was. It had to be you. Something about the description of her – "Ruby Mills, the Jewel of the Borough" – and only a woman would know who made her coat. A Poiret, you said, wasn't it?' She puts the fish into her mouth.

Harriet sits back in her seat, flushing. Someone has read her article. Mr Pickford declined to give her the byline, of course, but someone has recognised it as hers, simply from the style of her writing.

'I said I thought it was a copy.' She is aware of her mother's icy disapproval from the end of the table. 'It might really have been a Poiret, of course. The girl has a habit of taking coats – as well as jewellery.'

'You wrote about Ruby Mills?' Inspector MacKenzie asks in a very precise voice.

'Yes.'

He glares accusingly at his wife across the table. 'You didn't show me this. You didn't tell me she'd written about Ruby Mills.'

A troubled look crosses Mary's face. She has said something wrong, committed some sort of *faux pas*, but she doesn't know what it is.

'I didn't know… You don't always… Well, you're not always interested in the *Gazette*, are you? A silly local paper, isn't it? And… I think I assumed that you might know all about Ruby Mills and you wouldn't need Harriet to tell you about her.'

'Who is this person?' Gerald asks, fork halfway to his mouth. 'Ought I to know of her?'

'One of the Forty Thieves, Daddy. I wrote about her for the *Gazette.*'

'Ah. Yes. Of course.' He has not read the article.

'I don't need Harriet to tell me about Ruby Mills,' Arthur says, more to his wife than to the company at large. 'I encountered her myself in one of the vilest drinking dens in Southwark. She and her associate robbed Enderby's jeweller two weeks ago. They nearly killed Mr Enderby, and his daughter is a nervous wreck.'

'And then you arrested her?' Isabel asks, anxious about the turn in the conversation. 'This Ruby Mills?'

MacKenzie's face is ugly in the candlelight; his neck bulges above the starched white collar he is wearing. 'No. I know she did it, but unless we catch her with the stolen goods about her person or her property, then it's difficult to bring a trial.'

'Wouldn't Enderby testify against her?' Gerald asks. 'Surely that would be enough? He had a good look at her, yes?'

'No, it's not enough. Mr Enderby is an old man with a heart problem. Lost all his boys in the war. The strain of appearing in court would be too much for him. Besides, if we can't find the jewels, then Ruby Mills and her accomplice will hire the sort of lawyers who can turn an honest man's eyewitness account into a rambling stream of nothing.' He shakes his head. 'I've seen juries acquit villains often enough because the defence barrister twists the words of the witness.'

'I wonder why they do it? Why they steal?' Mary asks of no one in particular. 'The women, I mean. Do they become involved with criminal men? Allow themselves to be corrupted?'

'They're born into it,' her husband says firmly. 'If you saw what I saw, daily, you'd understand. The squalor, the iniquity, the lawlessness over the river. Ruby Mills will have been picking pockets when she ought to have been in school. The older ones teach the younger ones, and so it goes on. The lives they lead are hard and grubby. They might dress like ladies, but they are anything but. Foul, vicious creatures, all of them, and not, I should say' – he gives Harriet a severe look – 'the sort of women to be glamourised or praised in any way.'

'That's what I said,' Isabel puts in. 'When Harriet said she wished to write about them. *Don't give them any attention*, I told her.'

'I find them fascinating,' Harriet says with a shrug. 'Their ingenuity, even more than their style. Foul and vicious they may be, but these women seem so able to run rings around the police.' She takes a sip of her wine and gazes innocently at Inspector MacKenzie. 'Just think what they might be, were that intelligence harnessed for good.'

'They would still be thieves and brawlers, mark my words.'

'Oh, but Arthur, perhaps Harriet is right.' Mary's eyes brighten. 'If these women were working, perhaps? Doing something useful. You must get them *working*, Ralph!' She reaches a hand to Ralph's arm. 'You could do something about them. Factories, laundries, allotments, even. Honest work.'

Ralph tilts his head and gives her a soft smile. 'I shall do my utmost, Mrs MacKenzie, I promise, although I'm inclined to agree with your husband in his assessment of these people, more's the pity. They are a menace, and most of them far beyond reforming.'

'Tighter laws are what's needed,' Gerald opines from the end of the table. 'More power to the police.'

'That, too.'

'Well, I won't disagree,' MacKenzie says. 'They're using motor cars now. They've been known to leave the Flying Squad standing. If we had more men, more cars –'

'I can't imagine working in a factory would be half as much fun as stealing from Selfridges,' Harriet interrupts, suddenly annoyed. She cannot imagine a girl as bright and beautiful as Ruby Mills in factory garb, nor understand why this should be thought appropriate. 'You might be lifting them out of the mud, but you're hardly offering them excitement if you're consigning them to a mill or a munitions factory. They might just as well run wild and enjoy themselves, and then go off to sew mailbags or beat hemp in prison for a time.'

'Harriet!' Isabel is horrified. 'What a thing to say.'

'Don't be foolish, young woman,' MacKenzie snaps. 'You know nothing about them, nor the filthy, violent lives they lead.

You may sit here, offering your high-minded opinions; some of us must deal with these creatures in the real world. You might, more properly, leave the likes of Ruby Mills to those of us who understand them.'

An awkward silence falls over the company. Harriet stares at her plate: the mound of leeks and the half-eaten fish. The room is stiflingly warm. There are too many candles.

'Well,' says Ralph, breaking the silence. 'I'll be sure to do what I can as soon as I have opportunity. And perhaps Harriet will be able to channel her enthusiasm for justice into typing my speeches.'

'I shall look forward to writing your speeches,' Harriet says, tightly, still bristling.

'I said you can type them,' he laughs in a slightly forced way, catching her eye. 'I might draw the line at letting you *write* them. Goodness knows what would happen if you ever attempted to engage in politics.'

'Well,' Mary says, glancing across the table. 'Harriet certainly writes very well.'

'And on that, no one will disagree,' Ralph assents before turning to Gerald. 'By the way, talking of speeches, did I tell you that we saw Charles Haversham the other day? I can't recall whether I said. Harriet and I met him in Claridge's – a very pleasant lunch we had there,' he adds, nodding to Isabel next to him. 'He passed on his regards.'

And, with that, Ralph, the consummate diplomat, steers the conversation back to the party and people they know, and to the safer arena of Westminster gossip. Harriet concentrates on her meal and tries to quell the roar that is rising in her chest.

Ralph comes to find her later, relieving her of the tedium of the inconsequential chit-chat between her mother and Mary MacKenzie. They go outside and stand, shivering slightly, in the garden. The night is clear, and the sky is full of stars.

'I've escaped,' he says, finding his cigarettes in the inside pocket of his jacket. 'Your father was about to launch himself into a lengthy speech about the state of Ireland, so I excused myself. I've heard the speech before.'

'I expect Mr MacKenzie has heard it, too.'

'Ah, well, he probably agrees with your father. And he doesn't have the excuse of a lovely fiancée, does he? The glum inspector looked rather envious when I said I wanted to speak with you.'

'Envious of you having a fiancée or of you escaping my father's tirade against the Fenians?'

'Both, probably.' The match flares in the darkness, lighting his face yellow for one bright moment. 'But now I can stand out here, freezing, with you.'

He takes a draw on the cigarette and blows smoke out into the blackness of the garden.

'Insufferable man,' Harriet says.

'MacKenzie? Oh, he's alright. Like all policemen, he thinks every ruffian and good-for-nothing should be rounded up and locked away and that it is only lack of men and money preventing him from doing this.'

'He doesn't stop to question *why* girls like Ruby Mills might steal.'

'He's more concerned to catch her, you know, darling. That's his job. Emptying the streets and the stores of Miss Mills and her fellow thieves.'

'I'm not sure he stops to think about anything very much,' Harriet replies, reaching for the cigarette.

'He's expressing the opinions of thousands like him – people who wonder why we ever stopped hanging thieves or why people in prison need food. I didn't know you smoked.'

Harriet draws on the cigarette. 'I don't, really. Just when I'm annoyed or feeling undermined and belittled.' She hands it back to him. 'Or when I'm not taken seriously. God, I needed that.'

'I take you seriously, darling.'

Harriet shivers again, saying nothing.

'You're cold. Here.'

He takes off his evening jacket and wraps it over her shoulders. She is enveloped in his scent – the spice of the fragrance he wears, mixed with port and cigarettes. It makes her feel protected. She leans into him, wanting to be closer.

'One day, when you're in government, we'll have the chance to make a difference in the world.'

He kisses the top of her head. 'We shall.'

'Build hope as well as houses.'

'I might use that. That's a rather good line.' He puts an arm about her and draws her nearer. 'I knew I was marrying you for a reason. I thought your piece was splendid, by the way. For the *Gazette*. I felt very proud.'

'Not proud enough to let me write your speeches.'

'Not quite. But I'll expect you to comment, make suggestions, share in the process.'

'Well, you can't take all your ideas from my father and Arthur MacKenzie if you want to appeal to anyone under thirty. The time of the old men is passing, and you need to speak to the people who will matter in the future, even if some of them still haven't the vote.'

He chuckles. 'I'm quite sure you won't let me forget *them*. Neither will the strident harpies with their placards. Ow!'

She pinches him at the waist, giggling. 'No, I shan't let you forget them.' She rests her head on his chest and is quiet for a moment as he finishes his cigarette in the darkness.

She has never been this close to him: so close that the power of him almost overwhelms her. He is quiet as he looks out across the garden, and all she can hear is the strong and steady beat of his heart.

Together, they will conquer the world; she knows it. Their marriage, a union of equals, will offer inspiration for others.

She reaches out a hand, tentatively pressing her fingertips to the front of his shirt, exploring him through the starched cotton. She feels his muscles contract at her touch. He bends closer and kisses her hair again. She holds her breath and looks up at him, trembling a little.

Ralph flicks the cigarette away into the flowerbed and grasps the lapels of the jacket, drawing her closer still, kissing her, softly at first, and then as he did once before – as though he might devour her. Her whole body feels as though it is melting into his.

'I'm not surprised you're feeling the chill in this dress,' he murmurs, pulling his head away for a moment, allowing her to catch a breath. 'There's barely anything of it. Wonderful.' Then he kisses her again, his tongue in her mouth.

His hands begin to skim over her hips, up and under the jacket. The fabric of her dress is flimsy. She can feel his fingers running over her skin, touching, squeezing, probing, sending shivers through her body that have nothing to do with the cold air. He presses his hips hard against hers, while all the time kissing her.

He has never been like this with her before. His hands are everywhere. It suddenly startles her. She wanted passion, yes, but she anticipated tenderness and gentle kisses. This feels like some sort of attack.

Cold air whisks across the back of her thighs, and she realises with shock that he is pulling up her skirt. Touching her, higher and higher up the inside of her leg, where her flesh is soft and warm. The sensation is extraordinary – so extraordinary that she begins to panic. She cannot breathe.

'No,' she gasps as she struggles away from him. 'No, not that, Ralph. I don't want…'

He lets the skirt fall and draws her tightly to his chest. She can hear him breathing hard, his heart pounding. Her own pulse drums loudly in her ears.

'God, I'm sorry. Too much port. I forgot where I was. I'm sorry. Your dress. It's just too…' He groans quietly into her hair.

'Don't be sorry.' Her voice is muffled by his shirt. 'I'm sorry. I was just – I'm just – not ready for that. Not yet. And my parents…' She lifts her head and sees him frowning down at her. She buries her head back into his shirt front, abashed. 'It's not that I don't want… I was surprised, that's all. I'm sure, in time – I do want to, you know…'

'I won't rush you into anything, of course. I can wait. Even when we're married, we can take all that sort of thing slowly.'

'No, Ralph, I didn't mean…' The dress was a mistake. She should never have worn something so provocative. And now he will think her a tease or a prude. 'Oh, I don't know what I mean. Only that I'm sorry.'

She wraps her arms around his waist.

'I love you.' It seems like the right thing to say. The sort of phrase to make everything better.

He kisses the top of her head but does not reply.

24

Ruby stares into the window of the jewellery shop. The reflection is not attractive. The bruises have now disappeared, and the broken cheekbone has healed, but her face has grown hollow, and there are dark circles around her eyes.

Nearly a month has passed since Annie saw the piece in that leek-stinking newspaper and threw her out of the Forties. A month since she was last called upon to go out hoisting. A month since Billy Walsh last spoke to her. No one has spoken to her – not even Maggs. Annie's command has taken effect, and people cross the street to avoid her, or shout abuse. She is being shunned. Cast out of the Forties, receiving no share of their money. The roll of notes under her mattress is growing thinner. And it's not only the notes: her coat hangs off her bony shoulders. At least she didn't lose any of her teeth after Annie's beating, and her nose is still straight and neat.

She looks past her haggard face and focuses on the jewellery. It is early on a Friday morning and the shopkeeper is laying out his wares. Friday is always a good day for selling, she knows. Solly piles his goods high, so that everyone can see how much he has to offer. The whole place glitters and shimmers. By contrast, this shop is beautiful and elegant in its simplicity, and every pane in the wide bay window is clean. The display is understated: silken drapes in rich purples and blues unveiling sparkling diamonds dotted here and there, sitting in velvet-lined ring boxes, making each one look special. She sighs and presses her head against the glass to catch a better view of them.

She had thought that Solly would always take her side. He took pity on her, at first: when she half-walked, half-fell into his kitchen, he'd bathed her face in hot water and brandy, made her drink a glass of the same brandy and put some sort of ointment on her cuts and bruises. But, since that evening, he has avoided her. Somehow, from someone, he heard that Ruby had betrayed the Forties. And when he had stood in the little kitchen and asked her about it, he had not been content with her explanations. He couldn't understand her bewilderment and confusion. She had admitted, still nonchalant even with her battered cheek, that she had kept some of her steals, and he had recalled the crescent moon from South Kensington that he had prised from her fingers only to find that she had lifted it from under his nose later. He had been annoyed and frustrated with her then. Now, he is disappointed and angry.

He is also afraid. Solly needs Annie Richmond and the protection she, her brothers and Freddy Moss provide. He cannot afford to lose their business or their security. He allows Ruby to stay in the room above the shop because he cannot bring himself to turn her onto the streets, but he won't let her work in the shop anymore or even let her inside when there are customers present. And he cannot bring himself to speak with her, let alone sit and eat with her.

In those first few days, she did nothing but lie on her bed, waiting for her face to heal. Solly began to avoid her as best he could, and when she realised this, Ruby started to slip quietly into the kitchen when he was downstairs serving customers or arranging jewellery to make pots of tea and filch small plates of food for herself. She wasn't hungry anyway. And it hurt to eat.

When she grew stronger and more ravenous, and when her bruises began to disappear, she took to leaving the shop each morning, before Solly was awake, and crossing the river in the grey dawn. She needed air. She needed to walk among people who would not turn their backs or spit or mutter an insult as they jolted her shoulder when they passed on the street. She needed to look at loveliness. So, she walked miles, from dawn until dusk, wearing out the soles of her shoes, gazing up at the Natural History Museum or Westminster Abbey, or out over the Thames, rather than sitting in her small bedroom in Solly's flat.

No one spoke to her on this side of the river either, but at least there were no vile insults. At least no one called her a Judas. She could walk unseen. She could sit for hours in an old church to keep warm when it was raining, or in a park, watching the birds, when the weak early-spring sun shone. And she could, whenever she wished, visit her favourite stores – the large and the small – and run her fingers over silks and furs. She could not lift much, though. Not on her own. Not without the others to watch for her and run with her. Besides, she had nowhere to take her steals, so would have had no opportunity to exchange a fur coat or even a set of handkerchiefs for a few bob – and what else would she have wanted with four sets of handkerchiefs? And the thinner and grubbier she became, the more she attracted the attention of the store walkers, who watched her with hawk eyes whenever she picked up a hat or a scent bottle. So, lately she has gone back to the tricks she learned as a child on the street: picking pockets for a few pence so that she can buy herself something to eat. Then she returns, alone, to Solly's and lets herself into the flat without being seen.

It is a meagre existence, and it shows no sign of changing. She had thought her future looked dull when she was part of the Forties; now, it is bleak.

Not a single person believed her when she said that she had nothing to do with that newspaper article. Not Maggs. Not even Solly. The injustice of it still cuts her. It is one thing for her to want to plan her own operations or to take off with Billy occasionally or to keep some of her steals – it is one thing to break the rules sometimes. It is another matter altogether that she is being punished, shunned, *shamed*, for a breach of trust she has *not* committed.

The fury burns inside her every time she tortures herself, trying to work out how it could have happened.

The Forties, for all she wrestled with their rules, were her family. They have provided for her, cared for her. And now, like her six-year-old self with her nose pressed against the grubby window of Solly's glittering emporium, she is on her own again, straining to survive.

'Well, well, look who it is.' The voice, low, amused, is right behind her ear. She spins around and comes face to face with Peter Lazenby.

He grabs her by the arm before she can run and pulls her tightly towards him. He is, she is momentarily relieved to see, smiling. 'The famous Ruby Mills. The Jewel of the Borough. I wondered where you'd gone.'

Perhaps he doesn't know it was her who took the watch. Perhaps Ray Calladine did not tell him. The greedy little bastard would have been too eager to receive his reward to let slip exactly how he had come to have it.

'I was very disappointed that you skipped off after our evening of fun together,' he says. 'I had been looking forward to breakfast in bed.'

'Well,' she says, trying to pull away, but finding that she cannot. 'I had other places to be, like I told you.'

'You did. Walk with me?' It is an invitation, but the strength of his grip suggests that she has no alternative. He tucks her arm through his and clamps her firmly against him. 'We'll go this way, shall we? Back to the club.'

'If you like.'

They stroll past shops without speaking. A gentleman's outfitter, a bookshop, a tobacconist. He walks confidently and at a fair pace, but not briskly. A man of purpose, rather than a man in a hurry. All Ruby can do is trot to keep up with his long strides and try not to trip over.

They have not gone too far when he decides to break their silence. The street is already busy – people are out taking the air, beginning their day, thinking about the day's tasks – but no one else will hear his softly spoken words.

'I think you owe me, Ruby Mills.'

'Owe you? Owe you what?' She has no money.

'The price I was forced to pay to Raymond Calladine for the return of my pocket watch.'

She catches her breath.

'I don't know what you're talking about.' The words come out too quickly. Foolish.

He grasps one of her fingers and begins to twist it as they walk along. Ruby tries to pull away, but he is too strong and has her firmly caught.

'Well, you're a better thief than you are a liar, I'll give you that.' No one will notice what he is doing. They are simply two people, a man and a woman, walking arm in arm down a street. Only they know that one of them is about to dislocate the other's finger. Ruby fights the howl of pain and terror that is gathering in her throat. He twists a little harder and then releases her hand. He continues to walk, unconcerned by her agony, with her arm still held fast under his own.

'What do you want?' She whimpers out the words, desperately trying to pull away. She should shout, scream, attract someone's attention.

'I told you, when we first met, I could use a girl like you.'

'You think I'm a prostitute?' she asks, through gritted teeth. What would she tell a passer-by, even if she did call for help? That she stole this man's watch and he has twisted her fingers?

He smiles, looking at the street ahead rather than her. 'No, of course you're not. You're just a girl who likes a good time. And you're a thief.'

She tries to breathe steadily. 'Is that what you want, then? A thief?'

Still, he does not look at her. Instead, he nods to an older man they pass on the pavement and wishes him a polite 'good morning'.

'What do I want with you, Ruby Mills? I want you to work for me.'

'I'm not sure I want to work for you.'

Now he looks down at her, slackening his pace. 'Ah, but you owe me. That watch is worth a lot of money – more than you can afford. Raymond Calladine was greedy.'

'He's always greedy,' she says, unable to pretend anymore. 'He said you paid him a reward.'

'Is that what he called it?'

They reach the door of the Angel. The man on the pavement outside nods to Peter, ignores Ruby and opens the door for them.

Ruby expects that Peter will escort her upstairs to his flat, but instead he gestures downstairs, to the club itself. 'We'll go to my office. Business, not pleasure, this time.'

The club is empty except for a couple of women clearing and wiping down tables and a barman clanking bottles and glasses behind the counter. It is too early for revellers. Or perhaps too late. Peter passes a sharp comment about the state of the floor and tells one of them to see to cleaning it, snapping his fingers; they scurry to obey.

He propels Ruby to the door in the far corner – the one from which she had seen Billy emerge with the blonde. Beyond this is a corridor with a flight of stairs at the far end, which she supposes is the back exit. Any club selling unlicensed alcohol or serving non-members or providing a welcome environment for cocaine dealers is exactly the sort of place to be raided by police, and she is willing to bet the smarter gentlemen who come here will be ushered out onto a back street whenever the coppers come to call.

Peter opens the door to an office, ushering her through. The room is simply but elegantly furnished with a large leather-topped desk and a couple of solid, ancient-looking chairs that sit at odds with the modern styling of his flat two floors above. There are no windows since the office, like the club, is in the basement, but it is brightly lit by lamps. A dozen or so silver-framed photographs line the wall, and a crowd of faces that she recognises from the cinema smile out at her. She wonders briefly whether he knows these people personally. The photographs add a hint of softness, a romance, to an otherwise austere room. There is nothing else light or frivolous about it, and when he closes the door behind her, she is ill at ease. She can discern the lingering scent of whisky, cigars and men. This is the place where he brings customers, business partners, anyone he is not also wanting to take to bed. Men like Billy, she assumes.

'Are you involved in something with Billy Walsh?' she asks. 'Is he working for you?'

He picks up a silver case and offers her a cigarette.

She takes one and holds it as he lights it for her. Her hand is shaking a little, and she knows that he has seen it. She might be a thief, a scrapper, a member of the Forties, but she is not in a store or the Borough now. She is trapped in an office with a crook who knows that she stole from him. She is smart enough to realise that spending time in his bed will not necessarily have endeared her to him. She draws hard on the cigarette, shifting from foot to foot, trying to read his mood. This might end badly for her. Her stomach rumbles.

'"The Angel" – why?' She wants to draw him into conversation, to ignore the pain of her hunger. 'Why not call your club "Alhambra" or "Trocadero" or even "Lazenby's"?'

He smiles to himself, knowing that she is trying to distract him, recognising her discomfort. 'Well, I find those names rather uninspired. And two of them are taken. I named my nightclub after a girl I met in a brothel just south of Lille. An angel in my hour of need. Several hours of need, in fact. Sit.'

He points to a chair while taking a seat himself behind the desk.

'We deal with serious business here, Ruby. The club is becoming widely known and, on the surface, legitimate and clean. Some very wealthy and well-connected individuals come to dance and drink their nights away, and they enjoy themselves excessively. We are raided by the police every now and then, just like every dive in Soho, but, unlike the others, I tend to know when they are arriving.'

He grins and lights his own cigarette.

She had guessed correctly. He has his own system, just like Billy and Charlie Wagstaff at the Crown. It will not involve a small child like Alfie Hibbert, though.

'Away from the club, and the eyes and ears of our more distinguished members, we have concerns in other directions, of course. The buying and selling of goods and services, you might say. The usual sort of thing. Alcohol, cigarettes, cocaine, women. Here, too, we are building quite a reputation, but we manage to stay out of the line of vision of the police. They are much too busy chasing local gangs like the Elephants and Mr Kimber's ruffians from Birmingham to notice what happens here. And if they do notice, my many wealthy and well-connected associates are able to smooth over any perceived irregularities.' He does not take his eyes off her as he talks.

'What am I here for? I've told you, I work for Annie Richmond, not you.'

'That's not what I've heard. I've heard you found yourself in trouble with Diamond Annie – that you haven't been out with the

Forties for a month. You look like you haven't washed or eaten properly for days, and the bruises on your face are only just fading so she must have hit you pretty hard. You're a mess, sweetheart, and you'll need money soon, if not already. A girl like you won't manage without cash for her silk stockings. You can't live by pilfering on your own.'

'Billy,' she grimaces. 'What did he tell you? I don't need Annie Richmond or the Forties. I can manage on my own.' She tries to believe it. 'I've been hoisting for years.'

'It's your choice, but if you don't come and work for me, then I'm very certain that you'll be in prison by the end of the week. There are police officers who will follow you, watch your every move, wait until you've left a store and then ask you to hand over your coat. They'll pull up your skirts until they find what it is you've lifted.'

'The coppers can't catch me,' she scoffs, sounding braver than she feels. 'They never catch me.'

'Ah, but that's because they don't spend all day with you, following your every move. I can make sure that they do.'

'You can order the police around? Like the waitresses and the cloakroom boy?'

He says nothing. The question hangs in the air.

'So, what is it, exactly, that you want me to do?' She knows already. She needs the money. At least until Annie takes her back.

He watches her for a moment, as if he's deciding what to say.

'What is the most important commodity, Ruby? The most valuable thing a person can buy or sell… Or steal?'

She blinks at him. His question has surprised her. 'Diamonds?'

He smiles. 'Always the sparkles with you, isn't it? No. The most valuable commodity in London – in the country – is information.' He stubs out his cigarette and leans across the desk.

'I don't know how to steal information. I do hats, blouses, gloves, that sort of thing.'

'But you want to be so much more than a petty thief, don't you? You want to make something of yourself, enjoy the finer things in life. Champagne and diamonds, that's what you want. I knew it the moment I saw you. And for that sort of life, you need to be lifting more than a few gloves with Annie Richmond. You have to work for it, if you truly want it.'

She rubs the finger he twisted. It aches. He could have hurt her. Really hurt her. He could have brought her down to this office and beaten her black and blue for thieving his watch. He might do that still.

'How do I lift information? I don't know what I'm looking for.'

'You know more than you think. You're observant. The best thieves are. You act on intuition. You knew I'd have something in the rooms upstairs, something even better than a Cartier watch, something portable, light, that you could slip into a pocket. I don't begrudge it. I knew I'd catch up with you eventually and take it back. I only wish I hadn't had to deal with Calladine – I find the man so odious. What I want to know is, how did *you* know I would have such a thing? You might have taken the teaspoons, as you suggested.'

She shrugs. 'I don't know. You looked like old money, the sort who might have an heirloom – a Ming vase, a Renoir, that sort of stuff – knocking around his flat.'

'What does a girl from the Borough know about Renoir?'

'Solly. Solomon Palmer. I work at his jeweller's shop on the High Street. He brought me up like a daughter when Ma died. And when I was small, we would go and look around the galleries. He used to tell me about the paintings, and all the statues.'

'And you remembered it all?'

'Most of it.'

'Why did I look like old money? You said you knew that I was old money. You're right, of course, but I want to know how you knew.'

'Your ring, for a start.'

He lifts his hand to inspect the ring on his smallest finger.

'You thought I was only looking at the wristwatch. I saw the ring as well. The gold is old – last century at least – so your family is old. The sort that has paintings.' She frowns. 'And then there's how you speak, and how you stand and order people around. And…' She hesitates.

'And what?'

'You smell of it.'

'I smell of what?' He laughs. 'What?'

'Wealth. Not just money.' She gestures at the walls of the office. 'And not money from this. Anyone can smell of money, but you've been rolling in wealth all your life like a dog in shit.'

He sits back in his seat and presses the tips of his fingers together.

'And there you are, Ruby Mills. That's why you're going to work for me. You're a natural, but I'll teach you more than Solly Palmer, even. And you can pick up information for me, here and there.'

'I still don't understand –'

'A lot of people pass through this club. I do business with some of them. You listen to them, sit with them, charm them – like you charmed me. Take them to bed. They'll tell you things about themselves. Most of it will be worthless, but some of it will be gold. When you hear anything that might be of interest, then you come and tell me.'

'And what happens then?'

'For you? I pay you. For me? I make use of what you've told me.'

'Are you a blackmailer, then, as well as a pimp?'

He flinches. 'Ugly words, Ruby. Ugly words. It helps to know what a man's weaknesses are, what corruption he's involved in, who he deals with.'

A blackmailer and a pimp.

'What about Billy Walsh?'

'You should forget Mr Walsh. I know enough about him already. He's unimportant.'

'He met someone here. That night I came here. He called him "General". Looked like a soldier – tall, smart, important. Is he important? Does he work for you, too?'

A flicker of recognition crosses his face. 'Charles Haversham. We call him the General, because of how he throws his weight about. He wasn't a general in France – only ever a captain, as it happens – but he oversees a lot of what we do. He's engaging the Elephant Boys in our operations. I think he met your Billy Walsh when he was across the Channel and supposed to be shooting Germans. He's a business partner of mine. A silent partner – when he's not pretending to be a politician.'

'He's a politician? Doing business with you?'

He smiles. 'They're not all old windbags. Some of them are clever, some of them are… Useful to know. And most of them are as weak and corrupt and self-serving as you or I.'

'That I can believe.' Ruby takes a final draw on her cigarette and stubs it out in the small ashtray on his desk. That, too, looks like something old, special, now she sees it up close.

'It's the great game, Ruby,' he says softly, watching her fingers stroke the silver. 'Not so different from the games you play with Diamond Annie: using your skills, seeing what you can get away with, riding your luck, running from the coppers. But our games bring higher rewards when you play with higher stakes. Those of us who survived the war deserve to thrive now. We're untouchable.' He catches her eye. 'Come and join us.'

He's right: she'll never live the life she wants hanging around the Borough and lifting with the Forties. If she desires real money, real diamonds, she needs to work for Peter Lazenby. And, if he is as well connected as she thinks he is, then he offers even more protection from the coppers than Annie Richmond.

Plus, the ache in her belly tells her that she does not have much choice.

'Alright. I'll work for you. But not a word to Annie. Whatever she thinks of me now, the Forties are family and she'll take me back eventually, when she thinks I've served my time.' She wants to believe it.

'If you say so. Billy Walsh manages to work both sides of the river, after all.'

He stands, reaches into his jacket and pulls out a leather wallet. 'Here.' He hands her several notes. Her eyes widen when she sees how much he's given her. 'You'll need somewhere to work from – somewhere smart and nearby, not a hovel in the Borough. You'll find a letting agency a few doors down the street. Mortimer's.' He checks his wristwatch. 'They'll be open by now. Someone there will find you a flat to lease. Put down a deposit and pay a month's rent. Then go and buy yourself some new clothes, perfume, that sort of thing. Come back tonight, clean and dressed up.'

She folds the money and puts it into her handbag. 'You're far too trusting,' she says lightly. 'I might run off with it. Not come back at all.'

She has hardly finished speaking before he has her pinned against the wall, a hand around her throat. Her open handbag falls to the ground, and her powder compact and lipstick clatter out across the floor.

He squeezes her neck so tightly that she cannot breathe, cannot move. He says nothing, only holds her, suspended, while the room begins to darken. She cannot fight it. She is going to black out.

She falls next to the handbag when he drops her, suddenly, and lies, gasping, gulping the air. Her vision returns.

The tips of his shoes appear next to her nose. Shining leather, finely stitched, made by the best sort of craftsman in Jermyn Street, not an ordinary cobbler. She shrinks away from his feet before he kicks her, trying to protect her face, her head, with her arms, and squealing.

He does not kick her. He walks back to his chair and sits down. She hears him strike a match to light another cigarette. She is unhurt – only embarrassed by the chicken-livered noise she has made. She draws a deep breath and lifts herself carefully, shakily, from the floor, with as much dignity as she can find. She retrieves her make-up and closes the clasp of her bag before turning to face him, chin lifted high.

He is watching her, expressionless.

'Mortimer's, you said?' The sound that comes from her mouth is not her voice. It is hardly more than a whisper. She coughs.

'That's right. They'll find you somewhere decent.' He chats as though nothing has happened. 'Then buy yourself something pretty.'

She nods. 'Alright. I will.'

'And Ruby... Don't mess with me again.'

She forces herself to stand taller, stares at him for as long as she dares, and then walks out of the room, clutching her bag, trying to pull herself back to normal.

She has dealt with worse than Peter Lazenby. Far worse.

She'll go to Mortimer's, rent a flat, do as he's asked. It might suit her to spend her evenings in Soho rather than Southwark. Even if Annie Richmond calls her back to go out with the Forties, they never go hoisting at night. Far better to drink champagne and cocktails at the Angel than bad gin at the Crown, listening to Edith Lennox whining about everything.

But she'll go shopping first, whatever he says. She has money in her purse, after all.

Her stomach growls.

No. First, she needs to eat.

25

Friday, late morning

Harriet picks up a silk nightgown from the counter in Debenham and Freebody. The delicate fabric glides through her fingers. She touches the lace that decorates the edge of the décolletage and imagines it against her skin. Imagines Ralph's face when he sees her wearing it. Then she remembers what happened when she wore that foolish and insubstantial dress at dinner a few weeks ago and snatches her hand away.

It will be different when they are married. She will be ready then.

'Would you like to take a closer look, miss?' The assistant behind the counter smiles pleasantly.

'Thank you, yes.' Harriet blushes and the heat rises on her neck.

The nightgown is plucked by its fine shoulder straps and laid out in full.

'I should call it bridal,' the girl says. 'Beautiful, isn't it?'

It is lovely. Not quite white, but not dark enough to be cream, with scallops of lace.

'Champagne, they call the colour,' she adds, reading Harriet's mind. 'It will suit you, I think.'

Harriet asks the price and makes her decision. She shivers as the girl folds the gown lovingly, wraps it in tissue and fits it into a neat pink box.

*

Ruby stands next to a table of stockings, observing. It is the woman she saw – the one outside Enderby's jewellery shop. She has a keen eye for recognising people, and it certainly appears to be the same woman. It is the outfit she remembers most, though. She watches, fascinated, as the elegant creature, wrapped in a honey-coloured coat and wearing a brown hat, runs her fingers over a very pretty nightgown. She'll look lovely in that, too.

Ruby watches her talking to the assistant on the lingerie counter. The confident way in which she carries herself – like she knows her place, her worth in the world. Everything about her speaks of wealth and good taste. Her skin is plump and healthy, and her cheeks naturally flush pink as she blushes at something. She moves with an easy grace, tilting her head a little as she speaks.

Ruby tilts her own head, attempting to replicate the line of the woman's swanlike neck.

Her belly is full again, but her face, she knows, is still pale and drawn. It will take more than a pot of tea and plate of bacon and eggs to put colour back into her cheeks. And she really needs a wash and a change of clothes. Everything feels grubby. She lifts a hand and examines her fingernails, grimacing at the thin crescents of dirt under each one. Even the perfume she dabbed on herself at the Guerlain counter cannot erase the grime. But at least she smells good. Mitsouko. A new perfume. It is already her favourite smell in the whole world.

The honey-coloured woman laughs softly, a clean hand against her chest, and turns to gaze across the rest of the floor. Ruby leans back, her shoulders touching one of the store's wide, white-washed pillars, and catches a glimpse of a pearl necklace around a bare throat. The pearls are lustrous, she can see even from a distance – the sort of string a real lady is given for her twenty-first birthday or as a present from her mother. Ruby knows how these matters work. Solly has taught her, and she's read about it in the newspapers. She is meant to see them, admire them. That's why they are being worn without a scarf to cover them.

The woman reaches into her handbag for her purse and Ruby sees the ring glittering on her left hand. That's a large diamond. She squints, trying to get a better view. Marquise cut, so it makes her finger look slender, surrounded by smaller diamonds. How many? Twelve, perhaps?

Lucky girl. She's marrying a man with money to burn. Money to buy something so perfect as that diamond. Ruby looks down at the ring she's wearing – the one she's borrowed from Solly's shop without his knowledge. It is slightly too large and slips down her finger to the knuckle.

What would it be, to marry a man who could afford a piece that special? What would it be, to wander through life as comfortably and easily as this woman? Ruby squints at her. She's never known hardship or hunger, and no one is going to black this one's eye or cross the street to avoid her.

'Harriet? Harriet Littlemore?'

Ruby watches the honey-coloured vision turn to discover the flat-sounding voice that has hailed her. It belongs to an older woman, wearing a hat that was only ever fashionable before the war, if at all. But her coat suggests comfortable circumstances, despite her lack of taste.

Harriet Littlemore. Ruby notes the name.

'Oh, how lovely to see you.' Harriet Littlemore has a pleasing voice, not too high or low in pitch, neither dull nor overly musical, but coloured with the rounded tones of an affluent family.

Ruby widens the space at the back of her throat, listening to the greeting and imagining how she would make the sound. *How lovely to see you!* Such knowledge might be useful. She picks up a packet of stockings and stands, watching, listening, partially obscured by the pillar. Her girl, Harriet Littlemore, has lifted her shoulders and straightened her back to talk to the woman – someone old enough to be her mother. She nods her head gently, smiles politely.

They know one another well and are passing the time of day with amiability as well as civility.

'… And your Ralph is such a fine man,' the woman says. 'No wonder your parents are so pleased. Such a catch, my dear.'

Ruby picks up a second packet of stockings, as if she is comparing them.

Ralph. That must be the man with enough money for quality diamonds.

Harriet Littlemore speaks softly, so that Ruby struggles to hear. She takes a quiet step closer, catching snatches as Harriet turns away.

'... A lovely evening, yes it was... Turbot, I know, a wonder... No, not to worry. I wasn't offended at all. I'm sure he's right, of course. It was foolish of me, really...'

The older lady shakes her head and the feather on her hat bobs about. 'I'm sure that Ralph will be a very different sort of husband. And you are such a modern-thinking young woman, of course. I shouldn't say it, but I rather admire your spirit. And your *work*. Pay no heed to Arthur.' She reaches a hand to Harriet's and squeezes it.

There is some sort of understanding between the women. She sees it – but resists her own memories of camaraderie.

The assistant hovers behind Harriet, trying to hand her the pale pink box. Ruby watches Harriet turn, gracefully, to relieve her of it.

'Something new?' The older woman cranes her neck.

'Yes. A nightgown – very like this one.' She touches a similar garment on the table.

'Oh, that is beautiful.' She smiles and gives a little sigh. 'What it would be, to be young and in love again.'

Harriet dips her head. 'I should be on my way, Mrs MacKenzie. I'm dining with Ralph later and ought to go home and change. I can hardly visit the Savoy dressed like this.'

She gestures to her coat, as if there might be something wrong with it. Ruby frowns. Not at the coat, which is, to her mind, the epitome of elegance, but at the name: MacKenzie. It reminds her of that bastard copper.

'I'm sorry, I shouldn't keep you,' Mrs MacKenzie says. 'Do give my regards to your parents – and to dear Ralph, of course.'

Harriet gives another polite nod of farewell to the older woman and makes her escape, walking swiftly to the stairs as though she is gliding on water.

Ruby, still clutching the stockings, leans back against the pillar again and continues watching her.

'Are you intending to pay for those items, miss?' Another woman's voice interrupts her thoughts.

Ruby Mills snaps herself to attention.

She takes a deep breath and turns slowly; no need to appear troubled or panicky. All she has are two pairs of stockings, and they are only in her hands. There is nothing, unusually, in her pockets.

A woman sporting the store's black uniform is standing behind her with her arms folded.

'These?' Ruby holds the stockings away from her coat and lifts her shoulders, straightening her back. 'I was trying to decide which to buy.' She speaks in the same voice as Harriet Littlemore – rounded vowels and clipped consonants. She might look a little shabby, but she is a lady, not a thief, and will be easily affronted if the assistant is suggesting anything otherwise. 'I think I'll take this pair.' She can afford them easily enough with Peter Lazenby's money in her handbag, even though, looking at them now, she doesn't want either of them. She hands the stockings to the woman, as if she expects her to carry them to the counter for her. That is what Harriet Littlemore would do, or Mrs MacKenzie.

'Yes, of course. I'm so sorry.' The woman is flustered. 'We've had a series of shoplifting incidents recently – not that I was suggesting –' She breaks off when Ruby glares at her.

'How dare you make such an insinuation!' Ruby flares with righteous indignation. 'You may keep your stockings. I shall take my custom and my money elsewhere – somewhere I am not accused of thieving.'

The woman begins to make further apologies, but Ruby sails away towards the stairs, copying Harriet's stately glide.

She might pay a visit to Selfridges. It's not far, and she hasn't been for a while – and never with so much money in her handbag.

As she nears the ground floor, she gazes into the large hall where poor Alice Dunning was caught red-handed with powder, perfume and a few hairnets.

Alice will have settled into Holloway life by now. No one wants to be inside, but at least Alice will be glad to be far from her husband and his ever-swinging fists. Even while she's surviving on prison food and shredding the skin of her fingers picking apart coir rope, she will count this time as a blessing.

Ruby pauses on the lowest step.

Harriet Littlemore, clasping her pink box to her chest, is walking towards her.

Harriet has found a new powder compact and discovered a push-up lipstick in a shade that is darker than her usual rose. Satisfied with her morning's purchases, she makes her way to the main door, where the taxicab will be waiting for her. She might even head to the office before lunch.

Something causes her to turn and lift her eyes to the marble staircase.

The young woman descending the steps, with a sway to her hips, is unmistakably Ruby Mills.

Harriet stops dead and stares, her mouth forming a small 'O'.

Ruby stares back. A sly smile spreads across her face. And then she continues walking towards Harriet, slowly, like a cat stalking prey, until they almost touch shoulders in the foyer of the store. She says nothing, only looks at Harriet as other women, and a few men, drift around them, oblivious, on their way to buy or browse.

Harriet's heart beats harder inside her chest. The girl is smaller than she is. Up close, she is clearly underfed, and her skin is pale, but there is a ferocity about her, an energy, that is unnerving. Thrilling. Harriet swallows down her anxiety. She does, after all, hold the advantage.

'Ruby Mills,' she says, quietly but confidently.

The girl's eyes widen at the sound of her name. Green eyes. Now she flicks her gaze up and down, almost nonchalant, dismissive, taking in Harriet's whole appearance before looking directly at her face again.

'Harriet Littlemore.'

Harriet cannot prevent the nervous gasp emerging from her throat. 'How do you know my name?'

Ruby grins. The gaze is fearless. Defiant.

'How do you know mine?'

'I watched you escape Mr Enderby's shop,' Harriet says, hurriedly. The girl tilts her chin at this. 'And I know that you lifted a very beautiful mink coat – along with other items – from Hartleys before then.'

Ruby's eyes remain locked on Harriet's. 'I don't much care for mink. Nor for Hartleys.'

'No, diamonds are more your thing, aren't they?' Harriet stands her ground, but her breath is shortening.

There's a flicker of amusement in Ruby's face. 'Now you're talking. You don't happen to have any on you, do you?'

Harriet clutches the box. Her left hand, ungloved, answers.

'It's a lovely ring,' Ruby says, without looking at it. 'Marquise cut, surrounded by twelve smaller diamonds – am I right? Worth a lot.'

Harriet stands taller. She will not be intimidated.

'I pity you,' she says, as crisply as she can, her voice shaking only a little. 'You could never afford anything like this, nor will you, I suppose, find a man to give you one. You could only ever steal it – so it would never be yours.'

Ruby's eyes narrow at this. 'I can have whatever I'd like. If I see a thing I want, I just take it.'

'You look, most of all, to be in want of a bath,' says Harriet, in a tone that reminds her of her mother. The sound of it gives her confidence. She breathes deeply again. 'Perhaps you might take one – and use some soap.'

'I will be sure to do that,' says Ruby, without blinking. 'When I am next at home.'

Ruby leans in, just a fraction of an inch, so that Harriet catches a hint of scent that she half-recognises: like sweet jasmine on a warm summer evening.

'You should cut your hair, you know. It would suit you shorter. And emeralds. You should wear emerald earrings.' She steps back and winks. 'Perhaps I'll find you some before your dear Ralph does.'

Harriet lets out a gasping breath and puts a hand to one of her ears, almost dropping her pink box, as Ruby turns away, click-clacking across the marble floor towards the door, chuckling to herself.

Her heart pounds to the beat of Ruby's heels; the blush rises from her collarbone to her brows.

Four hours later, Ruby looks around the flat she's rented. No, not a flat – an *apartment*. She lets the middle syllable roll around her mouth like a gobstopper as she says the word out loud in her plummiest voice. Her Harriet Littlemore voice, as she has decided to call it, now that she has a model and a manner to copy. She's handed over one month's payment plus the deposit, as instructed. She's never been in a place so enormous, except Selfridges.

She trails her fingertips over a lacquered drinks cabinet. Everything has worked like clockwork. She can hardly believe how easy it was. The further liberal dabbing of French perfume in Selfridges, along with the exchange of what was left of Peter Lazenby's cash – and the dropping of his name – secured her the apartment from the letting agent. She had walked confidently towards the youngest man in Mortimer's Agency, having chosen him carefully from the array of men behind desks. He had a sharp and hungry look about him, like a man who sought his boss's position and would be keen to secure a lease.

She had decided to make an active effort to impress him. She was – in her own imagination – a lady. She had fallen down on her luck, briefly, but had money once again in her purse. She played her part by being cool and courteous towards him. She walked around, inspecting the apartment as though used to such luxury: confidently, and with a slightly disdainful manner. She talked airily, speaking of taking tea with her dear friend Harriet Littlemore and their plans to pay a visit to an art gallery later. She had studiously ignored the way his hand lightly grazed her arse every time he ushered her into a different room with a polite 'ladies first'. It was only after she had signed the lease and handed over the money that he suggested they adjourn together for lunch at a little place he knew and gave her a knowing wink. That's when she knew she had been too grubby and unkempt to fool him.

Everything in the apartment is clean. The walls of the living room are sparkling white – as bright as those of a department store. The polished wooden floor gleams in the hallway. She takes off her shoes in the lounge and her stockinged feet sink into a rug that is the colour of biscuits; it is so soft that she imagines she is walking on a cloud. The modest chandelier in the ceiling is entirely free of dust and when she pushes a switch on the wall – which she does delightedly several times – it lights up the whole room. The apartment block is brand-new; the man from Mortimer's told her that, when he wasn't trying it on. Built as soon as the war was over, in place of an older house that had been pulled down. Nowhere, not even the richest home in Mayfair, would be this clean. Even the bathroom is white, with chrome-edged mirrors on the walls.

She turns on the hot tap and empties more than a quarter of a jar of newly purchased bath salts into the tub. The sweet, pungent scent of old rose fills the air immediately, and she sheds her clothes where she stands, dropping them in a heap, desperate to scrub away the layers of grime on her skin. She rubs the bar of soap up and down her arms even as the bath is filling before lying back to enjoy the perfume and the peace.

Harriet Littlemore had told her to take a bath. She closes her eyes and lets her head sink under the water. The poor creature had been terrified, though. Ruby had seen it in her face. And something else, too – what was it? Fascination? Yes, Harriet had been fascinated by her.

Ruby reaches for a towel that is softer than any she has ever touched before and smiles to herself.

For a while, she stands at the open door of the wardrobe, admiring her purchases on their wooden hangers. They will be perfect for the Angel. She has three dresses – shimmering, modern, daring in their cut and fabric – in jewelled shades that she knows will suit her. She will be irresistible.

Unfortunately, she cannot walk around in the daytime dressed in clothes like this. She should probably collect one or two more appropriate items from Solly's. At least, now that she has a place to stay the night, she need not worry about bumping into him.

Still wrapped in her towel, she wanders to the lounge, picks up her handbag from the sofa and checks inside, counting over the last few pence. Peter is right: she can't sustain a life of bath salts and glimmering dresses by picking pockets. So, she will work for the bastard – drink his champagne and lift whatever information she can from bored rich men.

There will be nothing she cannot handle.

She sits down on the edge of the sofa and gazes about the empty room. It is quiet. She cannot hear the shouts of neighbours through the walls or the familiar calling and clattering of costermongers, scrap men and cats' meat sellers in the street.

She cannot hear a soul in this silent white palace.

26

Friday afternoon

Ruby reaches Solomon Palmer's jewellery shop deep in thought, deciding which of her clothes to collect. She should also find her jewellery. She might not have diamonds yet – or a honey-coloured coat – but she has one or two good pieces.

No one has spoken to her since she crossed the river. And the grimy streets have been busy with people. The only exception is a cart driver, who shouted for her to 'move out of the fucking way' somewhere just into Lambeth as he drove through the mud and shit.

They are still not speaking to her – and if they did, it would only be to curse.

She was going to be Queen of the Forty Thieves one day. Take over from Annie Richmond when the time was right. Billy had told her that the Forties would always watch her back – look out for her and look after her. Who's looking out for her these days? Not Maggs, not Annie. Definitely not Billy. Peter Lazenby is serving his own interests. If she's going to work for him, she will have to look out for herself.

She sniffs the putrid Borough air and wrinkles her nose as she pushes open the door.

Solly, behind his counter, turns and sees her. There are no customers.

She stands at the door, hesitating. Not wanting to greet him and be ignored.

'Where've you been?' It is he who speaks first. He is sorting small change. The till is open.

'I was over the river,' Ruby says. 'West.'

'Lifting?' His fingers close over the coppers in his hand, as if she might take them from him.

'No.'

Solly shakes his head and turns his back on her, dropping the coins into the drawer before closing it.

It is easier to leave from the back door, her suitcase in one hand and her favourite blue coat hooked over her other arm, than to face the shop – and Solly – again. The yard is empty, save for two small boys throwing stones against a wall.

She walks quickly down the High Street, oblivious of her surroundings, head down to avoid the stares and the sight of people she has known all her life turning their backs on her, until she is over the bridge.

'Here, watch out!'

She mutters an apology to the scurrying figure she has collided with in her haste.

'Ruby?' The figure calls after her.

Little Florrie.

Ruby checks the street. They are far beyond the Borough, but Florrie could still be in trouble.

'You don't want to be caught with me. Didn't you hear? Annie's orders.'

The girl grimaces, but she's spotted the blue coat. Florrie has always admired the Poiret. She doesn't move or turn her back. She stands, fidgeting on the pavement.

'How is everyone?' Ruby asks. She might not have another opportunity. Florrie has not yet learned to keep her mouth shut. 'Daisy, Maggs –?'

'Oh, Daisy's in a terrible way,' Florrie says, as if she's repeating someone else's words, eyes still on the coat.

'How do you mean? What's wrong with her? Florrie!'

Florrie snaps out of her reverie at the sharp tone. 'Maggs says she's taking in callers. Men from the docks.'

Ruby puts the suitcase on the ground. 'What?'

'Callers,' Florrie says, lowering her voice. 'You know…'

Florrie clearly does. She's old enough to understand.

'Why? I thought we were… I thought *the Forties* were helping her out. Giving her money, helping her make ends meet while Harry's away.'

'I heard Edith telling everyone that Harry had some debts no one knew of. Big ones. And Daisy didn't know of them, neither. Until some man came to tell her.'

Florrie, sitting quietly in the Crown, will have heard everything while everyone else will have forgotten she was there.

'What man? What happened?'

'No one had seen her for days. Not since you… You know. And then Edith said she found her with her face battered and Daisy told her that some man was very insistent she pay back Harry's debts.'

'Who was he? This man? Can't Ron go and see him? Or Freddy Moss?'

'They won't. It turns out that Harry owes money to them an' all. I don't know how they found out – from someone inside with Harry, probably – but he'd been doing the dirty on the Elephants on the quiet for years. Before the war, even. So, they've dropped him, Maggs said. And they've dropped Daisy with him.'

'The bastard.' Ruby purses her lips. 'And there we all were, thinking Daisy had found the only good man in Southwark. He was shit like the rest of them.'

'He was. He is.' Florrie agrees, biting a fingernail.

'The Forties are family, though. Nothing to do with the men. Why isn't Annie helping her out?'

It is not unusual for women to make ends meet by seeing men now and again, for a few shillings, but this is desperate. Daisy is young and still besotted with Harry. The men at the docks are hard, filthy, usually from foreign shores. They won't pay enough to clear a debt – not if it's as large as Florrie is making out. They will only keep calling.

Florrie shrugs.

'Annie says her hands are tied. Harry was leeching from the Elephants, and they have their own rules just like we do.'

'But that doesn't mean she can't help Daisy.' If she were still in the Forties, Ruby would make sure of it.

'Annie won't cross her brothers or tread on the boys' toes. You know how it is.'

It's not her brothers Annie is worried about, Ruby knows. Annie dominates that family. It is Freddy Moss she can't afford to oppose. They have a powerful and complicated relationship – complicated further by their own volatility. Annie runs the Forties, but now that she is looking to expand her business arrangements, she needs the goodwill – if not the support – of the men. Giving too much aid to Harry Gould's wife would be viewed as treachery. Annie will not risk the Forties' wider operations just for the sake of Daisy.

Ruby grinds her teeth. Loyalty to the Forties is supposed to mean looking out for each other. It ends up meaning doing what you're told. Daisy deserves better.

'What did Edith say? Did Edith help her out? You said she found her with her face bashed in.'

Ruby has scant regard for Edith, but surely even she wouldn't abandon Daisy.

Florrie shifts and drops her eyes. Ruby sees this and makes a swift grab for her shoulders.

'What? What, Florrie?'

Florrie wriggles free. 'Nothing, Ruby. I don't know about Edith, that's all.'

'That's a lie.' Ruby takes hold of her again, the Poiret slithering to the pavement as she digs her fingers into Florrie's arms. 'What's going on with Edith? Is she in trouble, too?'

There's dismay in the girl's face as she fights a howl of pain. 'She's seeing Billy Walsh again.'

Ruby drops Florrie's arm and takes a step back.

'I didn't want to tell you. I'm sorry, Ruby. But you weren't *around*, were you? You disappeared, and you know what he's like.'

She does. So, while she was shunned, blanked on the streets, spending her days peering through shop windows across the river and pilfering by herself in order to eat, Billy – always as uncontrollable as a tomcat – had gone wandering. But to Edith Lennox! And Edith, who has always been sweet on him, would have happily allowed herself to be courted. She tries to banish the image of dainty little Edith lying in Billy's muscular embrace. He'll grow bored of her soon enough, like he did before. It won't be long before he remembers the whining and the cajoling that goes with the fluttering eyelashes and the pouting. Anyone would grow tired of Edith after a while. Fuck Edith.

'I'm going to see Daisy.' She picks the coat up from the ground and flicks at the small amount of dirt that is on the collar.

'What?' Florrie, rubbing her sore arm, is even more dismayed now. 'You can't, Ruby. Annie... Maggs... The Forties... What will everybody say?'

'Someone's got to take care of her. And I'm not in the Forties anymore, am I? I can do what I want.'

'But you might be in the Forties. You might be back. Annie was saying only the other day –' She stops abruptly and claps a hand to her mouth with the comical melodrama of one who spends much of her time in the picture house. 'Aw, no, I mustn't say anything.'

'Well, you have said something. What is it? Is Annie expecting me to come crawling back? Spit it out.'

'She's had her eye on another jeweller's shop for a week or two – a really smart one. There's no one else who could turn it over except you. You're our best. Everyone knows it. Maggs would take you back in an instant. She said as much to Annie.'

Maggs had stood by when Annie blacked her eyes and had been just as hard-headed as the rest of them. 'Only because Maggs wants to be part of the action. But her cell has fallen apart, hasn't it? Alice is in Holloway, Daisy's banging dockers, Edith's banging Billy Walsh and I'm still the shit under everyone's shoe, in case you've forgotten. All she's got is Grace, who never goes out on raids, and you – and you've only done one or two stores and still jump about like an excited baby.'

'No, I don't.'

'She might as well try her luck at recruiting Doll again.' Maggs has called on Doll over the years, seeing how fast her fingers work when she's shelling peas, but Doll, though a good neighbour and loyal to the Forties, refuses to go raiding. She is devoted to her children – all the waifs and strays of the Borough she takes in. No one would be around to look after the children, she says, if she ended up in prison for thieving.

'I could put in a good word for you?' Florrie eyes the coat slyly. 'If you like. As a favour.'

Ruby purses her lips for a moment, considering the possibility of returning. She could be back in the Forties, back with the girls, and lifting jewellery. Back home. They need her. As long as she is prepared to grovel to Annie.

'Do what you want.' She hitches the coat into a better position in the crease of her elbow and picks up her suitcase, readying herself to return to Southwark. 'I'm going to see Daisy.'

Ruby doesn't wait for a response and crosses the bridge, with Florrie trotting at her heels and telling her more about Daisy's situation until they reach the High Street. There, Florrie, with one last doleful look at the coat, leaves her. Ruby takes a turn right, then left, and left again, and arrives deep in the heart of the slums. She knows this tangle of streets and alleys as well as the people who live here. Coppers fresh to the area fear this part of the Borough, where the tenements rise high and the daylight barely reaches the cobbles. It is a dark, foetid riddle of streets, that gives no clues to strangers; there are no helpful signs or comforting landmarks. Ruby wonders how the men from the docks have found Daisy's house – but then, of course, they always know where to find what they want.

Ruby bangs on a rickety door next to the brewery where Harry worked until recently. Dust and grime have begun to gather on the doorstep.

There is no answer immediately, so she bangs again. A window upstairs is hauled up. Daisy's face appears.

'Daisy, let me in.'

'Go away, Ruby. I'm not supposed to be talking to you.'

'You're hardly popular yourself, you silly cow. Let me in.'

Daisy disappears and in a minute the door is opened, just a crack.

'I can't let you in,' she hisses. Her eyes flick up and down the street. Children play, dragging sticks over cobbles and through the puddles, splashing dirty water over each other. Older boys are fighting, pretending the sticks are swords. A few women are leaning against the walls of their houses, passing the time of day in the chilly air, their housework done, their doorsteps swept clear of dust until the wind blows it all back again.

'You're with someone? A man?' Ruby strains to see into the

dingy hallway. There are no gas lamps lit in the house, even though it is growing dark outside.

'Who told you about it?'

'Never mind. Have you got a man here?'

'Not now, no.'

'Then let me in.'

The door is pulled back. Daisy's face is still faintly bruised, and her hair is unbrushed. Her collarbones stand prominently above the neckline of her nightgown. She was always on the scrawny side, but is now more flat-chested than ever. She lifts a single candle. The brass wedding ring is loose on her finger. She hasn't pawned it yet.

'You can come in for a bit, but someone will be here soon.'

Ruby has been inside Daisy's house many times before. Daisy was so proud of her home, her belongings, always pleased to show off a new teapot or cushion. She kept it so clean and tidy.

Today, there is nowhere to sit down. There is no furniture. Only a small stool in the kitchen.

Ruby's nose wrinkles at the smell of musk and sweat.

Daisy plants the candle on the floor.

'Do you want a drink?' she asks vaguely, reaching for a bottle and gesturing that Ruby should take the stool.

'Yeah. Alright.'

Daisy pours neat gin into a glass and hands it to her. 'It's all I've got.'

'Thanks.' Ruby takes a sip and coughs at the roughness of it. This is cheap stuff.

Daisy does not pour herself a glass but takes a swig from the bottle. There are no other glasses, as far as Ruby can see.

'Have you got any cigarettes, Ruby? I haven't had a smoke for days.'

Ruby feels inside her handbag – she can barely see in the gloom – and finds her cigarettes and a box of matches. She gives them to Daisy. 'You keep them.'

'Thanks.' Daisy lights up and enjoys the first few draws on her smoke in silence.

'They took everything.' She gestures around the empty house. 'My lovely coats. The car, of course. My jewellery. Hats.

Everything. Except the mattress. And that stool.'

'Shit, Daisy. How much…?'

'How much did he owe them? *Does* he owe them still?' Daisy sniffs, shrugs. 'A few hundred pounds, he told me. Might be more.'

Ruby says nothing.

'It was all going to be fine, he said. He had a job – the burglary – that would pay off more than half. He would do another one later. But then he was caught, and he tried to knife that man, and Freddy Moss refused to help him out…' Her voice drifts away with the smoke.

Freddy Moss had found out. Harry was only alive because he was relatively protected in Pentonville.

'Who did he owe money to, Daisy? Apart from Moss and the Elephants?'

'Some men he met in France, I think. He had such big plans, Ruby. He had dreams. The war changed him – but not like other men. Some of them came back screaming, but my Harry came back with *plans*. We were going to live the life of kings, he said. He had money from somewhere and he bought everything. The car, that lovely car…' She sighs and picks at the end of the cigarette with a dirty thumb nail. 'But he'd borrowed all the money for his dreams from men who had money to lend and more to spare. They wanted it back, with interest, and the brewery job and the other work weren't enough. That's why he started breaking into bigger houses. Took the silver, the jewellery, what have you – to pay them off. And then he got careless. And then he got caught.'

'And you?'

'The men still want their money.'

'You'll be paying it off forever.'

'Well' – she touches her face – 'they made it clear enough that I had to come up with some of it.'

'And this is how you're doing it? On the mattress with dockers?'

'What the hell else can I do, Ruby?' Her eyes flash, only for a moment, before returning to their vacant expression. 'Annie and Maggs came to see me. They won't help more than a few pence here and there for food because Freddy Moss has cut Harry off. The brewery don't want me anymore. I can go to a laundry, a factory, or I can go and clean an office or house over the river – but those jobs are scarce. I can hoist a bit, on my own, but the usual fences won't take my steals because of Moss and Annie. You know how it is, if you break the rules. I heard what happened to you.'

She looks, in the shadows of the kitchen, so much older than she was even a month ago. Eyes sunken into her cheekbones. Like a woman already halfway to the grave.

There is a knock at the door. A firm rap.

'You'd better go. Let yourself out of the back door and go down the passage.' She pats her hair and bends to stub the end of the cigarette in the candle stand. 'I have work to do. For Harry.'

Even now, Ruby thinks, as she lifts the latch to the back door, even now, Daisy is doing this for Harry. She might as well be in Pentonville with him. Or in Holloway with Alice. She turns back, about to suggest that gaol might even be a better prospect – at least she would be fed and the creditors would be far away – but Daisy has already answered the front door and Ruby can hear a man's voice.

27

Friday, early evening

The American Bar of the Savoy hotel is one long, gently sweeping curve of mahogany. Harriet sits on a high, velvet-cushioned stool, staring at the bright glasses and multicoloured bottles on the shelves behind the barman. They are dining here this evening. A little treat, Ralph has said. He is still trying to make up for the unpleasantness in the garden last month, she knows, although neither of them has ever mentioned it.

She has worn a demure outfit – fashionable, but modest – and is sporting her new rose-coloured lipstick.

'You choose for me,' she says to Ralph, twisting her fingers around the pearls at her neck. 'The only time I've drunk cocktails was with Charlotte Gibbs, at the end of the war. Do you remember Charlotte? We were at school together.'

'Round-faced girl with a dragon for a mother?'

Harriet laughs. 'That's the one. Charlotte is a sweet thing. I really ought to pay her a visit –'

'But not drink cocktails with her?'

'No. I don't think so. Do you know, we had the most extraordinary time. I can't even recall what it was that I drank then – only that I had the most appalling headache the next day.'

She is confident that Ralph understands cocktail drinking far better than she and Charlotte did, barely out of school, ridiculously naïve, sneaking from their homes to share in the great party taking place in London that wonderful night. Harriet had been captivated – and half-terrified – by the hedonism of it. She had watched, wide-eyed and dizzy with drink, as a man and woman grappled with one another in a shadowy corner of the room. They had been oblivious to her, oblivious to anyone other than one another, fumbling with clothing and limbs, juddering and groaning.

That was nearly two years ago. She blinks at the bottles of gin, vodka and coloured liquids in front of her. She is older and wiser now. She is certainly more sophisticated, here for an early evening drink with her fiancé. And this is the Savoy, not the unsavoury bar she and Charlotte stumbled into.

'Good lord, I shudder to think what two schoolgirls found themselves drinking,' Ralph grimaces. 'Probably a mixture of absinthe and engine oil, given to you by gentlemen with dubious intentions.'

'Yes,' Harriet laughs back. 'I think it was something like that. Charlotte was violently ill, so I tumbled her into a taxicab and we escaped back to Kensington. Our parents never found out, thank goodness. It was, for a short time, extremely thrilling – until it became awful.'

'Sounds like many of the nights out I had as a young man,' Ralph says, giving the barman a knowing look. 'Far too many mornings were lost to hangovers at Oxford. A White Lady, Craddock' he says to the waiting man in the immaculate white jacket. 'And I'll have a Manhattan.'

The barman plucks a delicate glass from a shelf and begins to measure out spirits.

'What have you been doing today?' Ralph asks. He is watching the man rather than her so does not see the colour rise to her cheeks.

'Oh, this and that. I went shopping in town this morning, looked at a few things, that's all, and then went into the office for an hour or two.'

She touches a fingertip to her earlobe, remembering her encounter with Ruby Mills earlier in the day. She can still, just about, smell her intoxicating fragrance. Or perhaps she is imagining it.

The glass arrives, with a curl of lemon peel half-attached at the saucer-sized rim. Harriet peers at it, recalling her last experience.

'You'll love it,' Ralph says. 'It's the latest thing. Mr Craddock here created it. Try it.'

She lifts the glass and sips cautiously. The taste is not sweet, but rich and bitter with orange and lemon. It is ice cold. And delicious.

'I do love it,' she says in some surprise. The barman smiles modestly and moves away.

She turns in her seat and surveys the room. Everything glitters. The rectangular lights on the walls make the room bright. The men and women here, sitting at tables and talking in polite tones, are, like she and Ralph, young, rich and attractive. Even perched on the high stool, she finds herself relaxing in such company. The diamonds dazzle on her engagement ring.

She expects that they will discuss the wedding but hopes that they will also speak of his work and his plans. *Their* plans. Visiting the constituency, perhaps. Looking for a house there, even. She sips her drink again and finds herself glowing at the thought of a bright-starred future with the sort of man who is keen to share his vision and his political life with his wife.

A man across the room hails Ralph. The familiar sense of disappointment plummets in her stomach. She wanted a quiet evening, something to settle her after that encounter with Ruby Mills; just the two of them, talking and discussing. They cannot go anywhere without Ralph being recognised and inveigled into a conversation that somehow excludes her.

She takes a deep breath. This will be her life, as a politician's wife. Everyone will want him. She must try to become used to it.

'Lazenby, what are you doing in this part of town?' Ralph returns the greeting. 'Checking on the competition, or are you hoping to swipe the bartender for the Angel?'

The gentleman is a little older than Ralph, but they are clearly acquainted. Yet another member of the party, from the look of him. He carries himself like one of them: confident and at ease with his world.

'My fiancée, Harriet Littlemore,' Ralph introduces her. 'This is Peter Lazenby, darling. A friend of mine.'

He looks rather dashing up close, Harriet thinks, reaching for her cocktail, needing something to hide behind as he nods to her.

'How do you do?' he says. Then, turning to Ralph: 'A fiancée, eh? I never knew.'

'Join us, why don't you?' Ralph suggests. Harriet bites down her frustration and smiles pleasantly, as if in complete agreement.

'How very generous of you. Shall we move to a table? There's more space. No, don't trouble, I'll find myself a drink and come over. I want to catch Craddock first.'

Ralph carries Harriet's drink to a small circular table surrounded by stiff white armchairs. They are only a little more comfortable than the stools, however stylish they look.

'He's full of entertaining stories,' Ralph says as she sits. 'But try not to let him charm you.'

'I'll try not.' Harriet watches the man chat with the barman before collecting a single glass of champagne.

'He owns a nightclub in Soho. It's called the Angel,' Ralph says, following her gaze as Peter saunters over. 'He's utterly disreputable.'

Peter Lazenby gives her a dazzling smile, once he has settled himself into the seat.

'Ralph tells me you own a nightclub, Mr Lazenby,' Harriet tries not to sound prim and disapproving, as though she meets nightclub owners every day.

He groans. 'Ralph Christie, you swine. You might have given

me a chance to make friends with your lovely fiancée before denting my reputation.'

'Not a chance.'

He doesn't look like Harriet's idea of a nightclub owner – if she had ever considered what one might look like. More like a gentleman of private means, even an aristocrat of some sort. He certainly has the manner of someone brought up to be refined.

He appears to sense her disapproval. 'I should say I have a very small interest in the actual running of the club. I provide the funds and other people come and enjoy themselves. I'd say we need a little latitude after all we've been through recently, wouldn't you? Just...' He winks at her. 'Please don't tell my mother, will you?'

She laughs at this. 'Your secret is safe with me, Mr Lazenby.'

'Peter. I insist.'

'Is it truly very disreputable? Ralph says it is.'

Peter raises his eyebrows at Ralph before turning his attention back to her. 'Extremely. You would be most welcome anytime. I'll give you the full tour.'

'Certainly not,' Ralph interjects. 'I won't allow it.'

Harriet giggles and reaches for her cocktail.

'How do you two know one another?'

'France.' Peter's eyes meet Ralph's. 'I found him in a hell pit just south of Lille.'

'That's right,' Ralph agrees, clearing his throat.

'We made some good friends in that particular hell. In fact, I believe it was there I had the very notion to open a nightclub, when we returned home.'

'The Angel, you called it,' Harriet says. 'I suppose it's fitting that the idea came to you in the hell of war.'

Peter raises his glass and nods, solemn-faced. 'When you have been surrounded by angels, you want to pay a small tribute to them.'

'Don't upset my fiancée, Lazenby.' Ralph leans forward, frowning at his friend. 'There are some things I'd prefer her not to hear about.'

'I'm sorry,' Harriet says, hurriedly. 'I didn't mean to... I'm sure the memories must be horrid.'

'Not at all,' Peter rests back in his chair. 'Not all memories of France are bad. Quite the reverse. I met Ralph there, after all.'

'You did,' she laughs, picking at her skirt, grateful that the awkwardness has passed. 'And now you must tell me about the Angel. I want all the gossip. And the more unsavoury the gossip, the better.'

'As the lady wishes.'

'Careful, now,' Ralph interjects. 'You should know that Harriet is a budding newspaper reporter. Anything you say might find its way to the front pages by tomorrow.'

'Spoilsport,' she says.

'A reporter? Well, in that case, I shall be very careful. Perhaps only the stories about politicians like Ralph –'

'Hey! Not even that!' Ralph grins. 'She won't want to marry me if she hears your tales. And her father will chase me out of town. Keep it clean and light, eh? Miss Littlemore is too innocent and virtuous for your sordid stories.'

'No, I'm not.'

'Littlemore, you said?' Peter cocks his head to one side. 'Not Gerald Littlemore's daughter?'

She pulls a face. 'Oh dear. That'll be the end of it, then. Once anyone mentions my father, everyone turns serious, talking only of politics or shutting me out of the conversation like a child.'

'Not a bit.' Peter takes her hand. 'If you're Gerald Littlemore's daughter, then allow me to regale you with a story that is anything but dull – and has nothing whatsoever to do with politics, because you will be bored by that. Only a singer, a trumpet player... And his trumpet.'

'Ah, I know this one,' Ralph says, settling back in his chair. 'You'll enjoy this, Harriet.'

Peter Lazenby is a natural raconteur. He has an ability to spin a richly tapestried tale, without, she realises, saying anything indiscreet at all. Everything is in the hint, the suggestion, the innuendo. She is not so innocent that she misses these and blushes deeply when she catches the vulgar meaning. He is witty, charming – probably even when one is not growing giddy with gin – and amusing. He alters his pitch and style when she laughs, hints at darker subjects, dishonest staff, drunkenness, adultery, love affairs. It all sounds like such a game. She is still being treated like a child, she knows, but he does it in such a lively and raffish way that she does not mind too much.

She sips her drink, laughing along. The bartender brings more cocktails and another glass of champagne.

Half an hour passes quickly with similar stories of crazy musicians and foolish waitresses. Peter finishes his drink and pushes back his cuff to study his wristwatch.

'I ought to go. I have business to attend to, and you, I think' – he looks fondly at Harriet – 'must be wishing me gone, so that you may have a delightful evening with my dear friend Ralph.'

'No, not at all –'

'I'll see you later I hope, Christie.' He squeezes Ralph's shoulder as he passes behind him. 'Lovely girl, by the way. Congratulations, again.'

Harriet watches him leave. He does not look back as he heads towards the door, stopping only to speak to the bartender once more.

'What did you make of him?' Ralph's query interrupts her thoughts.

She ought to have eaten lunch. Two cocktails have made her woozy.

'Oh, he's a charmer. A little too pleased to paint himself as the black sheep of his family, as if that would amuse me – I assume they are well-placed, his family?'

'They were. His parents are dead, despite his quip about keeping the nightclub a secret from his mother. But yes, he's extremely well-placed.'

'I wonder why he chooses to run a nightclub, then? Or own one, at least.'

Ralph shrugs. 'I can only imagine he would be bored otherwise. You've seen how he is. He enjoys the intrigues, the peccadilloes and indiscretions.'

'Although he chose not to share anything too outrageous with me.'

'Certainly not. He is, after all, still enough of a gentleman to behave properly.'

'At least while you're here to protect me.'

Ralph straightens his tie. 'We should move to the dining room, if we're going to eat.'

She needs something to soak up the cocktails.

'Yes, we should.'

He clasps her hand firmly and helps her up. His strength steadies her. Somewhere, in the back of her mind, she feels as though she has missed something, that she should have paid sharper attention to the conversation, beyond the foolish stories. But the cocktails have taken the edge off her critical thinking, and she does not really care about anything except the fluid sensation in her limbs and the warmth of Ralph's hand.

28

Friday night

The heels of Ruby's shoes click along the Soho pavement, matching the quickening beat of her heart. Daisy's dismal house is far behind her, over the river. She might as well be in a different country. Lights blaze from shops and pubs, scattering bright colour across her path. Even the streetlamps are like spotlights, following her as she walks, lighting up her way.

Ahead of her, somewhere between the groups of wandering people, laughing and joking together, out for a good time, Ruby sees that a motor car has drawn up on the pavement. Two men are carrying boxes, wooden crates, and loading them into the back of the car. She knows the men.

She would recognise Freddy Moss and Billy Walsh anywhere.

She pauses, watching from a distance, as they return to the doorway and emerge once again carrying more boxes. This is the work they are doing for Peter Lazenby, then. As Billy has told her, they are delivering goods – alcohol, cigarettes, cocaine, whatever he asks. She can't see Peter. She can't imagine he will be heaving boxes.

Another man appears in the doorway and she catches a glimpse of his face in the light. She does not know him. He is older. He scans the street, up and down, anxious for the Elephants to leave. Billy climbs into the driver's seat and starts the engine. Moss talks to the man in the doorway.

Ruby takes a step back, keeping out of sight. She recognises from the way Moss is standing, up close to the older man, that he is threatening or intimidating him. The man in the doorway cowers, cringes, as if he expects to be shoved or punched. Moss does not need to hit him. The threat of violence is usually enough from a man like him.

Moss climbs into the car and Billy pulls away.

The man watches them go, glances down the street and then scuttles back inside, pulling the door closed behind him. He has not seen Ruby – and none of the passers-by has taken any notice of men loading boxes into a motor car. People load and unload goods all the time. It is only the man's twitching that would attract attention.

She walks down the street and stands outside the door.

She had half-expected this to be the back of the Angel, but the small sign on the doorway tells her that this is the rear of the letting agency she visited with Peter's money. It is Mr Mortimer's office. The back door of the Angel is several steps further down the street.

So Mr Mortimer, as well as supplying flats, keeps stolen goods, or whatever was in the boxes, in the back of his office.

She turns the corner and continues to the Angel. The man at the door lets her in without question, barely acknowledging her.

The lobby is almost empty, but she can hear the music and knows that the club will be lively by this time of night.

'Evening, Ruby.' Daniel, the spindle-limbed young man at the cloakroom, greets her as an old friend. 'Welcome to the family. Mr Lazenby said you'd be in tonight.'

Of course she is expected. She puts a hand to her throat.

'Is Mr Lazenby downstairs?'

'He's in his office. He's not to be disturbed.' Daniel's eyes flick to the stairs.

'Who's he meeting?' It can't be Billy and Moss. She's just seen them leaving. It might be the General.

He shakes his head quickly. 'I don't know.'

He does know, she can tell, but he won't say.

Ruby shakes her shoulders. 'Well, I'd better go and see if I can find a drink.'

'Good luck, sweetheart. You'll do well here, I'm sure. Mr Lazenby seems to like you.' He gives her a sad smile. 'At least for now.'

The orchestra is playing loud and wild tonight, all shrieking clarinet and blaring trumpet. The sound vibrates up through the balls of Ruby's feet, filling her whole body with music and excitement as she walks around the dancefloor to the ladies' room to check her make-up. She should look her best.

The cocaine girl sits with her box of magic white powder in the corner, oblivious to the stink of the toilet, ready to dispense her wares to anyone that will pay. Ruby nods a greeting before peering into the cracked mirror and applying a fresh layer of lipstick.

'Do you want any?' the girl asks, gesturing to the box. 'Keep you going?'

'Nah.' Ruby grins. The music is enough for her.

Another woman staggers into the room. Ruby doesn't know her but recognises that she is in trouble. She looks haggard underneath the jewellery and the satin dress. Her eyes are wild, and one cheek is bright red, as though someone has just slapped her.

She stumbles to the sink. Ruby steps out of the way as she turns on the tap and begins to scoop water into her mouth.

'Need to sober up,' she slurs, pressing her cold, damp hands to her face. 'You got any lipstick? I've lost mine. Ah, thanks, sweetheart.' Ruby had not offered her own, but the girl has taken it from her hand.

Ruby watches as the girl paints her mouth; she is remarkably capable, considering.

'Is he in?' she asks of no one in particular.

'Yeah, but still in the office,' the cocaine girl answers. 'It's only just after ten o' clock.'

'Is it? I thought it was later. Lost my watch again.' The red-faced woman turns from her own reflection and stares at Ruby. 'I saw you with him, with Mr Lazenby, the other night. What's your name, darling? You just started here?'

'Ruby. Yes.'

'Well, good luck, Ruby. You seem like a nice enough girl.' She gives Ruby an appraising look, although she is not quite able to focus. 'Yeah, pretty. You'll have lots of admirers here.' She hands back the lipstick. 'Don't go taking them all from us.'

'Thanks.' Ruby slips it into her handbag, checking the mirror one more time. 'I won't. Have a good night.'

The dance music is growing insistent and is more appealing than this conversation.

Ruby sits alone at a table, nursing the champagne she's charmed from the barman for free, waiting for a man to ask her to dance. A girl might forget her troubles here, carried away on a tide of bubbles and music. She tries to relax her shoulders and let the sound and sensation of the club wash over her. Tries to ignore her unease at the conversation in the ladies' room, and her concern for Daisy. It is what Monte Carlo would be like, perhaps, or Hollywood. She half-expects to see film stars in the warm haze of light and smoke. Like the photographs on Peter's office wall. Daisy would love it.

'Ruby, it's good to see you here tonight.' Peter is there, next to her table, smiling at her as if she had a choice. 'But you're looking lonely, and we can't have a girl like you on her own, can we?'

The question needs no answer. He takes her hand, pulls her up from her seat and makes a point of considering her outfit, holding her at arm's length and turning her this way and that. 'Good choice.' He approves.

'I wanted to dance,' she says, over the music. 'You might dance with me.'

'Gladly.'

They dance for a time while the orchestra plays a foxtrot. He holds her tightly against him, and she can almost allow herself to believe that it is she alone who commands his attention and that he is just as entranced by her now as he was when they first met, when he had plied her with champagne. He dances well, leading her effortlessly, with grace as well as direction. For a moment, she is floating, lost in the music, in the press of his body and the sensations rising within her.

Peter wheels her abruptly from the dancefloor. 'Someone I'd like you to meet.'

She finds herself in front of two tall men. The first she recognises as the man Billy had called 'General'. Haversham, Peter had said his name was. He nods in recognition and smiles as enigmatically as last time. The other is handsome, as tall as the General, and obviously wealthy. She can spot wealth from a distance; at close quarters, she can smell it. Old money again.

'Charles Haversham, this is Ruby Mills. I think you may already have met.'

The General takes her hand, amused, and plants a light kiss on her knuckle. 'I believe we have. Hello again.'

'And this is…?' Peter does not appear to know the other man. But he is playing a game. She is alert to it.

'Forgive me.' Charles Haversham is involved in the same game. 'Alexander Somers. Alex, this is Peter Lazenby. He owns the nightclub. An old friend of our mutual acquaintance, Ralph Christie. And this, as you've heard, is Miss Mills.'

The men shake hands, make polite noises, assess one another. Mr Somers is a Member of Parliament. They establish other common acquaintances and share common views on the state of the nation, raising their voices as the music swells.

Ruby waits, listens, says nothing, because she is not expected to speak – and she has little to contribute.

'But we're not here for serious conversation, Lazenby,' Haversham says, after a time. 'I brought Somers here for light relief. Fun, dancing and all that.'

'Then you should spend the evening with Ruby.' Peter puts an arm around her waist and draws her closer to the group. 'I'm sure she can offer you a pleasant time – without needing to talk politics. Ruby?' He tilts his head. 'Would you like to take Mr Somers for a dance? He looks as though he'll be less clumsy than me.'

The handsome man laughs at this and nods to Ruby. 'Well, I'd be delighted, although I can't vouch for my dancing.'

'I need to go and greet a few people – always the duty of a good host – and Miss Mills needs to dance.' He hands her to

Alex Somers with a gentle squeeze of her fingers.

So, this is it. This is her occupation for the evening. This one. She smiles up at her dance partner. She takes a breath.

'I do need to dance. He's quite right.' She uses one of her better voices for this man. Not too plummy – he'll be used to proper ladies, and he'll soon recognise her for what she is if she tries too hard. She sounds as light as air, breathy, vague, girlish. Just the sort of girl to take his mind off weighty matters of state. He is a better prospect than a dock worker or smelter. She squashes down all thoughts of Daisy, standing in her grubby nightdress in the candlelit gloom of the Borough, and of the rough-looking girl in the ladies' room. She shivers. The tiny beads sewn on her dress catch the light, making her body sparkle.

Peter meets her eye as he takes his leave with Charles Haversham. He wants her for himself; she can see it. She turns away, briefly revelling in this, and leads Mr Somers to the dancefloor.

He is a competent dancer, but a little lazy. She far preferred dancing with Peter. This one, she suspects, has not danced in a while and she needs to pay attention in order not to be stepped on. He is the sort who would prefer to sit and talk, perhaps. After a couple of dances, she pretends thirst, and he readily escorts her to a table in one of the quieter alcoves and calls for champagne.

'It's good to dance,' he says. 'I hope I didn't tread on you too much. I'm woefully out of practice.'

'I would never have guessed,' she says. 'You move very well.'

'As do you, Miss Mills,' he touches his glass to hers.

'Ruby. Like the gemstone.'

'I like it. It suits you. Vibrant, mysterious, with a subtle charm. Although not as expensive, I hope.'

'You know your stones, Alex. I like that in a man. May I call you Alex? Yes? And no, I'm not expensive. Not really. Just shower me in jewels and bring me champagne, and I'm as happy as a sandboy.'

'Just a carefree, easy-going sort of girl, then?' He laughs. 'With simple tastes?'

'That's me.' She mirrors his laugh as she touches him lightly on his hand and shifts a little closer.

'Where are you from, Ruby?' His enquiry is polite.

'Oh, here and there. London.'

'You have family?'

'No. Just me. I prefer it that way.'

'It is easier, sometimes, I'm sure. You have a young man?'

He must know that it is unlikely if she's in a nightclub on her own.

'Died in France.'

'I'm sorry to hear that. I lost many fine young men in my regiment.' He stares at his drink. 'I'm sorry.'

'Don't be. I'm not the only woman in England to have lost a lover, am I? What about you? Is there a wife wondering where you are, pacing the floor at home while you're dancing with me?'

He drops his head briefly. She sees it.

'No. No wife. Nothing like that.'

She clasps his hand, her eyes shining. 'Then we're free to enjoy ourselves, Alex. You and me. Free to live life to the full, and what the hell.'

'Amen. I'll drink to that, beautiful Ruby.'

29

Saturday morning

The sun is clawing its way through the grey clouds into the morning sky when he leaves her apartment. He needs to be elsewhere, he says.

With his wife, he doesn't say. But Ruby knows.

She lies in the bath, turning the tap on and off with her toe, enjoying the way that the hot water creates a haze of perfume from the bath salts. The room is warm, growing pleasantly foggy and humid. The new towels wait for her on a rail. She will wrap herself in the softest cotton and make herself a pot of tea on the shining stove in her very own kitchen.

She lets her body relax and slips her head under the water, the warmth of it cradling her scalp.

It is still early. She might fall back into bed. Or perhaps she'll dress and visit a café for breakfast. He has left her money, after all. She grins. She might even buy a cake to take to Solly.

No, not Solly. He isn't speaking to her. She'll take it to Daisy.

She should help Daisy. Give her some cash. She won't give any of it to Annie Richmond, that's for sure.

Ruby pulls herself up from the bath and reaches for a towel, rubs the water from her hair.

There is a sound from beyond the bathroom door. The kitchen. Someone is inside her apartment.

She wraps the towel tightly around her chest and puts a hand to the door, readying herself, wishing that she had brought clothes into the bathroom with her. And a knife. She tenses, in preparation for a fight, and opens the door.

'What the hell are you doing here? How did you get into my flat?'

Peter Lazenby is setting the kettle on the stove.

'Good morning, Ruby. I have a key.' He picks up the key and balances it on one finger, as if to prove that he hasn't climbed in through the window. He is wearing the jacket he was wearing last night and there is a shadow of stubble on his jaw. He has not yet been to bed.

'Mortimer's. That creepy man from Mortimer's with the wandering hands. Fuck. Do you own their business, too, as well as the Angel?'

'After a fashion.' He puts the key down, finds cups and saucers from the cupboard and begins to search for sugar and milk as though he's in his own home. He is, after all, paying for the apartment. 'I own Mr Mortimer, certainly.'

'Why are you here?' Her hair is damp when she touches it.

'I'm here because you're going to tell me all about Alex Somers, and because you owe me breakfast in bed.' He pours milk into a jug and adds it to the tray.

'What do you want to know about him?'

He scoops tea from a small cardboard packet into the teapot. 'I want to know whether he will do business with us. Haversham thinks he will.'

'The General?'

'What did you make of Somers?'

Ruby pulls a face. 'Full of himself. Dishonest. There's a wife, I'm sure of it, but he didn't mention her, even when I enquired.'

'He's married. I know that already. I can't imagine this is the first time he's strayed from home. And he's a politician, so dishonesty and pomposity come naturally to him. What else?'

She is feeling cold and uncomfortable, standing in a damp towel with damp hair. The kettle is taking an age to boil. She would love a hot cup of tea. 'He's short of funds.'

'Ah. Haversham was right.'

'Then why…?'

'It was a hunch. We needed to test it. What did Somers tell you? Come on, I want details.'

The kettle starts to rattle.

Peter has not noticed that she is cold. He is paying no attention to her at all. He only wants the information.

'He gambles. Heavily. Horses. Usual story: he had a dodgy inside tip a week or two ago and made an unwise bet that didn't pay up. He says it's practically cleaned him out.'

'He paid you?'

'Not enough. And he grumbled about it. I think he thought I was on the house. He sounded desperate when he talked about the gambling, mind you. Must be hard, strutting around like the lord of the manor when you've mortgaged your wife's diamonds.'

Peter reaches into his jacket and pulls out a pile of folded notes. He counts five onto the kitchen table.

'Helpful information. You've done well.'

The kettle screeches to a boil. He takes it off the heat but does not pour the water into the teapot.

'Now tell me, how do you know Harriet Littlemore?'

'Who?'

'You're a very poor liar. The young man at Mortimer's – the one with the wandering hands – he told me that you paraded about, *all la-di-da*, although evidently you were no lady. He said you were trying to impress him, and that someone called Harriet Littlemore was a particular friend, apparently. You were taking tea with her. Why would you tell him that?'

'Oh, I was playing pretend, you know? That was just a name I thought of.'

He tuts. 'I've warned you before not to mess with me. You see, I've met Harriet Littlemore. Sweet and stupid, but terribly well-connected. I know her father, too, and she's about to marry another associate of mine, Ralph Christie. So, the question is, how would *you* know her? Did you steal something from her?'

Ruby shakes her head, uneasy. 'We met. Yesterday. Before I rented this place.'

'You met? I can't see the two of you moving in the same circles.'

'We met in a shop. We had matters to discuss. Interests in common.' She bites her lip.

'I doubt that. What could the earnest and thoroughly respectable Harriet Littlemore possibly want to discuss with a little tart like you?'

'You wouldn't understand.' She folds her arms across her chest, trying to keep warm. He would never understand her longing to move through the world as comfortably as Harriet Littlemore. Or why she might spend hours tilting her head, walking slowly, speaking in that soft voice, mimicking the rounded vowels. He does not need to pretend wealth and class, after all. 'Personal stuff.'

He rummages for teaspoons in a drawer, pulls out two and lays them neatly in the saucers. 'Your shared appreciation of silver teaspoons, perhaps.'

'Yeah. That's right. 'Cause I have so many of them.'

He turns away from the tray to face her.

'Well, those are probably mine as well.'

They stand in the white quietness of the apartment. All she can hear is the low hum of an electric lightbulb. He watches her with the same expression on his face that she had seen in the club, when he had given her to Alex Somers, and now there is only a cotton towel between them. The skin on her collarbone puckers with tiny pimples and she shivers.

'You were making tea,' she says, caught between desire and fear. 'And I should find some clothes. I'll catch my death.'

The hairs on her forearms prickle when he unfolds them, silently. He lifts her wrists above her head in one hand and tugs the edge of the towel so that it slides from her chest to the ground.

He raises her wrists higher for a few seconds, so that she is forced to stand on tiptoe, her breathing ragged, before leading her to the bedroom without a word.

30

Saturday, late morning

Harriet presses the neat stack of envelopes into her handbag. There are five in total, and each one contains a letter to Robert Pickford. He has handed them to her because, although each one begins 'Dear Sir' or 'Dear Editor', they are commenting on her Forty Thieves piece. She had been surprised, at first, when he dropped them on her desk. He has not shown her any great regard until this moment – quite the opposite, indeed. She knew what they were, of course. Jimmy Cartwright has many such envelopes on his desk. He takes it for granted that he will receive them. Members of the public always write to the editor to praise or critique an article or report, and Pickford hands them to his reporters. They learn very quickly, Jimmy has told her, that real people read their words. He has also told her not to pay too much heed to such letters. He assumes she has received them already.

'Read them, enjoy the praise where you find it, and try not to argue with the negative remarks,' he said. 'Learn from them. People like what they like. Oh, and some people are mad.'

Some people, if these letters are any indication, are, indeed, mad – or at least hold odd opinions. Mostly, they are diatribes against shoplifters and thieves, but there are a few words of praise for her writing scattered here and there.

These are the first such letters she has received, and they feed a growing hunger within her. She is worth more than the women's pages – she always knew it – and, in a matter of days, five people have written to the editor, confirming her ability. She clings to the positive words, reciting them in her head. She will read them over again later, perhaps.

She stares at her typewriter, wondering what excitement she might give her readers today. Now that she knows she has readers beyond Mrs MacKenzie and, occasionally, her mother. Mr Pickford has made it clear yet again that she is to confine her energies to the women's section and to what he terms 'feminine interests', despite the evident enthusiasm for her piece about Ruby Mills.

It is Ruby's story, though, that was the inspiration. And Ruby herself.

Harriet touches the knot of hair at the back of her neck. She has twisted it into the same style today as she has every day since leaving school.

Jimmy Cartwright breezes in, a leather satchel slung across his body as always, and heads straight for his desk without speaking.

Harriet feeds a sheet of paper into her typewriter, observing him. He throws the bag on his desk and pulls out his notebook, oblivious of everything around him. He is like this when he is investigating. This is not reporting; it is scenting out news, and he is like a dog after a fox. When he is writing about something that has already happened – the robbery at Mr Enderby's, for instance – he is gregarious. He laughs with the other men, slaps them on the back, hail-fellow-well-met. But when he is investigating, operating on a hunch, a tip from an informant, an overheard conversation, a whisp of a story on the wind, Jimmy becomes withdrawn, secretive, focused.

Harriet pulls the sheet out of the typewriter, feeds it in a second time – straighter – and taps the carriage return twice. She puts her fingers to the keys, pauses, then types: 'The Cocktail Hour'. She will write a piece about the American Bar at the Savoy.

Jimmy is flicking through his notebook, a well-chewed pencil between his teeth.

The clock on the office wall tells her that it is already nearly eleven. She has written only three words. It is time to go and make the morning tea.

When she reaches Jimmy's desk with the tray, she sees that he has finished reading his notes and has pulled a copy of the *Daily*

Express from his satchel. She puts a cup of tea in front of him.

'Thank you.'

'Are you seeking inspiration?'

'Just seeing what they're leading with today. How about you?' He folds the newspaper and drops it on the corner of the desk. 'Are you still basking in adulation for your girl-thief article?'

She feels the heat rising at her neck. 'No. Not really. I had some letters… Mr Pickford…'

'Good. I'm glad. It was a great piece. Are you following it up?'

The compliment is unexpected. 'No. At least, not immediately,' she flusters. 'I'm back to the women's section. Trying to conjure something breathlessly exciting.'

'Hats or handbags?' he laughs, not unkindly.

'I thought I'd try cocktails.'

'Really? For the matrons of Holland Park? Audacious.'

She giggles. 'I know. My mother and her friends will have kittens. What about you? You were distracted when you came in. What are you chasing? A murder?'

'Corruption.'

'My father is always fulminating about corruption, usually from behind the *Times*, over the breakfast table. What is it now? More American businessmen paying to become peers?'

'Viscount Astor, you mean?' His eyebrows raise. 'That was a couple of years ago, and I'd hardly call his peerage corruption.'

'My father would disagree. Says he bought his title when the war was at its height. That greedy Yankee, he calls him.'

Jimmy shrugs. 'Well, he may have done, but Willy Waldorf shared his wealth – at least a little of his vast empire – unlike so many others. A philanthropist as well as a newspaper proprietor. No, this is different – shabby stuff.' He runs a finger down the scrawl in his notebook, open on the desk. 'Illegal buying and selling, gambling and drugs, prostitution, that kind of thing. I'm picking up straws in the wind so far, but there's a story here, I know it. I can smell it.'

The door to Pickford's office opens. The editor, in his shirt sleeves, collar off, cigarette in hand, summons Jimmy.

'On my way, sir.'

He rolls his eyes at Harriet and gulps down a mouthful of tea. 'Good luck with the cocktails. Let me know if you need anyone to help with your research. Unless you already have a young gentleman to escort you around the bars.'

She turns her head, avoiding direct eye contact. 'Of course, Jimmy. I'll let you know.'

He strides towards the editor's office and closes the door behind him.

He has left his notebook on the desk, open. As she moves to collect the half-drained teacup, Harriet cannot resist taking a look.

His writing is appalling. He has a shorthand all of his own, but one word is legible, circled twice at the top of the page: *Angel*.

She stares at the word.

'Forgot my notebook.' Jimmy is beside her. He reaches for it, snapping it shut as he scoops it off the desk. 'Ah, thanks.' He takes the teacup from her hand. 'I hadn't quite finished it. Don't want to waste your lovely tea, do I?' He jerks his head towards Mr Pickford's office. 'He's in a filthy mood, by the way. I'd get back to your typewriter, if I were you. Don't let him see you standing idling.'

'No. I won't. Thank you for the warning.'

She returns to her desk deep in thought, recalling the charmingly aristocratic Peter Lazenby. The stories he told her had been racy, to be sure. The goings on at the Angel lay on the outer edges of morality, but there was nothing more to them than that.

Straws in the wind, Jimmy said.

She shakes the Angel from her mind and tries to concentrate on her piece. She scribbles headings and comments in her notebook, describing the colour, the taste, the sensations of the American Bar as best she can remember, before typing the requisite number of words.

The sentences come, slowly, painfully, until she finishes. It is a poor article, but it is something, and she is sure that it will suffice. She tugs it from the typewriter and lays it on her desk.

She pulls her new powder compact from the handbag under her desk and checks her appearance in the tiny mirror. A strand of hair has fallen out of her comb. She hooks it back behind the teeth of the comb with a frustrated sigh, knowing that it will work its way loose again before the end of the day.

Perhaps it is time to do something about it.

31

Saturday afternoon

Harriet catches her reflection in every window she passes. In every pane of glass, she is smiling. The thrill of what she has done washes through her in waves. Excitement. Joy. Anxiety. Mostly excitement. Her mother will be furious. Wave after wave. She is dancing over waves.

She would rather like to cast her hat into the street so that everyone can admire her new hairstyle, but this might draw too much unwanted attention. Even so, she would like to show it off. Instead, she pulls off a glove and touches the edge of the cropped hair. It is not even two inches below her earlobe. Another ripple of joy.

This is the single most daring thing she has ever done. Even more daring than visiting the gaol. She had left the office and walked for what seemed like miles into Chelsea, along the King's Road, until she found exactly the sort of hairdressing salon she was looking for. The type of place where people understood her *need* to cut her hair, where the walls were lined with photographs of film stars, where the man who wielded the scissors fussed her, complimented her and spoke with the hint of a French accent.

An hour and a half later, she had gazed at herself in the mirror: a modern woman with a waved cut. It was everything she had wanted.

Ruby Mills had been right; it does suit her short.

But now the hat feels wrong. Too large and wide and old-fashioned for the hair underneath.

There is nothing to do but find a new one. At least, by trying on hats, she can study her reflection as much as she pleases.

'No, don't wrap it,' she says to the assistant. 'I'd like to wear it now.'

The shop assistant takes the money, and Harriet angles the new hat low over her brows. It is small and neat. A pleasing shade of blue – something a little different, a little bolder.

'I don't want that one,' she nods to the old brown hat, lying discarded on the counter. 'You may do with it as you wish. You keep it.'

The assistant raises her eyebrows only a fraction. She has already noticed and complimented the hairstyle and appears unsurprised that the brown hat has been abandoned.

'Thank you, miss, if you're certain.'

Harriet does not hear the girl's response. She is too taken with her new purchase and is already several feet away.

Only occasionally does the anxiety flicker in her stomach as she wanders through the store. *It is only hair*, she tells herself firmly, in answer to the anticipated criticism. *My own hair. Mine to dress – or cut – as I wish.*

She stands at a counter in the lower hall of Debenham and Freebody, examining a row of manicure sets. She pulls off a glove, reaches out a finger and strokes one or two. The tortoiseshell boxes are shiny and smooth, cool to the touch. She covers one of them with her hand, so that it nestles under her palm.

This is what Ruby does. What the Forty Thieves do. She knows the tricks now. Alice Dunning told her.

How easy would it be, to curl her fingers around this one inexpensive and insignificant item and slip it into her pocket?

Harriet feels the energy rush through her body so violently that it makes her giddy. She staggers, snatches her hand from the manicure set and walks away hurriedly, her heart beating at a frantic pace.

No one appears to have noticed her.

She makes her way to the perfume counters across the hall, calming herself, drawn by the glass bottles glimmering under the chandeliers. She catches a hint of a scent, something warm and exotic, and turns to locate the bottle from which it is emanating.

She sniffs at a few and asks to try the one that she recognises.

Mitsouko, it is called.

'It doesn't suit everyone,' the assistant tells her, dabbing a small amount on her wrist. 'It's very modern. You might prefer something a little more delicate, perhaps with lily of the valley?'

Harriet shakes her head and breathes in the perfume, rubs her wrists together, continues walking around the store. She does not want to smell like an English garden.

She browses, examines, assesses sundry items around the hall, as she ordinarily would, taking her time, revelling in the luxurious scent that envelopes her. She returns to the manicure sets and, once more, rests a hand over the smallest of them. The tortoiseshell case is hardly bigger than a duck egg under her palm. She quietens her breathing, smiles softly, takes a graceful, languid look about her – then closes her fingers and lifts the case from the counter.

She turns from the table and, as she does so, slips the case into her coat pocket.

No one has seen her do this. She is almost certain. Her heart begins to beat faster again and her eyelids flutter as she stares around the hall. It is busy now. Saturday afternoon, and the aisles between the counters are full of women just like her, examining the fancy goods.

But no one has seen her take the case.

She makes her way, without rushing, towards the main door, beyond the marbled foyer where she had run into Ruby Mills only yesterday. She breathes deeply. The doorman nods politely and opens the door for her, and she steps out on to the street.

Nothing has changed. The London traffic is as it ever was – noisy and smelly. The world continues to turn.

If she takes a single step further, if she walks away from the store, then everything will have changed. If she moves her feet, she will be a thief.

She grips the handle of her handbag so hard that her knuckles hurt.

All she needs to do is walk now. Walk purposefully along the pavement without regard to her direction. She must turn into the first street she comes to, and then turn several times more, until she has put nearly a mile between herself and Debenham and Freebody. She knows how they do it, the Forty Thieves. Alice Dunning told her all about it. It is easy.

Just one step.

She stares at her shoes. She can feel where the edge meets her stockinged toes. One shoe has a scuff mark near to the strap. She frowns. It will need polishing. She will leave them out for Hanson later.

She hesitates.

From somewhere down the street a car horn blares – a hard, raucous sound – swiftly followed by another, deeper honk. Two motor cars have collided, and their drivers are shouting, commanding the attention of passers-by.

A pair of magpies on the roof of the store opposite take off, chattering in annoyance, soaring away to find a better perch, tails fanning gracefully behind them, flashing blue-black.

Harriet feels for the case in her pocket and clutches it as she steps out, walking in the opposite direction from the motor cars, as though she has urgent and important business elsewhere, the sort that will allow for no distraction.

She walks and walks, not caring where she is going, only away, until she no longer expects a hand on her shoulder or the shout of a shop assistant.

Finally, in a small park, she takes the manicure case from her pocket and cradles it in her palms. Such a small and mundane item. Her heart races even to look at it.

The sensation makes her quite giddy.

32

Saturday evening

It is nearly eight o'clock that evening when Harriet finally considers abandoning her attempt to find the entrance to the Angel.

Since six o'clock, she has been walking the streets, trying to dissipate the restless energy that has been fizzing inside her.

She must have walked the whole of London, touching the smooth tortoiseshell case in her pocket every now and then, each time overwhelmed by that same heady concoction of fear and excitement she had experienced in the park. For a while, this had been all she wanted to do: return to the thrill over and over, the surge of electricity, as she walked along as calmly and nonchalantly as she ever did – as any decent and honest woman might. To an observer, she was a young and fashionable lady of means, returning from visiting a friend, perhaps, or someone who, having completed her shopping, was now making her way home for supper. No one would suspect that, in her own mind at least, she was as wild and vital as Ruby Mills.

Then it grew dark and, still not desiring to return to Kensington, she had begun to turn over in her mind that single word she had seen in Jimmy's notebook – *Angel* – until a new possibility possessed her. Thinking blithely that she might visit Peter Lazenby's club, she had made her way to Soho.

Now, the dark and heavily clouded sky matches the growing gloom of her mood. She has no idea where the Angel is located. She cannot find it, and she has been walking for nearly two hours. Her feet hurt and she feels frustrated and foolish.

She really ought to go home.

She stands on her own in Gerrard Street as people pass by, twisting about, trying to imagine where a club owned by an elegant aristocrat like Peter Lazenby might be. She wonders whether she might ask someone. The night makes the bright lights of the many shops and pubs seem brazen and garish. They dazzle her eyes, assault her vision, so that she strains to see properly.

'Miss Littlemore?'

She turns around to see Peter Lazenby himself walking towards her, his puzzled expression lit up by the vibrant primary colours emanating from a shop window.

'It *is* you, Harriet. I thought I recognised you. What are doing here? Is Ralph with you?'

'No.'

'This is not really the sort of street for a lady to wander down by herself, you should know.'

'I was with a friend. A girlfriend. We had dinner nearby. She went home.' Harriet falters.

'And... Now... You're looking for a taxicab?' he ventures.

'Yes,' she says, as if that was her intention. 'Yes –' more firmly – 'a taxicab.' But then he smiles, and her previously dampened excitement sparks to life again. 'Is your club near here?

'My club? The Angel? Yes, that's where I'm going now. It's still early, but I should be there, ready to greet the guests. Saturday is usually busy.'

'Oh. Yes, of course. And... You must make sure that the trumpeter is...'

'You remembered my little story.' He laughs. 'Well, no one ever forgets it, of course. I'm not sure he's playing tonight.' The colours dance about his face as he moves.

'I should like to see it. The club.'

'The club? I thought you wanted a taxicab?'

'Well, yes, of course. But would you show me the Angel? It sounded so wonderful, when you described it.'

'I'm not sure it's the place a lady like you should visit on her own.'

'But I'm not on my own, am I? I'm with the owner. Is it far away?'

'No. It's just here.'

He points to an ordinary doorway. It might be a solicitor's office. Unlike the shining pubs and shops, this is a door that pulls itself back from the street, hides in the darkness, makes itself indistinct. There is a man standing outside who looks similarly anonymous, in a dark overcoat that makes it seem as though he is blending into the wall, camouflaged.

'This is it?' She cannot keep the disappointment from her voice.

'This is it.'

'Sorry, I didn't mean –'

'Not at all. I prefer a discreet entrance. We have an exclusive clientele, and there's nothing worse than appearing brash, is there?'

'No. Of course. I see.'

'Harriet, I really think that you should go home. Your parents will wonder where you are.'

'I'm not a child, Peter. And I really should like to see inside before I go home. I'll take just a quick look, and perhaps a drink, and then I promise I'll climb into a taxicab.'

For a moment, he does not move; and then, apparently coming to a decision, he gestures to the doorway. The man standing guard nods to him and opens it. Harriet is ushered into a small lobby. It is already full of people milling about, which is strange because she had not noticed anyone entering. But then, she had not noticed the door at all. She had been expecting something 'brash', from his talk of it. Instead, the place looks reassuringly respectable. She is mildly disappointed.

Peter guides her to a cloakroom at the side of the lobby, and to a languid young man who is embracing someone else's coat – stroking the collar, lost in thought. He's a beautiful creature, slight and almost feminine in the way his thin fingers caress the fur. His manner fascinates her.

'Daniel will take your coat and hat,' Peter commands.

The young man starts from his reverie and hastens to hang the coat the moment he hears Peter's voice.

'It's warm down there,' Daniel says, smiling, as he takes her coat from her.

She sees him squeeze the sleeve, as if he is assessing the quality of the wool. 'Thank you. Yes.'

'I say, you've cut your hair!' Peter laughs. 'How very fetching you look. Will Ralph approve, do you think?'

She blushes, touching the soft waves near her cheek. 'I don't know. I hope so. Do you really like it?'

'I do. Very fashionable and, I have to say, it suits you like that.'

She colours again.

The young man circles a finger over one of her coat buttons as he carries it away, totally oblivious to her.

Down there, he had said. She takes a deep breath. She can already hear music.

'Harriet?' Peter's voice is there in her ear, above the sound of her own breathing. 'Shall we?' He puts a hand to her elbow and guides her to the top of the staircase. Each step takes her closer to the noise, the dancing, the heat of the club.

When she reaches the final step, she finds herself in a large, low-ceilinged, dimly lit room set with equally low tables, chairs and sofas. It is humming with people and with the insistent, syncopated beat of the music. The sound reverberates through her heels, into her ribcage, and makes her body itch to move. It is a pity she is not dressed for dancing; she is still dressed for the office, in a modest blouse and long skirt. Not at all decked out like the other women here. At least her hair is right. Fashionable. She stands, taking in the scene before her. She tries not to stare, tries to stand casually, as though she visits nightclubs every evening. The cavern is almost macabre in the way it is lit. Lamps on the tables give off little glow, just enough to illuminate the laughing features of men and women bent on a good time. One woman, with carefully painted red lips, walks across her path, and Harriet notices that she has a dull look about her eyes, as if she is only present in body and her mind is absent.

A waitress appears with two glasses on a tray. Champagne.

'This isn't quite your scene, is it?' Peter asks in an affable tone as he gestures to seats at a table. 'Not the Savoy, certainly – although our seats are a darn sight more comfortable.'

She smiles, making light of it as she sits and surveys the room from a new perspective. Two young women walk past in gossamer-thin dresses. 'I'm only concerned that I'm rather overdressed. Do I stick out like a sore thumb?'

'Not at all. We keep the lights low, so that everyone feels relaxed – even the people who are making their first visit. But tell me, how do you like it so far?'

She can just about make out a couple locked together in a passionate embrace on one of the sofas – the woman is sitting on the man's lap. There is a dense, smoky heat to the room. She is finding the experience strangely dangerous, and intoxicating.

'It's…' She cannot think of the right word. 'Lovely.'

He gives a short bark of laughter. 'Lovely? Is that what it is? Well, I've never heard the Angel described as lovely before. I adore it. Perhaps I'll use it on my advertising – "Come to the Angel: it's *lovely*."'

She blushes, grateful for the low lighting, and sips her champagne. 'I'm sorry, I shouldn't tease. You shouldn't be here, though. It's a good thing I know Ralph so well, or he would black my eye for allowing it.'

She regards him, safely behind her glass. He is an attractive man, forties or thereabouts, judging by the flecks of silver at his temples. He keeps himself fit, and his face is unlined, despite the nightclub hours. He is a charmer, as she had already decided in the Savoy, with his lazy smile and soft voice.

'Does Ralph ever come here?'

It is a gauche question, and she regrets it immediately. She should know the answer, surely, as his fiancée.

'You might bring him.' Peter's answer is diplomatic. 'Now that you know where it is.'

'I'm not sure it's really his scene either,' she says. 'He's much more comfortable in a place like the Savoy or his club – or, better still, in the House of Commons. He says he hates dancing. He would always prefer to sit and talk politics over whisky or port than drink champagne in a room where dancing might be expected.'

'That's terribly dull of him,' Peter says. His eyes crease a little in the corners as he smiles. 'Then it will be up to you to liven him up when you marry, even if you can't drag him to my dancefloor.'

He is distracted for a fraction of a second, looking beyond her, towards the dancers. She turns instinctively to see what he is looking at. One young woman has thrown her arms around a man's neck and sways, draped against him like a long scarf. They look so peaceful and carefree – as though, in the dancing, they have shaken off the sadness of the last few years. She decides she might write an article for the *Gazette* about dancing, and turns back to share this thought with Peter.

'Do you normally write about dancing?' he asks, his focus half on her, half on the dancefloor.

'Oh, I write about all sorts of nonsense,' she says, taking another mouthful of the champagne. 'I write of hats and gloves and what the best-dressed Kensington lady might expect to find in the stores. Mr Pickford – that's the editor of the *Gazette* – he says this is what his female readers want to read.'

'You don't agree?'

'I think women want to read about more than fashions. I wrote about the Savoy this morning.' She pulls a face, recalling how bad a piece it was. 'But my best so far was a page on one of the famous Forty Thieves. She was something of an inspiration. Ruby Mills, her name is.'

He raises his brows. 'It was *you* who wrote that piece about Ruby Mills?' He sounds mildly incredulous. 'I never knew that. The Jewel of the Borough, you called her. Ha. It seems you really did meet her… Well, well.' He shakes his head, laughing at some private joke. 'And you wrote it?'

'I did. Did you read it?'

'Certainly. You captured her rather well, if a little too admiringly.' His attention has moved again to the other side of the room. He frowns at something.

Harriet starts. 'You *know* her? You know Ruby Mills?'

'Yes, I do… Damn it, what's he doing –?' A flicker of annoyance crosses Peter's brow. 'I apologise, Harriet. Do you mind if I leave you here for a moment? There's something I need to deal with.' He is already leaving.

'Not at all. I'll just enjoy all of this.' She gestures to the dancefloor.

She watches on as he strides away – so much the man in charge. At the bottom of the stairs, he meets the young man from the cloakroom. He upbraids him about something, so that the man hangs his head. It looks as though he is bleating some sort of apology, twisting his hands one around the other.

Peter pushes him rather roughly out of the way and runs up the stairs, taking two steps at a time. The young man, almost in tears, trails after him.

Something has happened upstairs, perhaps. Something that the young man is incapable of dealing with.

Harriet drains her glass and turns her attention back to the dancing. They are beautiful, the women. So very young and bright-eyed, they all seem. One of them is laughing at something her dance partner has said – in that forced way one does when a man is particularly tedious, but you are trying to be polite – throwing back her head, mouth wide open.

She watches for a while, but Peter does not return. There is little point in staying if he is busy. She will go home, now she has seen the club and it is not quite as outrageous as she had imagined or hoped. She will find a taxicab and invent some excuse to her mother for her lateness. Deal with the consequences of her haircut. But she needs to find some relief first. She has drunk too much, and she will never make it back to Onslow Square. Surely, there will be somewhere.

Across the dancefloor, beyond the bar, she spies a pair of women emerging from a doorway, swaying arm in arm, and guesses that this is where she might find the room she is looking for. She picks up her handbag and makes her way over.

A group of men are gathered in a small cluster by the bar, drinking whisky as they talk. They look like factory workers, she thinks, muscular and thick necked. Harriet will have to pass them. Her shoulders tense, and she clutches her bag to her body, but they are watching the women whose skirts ride high to their calves as they bob and skip. They won't be interested in her.

One man, eyes on the dancers, is, from the look of his gestures, outlining a plan or telling a story while the others listen, nodding and commenting occasionally. She is alarmed to realise that she recognises him. His suit is smart, but also 'flash'. He has a handsome face, cleanshaven and with a strong jawline, but his expression is hard.

He was the man with Ruby Mills. The man who robbed Mr Enderby's shop and pushed little Cecily to the ground. *Billy Walsh*. That was the name Alice Dunning had given to her. An associate of the Forty Thieves and a hardened criminal, according to Inspector MacKenzie. And here he is, lounging against the bar of the Angel, holding court, as though it is he who owns the club and not Peter Lazenby.

Harriet remembers to breathe. Raises her shoulders. He will not recognise her. She will not be afraid.

The men do not move as she nears them. They are committed to their own conversation and ignore her. There is a lull in the music as the dance comes to an end and the musicians pause for a drink.

'– taking the goods to Mayfair tomorrow –'

'– and the General wants the boys to collect another load from here. Mortimer's keeping it all warm –'

She slows her steps, trying to make sense of what they are talking about. They are carrying, fetching something. Jimmy had spoken of illegal buying and selling. Perhaps this is it. This is what he was talking about. It would be the sort of thing Billy Walsh might be involved in, alongside raiding jewellery shops. She turns back to the dancefloor as if looking for someone and continues to listen.

'He will, if he knows what's good for him.' The voice is jocular enough, but the men respond with dark laughter. The sound of it bothers her.

'Another one, Billy?'

'Yeah, go on.'

The discussion of 'goods' is lost to her as the men turn towards the bar for more whisky, so she proceeds on her way to the door beyond where they stand.

She enters through and finds a narrow corridor with the room she is looking for visible at the end. A woman falls out of the doorway, laughing wildly while cursing. Harriet, startled, steps aside to let her pass. The woman does not even notice, let alone thank her.

She finds three more women inside the small, stinking room. She puts a hand to her nose in a vain attempt to cover the smell of excrement. A girl leans over a basin, seemingly oblivious to the odour, examining a spot on her chin in a cracked mirror that hangs on the wall. The other two are giggling, bent over a table, heads almost touching. One of them sits back and stares up at Harriet, wide-eyed, revealing a small silver box from which the other is drawing white powder in her fingertips and pushing it up her nostrils. She is sniffing noisily.

'You want some?' The girl at the mirror asks, seeing Harriet's fascinated stare.

'No. Thank you. I came to find…' She closes her mouth. She has only ever read of it, but she is almost certain that the two women are taking cocaine.

'It's there.' One of the giggling women nods to a wooden door. Harriet pushes open the door. The stench is so strong that she gags, but there is nowhere else, and she is desperate.

By the time she has finished, the two women have gone, leaving only the creature with the spotty chin guarding the box. Harriet eyes it.

'You sure you don't want any? It'll perk you up. You look like you need it.'

'Quite sure. Thank you.'

She rushes out of the room without washing her hands.

The musicians are playing again when she reaches the dancefloor. The music is louder now. The men at the bar have disappeared, their glasses abandoned on the counter, yet to be cleared away. The whole place is filled with noise, smoke and alcohol. Harriet's head starts to throb with the pulse of the drum's beat and the shriek of the clarinet. She thinks that she might be about to be sick.

The languid young man from the cloakroom is suddenly in front of her. He is holding her coat and her new hat.

'Mr Lazenby sent me to look for you.' He is in a state of agitation. 'I couldn't find you. Thought I'd lost you. You must leave, he says. Now.'

'I was about to leave,' she shouts over the noise of the music, trying to move past him. 'I want to go home.'

He grasps her arm. 'Not that way. Out the back. Quickly.'

She is escorted to a door across the dancefloor. He pushes it open to reveal another narrow corridor.

'What's happening?' Harriet pushes her arms into the sleeves of the coat he has held open for her. 'Why are we going this way?'

He continues to propel her down the corridor, towards a set of stairs leading upward. The music fades behind her.

'A raid. Mr Lazenby says he doesn't want you caught up in it.'

'A raid? What do you mean?'

'The police call every so often. They usually arrive later in the evening on a Saturday – after hours. Mr Lazenby is furious that they're coming here at this time of night. It's far too early. He'll give them hell, I'm sure. It's a nuisance, but they have to do it, I suppose.'

'There are women, I saw them. They were taking cocaine, I think.'

'We don't worry about it.' He shrugs. 'They'll pack it away and no one will know by the time the police arrive. Here you are.' He gestures to the stairs. 'Back door. It's where we send all our better guests when we've had the call.'

She follows him up the stairs, pausing only once to look behind, down the corridor, her heart thumping in fear. All her earlier bravado has vanished. She does not wish to be in the club when the police arrive. Her parents would disown her. The newspapers would hear of it and make much of Gerald Littlemore's daughter being found alone in a nightclub... A wave of nausea threatens again.

'Are the police here?' she asks, her voice rising. 'Are they in the club already?'

'No, no. We always have plenty of warning. They won't be here for another half an hour.'

'Not much of a raid, is it, if they warn you?' she comments as he thrusts open the back door to the street. She is jittery now, shaking, trying to keep herself calm.

'God help us if we lose our informer. And God help our guests. Here you are. Can you find your way from here? I need to go back and send a few other people out this way.'

She stands on the pavement, still trembling, trying to find her bearings. 'Yes. I shall look for a taxicab.' How ridiculous to be so terrified. She stamps her feet, as if she is cold, to stop the shaking in her legs.

'Down there. That's where you'll find one.' He points along the street. 'Sorry that your evening ended so early. Come again, won't you? You know Mr Lazenby?'

'I do.' She buttons up her coat. 'He's a friend... Wait –' She remembers. 'I saw Billy Walsh at the bar earlier. Who were the men with him?'

He shrugs, handing her the hat. 'Elephant Boys, I should imagine. Freddy Moss, maybe? I think he was around. They do some work for Mr Lazenby. How do you know Billy Walsh?'

An acquaintance with such a man would be unlikely.

'Oh, I don't know him.' She turns away, embarrassed to lie directly to his face. 'I know his – *friend*. Ruby Mills.'

'Ah. Now, she's a darling. Mr Lazenby likes her. Likes her a lot, if you know what I mean. And he's not always so partial.' He laughs. 'Wouldn't have thought you would know people like them.' There is a hint of curiosity in his voice now.

'Well,' she shrugs. 'It's a small world.'

He bids her goodnight and disappears back inside. The air outside is cold, and, compared with the club, even this sordid street smells clean. The clouds have lifted to unveil the crescent of the moon – but with hundreds of bright lights shining out from public houses and restaurants, Harriet cannot make out many stars. She takes a deep breath and goes in search of a taxicab, hat in her hand, clutching her bag close to her side, her heart still thumping.

33

Saturday evening

Ruby shivers. The night is chillier than she expected – but then, she has only just emerged from her flat, so how was she to know?

Peter left two hours ago, telling her to dress and to be at the club. Saturday is the club's busiest night, and he wants her there.

She shivers again. Her coat is undone, so she wraps it tightly around her and folds her arms, concentrating on the pavement, hurrying her steps.

'Sorry,' she mutters as she bumps into another woman. 'Oh.' She blinks in surprise, seeing the honey-coloured coat. 'You.'

Harriet Littlemore takes a step back. She is in a state of agitation, fiddling with her hat.

'Are you alright?' Ruby is curious. 'What are you doing here?' This is no street for a lady like Harriet Littlemore – even she should realise that.

Harriet straightens herself and stands taller. A habit, Ruby assumes. Something she does when she's anxious or nervous. Like you would if you were in a fight. Ruby straightens up herself, instinctively, and is amused by her own response. She is the shorter of the two by a couple of inches, but it would not be an even match if it came to throwing punches.

'I came to the club, to the Angel,' Harriet says. Her voice trails away, lost in the sounds of other people out on the streets for the evening.

'I wouldn't have thought it was your sort of place.' Ruby just about holds back the laugh.

Harriet bristles and steps back, the top of her head briefly illuminated by a streetlamp, surrounding her with a bright halo. 'Why not? It might be. You don't know where my sort of place is.'

Ruby stares, transfixed by Harriet's hair.

'You cut it!'

Harriet puts a hand to her neck, feeling the edge of her crop.

'I did.' She pauses, a neatly waved lock of hair brushing the tip of her finger as she moves her head just a little. 'What do you think?' She asks in an intense way, as if Ruby's opinion, here in the street, really matters.

Ruby Mills is an arbiter of fashion now. She stands, considering, tipping her own head this way and that to assess the cut.

No one ever asks her opinion of anything.

'I like it,' she concludes. 'I told you it would suit you. Makes you look…' She searches for the right word. 'Fresh. No, not fresh. It makes you look *alive*.'

Harriet lifts her chin a fraction, and, under the streetlamp, her face glows. Her eyes are shining.

'New hat, too,' Ruby says. 'I like that as well.' It is nearly the same colour as her best coat – the blue Poiret she took from Grace Bartlett's warehouse, after much pleading. She recalls that she was wearing the coat when she and Billy raided the jeweller's shop.

Harriet stands as if she is waiting for approval, acknow-ledgement, eyes wide, mouth slightly open. Something about this pleases Ruby. She has seen younger girls in the Forties look at Annie Richmond like that, or sometimes Maggs. Like they are waiting just to be noticed, to be blessed by a nod or a smile from the Queen of the Thieves.

'Really, though, what are you doing here, Miss Harriet Littlemore?'

Harriet does not answer immediately. She appears uncertain and her response is vague. 'I know the owner, Peter Lazenby. We met yesterday evening, and he spoke of it. I wanted to see it for myself.'

'Yesterday evening?' Last night Peter Lazenby was in the club, pushing her in Alex Somers' direction. 'When?'

'Oh, early. We were dining at the Savoy. We had cocktails – my fiancé and I, I mean – and then Peter arrived, and we were introduced. They were in France together, you see.'

'Ah.'

Sweet and stupid, Peter had called her. And Ralph, the fiancé with money for diamonds, was one of his associates. He had told her all about Ralph Christie this morning – when he had not been screwing her or draped over her, fast asleep. 'But he isn't with you tonight?'

'Ralph? No. No. But I wanted to see the club, so I came alone.'

Harriet may or may not be stupid, but she is certainly an innocent. Ruby would bet her best jewellery that she has no idea what Ralph involves himself with – or Peter, for that matter.

'I can take you into the club if you like. Show you around. I know the people. I'm often around here, these days.' It wouldn't hurt to take her inside, introduce her to the barman, dip into the pockets of her coat…

'No, I've been inside already, but I have to leave. The police are on their way. That's why I was sent out of the back door.'

'Coppers? Shit. Peter'll be livid,' Ruby mutters to herself. She narrows her eyes at Harriet and asks sharply, 'When are they coming, do you know?'

'No. Soon, I think. Half an hour, perhaps? Earlier than usual, the cloakroom boy said.'

'I should go and see what's happening.'

'Do you think so? Shouldn't you walk away? You might be caught.'

Ruby shrugs. 'Doing what? Coppers don't bother me.'

'A notorious thief. One of the famous Forty Thieves. Why wouldn't they be interested in you?'

'You're right.' Ruby winks at her. 'I could be up to anything, couldn't I? But you should go. No, I mean it. Not for your own sake. If Peter Lazenby is having to deal with coppers, you'll be a distraction.' Harriet looks oddly vulnerable. It's the short hair, perhaps, that gives her a childlike appearance. Ruby reaches out a hand and touches her sleeve. 'You'll be alright? Getting home?' The coat is as soft as she imagined. She folds her fingers around Harriet's arm and squeezes it. She can feel from the nap that this is a recent purchase. It's not yet been caught in the rain or left over a chair in a smoky pub. The edges of her own coat fall open. Her dress – red spangled satin – is flimsy in the chilly air.

'Yes. Quite alright.' Harriet stares at the dress, and then at the hand, but does not move. 'I can find a taxicab easily enough.'

Two other women hurry past, arm in arm, clutching each other and swaying a little as their heeled shoes meet the uneven pavement. Ruby recognises them from the Angel and steps away from Harriet.

'Trouble,' one of them says, calling over her shoulder to Ruby as her companion tugs her along. 'We're off to Dalton's. You want to come?'

'Later,' she shouts after them. 'I'd better go,' she says to Harriet. She does not wait for a response but pulls her coat back around herself and heads towards the front entrance of the club.

The foyer is almost empty when the doorman lets her in. The only person there appears to be Daniel, the cloakroom attendant – and he is barely recognisable.

'What happened?'

Daniel's left eye is swollen and there is blood all over his nose and mouth. He is half-standing, half-sitting against the wall; his lanky frame has folded in on itself, like a broken branch that has fallen from a tree in a storm.

He shakes his head. Whether he cannot speak or is unwilling to speak, Ruby cannot tell.

'Who did this, Daniel?' She knows the answer, even as she asks.

His right eye waters, causing the kohl to run black tears down his cheek.

Peter emerges from the stairwell, hair ruffled and tie loose, an ugly look on his face.

'Are you still here? I told you to get out. Fuck off, before I throw you into the street.'

Daniel shrinks further against the wall, scrambling to stand up. Ruby does not move to help him. You do not help someone when the man who punched him is only a few feet away – she learned the rules years ago.

Daniel stumbles, falls through the door of the club and disappears into the night.

'Where've you been?' Peter snaps at her. 'You're late.'

'Nowhere,' she says. 'What did I miss?'

'That simpering bloody fool told me we were about to be raided by the police. He'd had word, he said, that they were coming early.' He is furious. 'I emptied the club, sent people elsewhere. But he was wrong. He misunderstood the message. We are not expecting the police for several hours, and I have sent my paying guests to Soho's many other clubs, hotels and bars to spend their money. And I can't send out my staff to invite them back if the police are still going to arrive after hours. Can't call them back only to send them away again.' He runs a hand over his hair, smoothing it down. 'He's cost me money on the most lucrative day of the week, and he's lost me credibility – which is worse.'

And he's lost his job for it, Ruby thinks. And possibly a tooth. Peter certainly doesn't need the money, but he does not like being made to look stupid or incompetent.

'This is the best nightclub in London,' she says quickly. 'Everyone knows that. They'll be back tomorrow.'

He stands chewing his lip, angry, then reaches for her, blood on his knuckles, and pulls her close.

'Ruby, Ruby...' he murmurs into her ear, voice thick. 'Come and dance with me, eh? Make it all better?'

Still in her hat and coat, she follows him downstairs, her hand clasped in his. The orchestra have packed their instruments away, but the pianist is still playing – something old from years ago. They dance slowly as the barman moves around the tables, gathering up abandoned glasses and ashtrays.

Daniel picks himself up from the pavement and rubs the back of his hand across the black slime oozing from his nose. He spits a glob of blood on to the ground.

'Here.' A clean handkerchief is thrust into his hand. 'You'll need this.'

He stares at the white handkerchief, neatly folded. 'I'll ruin it,' he says, his voice little more than a sigh.

'I have another. Wipe your face and I'll buy you a drink. You look as though you need one. The pub across the street is decent. I've been sitting in it for a while. I saw what happened.'

Daniel looks up from the handkerchief to see a man in an ordinary grey coat and hat, with a brown leather satchel across his body. He looks like an overgrown schoolboy.

'Thank you. I think I do need a drink.'

'James Cartwright,' the man says, offering his hand. 'Let's go and find you a pint.'

Harriet fidgets in the back of the taxicab, trying to put her thoughts in order. She crosses and uncrosses her legs.

The driver concentrates on the road and the route to Kensington, the last half-inch of a cigarette dangling from his lip. Harriet pays him no attention either. She is still standing outside the Angel with Ruby.

The girl's coat and hat had been dark and plain. Brown, perhaps, or grey; she could not quite remember. But underneath the coat, when Ruby had grasped her arm, so concerned that she would be safe, Harriet had seen a flash of scarlet. Ruby had been wearing a red dress. And it must have been covered in spangles because it had glimmered under the streetlight. And red lips – she had painted her lips in such a daring shade, so that Harriet had been mesmerised by her mouth.

What had Ruby said to her? She tries to remember everything, savouring every detail of the conversation that had been curtailed too soon. Ruby had offered to show her around the club – she knew people there – and she liked her new hat and thought the hairstyle made her look fresh – no, *alive*.

She *is* alive. Her body is fizzing with an energy that has nothing to do with the glass of champagne she drank but feels like a million tiny bubbles rising inside her.

34

Harriet needs a new pair of gloves. She stares at the display in the shop window. Gloves of different hues are laid out in an arc, creating a rainbow effect that is rather pleasing to the eye. She has managed to lose her usual pair on Saturday – in the Angel nightclub, perhaps, or in the taxicab – and rather than retracing her steps and hunting for them, she will buy herself something new. The old ones had become a *little* worn, after all.

Now she must choose the style and shade.

She has returned to Soho on Monday morning instead of going directly to the offices of the *Gazette*. This is not her usual haunt for gloves, but she found that her feet brought her here again, and these are very pretty. The newspaper can wait.

Besides, she needs cheering up.

She rests a gloveless hand on her arm and the weight and warmth of it returns Ruby Mills to her thoughts – the fondness of her gesture, clasping Harriet's arm like that outside the Angel nightclub. Ruby is the reason why she has returned to Soho, even if she would not like to admit it. Ruby – who had declared that she was often around here.

Ruby has not really left her thoughts since Saturday night. It has been to Ruby that she has turned, if only in her daydreams, to escape her mother's anger. She had known that cutting her hair would cause a scene and had anticipated her mother's barbed comments – she had even rehearsed her own responses – but the depth of her parents' shock had taken Harriet by surprise. Her father had not noticed, of course, when she first sat down to breakfast on Sunday morning, but, caught up in the hailstorm of Isabel's comments, he, too, became cross. And as Harriet had responded to her mother's criticisms first with what Gerald described as 'insolent disregard', and then with 'disrespectful petulance', his anger was exacerbated. Infuriating her mother was part of everyday life – something she appeared to do merely by breathing. Upsetting her father was more serious. He was so often her ally. Cutting her hair short was, according to him, yet another sign that she was growing wild, that she had lost all respect for decency. She had not joined them at church but retired to her room for most of the day.

By Sunday evening, Isabel had declared in pinched tones that perhaps she might grow used to the style after all. The storm abated, the frost began to thaw, although her lips still tightened a little every time she glanced at her daughter's head. Harriet knew that this shift had only begun at all because Gerald had decreed that it should. Even so, at the first opportunity, she has escaped the disapproving atmosphere of the house.

Ruby would understand. Ruby had told her that she looked *alive*. She is living, really living, for the first time in her life.

She squeezes her forearm, as if by doing so she might conjure Ruby onto the pavement next to her.

The blue gloves, perhaps. To match her hat. The one that Ruby admired.

'Are you lifting or just looking?'

Harriet jumps. Ruby is there beside her, as though she really had summoned her, or as if they might have arranged a rendezvous on Saturday night and she has been waiting for Harriet to arrive. Without thinking, Harriet clasps her warmly, as she might an old friend from school. Ruby does not return the embrace, so she shrinks back, full of embarrassment and confusion.

'I'm so sorry. I was thinking about you, and then suddenly here you were. I need new gloves, and I was just looking, but I was remembering you and the Angel. How did you find me, I wonder? Did the police arrive? Was there a raid?' The words tumble.

Ruby laughs. 'Easy, girl, easy. I saw you from across the street. Recognised your coat. The Angel was quiet as the grave when the coppers eventually turned up. Just me and Peter, sharing a cup of tea while the barman washed glasses. They went away.'

'Thank goodness.'

'That's exactly what I said. So,' she nods at the window display, 'are you looking – or lifting?'

Harriet's eyes widen. '*Buying*,' she says firmly.

"Course you are. I'll come in with you, if you like. Keep you company while you choose.'

The surge, the thrill, runs through Harriet. Fear and excitement. She knows. She *knows* what will happen, if Ruby is in the shop with her.

'I'd like that,' is all she says. She grips the door handle tightly as she turns it. 'But we won't be long. I know which pair I'm buying.'

Ruby doesn't need long. Alice Dunning said her hands moved like lightning.

Harriet tries to remain calm, steady, the picture of Kensington respectability, as she greets the shop assistant with a polite 'good morning'.

Ruby is at her shoulder. 'Shame not to try on a few pairs… See the colour of them… You should do that.'

'Suits you, that blue.'

They sit at a cloth-covered table in a café, sharing a pot of tea and plate of cakes. Harriet's new gloves, pale blue kid leather, lie next to her saucer. Harriet is treating them both.

'Thank you.' She pours milk into Ruby's teacup. 'And what did you find, while I was paying for them?' She sounds prim. More disapproving than she intended. She had, as Ruby suggested, tried on several pairs of gloves before deciding, aware that Ruby had, at times, been distracted during the transaction.

'I didn't buy anything,' Ruby says, picking up an iced bun and inspecting it.

'I know. That's not what I asked.'

Ruby says nothing and bites into the sweet dough.

'How many pairs did you take?'

Ruby shrugs, chewing. 'Half a dozen, maybe.' She speaks with her mouth full. 'And a bag.' She nods towards the floor.

Harriet had not noticed a handbag. Ruby must have tucked it under her arm just as they left the shop. Now it sits by her feet, small and neat, dark green leather with bone handles.

'I shan't be allowed to return to that shop, you know,' Harriet says.

'You have new gloves. You don't need to go back there, do you? And other places sell gloves.'

Ruby is right. Even if she did ever return, the staff will have long forgotten her – and the fact that she harboured a thief and pretended to know nothing about it. She presses her legs together tightly, remembering how she felt when they left the shop. Knowing that Ruby had stolen something.

'Where did you hide the gloves? In the pockets of your coat?'

The question is unanswered.

'What will you do with them? You can't wear them all at once.'

Ruby licks her fingers and dabs up the remains of the bun from her plate.

'I'll keep them, for now.'

She is nonchalant, as if hiding several pairs of stolen gloves might be an everyday habit. It surely is. In their brief quarter-hour together in the Holloway cell, Alice Dunning had not elaborated much on what happened to the lifted items. Harriet had been keener to know about Ruby, aware of the warder outside and the certainty that they would be interrupted at any moment. It was Jimmy who had told her that the women traded the items for money, rather than keep them for themselves. That they would use an intermediary – a fence – to do so.

Ruby has eaten every crumb. She eats at speed, not daintily – like someone who doesn't know when she'll eat again.

'Would you like another one?' Harriet says. 'Or would you like mine? I really shouldn't be eating cake.' She pushes the plate across the table.

'Why not?'

'Oh, my mother thinks I'm growing fat,' she says. 'I have a wedding dress to fit into in the summer.' She picks up the tongs from the sugar bowl and taps the prongs lightly together. 'I'm not even supposed to put sugar in my tea – can you imagine?'

Ruby lifts her eyes from the cake. 'Bloody hell.'

Harriet giggles. 'Shush. You'll have us thrown out.'

Ruby takes the tongs from her and drops a lump of sugar into her own cup – and another into Harriet's.

'You should never go without sugar if it's on offer. Life needs sweetening.'

Ruby has very delicate hands. Long fingers and the nails –

which had been full of dirt when Harriet met her in the lobby of Debenham and Freebody – are scrubbed clean. She wears a ring on her right hand – an opal surrounded by silver marcasite. Harriet wonders whether this is something she owns or whether it has been stolen. It's pretty rather than expensive, and it suits her, somehow.

'No, you're quite right.'

'Is he worth it? Worth going without a sugar lump for?'

Ralph. She has barely thought of him today. She twists the engagement ring, straightening it so the stone sits squarely on her finger. The diamonds twinkle at her and she thinks of his warm smile and the way his hair falls over his brow and how handsome he is when he laughs.

'Yes, I suppose he is.'

'You're lucky.'

'Do you have a young man?'

'No one I'd give up cakes for.' She sounds weary of the world, or perhaps just of men.

'What about Billy Walsh?'

Ruby sits up. 'What do you know of Billy Walsh?'

'I…' Harriet is taken aback by the sharpness of her tone. 'He was with you, wasn't he? At Mr Enderby's jewellery shop. I saw you, both of you. You saw me there, too, don't you remember?' She presses her lips together. She will not betray Alice Dunning. She must not give any intimation that Alice has shared so much. Alice was perfectly clear what would happen to her – even inside Holloway – if the Forties heard that she had spoken about them.

'Yeah, I saw you.'

Harriet's neck is warm.

'Billy Walsh is nothing. Just a man.'

'Not… Someone you step out with?'

'No.' The single word is final, decisive. Harriet decides not to pry. There is history between Ruby and Billy Walsh, but it is clearly causing her new friend distress. Ruby sits in silence, frowning.

'I took something once, you know.' Harriet stirs the sugar into her tea, staring at the swirl of the liquid. 'Like you do.'

Ruby doesn't comment.

Harriet lays the teaspoon in the saucer. 'I said, I took something once. From a shop, I mean.' She leans forward and drops her voice. 'I *stole* something. *Lifted* it.'

'I don't believe you. Why would you do that?'

'I wanted to know what it felt like to take something that wasn't mine.'

She wants Ruby to ask her how it felt. She wants to tell her, to share the experience, but Ruby is concentrating on the cake.

'It was a manicure case. Tortoiseshell. Smooth as glass and small enough to fit under my palm. That was how I did it. I just closed my hand around it and slipped it into my pocket.'

Ruby smiles.

'That's good.'

The skin on Harriet's cheek turns a little redder. 'I felt something, you know. It was like you said. I felt *alive*.'

'Weren't you scared you'd be caught?'

'Terrified. I walked and walked for miles, very quickly, and then I stopped and pulled it out of my pocket, just to make sure I really had taken it.'

'Where is it now?'

'It's in the drawer of my dressing table with some other trinkets. I didn't think it was wise to carry it around with me.'

'No. It's never a good idea to keep your steals, although I don't imagine the coppers will come banging on the door of your house in…'

'Kensington,' Harriet supplies. 'Onslow Square.'

'In Kensington,' Ruby nods. 'Onslow Square, you say? Nice to know. Well, they won't be tipping out your drawers and cupboards hunting for it there, will they?'

'Goodness, I hope not.' The thought of the police confronting her mother with a story about a stolen manicure case makes her suddenly cold.

She grips the delicate handle of her teacup to stop her fingers from trembling and savours the tea, calming herself. Ruby is surely right – no one will ever know about it. No one will be looking for it, even. It was just one item from a large store, and she is not the sort of person who would be suspected of stealing. She closes her eyes and takes another reassuring sip of sugared tea. Life does need sweetening, now and then. Ruby is right about that, too.

When she lowers the cup, Ruby's plate is empty again. She is studying herself in the mirror of a silver powder compact and applying lipstick. Sunlight falls on her hair, making it shine.

'You look like a film star,' Harriet says, recalling the comments of the tearful assistant in Hartleys. 'Like you've just stepped out of the screen at the picture house and sat down here to tea with me.'

Ruby lowers the compact, her green eyes bright. 'Do you think so? Oh, I'd love that. To be in a picture.'

'You would be perfect, I'm sure of it.'

Ruby beams at her, and at her own reflection. 'Yeah, I know.'

A waitress in black uniform and white apron hovers nearby.

'Let's walk, shall we?' Harriet reaches for her handbag to find her purse.

They walk, arm in arm, along the pavement. Harriet does not notice where they are going, nor does she think that Ruby is walking in a specific direction. She is too caught up in Ruby's chatter. Ruby is obsessed with the picture house. She prefers the American films, she says, the romances and dramas – although she likes comedy, too. She adores Katherine MacDonald and Mary Pickford and Douglas Fairbanks, *of course*, and Rudolph Valentino, who she saw only recently in *Passion's Playground*, and whose eyes are so beautiful and soulful.

Harriet has been once or twice to the picture house with Ralph, but mostly she goes with girlfriends, and only occasionally. Ruby's knowledge is impressive, encyclopaedic, and her delight is infectious. This is how she exists, then, when she is not stealing from shops; the make-believe world gives her such joy. The picture house is where she escapes from what Harriet imagines is the squalor of her everyday life. A life that has been hard, brutal even.

She doesn't want to think about that. Doesn't want to think of Ruby keeping company with someone like Billy Walsh, nor the men she encountered in the Angel. Nor Alice Dunning, with her coarse features and broken nose. She squeezes Ruby's arm tightly. Perhaps she might help her in some way.

Ruby drags her to look at a copy of *Picture Show* on a stand outside a newspaper shop. She drops Harriet's arm and picks up the magazine, better to examine the image of Mary Pickford that graces the cover.

'Excuse me, young lady, do you have the correct time?' An elderly man leaving the shop makes enquiry of Harriet, who, feeling a little abandoned by Ruby, is scanning the headlines of the various newspapers on sale.

She pushes back her coat sleeve and consults her wristwatch. 'It's a quarter to midday.'

He makes some bland comment about the morning, the weather and the need to return home for lunch. Harriet responds politely, aware that Ruby has finished her survey of the magazines and is waiting to leave. The man raises his hat and thanks her before shuffling away.

'What a dear sort,' Harriet says.

'He was,' Ruby loops an arm through Harriet's again and pulls her away from the shop, walking smartly. 'Most agreeable.'

Something about her chuckle makes Harriet uneasy.

'No, keep walking,' Ruby says hurriedly, clamping her arm under hers and dragging her on. 'Don't slow down, for God's sake. Not until we reach the turning.'

'Ruby, what did you do? Did you pick his pocket?' Harriet stops still and wrenches her arm free.

'Just keep walking.' Ruby strides on ahead.

Harriet jogs to catch her. 'Ruby!'

They turn the corner and Harriet takes her elbow, horror on her face. 'What did you take? How dare you! He was just a sweet old man. A decent man.'

'How do you know he's decent? Because he had a plummy voice and a smart overcoat? Don't be fooled by that.'

'I can't believe you did that. What did you take from him?'

'He had a couple of notes in his pocket.'

'Stealing gloves from a shop is one thing but taking money from an elderly man in the street is quite another matter. And you did this while I was telling him the time – why?' Her voice cracks.

When the elderly gentleman discovers that he is missing some money, he will believe Harriet to be guilty – that she deliberately distracted him while Ruby picked his pocket. She is appalled.

Ruby pulls the notes from her coat – along with the magazine. 'Why not? Do you want to share?'

'No, I do not.' Harriet recoils, horrified by the thought. 'How could you do such a thing? The poor man.'

'But he's not poor, is he? Not if he wanders about with this much money in his pocket, without worrying about keeping it safe. If he can afford to be so casual, then he's not poor. And he's fair game.'

Harriet has no response. Instead, she gazes around her, only now wondering where she is. They are at the river. Waterloo Bridge.

'It's alright for you,' Ruby says. 'With your wealthy father to look out for you, and your rich fiancé who buys you diamonds. I don't have anyone. So don't stand there judging me for taking an opportunity when it offers itself.'

'I'm not judging you – truly, I'm not.' She is chastened by the accusation.

'You are. Everyone does.' Ruby pulls the green handbag tighter under her armpit and leans forward to kiss Harriet on the cheek. 'Thanks for the bun, though. I enjoyed that.' She grins and her face is full of that same vitality and energy that Harriet had glimpsed outside Mr Enderby's. Now she cannot help but smile back.

She watches Ruby disappear over the river, a hand on her cheek, trying to decide whether she should call after her, until it is too late and she is too far away to hear.

Then she sees the small figure turn and raise an arm; Ruby is waving to her. Harriet waves back and keeps waving even when Ruby gives up and continues on her way. She waves until Ruby has disappeared, her face glowing and her heart almost bursting.

35

Ruby pulls the bank notes from her pocket and sits counting them on her bed at Solly's, along with the money Peter gave her. The green handbag and the half a dozen pairs of gloves have been shoved under the bed. Perhaps she will take them to Grace Bartlett's warehouse one day. Perhaps not. She is determined to share some of her money with Daisy. Daisy is the main reason she crossed back over the river when it would have been easier to remain in Soho. Maybe she'll take her some smokes and a bag of sweets as well. Aniseed balls. Daisy loves those.

Ruby has a lot of money now. Hard cash, and it's all hers because she is no longer a member of the Forty Thieves.

But what is she?

She is hardly the same as Daisy Gould. Not with so much money in her hands.

She picks up a diamond earring that is lying next to the bank notes and watches it catch the light that is streaming in through her bedroom window. She brings its twin close to her eye, letting her gaze shift out of focus so that she can see only a rainbow of colour. There is a tiny glimmer of fire in every stone.

A gift from Peter.

When the police had finally left the club, he had carried her upstairs to his flat. They had spent the whole of Sunday in bed.

She is his Venus, he tells her. His evening star. The one who allows him to forget his troubles.

She ignores the memory of the blood on his hands and the disquiet lurking deep within her bones. She knows what he is. But, for now, he says that he adores her, and, for now, that is all she wants.

She hears a familiar voice. Maggs is in the kitchen with Solly, shouting for her.

Ruby slouches out of her room, shoeless.

'I thought I heard you,' is all that Solly says as he reaches for an extra teacup. 'Told Maggs you were here.'

'Maggs.' The last time they saw each other was when Annie was blacking Ruby's eye.

'Annie wants you on a job.'

And that's it. With one breath, she is back in the Forties. There is no question in Maggs's mind that this will be a welcome invitation.

Ruby shrugs and sits at the kitchen table, reaching for the tea that Solly has poured for her. 'I don't work for the Forties, remember? And I don't need a job, Maggs. I don't want one.'

'You'll want this one. Annie asked for you specially.'

The floor is cold against her stockinged toes.

Maggs carries on, ignoring Ruby's sullenness, leaning against the sink, cup in hand.

'It's another jeweller. A small place off Bond Street. Very smart. Annie's had an eye on it for a while and she'd like you to see what you can find.'

Ruby shifts on the stool. Her fingertips begin to tingle, as though her old life is stroking magic into her hands.

'How do you mean, see what I can find?'

'It's a two-stage operation,' Maggs says, sensing interest. 'You pay a visit and view the pretties. You try on a few things. You identify the better goods.'

'Just trying on? What's the point of that?'

'Let me finish. You come back, and you tell Solly what you've seen. He finds imitations here, paste and glass, or he makes them, and then comes stage two. You return to the store when there's a different assistant. You ask to see the same pieces as before and you swap them over.' She drinks a large mouthful of tea and sloshes it around her gums. She has bad teeth and always drinks her tea scalding hot.

'You slide my knock-offs into the boxes and walk out with the real diamonds,' Solly finishes.

'Why not just run off with the stuff in the first place?' Ruby frowns. 'It sounds like a lot of bother. I could just put a few rings in my pocket. Or I could go with Billy Walsh and distract the assistant, like we did in the other place.'

Maggs shakes her head. 'There's a guard on the door. He provides the brawn. I told you it was high class. If the assistant suspects you've pocketed anything, the man on the door will have you, and you're straight to Holloway.'

'But if I've replaced the goods with Solly's stuff, the assistant won't notice – at least not until I've gone. Clever.' She picks up her teacup. It is clever.

'Annie's idea.'

Annie Richmond wants her back. Just like Florrie said. They can't manage without her.

'Why does she want me to do it? And why not just take some of Solly's jewellery on the first visit?'

Maggs grins, leans over the table and punches her softly on the chin. 'You're so naïve sometimes. Still so much to learn. A fancy jeweller will notice if one of the girls sticks a ruby ring where an emerald is supposed to be. This is why we're sending you: you've got an eye for the best goods. You identify the choicest pieces first of all, and Solly finds you a match as close as he can make it. That way, it won't be so obvious when you switch them.'

'I see it now.'

'Thought you would. Anyway, Annie wants you there right away. You're back with us, Ruby.'

'Now?'

'Yes, now.' Solly interrupts. 'You'll have a clear view of the jewellery in decent daylight. If you wait until later, it'll be too dark. You've a good eye, like Maggs says. Make use of it, little Magpie.'

An opportunity to prove herself. To be back with them all again. To have them talk to her, rather than ignore her. Have Solly call her Magpie. And no grovelling. 'Alright.'

She will visit Daisy afterwards. Or maybe tomorrow.

'Grace has sent you a decent coat to wear,' Maggs says, nodding at the biscuit-coloured creation draped over Solly's chair. 'Fetch yourself a string of pearls from downstairs. Elegant but not too flash. This is upmarket.'

It is upmarket. She can tell that as soon as she stops outside the big bow window. It sparkles. There are only a few choice pieces on display, and everything that she examines is blinking back at her – even through the glass.

She stifles a yawn, curling her gloved hand into a ball as she holds it to her mouth. She can be a lady, when she wants to be – one who has not had much sleep recently and has filled her stomach with nothing but cake this morning. Someone like Harriet Littlemore, who sleeps in a chaste and comfortable bed, who offers her food so easily because she has never known what it is like to go for days without, and who frets about a single trinket she has lifted. Ruby was nicking items like that before she was tall enough to see over the shop counter.

She straightens her shoulders trying to recall the last time she was ever so innocent. Too long ago. Before Solly sent her to Ray the Rat. It's hard to remember.

Instead, she pictures Harriet's face. The way her lips part a little, and how she grows slightly short of breath when she becomes anxious or nervous. Sweet, really.

Harriet Littlemore is not only sweet; she is useful.

Ruby inclines her head towards the shop window in a slow and graceful movement. She widens the back of her throat, ready to stretch the vowel sounds when she speaks.

Maggs is watching from further down the street. She is pretending to be interested in the flowers outside a florist's shop. Who is ever interested in orange chrysanthemums? She will be bored already.

Ruby moves to the door of the shop and finds that it is opened for her. A man in a perfectly cut dark suit lets her in. He is twice her size and has an unblinking stare. She knows the look. She has seen it often enough. He's another one back from the war. She wonders, as she passes, nodding politely, what he was before – before the guns stole his peace of mind. He might have been a banker, a stockbroker, a lawyer. He looks like any of those in his smart suit. But now he is employed for the size of his shoulders, doing a job where he does not need to think, only do as he is bidden. At least he has a job.

The man behind the counter is altogether different. He is

a hawk, an aging bird of prey with a small sharp nose and tiny bespectacled eyes that watch her with interest, as though she is a mouse approaching his nest. What is he looking for? Is he expecting a thief? She gazes around the shop like someone who has time and money on her hands, breathing carefully. No. He is doing exactly what she would do: he is estimating her value. He is costing the pearls at her throat and the jewels in her ears. He is looking over her coat and deciding whether it is made by a reputable fashion house, or whether it is a cheap imitation made by a friend on a sewing machine at home. This is a man used to wealthy customers. He will spot a fraud as easily as he will pick out a glass bauble in a tray of diamonds.

But she is not a fraud. She is not a thief. Like an actress in a film, she is playing a part. She smiles, imagining herself as languid, gracious and moneyed.

This is what she loves. This is the best part of it. Observing herself becoming someone else. She would like to be someone so untroubled by life. Someone who does not need to earn her money with men like Peter Lazenby. Or Ray Calladine. But for now, she can pretend.

'May I help you?' The bird-featured man narrows his eyes. Only a fraction, but she is aware of the scrutiny. The first impression she makes is the one that will determine whether she looks at jewellery or finds herself thrown out by the guard.

She throws the jeweller a bored look, as though she is hardly bothered by his bracelets and cuffs. She has so many already.

'I have a birthday approaching. My parents wish to buy me something. I don't know. I really don't know what I want. They suggested we might come here, so I thought I'd take a look.'

She gazes about her. 'What have you got that might tempt me?' Now she offers the smallest of smiles, as if daring him to find her something that will hold her attention.

'Might I know your parents?'

A lesser thief would be thrown by such a question. She takes a risk.

'I don't know,' she says, airily, turning away from him. 'Might you? The Littlemores. From Kensington.'

'Gerald Littlemore?'

Shit. He does know them.

'That's right.' She touches an earring – a drop of fire opal from Solly.

'Then I'll be delighted to find you something, Miss Littlemore. It's been many years since you were last here.'

'Indeed, it has. But how lovely to return.'

She breathes evenly. She has made a mistake, but there is no need to panic. *Many years.* He has not recognised that she is not Harriet. Besides, if he becomes suspicious and she needs to run, she will be faster on her feet than the giant at the door with the vacant expression.

The old man pulls out trays of rings, bracelets and necklaces for her to examine. Nothing is too much trouble for Gerald Littlemore's daughter. He enquires after her parents and she makes a few bland comments – enough to convince him that she is Harriet, or at least to assuage any doubt.

Other customers come and go, but Ruby is left, trusted, to view the jewellery. When the jeweller is forced to abandon her and serve the others, she examines the goods more carefully. She shouldn't linger – she has a job to do – but these are items to be appreciated and enjoyed for their intricate beauty and craftsmanship.

She memorises what she sees, ready to describe everything to Solly.

The jeweller has begun serving an older gentleman customer when she decides it is time to leave. She has seen what she needs to see – he has shown her his treasures.

'Thank you. I do believe I have chosen one or two items. My father will be along in a day or two. No, no, I can recall them perfectly. I shall look forward to my birthday after all, thanks to you.' She flashes him a coy smile and waltzes to the door, which is opened for her.

'Give your father my regards, Miss Littlemore. Tell him that I am here every day except Thursday and will be delighted to renew my acquaintance with him.'

She does not ask how he knows her imagined father. She does not care. She has forgotten about Harriet Littlemore for now. Her mind is full of diamonds, full of the designs that she will share with Solly. It will be just like old times: the two of them, setting glass in paste and imitating wonders together.

She will return on Thursday, her pockets full of pretend.

36

Monday afternoon

Harriet runs her fingers through her hair as she stares at the blank piece of paper in her typewriter. She caught a taxicab from Waterloo Bridge and is pretending that she has been at her desk all day – and not just since lunchtime. So far, she has avoided Mr Pickford.

'You've cut your hair.'

Jimmy's comment, as he passes her desk, makes her jump.

'Yes.' She waits for a further remark or criticism, but he makes none. It was a mere observation, a telling of the fact. He swings his satchel from his shoulder and drops it onto the floor next to his desk. She sees him light a cigarette and leaf through his notebook. He is not interested in her hair – or her – only in his work. She types half-heartedly and observes him.

'Are you still embroiled in corruption?' she asks, half an hour later, placing a cup of tea at his elbow.

He doesn't look up from his notebook. He is scribbling intensely.

'I am. More than before. Although Pickford thinks I'm writing a report on a burglary in Knightsbridge, so I really ought to get on with it.'

'How much corruption have you found at the Angel nightclub?'

His head jerks up. 'Why? What would you know of the Angel?'

'I was there on Saturday night.'

'You were what?' He nearly drops his pencil. 'The Angel?'

She ducks her head. She will not tell him that she was reading his notebook. 'You told me about it, remember? When you were telling me about corruption and illegal goods the other day.'

'Did I? I don't recall –'

'Well, you did,' she says, becoming more confident in her lie.

'And I decided I would go and find out about it.'

He frowns, puzzled. 'Why would you do that?'

'I know the owner.' She tries to sound casual. 'Peter Lazenby. So, I paid a visit to his club.'

Jimmy turns around and drags a chair from the desk behind his. She sits.

'How do you know Peter Lazenby? Are you often at his club?'

She is beginning to regret telling him. His questions are sharp.

'No. No, I'd never been before. It was my first time there. I don't visit clubs like that at all. But I know him. Well, I sort of know him. He's a friend of…' She does not mention Ralph. It is too complicated. 'He's a friend of a friend. As I say, I don't visit nightclubs as a rule, or bars – well, certainly not on my own.'

'You went alone?' He cannot disguise his shock.

'I thought I might take a look. See what I could see.'

'You've got guts, I'll say that for you. And?'

'Well, I didn't… I didn't stay long. There was a raid. Police. I left long before they arrived, through the back door. The cloakroom attendant told me that they received a warning at the club.'

'That's not quite what happened…'

Harriet is surprised. 'What do you mean?'

'Never mind. I'm intrigued – tell me about the Angel.'

'Um. I saw some women sniffing cocaine.'

'Really? Do you know what that looks like?'

'I'm not so very naïve,' she says. 'They were pushing white powder up their nostrils – that *is* cocaine, isn't it?'

'It is. Anything else?'

'I saw the man who robbed Enderby's jewellers with Ruby Mills. Billy Walsh, he's called. He's one of the Elephant Boys and a hardened criminal, according to Mr MacKenzie.'

'Inspector MacKenzie? Of Scotland Yard?'

She colours. 'Embarrassingly, I know him, too. He's a friend of my father's. He says Billy Walsh is a violent man. I saw him shove Cecily Enderby into the street, certainly.'

'He's capable of more than that, but he's a small-time crook, at the moment. I think the Elephants are becoming involved in operations on this side of the river. Illegal betting is usually their thing, racecourses and dog tracks, but I hear they're trying to involve themselves in the cocaine market.'

'The men with Billy Walsh, they were more of the Elephant Boys, I discovered. The cloakroom attendant told me. When I walked past, I heard them mention something about taking "goods to Mayfair". Someone called Mortimer is looking after them. Would that be cocaine as well, do you think?'

He rubs his eyebrow and stares pensively at the notes, talking more to himself than to Harriet. 'There's an office not far from the club, a letting agency. That's Mortimer. I want to speak with him. I know that I can tie Lazenby with the Elephants, and with some of the other crooks around, and, of course, Kimber and the Brummagems might be part of it, but I doubt it, and my real suspicion is that there are Westminster men involved…'

She starts. He looks up.

'What do you mean, Westminster men?' she says.

'Why do you ask?'

'No reason. I suppose it's just that, with my father's connections, I've been around Westminster men all my life. They are good men. Upright, decent people. Not drug dealers, certainly.'

'I'm sure they are. They're not all bad.' He pauses. 'Stay away from Peter Lazenby, Harriet. He's not a good man. Not at all.'

'He's certainly a charmer,' she says, remembering his stories.

'No, he's not a charmer. He's a crook. And a nasty piece of work, running prostitutes and selling stolen goods. And he beats up his staff.'

Harriet puts a hand to her mouth. 'Really?'

'I picked one of them up from the street on Saturday. I was watching the place from a pub opposite – watching who was coming and going. I didn't see you, but maybe you'd gone by then. Ah, no, you said you left from the back. But that cloakroom attendant you spoke of? His face was covered in blood when I found him. He'd made some mistake about the time the police were arriving – just a simple error, I gather – and Lazenby punched him several times. He nearly passed out in my arms.'

'Oh, goodness. Terrible. Why would he do that?'

'The boy lost him business. Saturday night would normally be busy, and Lazenby sent his customers away expecting the police were arriving.'

She lets out a long, shaky breath. 'I see. And prostitutes? In the club?' She recalls the brightly dressed, shimmering girls she saw dancing, snuggling up to laughing men. And Ruby standing under the streetlamp, a sparkling gown underneath her coat. 'That's what he does?'

'He does.'

Peter Lazenby had left her sitting on her own in his club. What must she have looked like? And Ruby, is that what she does, when she's not stealing from shops?

'But he's not acting alone. He's protected. His illegal activity is overlooked. And that's what really interests me.'

'This is the corruption you spoke about?'

'Exactly. And hypocrisy. This is the heart of it, for my money. Crooks, even fancy ones like Lazenby, are one thing. But there are other men who involve themselves in Lazenby's work. You won't see them, of course, but they'll be there in the shadows. They say they're building a better society for us, for those of us who came back from the war. But they're not. They're making their money off our backs and the backs of the poor – like they've always done – and that's what I want to expose. That's what I want people to read about, what I want them to know. All I need is proof. Something I can put into a newspaper.'

Harriet has never heard him speak like this. She has not heard anyone speak like this. Not even Ralph. She has been surrounded by politicians and high-minded, moralising men all her life, but none has spoken like this.

'But for the moment, I am supposed to be typing something for tonight's edition, and if Pickford sees me idling with you, he'll tear me to pieces.'

'I'm sure that all will be forgiven when you present him with something as sensational as this.' She stands, and gestures to his notebook.

'Maybe. But don't say anything about it, will you?'

'Of course not.'

'And Harriet, I meant what I said. Stay away from Lazenby.'

She returns to her desk.

Peter Lazenby had been nothing but politeness to her. He was Ralph's friend; they had fought together in France – been through hell together, he had said.

Despite her assurances to Jimmy about keeping quiet, she must surely talk to Ralph.

37

Tuesday morning

Ruby bangs on Daisy's door for the fifth time. It rattles on its hinges, but no one answers.

'She ain't in!' a voice pipes up from somewhere behind a window of one of the dilapidated homes on this most dismal street. 'I saw her go out at first light.'

Ruby squints up at the houses. It is not much beyond first light even now, and they are all still in shadow. She cannot tell which window the voice has come from. News has not yet reached this part of the Borough that she is back with the Forties. No one is supposed to be speaking to her – on Annie's orders. The woman shouting will not reveal herself.

Someone has risked their own skin for her, and she is grateful for the kindness, even though she had already concluded that Daisy was not at home.

She leaves a small bag of aniseed balls on the doorstep, pushing them as close to the edge of the door as possible, knowing that, in all probability, some light-fingered child will have taken them before Daisy returns home. The doorstep is still thick with dust.

At least if Daisy's out, she's not on a mattress upstairs. Ruby imagines her buying food or a packet of tea, over the river, perhaps. She hopes that's what Daisy is doing. She straightens up and stares, for a moment, down the empty street, knowing that everyone will be watching her from behind their ragged curtains. She walks slowly, swinging her hips and holding her head high, back to Solly's.

There are jewels to be set after all, and Solly is keen to make an early start.

Solomon Palmer leans over the kitchen table, his eyeglass glued to his socket. He picks up a small piece of green glass with his finest-tipped pliers and drops it into the claw of the ring.

Ruby watches him as he folds the fingers of the claw into place. She always loves observing his work. He will pay as much attention to a chip of glass – setting it exactly right – as he will to a real emerald. He sits back in his seat for a moment and wrinkles his nose, examining the result.

'Not bad.'

'You're a master, Solly. It's exactly what I saw.' It won't fool any jeweller who might examine it closely, but it only has to fool one particular jeweller for the length of time Ruby is still in the shop. Even so, Solly is a craftsman who takes pride in his work.

He lays the ring on the battered wooden tray next to his jar of green glass, each sliver fractionally different in shade from its neighbour, from bright yellowy grass to darkest bottle or Hooker's green. He has collected them, over the years – picked them out of mud and dust on the streets and added them to his jar. Ruby, who will notice anything that catches the light, used to do this, too, when she was younger. Even now, sometimes she will stop mid-stride, bend down, lift a chip of glass from the gutter, pocket it and bring it home. Solly has four jars, respectively containing various red, blue, green and clear glass splinters.

'Well, we're relying on your eyes, Ruby. I hope you haven't lost your knack.' *While you've been out of the Forties*, he doesn't say.

'I haven't.'

He sits back in the chair and surveys her with nearly the same attention he gives the stones: as if checking for a flaw or crack.

'Tell me about it, how it went. Maggs said you did well.'

Maggs wouldn't know. She was outside all the time. If anything had gone wrong, if the shopkeeper had suspected her at all, she would have been on her own. Annie Richmond wanted Ruby on the job, but she would have sacrificed her to carry it out.

It had been a test of both her skill and her loyalty – her willingness to act without anyone to help her, for the Forties.

'I played the part, like I always do. Pretended I was someone else.'

'Who were you? Leading lady from one of your moving pictures?

'No, not this time.' She hesitates, wondering whether to tell him. 'Someone I met.'

'Oh? Anyone I know?'

'Hardly. This one's a proper lady. From Kensington. Soft around the edges. She walks like she's gliding on air. Rich – and about to be richer still.'

'How come?'

'She's marrying a man who's loaded with money. You should see the ring he's given her, Solly. Marquise-cut diamond the size of a thumbnail, edged with twelve smaller stones. It's the most beautiful thing I've ever seen.'

'I'm surprised you've not nicked it, then,' Solly laughs.

'I'm surprised myself.' She picks a chip of apple-coloured glass from the tray and lifts it to the light. It's the first time he's laughed with her for ages. Weeks.

'How did you meet a woman like that?'

'I don't know. It's like she's following me around. She saw me with Billy, when we did that jeweller's shop in South Ken. She just stared at me, like she was peering into my soul. And then I saw her in Debenham and Freebody and she knew who I was.'

'Doesn't everyone?' he chuckles, picking up the spare chips and dropping them back into the jar.

'Everyone in Southwark knows me, but not someone like that. How would Harriet Littlemore know my name?'

'How do you know hers?'

'I overheard someone talking to her. She was buying a silk nightgown, for her wedding, I think, and another woman called to her. She was really shocked when I said her name, though – like she'd thought she had an advantage, knowing mine. That made me laugh.'

'And what? You got talking, you and this Harriet woman? What about? Common interests in expensive jewellery?'

'Ha. I like that. No. She told me to take a bath.'

'How rude.'

'She was right. I needed one.'

'I hope you told her where to stick her bath, though.'

'I told her she needed a pair of emerald earrings. And that she should cut her hair.'

Solly prises the glass from her fingers and adds it back to the sparkling green jar before screwing on the lid. 'You're a charmer, Ruby Mills. Fancy telling a lady she should cut her hair.'

'Well, she did it,' Ruby says, looking at him with a serious face. 'She cut it short. I saw her again on Saturday night. And her hair was cut short.'

Solly rubs an eyebrow and shrugs. 'Well, maybe she sits in the picture houses as much as you do. Maybe she wants to look like those American actresses, too.'

'Nah.' Ruby shakes her head. 'It's more than that. She wanted me to see it; it was like she wanted my *approval*. Like it was important to her, what I thought. And she had a new hat that was exactly the same colour as my best coat – the same blue.'

'She wants to be like you, you think?'

'She wouldn't, if she knew what my life was, would she? Besides, she disapproves of what I am.' Harriet Littlemore had lifted a trinket, probably out of boredom; it didn't give her any sympathy for the Forties.

Solly puts the eyeglass into a leather pouch, which he then shoves into his pocket. 'Odd, though. Her mimicking you. Maybe she's just fallen for your pretty face. Easily done, I imagine.'

'Maybe.' Ruby fiddles with the opal ring on her finger. 'I don't know. But while she's around, she's bloody useful. It's why I used her for this job. Spoke like her, even used her name.'

Solly tuts. 'That was unwise, Magpie. What if she finds out?'

'She won't.'

Solly frowns as he tidies away the tools. 'There's something you're not telling me, Ruby. I can hear it.'

Ruby is quiet for a moment.

'There's nothing, I swear it.'

Solly licks his lower lip. Ruby's oaths are worthless, he knows that.

She stands and stretches her arms. 'I'm going back to Soho,' she says.

'If that's what you want.'

'You don't need me. I'm only distracting you.'

He stands, too. 'Your place is here, Magpie. With the Forties. And with me.' Annie Richmond may still be testing her, but Solly has made his own decision.

'I know. Thanks.'

She is restless.

She returns to her room and unpacks and refills her handbag with items she might need tonight. She replays yesterday's conversations with Harriet Littlemore. They had shared their enjoyment of the moving pictures. Harriet had offered her cake. They had laughed at the idea of giving up sugar for the sake of a man. And Harriet had watched her cross the bridge. She had been standing there, waving, when Ruby turned around.

Peter Lazenby had called Harriet sweet and stupid. He was not wrong. She can afford to be generous with a piece of cake because she is wealthy, and she can afford to be ignorant of how the world works because it has always worked to her benefit. It does, for people like that. But like the sugar lump in her tea, Harriet Littlemore will dissolve into nothing if anything or anyone hurts her because she is soft as well as sweet.

Ruby had kissed her on the cheek quite deliberately, guessing as Solly had guessed.

Now, she fiddles with the catch on her powder compact, opening it and snapping it shut, over and over.

Ruby has never felt ashamed before.

38

Tuesday evening

Ruby is still deep in thought when she reaches the Angel later. She trails down the street where she had met Harriet on Saturday evening. It was busier then, but it is Tuesday tonight. She sees only one or two men on their way out for a drink. A skinny dog cocks its leg against a streetlamp outside the entrance and limps away as Ruby approaches.

There is a new man attending the cloakroom – older, less attractive than Daniel. He takes her coat and hat without comment, boredom on his face. He doesn't even appear interested in her dress – a vibrant turquoise green that brings out the colour in her eyes. Daniel would have noticed immediately. He would have complimented her, told her she was beautiful and sent her downstairs with a smile. He was a sweetheart.

Her mood is not lifted by the music. The orchestra is small in number, and the tune they are playing is as lifeless as she feels. There are a few customers, but no one who looks ready to buy her champagne and dance with her. She drifts to the bar, exchanges pleasantries with the barman and buys herself a drink using the money in her handbag. Champagne. She only drinks champagne at the Angel.

The door across the dancefloor opens and Peter appears, in company with the General, Billy Walsh and another man. She brightens when she sees him. She is wearing the diamond earrings he gave her and hopes that he will approve, but he is deep in conversation and does not notice her. Instead, it is Billy who catches sight of her and crosses to the counter.

He gives a low whistle. 'You look like a film star. Can I buy you another drink?'

'I don't think you can afford my company these days, Billy Walsh.'

He pulls a face. 'I heard you were working for Mr Lazenby.'

'Well, I wasn't going to starve waiting for someone in the Borough to throw me their scraps, was I? Besides, Peter knows a diamond when he sees one. He appreciates my many talents.'

'Really? What other talents do you have?'

'Fuck off, Billy. Does Edith know you're out? Don't look at me like that. I know you're back with her. You might have waited. You might have said something. I had to hear it from Florrie.'

He stares sullenly at the counter. 'What was I supposed to do? After what you did? But I know Annie's taken you back now. Maggs told me you were on a job near Bond Street. You should go home. Stay with the Forties. This is no place for you.'

'And I've told you, I please myself. I look out for myself. I always have. I certainly don't need you telling me what to do. Why don't you skip home to Edith Lennox? I'm sure she'll have made you a lovely supper. She's probably waiting for you now, wondering where you are while your cabbage is going cold.'

A man at the bar, a leather bag slung over his shoulder like a telegram boy, watches them. He's not the usual sort of Angel customer. He is cradling a small glass of whisky as if he is trying to make it last all night. No money. Ruby dismisses him.

'Aw, come on, darling, don't give me a hard time,' Billy entreats her, turning on the charm. 'You know how it is with Annie, how we all have to dance to her tune, but now you're back, how about it…?' He runs an arm around her waist, and she feels the familiar sensation of his thumb stroking her back, where he knows she likes to be touched. 'You and me?'

Peter is suddenly there, behind Billy, with a hand on his shoulder, gently prising him away.

'It's been useful to see you tonight, Mr Walsh. I'll leave the situation with you, yes?' He is businesslike, but he is telling Billy to leave – and to leave her.

Billy knows it, too. There is little doubt who is in charge in the club. He shoves his hands into his pockets.

'Goodnight, Mr Lazenby. You can consider the work already done.'

He nods to Ruby before leaving. 'I'd better go. I'll see you around.'

Ruby leans into Peter's chest before Billy has taken three strides. 'Do you want to go upstairs? It's quiet tonight.'

He eases her away and holds her by the shoulders, studying her, approving. 'Not now. It'll be busy in here soon enough. And I have work to do.'

'You're always working. Who's that you're with?' She nods towards the office door. 'The man with Charles Haversham?'

'Ah, I think you'll be interested in this one. A sweet treat for you, perhaps.' He leans close to her ear. 'That's Ralph Christie. Your friend Harriet Littlemore's fiancé. The one I told you about.'

'Really?' She cranes to take a better look.

'You'll like him; he's immensely rich. He plays our game exceptionally well. You'd never know it, but he's as much of a thief as you are. In truth, he's a better one. He's made most of his money quietly manipulating the stock exchange over recent years.'

'How do you do that? Is it like fixing a horse race or a boxing match?'

'Cleverer. Do you know, even with the restrictions on the stock markets during the war, Ralph Christie was able to make money. We were in France at the time, so I've no idea how he managed it. Fiddling the government bonds, probably.'

'Stinking rich, then?' The diamond on Harriet's hand springs to mind again.

'Positively reeking. He's a useful ally, as well as a wealthy one. He's going to be a big noise in government very soon, and we need the protection of people in power. If you find yourself in trouble, it's wise to have powerful friends.'

'Are you in trouble?'

'Not at all.' He fingers a lock of her hair, smiling softly as he tucks it behind her ear. 'But it's always smart to have insurance. Bubbles burst, now and then.'

Ruby watches Ralph Christie. A confident man, from the way he stands.

'So, how about you come and keep us company?' Peter touches the diamonds in her ear, then trails a thumb gently down her throat and strokes her collarbone. 'Drink champagne? Give us something lovely to look at?'

'Well, given you've asked so politely, I suppose I shall.'

'Good.'

'What's Billy Walsh up to? You sent him away; where's he gone?'

Peter's thumb reaches her clavicle, pauses, then presses a little harder. 'I told you before not to worry about Mr Walsh. He's taking care of some business for me. Tedious work, carrying some merchandise over to Mayfair. Come and meet Ralph.'

He takes her hand and escorts her past the watching man with the satchel, who's sitting nursing a now-empty glass.

Ralph Christie might be thought a handsome man, Ruby decides, even without his money. Smooth skin; round cheeks;

pleasant, open features. But it is the wealth that makes him so attractive. And perhaps also the way he holds everyone's attention as he speaks. Something in his manner fascinates her; the quiet power he exudes. Without imposing himself, he dominates the circle. Even Peter is oddly smaller, less significant, in his company.

The four of them talk of this and that, and nothing in particular – music, film stars and people they admire – laughing and drinking at a small table.

Ralph's eyes keep returning to Ruby, roving the neckline of her dress and curves of her body.

She knocks back a large mouthful of champagne and tries to forget Harriet Littlemore.

A few extra members of the orchestra turn up to the stage, and they strike up an exotic-sounding piece. Couples that she had not noticed earlier, hidden away in alcoves, appear on the dancefloor. The heavy, syncopated drum throbs deep in Ruby's stomach, and the wailing clarinet makes her feel alive and free, and sensual. She cannot prevent her body from swaying, the edge of her skirt's hem tickling her calves as her feet tap and twist under the table.

'Would you care to dance? You look as though you would.' Ralph leans in close to her.

A tiny twitch on Peter's lips allows her the answer.

'You're right, I would love to dance.' She lays a hand on Ralph's thigh. 'Will you dance with me?' She does not dare imitate Harriet with him but still uses one of her better voices.

'I should like nothing more.'

He dances well, like someone who has been taught properly, but he moves stiffly at first, revealing that it is not something he does naturally. She cannot help but compare him unfavourably to Peter, who is fluid as water. Nevertheless, she compliments him as a matter of course.

'I took a few lessons, a while ago,' he says, swirling her around. 'The sort of thing one should do, I believe. I'm glad to know they paid off.'

The music comes to an end, and they collapse into one another. He pulls her tight against his body and they stand on the edge of the dancefloor, waiting for the orchestra to begin again.

'You're the most beautiful creature here,' he says, breathing heavily into her ear, his hand sliding over her hips, fingers groping. 'I've been longing to meet you for a while.'

'Really?'

'Really. And now that I have you, I should like to take you home with me.'

'Do you think I'm a fast sort of girl?' She tries to pull away, laughing.

'I'm very much hoping so, from what I've heard from Peter.' He won't let her go, but grips her, pinning her arms to her sides as he tries to kiss her. 'How about you let me find out?' He pulls her closer again, his lips at her ear, breath sweet with the champagne. 'Do you know how much I want you?'

'Don't you have a wife at home? Or sweetheart you should be staying true to?' She wants to know exactly how he will lie to her.

'No. No wife. And no sweetheart at all. Just a man who looks after me, and a housekeeper, a cook and a maid, but they won't bother us.'

'How do you know? Are they used to you keeping company?'

He nuzzles into her neck. 'They are always very discreet. That's why they work for me. And they are probably turning in for the night already.' He takes a watch from his pocket and consults it, still with his arm around her. 'Quite definitely.'

It is the watch that decides it.

'I think, perhaps, you should speak to Peter.'

'Speak to me about what?' Peter is behind her, a glass in his hand.

'Ralph wants to take me home with him.'

'Lucky Ralph.' He salutes his friend. 'And lucky Ruby, of course.' His smile is warm enough, but she cannot quite read his face. 'Go and find your coat, then.'

Ralph picks up her hand and presses it to his lips. 'A jewel indeed.'

Peter meets her at the cloakroom, no longer smiling.

'He's speaking with Charles Haversham,' he says, when she enquires where Ralph is. 'He's on his way.'

He straightens her coat, tugging the lapels and drawing her closer. 'Look after my friend,' he says. 'As I told you, he's useful to me.'

'He's getting married soon,' Ruby says, frowning. 'I'm not sure...'

'You're not growing prudish, surely?' His brow lifts, mocking her. 'Don't trouble yourself about that. He'll make the evening worth your while. And I shall have his continued support – which is what matters to me.'

She says nothing. Something does not feel right.

'Ah, it's Harriet you're thinking of, isn't it? Harriet Littlemore, your reporter friend?'

'My what?'

'Your loyalty to your friend is rather touching, sweetheart, but this is business.'

'What do you mean, my reporter friend?'

'Only that I suppose if you tell her all of your secrets, it's no surprise that you would feel close to her.'

'Tell her all of my secrets?' Ruby is puzzled. 'I've never told her anything – except that she should cut her hair and some nonsense about film stars.'

'Don't be foolish.' He smiles, stroking her face. 'She wrote about you, yes? In the *Kensington Gazette*? The Jewel of the Borough, she called you – a rather admiring piece, on the whole, if I recall, but I still can't help thinking that she was right. As Ralph says, you are a jewel indeed. My diamond girl. I'm finding it almost painful, you know, to see you leave with him –'

Ruby pulls away from him. 'What are you talking about? Harriet Littlemore wrote that piece about me? With all the tricks of the Forties, and what I did, and everything? She's a reporter? *She* wrote it?'

'Well, of course she did. I assumed that was the reason you knew her. That's why Annie Richmond threw you out of the Forties, isn't it? For telling a newspaper reporter their secrets.'

Ruby puts a hand to her face, remembering how Annie had broken her cheek. How she had been humiliated in the Crown, in front of everyone. Harriet Littlemore had written about her. Harriet had found information from somewhere and made it look as though she, Ruby Mills, had betrayed the Forties. She had been ignored, spat at, shunned by everyone in Southwark for weeks. And she had ended up working for Peter Lazenby – hardly better than Daisy Gould on her mattress – because there was no one else offering her work and she had been running out of cash.

'What's the matter?' Peter sees her expression.

'I never knew… I didn't speak to her about the Forties… I didn't know it was her that wrote it…'

Ralph appears in the doorway. 'Ready?' He smiles. He wants to take her home. He's read about her, and now he wants her: the Jewel of the Borough. 'Everything alright?' he asks, seeing her face.

Harriet Littlemore had not followed her for nothing. She had wanted more information. She had not sat in the café mooning over her in awe and adoration. She had been scrutinising her – oblivious of the damage she had already caused. Offering cake, sharing stories about her own life, hoping to draw more from Ruby, more secrets. And she, like a fool, had prattled on about films and movie stars. She had trusted that Harriet's enquiries had been entirely innocent, or else motivated by some sort of affection.

How could she have been so stupid as to pity the woman?

'Perfectly alright,' she says to Ralph, shaking her shoulders and lifting her chin, trying to smile. 'Let's go.'

39

Wednesday morning

It does not take Harriet long to reach Mayfair. She has taken a taxicab to Ralph's home, rather than going directly into the offices of the *Gazette*. Mr Pickford won't mind her absence, and she needs to speak with her fiancé about Peter Lazenby. Jimmy's comments have troubled her. She brooded over them for much of Tuesday, and then slept badly, restlessly, trying to recall the conversation with Peter at the Savoy. She drank too much that evening and her memory is patchy.

If Peter Lazenby is as deplorable as Jimmy has made him out to be, then Ralph ought to hear of it. His career may suffer if he is known to be associating with such a man.

She presses the doorbell and waits for Ralph's butler to answer.

The house is a fine edifice, with an immaculate white frontage, a shining black door underneath a colonnaded porch and black railings that have not a speck of dirt or soot on them. Solid, respectable, polished and elegant. She breathes deeply, contentedly. She likes what she sees.

The door opens and Ralph's man, who is not usually perturbed by life, is startled to see her on the doorstep.

'Miss Littlemore – we were not expecting you.'

'No, of course not. I sent no word. But I should like to see Mr Christie.' She waits for him to open the door and let her in, but he makes a small bow and tells her that he will enquire whether Mr Christie is receiving visitors – then he closes the door.

His behaviour is irregular, if not downright rude. She might reasonably expect to be allowed across the threshold of a house which, in a few months, will be her own.

After a minute or two, the door is flung open and Ralph, pulling on his coat, barks an instruction to his servant before closing the door behind himself.

'Darling! This is an unexpected delight. What brings you to this part of town so early?'

Harriet glances at her wristwatch. 'Is ten o'clock very early, Ralph?'

'It is for me,' he laughs, slipping her arm through his. 'Let's walk, shall we? It's a beautiful day. How about we find a café? Breakfast?'

'If you like.' She glances up at the heavy grey clouds overhead and admires his light-heartedness. 'But I've already eaten breakfast. A pot of tea would be lovely, perhaps.'

He walks quickly away from the house, half-pulling her along the pavement so that she has to trot to keep up. 'Are you going in later?' she asks. 'To the House of Commons, perhaps?'

'Perhaps. Here we are, this one will do.'

He stops outside a drab sort of place. It has dusty windows and there are no curtains. Harriet might have preferred somewhere that was decked with pretty tablecloths and flower vases, but Ralph ushers her through the door and asks for a table.

A distinctive scent slices through the warmer fog of tea, bacon, toast and tobacco.

Harriet turns, half-expecting to see Ruby standing behind her, but the only person there is Ralph.

'I'm famished,' he says, as they make their way to a wooden table in the corner. 'Eggs and bacon it is. Are you sure you won't join me? Just a pot of tea?'

'Quite sure, thank you.'

'Is everything alright?' he asks, leaning across the table to grasp her hand. 'You seem out of sorts.' She shakes her head, uncertain of the sensation she feels. 'But you came over to see me,' he presses on. 'I was too distracted by hunger, I'm sorry. What brings you here?'

She perches on her seat, her handbag on her lap, wondering what to say and how to phrase it.

'Your father tells me you've chopped your hair. Is that what it is? Are you needing some sort of approval – I meant it when I said I really didn't mind what you do with it.'

'No, that wasn't it,' she says. 'But –' She removes her hat, glancing about to make sure that none of the other diners will mind. 'What do you think? Mummy was furious, of course. You would have thought I'd committed a murder.'

'Well, I think it looks lovely. It rather suits you.'

'Thank you. I never cared for all those pins,' she says, replacing the hat. 'And the endless combing and brushing. It feels quite liberating.'

Ralph's plate arrives, and she pours the tea. He really is hungry and devours the bacon with the speed of a schoolboy. His own hair is uncombed and ruffled; he looks as though he's been out for an exhilarating drive in the country.

'But, no… I came to ask about Peter Lazenby,' she says, touching the handle of her teacup with a fingertip.

'Lazenby? Why?' He continues to attack the meal.

'How well do you know him, Ralph? Really?'

'As he told you, we were in France. War tends to bring you close to other men, for a time, although we're less involved now, of course. I hardly see him, really.' He sees the serious expression on her face and lays down his fork. 'What's this about, Harriet? Why the sudden interest in Lazenby?'

She frowns at the teacup. 'I've heard some stories about him, Ralph. They bothered me. I don't think you'll like it, but I need to tell you that he is involved in some very dark affairs. Drugs, stolen goods – *prostitution* even,' she whispers the last word. 'I'm so sorry. I know he is – or was – your friend, but that's what I've heard.'

Ralph returns to his breakfast, cutting the crisp white of his second egg, deep in thought.

'And I'm sorry that you've been bothered by such unpleasant matters. You shouldn't have to listen to that sort of thing,' he says, after a while. 'Peter Lazenby is – as you'll remember from meeting him – a man who lives what can only be described as a reckless life. I doubt he could own a nightclub and be any other way.'

'It's true, then? What I've heard? He's involved with criminals? Corruption?'

'I don't know exactly what you've been told.' Ralph sighs heavily and looks up at her. 'He sails close to the wind, I'm quite sure of it, but he's not a criminal himself. He's from a good family.'

She studies the tea in her cup. It is already too dense and dark for her taste. She does not want to drink it but takes a small sip, for politeness' sake, wondering whether she might ask for a pot of hot water.

'And you… You don't have much to do with him, do you? I heard that there were politicians involved in his business –'

'Don't be ridiculous, Harriet.' He grips his cutlery and leans over the table, speaking with a quiet, tight voice. 'I can only assume that you've been listening to vulgar gossip in the newspaper offices. No politician I know would involve himself in anything illegal or corrupt. And no one that you know, either.'

'I'm sorry.' She shrinks a little at the sharpness of his response. 'I only wanted to warn you about him, and perhaps… Suggest that you keep your distance.'

'I barely see him. Hadn't seen him in months until the other day.'

She lets out a sigh of relief. 'Oh, I'm glad of that, Ralph. Very glad.'

He finishes his meal in swift silence and downs the last mouthfuls of his tea.

'I should be heading to the House. Are you returning home or going to work?' He reaches into a pocket, and then a second pocket, frowning. 'Blast. I appear to have left my watch at home. Do you have the time?'

'It's nearly a quarter to eleven,' she says, checking her wristwatch again. 'I have no plans, so I expect I'll go to the office for an hour or so.'

'Then I ought to go. If you'll forgive the urgency.' He pulls coins from his pocket and hands them to the man hovering a few feet away. 'I'm sorry, darling, you've caught me in a rush. Still living the bachelor life, I think.' He helps her with her coat. 'Thank goodness you'll be rescuing me very soon – I can look forward to a calmer start to every day.'

She smiles at him. Privately, she is sure that his staff would happily wake him earlier and cook his breakfast. There is, surely, no need for such a rush – or breakfast in a dismal café. Perhaps he is embarrassed that she has caught him behaving like a sluggard.

They part affectionately on the pavement outside the café, preparing to travel in different directions. Ralph suggests she takes a taxicab, but she declares a desire to walk. The office is not far, and she would like some air after sitting in the cramped, cigarette-and-bacon-scented café. He kisses her cheek, and she is, once again, assailed by a fleeting memory of Ruby.

As Ralph strides away towards Westminster, she lingers and, for reasons that she cannot put into words, turns back towards his home.

This will be her street soon. These fine houses contain her neighbours – as yet unmet. She will take tea with women like herself, discuss matters of importance over dinner, share the usual grumblings about housemaids and cooks. In time, the nanny will wheel her children along these pavements in the perambulator, as they go in search of parks and places to run about.

It will be enjoyable, she tells herself, noticing a woman in a subdued but tidy uniform sweeping one of the doorsteps. There is much to look forward to.

What does the future hold for Ruby Mills? A life of crime, including prostitution – Harriet does not want to imagine it – and undoubtedly there will be time in gaol to come. Perhaps Mary MacKenzie had been right: what might someone like Ruby become, given the right education and work? Wasn't Ruby Mills exactly the sort of woman that the suffragists had sought to raise up? Could Harriet, once she is married to a Member of Parliament, help her in some way, find her a job that makes the best use of her talents? Save her from a life of criminality? Keep her as her own, dear friend?

She walks on towards Kensington, turning over possibilities and plans in her mind, wondering when and where she will next see Ruby. Envisioning a time and place where they might have opportunity to talk more deeply about Ruby's future, and her own part in it.

She is nearly at the *Kensington Gazette* when a man walks past her at speed, bumping her hip and causing her to stumble.

'Oh, I do apologise, miss,' he begins, acknowledging his clumsiness. 'Harriet?'

'Jimmy?'

Jimmy Cartwright hitches his satchel in front of him, so that the bag does not nudge her again. 'Sorry about that. I'm late and not looking where I'm going.'

'Oh dear, it is rather late in the morning to be arriving for work, isn't it?'

He grins. 'We can face the wrath of Pickford together.'

'Safety in numbers.'

Up ahead, coming towards them, is a young woman, little more than a girl, pushing a skeletal man in a bath chair along the pavement. It bumps and squeals as it moves, the iron wheels dropping into every hole and crack, causing evident distress to the man. He has no legs. Harriet swallows, lowering her eyes, unable to look at either the man or the girl who pushes him along.

'Spare us some change?' the girl asks as they step aside to let them pass.

Harriet clutches her handbag.

Jimmy rummages in his pocket and pulls out some coins. 'Where were you?' he asks the man in a quiet voice.

'Ypres.'

Jimmy presses the coins into his hands. 'God bless you for it.' He glances at Harriet, dropping his eyes to her handbag.

'Of course,' she says, flustered. She pulls off her gloves and opens her handbag to find her purse. She has no idea how much to give to the girl. Half a crown, perhaps? She hands it over with a weak smile.

'Thanks, miss. Much obliged to you.'

The sad pair trundle on, the girl pushing hard on the handles of the chair.

'Poor bastard,' Jimmy mutters, under his breath.

'He came home,' Harriet says, watching them.

'To what sort of life, I wonder?'

She has no answer. She drops her purse back into her handbag and snaps it shut.

'Well, there's a diamond, if I ever saw one,' Jimmy says, indicating her engagement ring. She has forgotten to remove it. 'I've seen eggs smaller than that.'

'Oh, heavens, my ring.' With haste, she pulls the handkerchief from her pocket. 'Please don't breathe a word, Jimmy,' she says, in a state of agitation. 'Mr Pickford mustn't know. Please don't say anything.'

'Of course not. Not my business. Who's the lucky man – do I know him?'

'I don't know. You'll have heard of him, possibly. People have.' She wraps the ring in the handkerchief and folds it over and over until it forms a small square. 'His name is Ralph Christie. He's an old friend of the family. But really, please don't say anything. I'll have to leave my job when I marry – in July – but I'd rather like to keep it until then. I'm sure Mr Pickford would be glad of an excuse to get rid of me sooner.'

They reach the doors of the *Kensington Gazette* and the doorman lets them in.

Harriet pushes the folded handkerchief into her coat pocket.

She does not see the troubled look on Jimmy's face as they climb the staircase together.

40

Wednesday, late morning

Ruby has been walking for nearly half an hour, and the heels of her shoes are caked with the mud and slime of the cobbles. The taxicab would not bring her to the Borough – and certainly not to a street like this. Even Ralph Christie could not give her enough money to buy that sort of service. It had been as much as she could do to persuade the driver to cross the river at all. He had taken her as far as St Saviour's Church, and only when he heard her natural Cockney did he allow her to leave the vehicle, secure in the knowledge that she – and his hubcaps – would be safe enough.

She is still wearing last night's dress, having not returned to her flat or to Solly's. It peeps from the folds of her plain coat as she walks, an emerald flash of brilliance on an otherwise dull day. Her shoes are probably ruined. She does not care. She can afford a new pair now. Her insurance paid up.

It is early afternoon, she guesses. Most of the ordinary shops are already shut up for their half day. She slept in Ralph's bed for what seemed like hours after he left. She had not slept at all during the night.

She reaches into her coat pocket and plucks out a fine gold pocket watch to check the time. Ten past two. She runs a thumb over the case before hiding it away again. Her stomach rumbles as she catches the scent of pastry from a pie shop that is still open. She stops to buy two pies and continues on her way, eating one of them from the paper bag.

She reaches Daisy Gould's house and bangs on the door.

It is ajar, so she pushes it and shouts a loud 'hello' as she enters.

'Ruby? Is that you?' Daisy's voice is tentative. She inches herself down the staircase like an animal in pain.

'I brought you some breakfast. Pie.'

'Thanks.' She lingers on the stairs, in the shadows. She is still in the dirty nightdress.

'You on your own?' Ruby holds out the paper bag.

'Yeah.' She takes the bag and sniffs it, before tearing it open and bolting down the food as though she's not eaten for days.

'Careful. You'll make yourself sick.'

Daisy doesn't answer. She shoves the food into her mouth, making small grunting noises as she eats. Finally, she lets out a sigh. 'Oh, that was good, Ruby. You're a good friend. I needed that.'

'I can see.' Daisy is even thinner than the last time she saw her. 'I brought you something else. I've got money. Lots of it.'

Daisy's body starts to tremble. 'You brought me money?' She presses her lips together to stop herself from sobbing.

'I had a lucky night,' Ruby says, reaching into her handbag. 'I don't want it to go to Annie Richmond, Daisy. If I take it to Annie, you'll only get a cut of it.'

'I thought you were steering clear of Annie anyway,' Daisy sniffs and wipes a hand across her nose.

'I'm back in the Forties. You won't have heard, but Annie called me back. I'd served my time and she wanted me for a jewellery job. But she doesn't know anything about this, and I won't be telling her, so it's all yours.'

She hands Daisy a pile of notes. Daisy drops the paper bag to the floor and shuffles the notes in her hand.

'I can't take this, Ruby. This is too much.'

'Will it pay off your debt? Harry's debt?' Ruby pushes the notes back towards her.

'Very nearly, yes.'

'Well hold on to it. Keep it safe and add it to whatever Annie gives you on Saturday night. And whatever else you make here before then. I'll bring more when I can.'

Daisy clutches the notes to her chest. 'Why are you doing this, Ruby? Why are you helping me like this?'

'Because I landed in a lucky spot. And we outcasts have to stick together. You'd do the same for me.'

'I would.' Daisy nods vigorously. 'I would.' She stares at the cash. 'Where did you get it? It's so much. Did you rob a bank?'

Ruby cackles with laughter. 'Pour me some of that filthy gin of yours, and I'll tell you all about him.'

'This is all extremely odd.' Gerald Littlemore stretches out his legs from the chair where he sits and gazes from his daughter to his wife, and to Inspector MacKenzie.

'Mr Carrington was most perplexed about it.' Arthur MacKenzie is sitting on the sofa opposite, bent over his cup and saucer, stirring in sugar. 'Do you know anything that might help us, Harriet?'

'No, not at all.' She is only half-listening. She had spent only an hour at the office, fiddling with some words on the typewriter, before returning home. Her parents had eaten lunch already, so she found a slice of bread and butter in the kitchen and sat flicking through a novel until Mr MacKenzie arrived, and she was compelled to join him and her parents for tea.

Gerald starts up again. 'Why would Anthony Carrington have thought you would go to his jewellery shop alone, I wonder? If we were buying you a birthday gift, we would simply have taken you.'

Anthony Carrington is a long-standing friend of her father, although it has been many years since Harriet saw him. She had been a child when they had last visited his shop together and her father had bought her a small silver locket to wear at a party. She had been, what, twelve? She had felt very grown up at the time. It was so long ago.

Mr Carrington had been puzzled by Miss Littlemore's visit to his shop on Monday afternoon. Something had not been quite right. He really could not believe it had been Gerald Littlemore's daughter, although it had been years since he had seen her. There had been something affected in her manner. And then, recalling the theft at Enderby's in Kensington, he had decided to call Scotland Yard. Arthur MacKenzie had listened very carefully as the jeweller had voiced his suspicions.

'It wasn't Harriet,' the inspector says now. 'That is my point.'

'It's not even your birthday.' Gerald carries on, ignoring him. 'Your birthday is November, not March.'

'He might have been confused,' Isabel says, handing a small slice of cake to MacKenzie. 'He is getting quite old.'

'He's not that much older than I am,' Gerald huffs.

'A young woman, short hair' – MacKenzie looks at Harriet – 'in a smart beige coat and wearing a string of pearls. She *said* that her name was Harriet Littlemore, but it was not Harriet. She was dark-haired, for a start.'

Harriet reaches a hand to the pearls at her throat. Dark hair, calling herself Harriet.

'Well, I have not set foot in Mr Carrington's shop since I was a child, I can assure you. I have no idea who it might have been. I cannot help you, I'm afraid.' She gives MacKenzie a polite smile.

'One of the thieves you seem so enthralled by?' he responds, still staring pointedly at her. 'Ruby Mills, perhaps? I can spare a man to watch the shop, I suppose. Keep an eye on the place in case she returns.'

'Ruby Mills?' Isabel holds the cake knife in mid-air. 'That dreadful creature you wrote about, Harriet? I told you she would come to no good. And if she's making use of your good name – *our* good name – then that really is the limit.' She cuts firmly into the fruitcake. 'You should never have had anything to do with her.'

'I've not had anything to do with her,' Harriet lies, taking the proffered cake. 'Except to write about her.'

'Carrington said she had excellent taste,' MacKenzie says. 'Found the best quality diamonds like an expert.'

Harriet hides her smile by biting into the cake.

'I don't want Harriet's name mentioned, Arthur,' Gerald says. 'When you catch this girl, I mean. It wouldn't do for her to be associated in any way with a criminal like that.'

'Of course not.'

'Harriet wouldn't take tuppence worth of tea that she didn't pay for, let alone diamonds,' Gerald concludes, his moustache twitching as he chews his cake.

'I would not,' Harriet says, with feeling. The heat rises at her neck as she remembers the tortoiseshell manicure case in her bedroom. 'Certainly not.'

41

She must warn Ruby. The thought burns in Harriet's mind as she walks towards Oxford Street.

It had been growing dark when Arthur MacKenzie had left the house yesterday, and she could manufacture no pretence for escaping and travelling to Soho. Besides, not long after the inspector had gone, Ralph had arrived, for no reason other than to bring her a bouquet of flowers and to apologise for leaving her so hastily that morning. So sweet of him. And then she had quite forgotten about Ruby. Her mother had persuaded Ralph to stay for dinner and fussed about the meagreness of the lamb chops the kitchen had prepared, and Ralph had made them all laugh with impressions of various men of note that he knew.

When she woke this morning, however, it was Ruby – not Ralph – who was the focus of Harriet's first thought. Ruby had pretended to be *her*, to be Harriet Littlemore, as she studied Mr Carrington's very fine diamonds. She had lain in bed for a while, imagining Ruby standing just a little taller, copying her own mannerisms as her slim fingers stroked the bracelets and brooches so that the jewels caught the light. Ruby becoming Harriet, just as Harriet, when she had taken the manicure case, had pretended to be Ruby. She then found the case at the back of the dressing table drawer where she had hidden it and ran her thumb over the tortoiseshell.

Ruby was a clever thief – a brilliant one – but the inspector was certain that she was planning to raid Mr Carrington's shop, and he would be watching and waiting for her.

Harriet had abandoned all thoughts of the office and decided to spend the day searching the larger department stores in the hope of finding her friend.

She walked every floor of Debenham and Freebody, traipsing up and down the marble staircase to wander around coats, fabrics, furs and cosmetics. It was possibly the first time she had ever been into the store without intending to make a purchase. She barely glanced at the new gowns.

Now, she reaches the corner of Duke Street and the impressive façade of Selfridges. The flags on the roof hang limp in the grey morning, but the recently cleaned colonnade is shining, and the new extension has made the building even more imposing on this section of Oxford Street. Privately, Harriet thinks Selfridges a little vulgar, but never says so in public because this is her mother's view. Instead, she vigorously defends Mr Selfridge's stance on women's suffrage and lauds his store's imaginative window displays and spacious interior – received opinions she has heard voiced by people more forward-thinking than her parents.

She breathes deeply as she enters through the vast doorway and is greeted by the beautiful fragrances. She closes her eyes and revels in the appealing amalgamation of scents.

She must concentrate. She decides to begin at the top of the store and work her way down. She will ignore the restaurant, the bookshop and the gentlemen's clothing. She cannot imagine that Ruby will be booking theatre tickets or sending parcels at the store's postal service, either. At least here, unlike other places, she may ascend and descend the floors at speed by using the lifts.

It is almost an hour later, when she is on nodding terms with one of the female lift attendants because she has ridden in the lift so much, that she catches sight of Ruby.

She is at a counter near the rear of the ground floor. It does not surprise Harriet to see that she is examining jewellery. It is not fine quality, such as one might find at Mr Carrington's, but mere imitation. Glass beads threaded on string, paste diamonds fashioned into brooches or hatpins.

Ruby is wearing her pale blue Poiret and a light brown hat. It sits close to her head and is pulled low on her brow, but Harriet would recognise her anywhere; she moves with such grace and poise. Harriet watches, transfixed, as Ruby lifts strands of purple beads from the metal stand and dangles them above her head, to see how long they are. She tilts her head to one side, as if considering whether to make a purchase – or possibly whether to steal them.

She might have a care in this store. Selfridges has recently, and very publicly, employed more floorwalkers in an effort to deter thieves. Harriet readies herself to fly to her aid, to buy the beads herself if Ruby slips them into her pocket.

Thankfully, she sees Ruby speaking with the assistant at the counter. It appears that the girl is buying rather than stealing today.

Something lifts in Harriet's own spirit, seeing this. She is not a thief by nature, Harriet thinks; Ruby is a woman who needs to be surrounded by beautiful things. If Harriet were able to help her in some way, then Ruby might work in a store like Selfridges. It would be beneath her to be in a factory or to char in an office, but she might be a shop assistant, where she could live every day next to the fur coats and fashionable gowns that she adores. She knows about jewellery, certainly. Arthur MacKenzie said that she had picked over the diamonds like an expert. Could she work in a jewellery shop and not be tempted to lift the goods?

Perhaps Harriet could speak to someone at Hartleys and put in a good word for Ruby. Her mother's regular custom there must count for something. Yes: she is determined to do this, to help her friend live a moral and law-abiding life and earn a little money. Her own job – when she goes to the office – gives her personal satisfaction as well as money in her purse that is earned and her *own*, not her father's. She could accord Ruby this same dignity. They might even laugh about it together, when Harriet calls into Hartleys and finds Ruby in the smart navy uniform of the store, setting out the fur stoles and hats.

'Those are pretty,' she says now, nearing her friend at the counter. 'They'll suit you, I'm sure.'

Ruby turns and, on seeing Harriet, a strange expression crosses her face. Not the grin that Harriet expected or even a smile of recognition, but something nearer to contempt or even hostility.

'The beads, I mean,' Harriet says, as the assistant hands a paper bag across to Ruby. 'I saw you buying them. They look very lovely.'

Perhaps Ruby is embarrassed that someone has caught her buying imitation beads. She need not be – they have become quite fashionable, although she would never wear them herself.

Ruby's features soften a little, but her mouth twists into a sneer rather than a smile.

'Perhaps you'll write about me buying them.'

'What?'

'Put it all in your newspaper.'

'Oh, what? The *Gazette*, you mean?' She must have mentioned the newspaper to Ruby, although she cannot recall doing so. 'Yes, you're right. I think I wrote about imitation jewellery a month or two ago.' It thrills her, to imagine that Ruby might read her articles.

'I'm sure you did. Because things aren't always what they seem, are they? Glass beads pretending to be semi-precious stones.' She rattles the paper packet and drops it into her handbag. 'People pretending to be what they're not.'

'Yes.' Harriet cannot quite catch the meaning of this comment, but it jars with her. She does not wish to deal with Ruby in such a prickly mood so close to the shop counter – and the watchful assistant – so tucks a hand under Ruby's arm to draw her away.

'Get off me,' Ruby growls at her.

She drops her. 'I'm sorry, I didn't want –'

'I don't care what you want.'

Something must have happened. Or else Harriet has interrupted her in the midst of a hoisting spree. Women of all ages, shopping, browsing, trying on jewellery at the counters, pass around them. She lowers her voice, conscious that she should not draw attention to their conversation.

'What is it, Ruby? What's wrong? Are you in trouble of some sort? Tell me.'

Ruby regards her with disdain. 'Why, so you can write about that and all? Put it in your newspaper?'

'Why do you keep talking about the newspaper?' Harriet frowns, struggling to understand.

And then she knows.

Ruby watches the realisation dawn.

'Oh!' Harriet breathes. 'The article.'

Ruby does not respond. The look on her face is sour.

'The piece I wrote. I wrote about you. Is that what this is about? Is that why you're cross with me? *Are* you cross?'

'Cross?' Ruby is incredulous at such a word. She folds her arms, but her fists are clenched hard, as if she is fighting to contain emotion. 'Do you have any idea what damage you caused me?' The voice is hard and bitter, and it fills Harriet with such dismay that she wants to sob – right in the middle of Selfridges.

Alice Dunning had sat on the bed in her cell at Holloway and told Harriet what happened to those who broke the rules of the Forty Thieves. *You don't keep your stolen goods. You share everything with the group. You don't betray your friends. You don't speak to the police.* Alice had ventured the information not because Harriet had paid her so handsomely, but because she believed she was *safe.* No one in Holloway knew that Harriet was a reporter. No one would connect Alice with Harriet's article. She had been so proud of her cleverness in how she had protected Alice. Without a thought to the consequences that might come of focusing the article on Ruby.

'Damage?' She swallows the lump in her throat and puts a hand to her pearl necklace, remembering. Alice had told her about the brutality of the Forty Thieves. And if they believed it was *Ruby* who had shared the information, shared the methods and tricks that she had treated so lightly in her article, then Ruby will have been ostracised, at the very least. 'Did they hurt you?' she asks in a whisper, not wanting to hear the answer.

'What do you think?' Ruby says, unsmiling. 'Someone put my face in the newspapers. Drew a picture of me. Someone wrote about me, told the whole world how the Forties operate.' Her voice grows harder. 'Someone made me out to be something special, gave me a nickname: the Jewel of the Borough. That sort of thing doesn't go down well with the likes of Annie Richmond.'

'Oh.'

'Oh.' Ruby glares at her. 'Yeah, that's exactly what Annie said, when she saw the paper.'

Harriet's stomach clenches in fresh horror. The Queen of the Thieves. Alice had spoken of her in awe as well as terror.

'But it was only meant for Kensington. I didn't think anyone would have read about it in Southwark, surely. Were you in trouble for it? Oh, please say not.' She reaches out and grasps Ruby's arm. Ruby pulls away again and lifts her chin.

'Annie Richmond beat me, in front of everyone; broke a bone in my cheek and battered the face that you put in your paper. I was spitting blood. Then she threw me out of the Forties.'

Harriet's throat constricts again. She can barely talk. 'Oh, I'm sorry. I'm so sorry... I never knew... How could I know...?'

Ruby, by contrast, is oblivious to everyone around them, taking pride in sharing her dreadful tale with Harriet, seeing how she cringes. 'I had no one. I had no money and no food for weeks. That's why I went to work at the Angel, for Peter Lazenby.'

Harriet cannot hide her anguish. She is the one who has driven Ruby to this life. 'I had no idea the trouble it would cause you. Forgive me. It wasn't meant to harm you.'

'I don't forgive. Never have. I prefer revenge.'

'Revenge?' Harriet feels cold fear wash over her now.

'It's remarkable, you know, who you meet in a place like the Angel. Such rich men. Men like Ralph Christie, for example.'

'Ralph?' Harriet blinks. 'You met Ralph there? Oh no, I don't believe it. It's hardly Ralph's sort of place –' She is conscious that people might overhear.

Ruby is unconcerned by her evident discomfort. 'It's very much his sort of place. The champagne, the dancing, the women. Very generous he is, too, if he gets what he wants.' She reaches into her pocket and pulls out a gold watch, as if to consult it. 'Which, of course, he did, all night, because he fucking well paid for it.'

Two older women, arm in arm, turn their heads in alarm at Ruby's profanity, as if they cannot quite believe such a word might exist in a place like Selfridges. One of them tuts. Perhaps she has misheard. They move away, just in case, to avoid having to overhear such language again. Later, they will murmur together about how vulgar young women have become in recent years.

Harriet, now no longer noticing nor caring what other people think, is in shock.

She can smell that fragrance again. Mitsouko. Unmistakable.

Ralph had smelled of Ruby the other morning. He had reeked of her. She understands why, now.

'How dare you?' It's all that she can think to say. 'How *dare* you!'

'I don't know.' Ruby gives the smallest shake of her head, as if nothing really matters to her, and slips the watch back into her pocket. 'I never know how I do dare. I just do.'

She makes to pass Harriet, but the movement is awkward. Harriet reaches out, and, for a moment, the girls grab and grapple with one another. Harriet takes note of the feeling of Ruby's arms – their leanness, hidden from view underneath the fabric of the coat. She is thin. Quite thin. Not Ralph's sort at all.

They both know that Harriet will not fight her in the middle of Selfridges. Ruby is as wiry as a cat, a creature of the gutter, born into fighting. She brushes Harriet aside with relative ease and turns away, walking to the door, then out onto Oxford Street, her head high.

Harriet puts a hand to her mouth to prevent the wail that is rising in her chest. Ralph and Ruby. She cannot believe it – does not want to believe it. And yet, she knows that Ruby is telling the truth. The truth is Ruby's revenge for her article.

And everything she believed she understood about Ruby, and about Ralph, is wrong. False. As much an imitation as the strands of pearls in her fingers, necklaces she has plucked from the stand and is twisting mindlessly in her agitation.

Her life is a sham, all of it.

She stumbles to the door, needing air, needing to be away from this place, from the glittering, shimmering, sweetly scented world. She needs to walk, to think, to work out what she will say to Ralph, how she will confront him. How she might begin to tell him that she knows he paid to spend the night with Ruby. How insulted she has been. She will tell him that she feels sick when she thinks of it.

She will not say that she is ashamed of the feeling that rises within her when she imagines them together.

She pushes the pearls into her coat pocket and stands on the pavement. She takes a deep breath. Even the putrid air of Oxford Street is now preferable to the cloying perfume of the cosmetics hall.

She will return home. Tell her parents that she no longer wishes to marry Ralph. No. She will speak to Ralph first. Have it out with him. Break off the engagement.

Oh, but Ruby. Ruby.

Will she ever forgive herself for everything that has happened to Ruby? Her silly little article, that caused such pain to the girl. For what? A few admiring letters and a word of congratulation from Mr Pickford? Vanity. Nothing but vanity. And she had not even had opportunity to warn her about Inspector MacKenzie's suspicions about Carrington's.

Harriet has not reached Marble Arch when she feels the hand on her shoulder.

Ruby! Ruby has run after her.

It is not Ruby, but a man in a dark suit, accompanied by a woman, equally sombre. The sort of woman who might fade into any background. The sort you would not notice was watching you.

'You did not pay for those necklaces, miss,' the man says. 'You'll need to return with us to the store, please.'

42

Thursday

The little bell over the door jangles as Ruby enters the shop on Borough High Street. The longcase clock chimes noon.

Solly is exactly where she expected him to be – behind the counter with an eyeglass stuck into the socket of one eye. He is examining a bracelet. He doesn't look up. He knows, from her step, who it is.

'Afternoon, Magpie.' The comment causes the other man at the counter to turn around.

Raymond Calladine.

'It stinks in here, Solly. Think we've got rats again.'

'Afternoon, Ruby. An unexpected pleasure to see you.' When Ray smiles, his marble eyes squint behind his glasses and he reveals a row of tiny yellowing teeth.

'Like I said, I think we have rats.'

His smile fades a little. 'I hear you're out whoring for Peter Lazenby.'

She ignores this. 'I'm not stopping long, Solly. Just changing my dress. I'm supposed to be meeting Maggs in' – she pulls out the watch again – 'an hour and a half.'

'Another watch, Ruby?' Ray sneers. 'Who've you lifted this one from? Have I got to find the owner again?'

'Fuck off, Ray.' She strides past him to the stairs.

He catches her arm. 'Don't grow too fancy, Ruby Mills. Don't forget where you come from or who your real friends are, when you need us.'

Solly removes his eyeglass and spreads the bracelet on the counter, looking at Ruby from underneath thick eyebrows as she shakes herself free from Ray. 'I think we're done here, Raymond. You can take the items now, if you like.'

'No,' Ray says, picking up his hat. 'I don't carry that sort of money this side of the river. You can send them over, like normal.' He runs his tongue around the inside of his gums. 'If your delivery girl can spare the time.'

'I'll bring them myself, tomorrow.'

Ray bids him farewell and puts on his hat. The hair at the back of his neck is thick with oil. It has ruined the hatband.

'I have the goods for you,' Solly says, with a degree of weariness in his voice, when Ray leaves the shop. 'For the Forties' job you're supposed to be doing today. Don't you want to see?'

Ruby lingers at the bottom of the stairs, torn between needing to change her dress and wanting to see the jewellery.

'I'll lock the door.' The jewels always win.

He scatters several rings, a bracelet and a brooch onto the counter, pushing them apart from one another so that she can take a closer look.

She examines each of them carefully, remembering the pieces from the jeweller's shop.

'Perfect. These are a close match to what I'll lift.'

He puts a hand over the jewels to collect them up, pausing for a moment. 'When you pick up the real stones, they'll be worth a lot, Ruby. I mean a lot. You chose well.' He scoops them into a velvet bag. 'But you need to be careful. This isn't a little place like Enderby's, run by an old man and a silly girl. It's the sort of store where they will be watching you. Like hawks.'

'I know. I know what I'm doing.'

'I know you do.'

He hands her the pouch and sighs.

'I don't like Ray Calladine any more than you do, Magpie. But we have to do business, don't we?'

She opens her mouth to say something, but then closes it again.

Gerald, Isabel and Harriet sit in silence, contemplating their lunch of cold cuts and potatoes. They are eating far later than usual, and Isabel has already commented that the meal is now ruined. Inspector MacKenzie left a quarter of an hour ago, having declined to stay. He did not want to intrude, and besides, he had said what he believed needed saying when he had brought Harriet home.

The fire roars in the hearth, but the stony atmosphere makes Harriet's teeth chatter. She wishes that she might escape and return to her room, as if nothing has happened.

She has a miserable headache. Her eyes are red and puffy with crying. She has no appetite.

She gazes over at the chair that Ralph usually occupies on the occasions when he has joined them for dinner. Ordinarily, she would welcome his presence and support in such circumstances; he would know how to placate her parents. Instead, a maelstrom formed of several emotions swirls through her. She identifies each of them as she prods at the fat on a slice of ham. Rage, hurt, frustration, shame and, oddly, curiosity.

'Arthur MacKenzie is quite right.' Isabel slices through a potato. Her voice has that clipped, frigid tone with which Harriet is all too familiar. She has brought disgrace upon the family, and her mother – silent and tight-lipped while Inspector MacKenzie was in the house – is about to unleash the full torrent of her fury. The servants, sensing something is brewing, have wisely vacated the room. Harriet braces herself for what will come.

Isabel remains contained, for the moment. The longer she holds on to her anger, the more intense and vicious the outburst will be when it comes.

'He won't say it in so many words, but he believes you have

been allowed to run wild. He believes' – she makes a second slice though the potato, as though she wishes only to dissect it rather than eat it – 'that we, your father and I, have lost control of you.'

Nothing that Harriet can say will make the situation better for any of them. She had, albeit unconsciously, walked out of Selfridges with two imitation pearl necklaces in her coat. The store walker had followed her for several yards and then, once she had witnessed enough to believe that Harriet had intended to steal them, ran to call the male colleague who apprehended her.

Harriet had apologised profusely and offered to pay for the necklaces immediately – not that she wanted them – but there had been something of a fuss. The staff at Selfridges had decided to call the police. One of the store walkers had read of the spate of shoplifting in the larger department stores, of the raid at Debenham and Freebody a little further along Oxford Street, and believed that they had apprehended 'the Jewel of the Borough' – despite Harriet's protestations to the contrary. The senior manager judged that a thief of such notoriety, who had been written of in the newspapers, at least warranted a telephone call to Scotland Yard.

There was no talk of prosecution or any sort of trial, of course. As she had stood, weeping quietly into her handkerchief, Arthur MacKenzie had smoothed matters over with the staff at Selfridges. He had talked of a 'misunderstanding' and of there being 'no intention of criminality' before escorting her home. He had spoken to her most unkindly in the motor car, and she had been forced to endure his criticisms of her attitude and her misbehaviour as well as his scolding about the necklaces.

'And I am inclined to agree with him,' her mother continues. 'This ridiculous need to work in an office, your fascination with common thieves, the clothes that you wear, your hair...' She begins to slice another potato, having carved the first into several slender pieces and abandoned it. 'I said that no good would come of it.' This last comment is addressed to Gerald, who is the only one who appears capable of eating.

Isabel reaches into her skirt to find her handkerchief. She dabs her eyes and blows her nose before returning to her potatoes, saying no more. This is ominous.

There is a lengthy silence, punctuated only by the sounds of Isabel's knife scraping the plate and Gerald chewing mouthfuls of cold beef and horseradish sauce.

Then, her father rests his knife on the edge of his plate and makes a contented huffing sound, as though he has reached an answer to a tricky conundrum. His moustache twitches as he chases a small piece of meat from a tooth with his tongue.

'I wonder...' He speaks to Isabel rather than Harriet. 'Might we see whether young Ralph will bring forward the wedding by a month or so. He's a steadying influence. He was very good over that suffragette business.'

Isabel considers this. 'That might be an idea. It would give Harriet something to think about besides herself. I'm sure that the dressmaker could be encouraged to work faster, and the other arrangements could be made easily enough.' She pauses. 'It wouldn't look like unseemly haste, would it? They've been engaged for a while. When would you think best? Next month? After Easter, perhaps?'

'He hadn't settled on a date, the last time I spoke to him. There was just a vague notion of July, as we know. But I'm sure that if I have a quiet word –'

The noise in Harriet's throat emerges unbidden. A strangled cry of frustration that turns into a second, more violent sob.

'Good heavens, what on earth is the matter?' Isabel frowns at her.

'Ralph,' is all she can say. Then the words splutter out: 'Ralph is the matter.'

Her mother drops her knife with a clatter. 'Oh Harriet! Don't tell me that you've had an argument with Ralph along with everything else. What have you done, foolish girl?'

'What have I done?' Harriet stands abruptly, throwing her napkin on the table. 'What have *I* done? What makes you think that *I* am at fault?'

'Don't raise your voice,' Isabel snaps. 'Sit down at once. The servants will hear...'

'I'm not raising my voice.' She draws a long breath as she resumes her seat. 'But you should know that I have been reconsidering my engagement to Ralph.'

'What?' Now Isabel's voice begins to rise.

'Calm down, Isabel,' Gerald soothes from the other side of the table. 'It's likely as not just a tiff. What's happened, Harrio?'

The use of her childhood name upsets her.

'Oh, nothing,' she says, failing to keep the misery from her tone. 'Nothing at all, apart from his consorting with other women. Prostitutes. It's little wonder that I lost my mind in Selfridges when I discovered it.'

'Harriet, you're being ridiculous!' Isabel is on the verge of shouting, held back only by a lifetime of frigid decorum. 'This is Ralph Christie you're talking about. We know Ralph. He's devoted to you. To us. In light of your recent behaviour, he will prove your salvation. A steady influence, as your father says.'

'You don't know anything, Mummy. You may think that you do, but you do not. I didn't, but I do now. And the Ralph I have discovered is not a man I wish to marry.'

'Harriet, you're talking utter nonsense. I don't know where you've had your information, but –'

'I cannot marry him.'

The silence that greets this declaration is so thick that Harriet can hardly breathe.

It is broken by Gerald, clearing his throat and straightening his knife and fork on the plate. He looks thoughtfully at his daughter.

'Well, I suppose that the only way to sort this out is for me to speak directly with Ralph. No, Isabel, I shall talk to him.' He raises a hand to quieten her. 'I shall ask him about his – *friendships* and discover if there is anything that might prevent my daughter's happiness. I do believe him to be an honourable man, but… If Harriet has concerns, then I must ask.' He returns his gaze to Harriet. 'You should know, my dear child, that a man – any man – and especially one who has been abroad, might have a *history*. That doesn't mean he won't make a good husband in the future.'

Harriet stands, picks at her skirt, tries to remain calm. She speaks in a low voice to her father.

'I don't care if he has a *history*, as you put it. I'm not naïve. I work in an office full of men, and I do, despite your efforts, have some understanding of the ways of the world. But I do care that he has been to bed with a woman he met in a nightclub while he is engaged to me. Two nights ago.'

Isabel draws a sharp breath and puts a hand to her mouth.

'You may speak with him, Daddy, as you wish. But I doubt you will change my mind, whatever excuses he gives. I am sorry that I have disappointed you, but you have given me little opportunity to explain myself. I did not mean to steal those bead necklaces, nor to walk out of Selfridges without paying for them. I was distracted, *distressed*, because I had just learned about Ralph.'

She walks out of the room and directly upstairs. She decides that she will not cry any more.

Isabel follows her swiftly into the bedroom and closes the door behind her. Harriet can't decide whether she sees shock or fury in her mother's eyes.

'Do you really think you'll find another man to marry you, with so few of them left?' Isabel's voice wavers. It is Isabel who is on the verge of tears now. Harriet has never seen her mother like this.

'I'm not certain I wish to marry at all.'

Isabel slaps her cheek. 'Of all the selfish creatures! There are young women desolate out there. Poor girls, whose fiancés died in that dreadful war, and you, *you*, are turning your nose up at the best match you could possibly hope for when you are in such disgrace. And why? You've heard gossip? Is that it?'

Harriet stands squarely to her mother, her cheek stinging. 'It isn't gossip. I know it.'

'You know it? How do you know it?'

Harriet slumps onto the bed. 'Because I know the woman. I saw her in Selfridges this morning, and she told me that Ralph was her lover.'

'Nonsense.'

'It's true, Mummy. It really is.' She hangs her head. 'I can't bear it…' What it is she cannot bear she has no way of describing to her mother. Her part in Ruby's expulsion from the Forties, the way Ruby had spoken to her, as well as Ralph's betrayal. Ruby. All of it.

Two fat tears form in Isabel's eyes. She brushes them away and sits beside her daughter. She picks up Harriet's hand and strokes her daughter's knuckles in silence.

'He was supposed to be marrying me in July,' Harriet says eventually. 'But he might even be with her now. He won't want to bring the wedding forward – even if that is what you and Daddy decide.'

'She will mean nothing to him,' Isabel says, sniffing, her profile proud in the light coming in from the window. 'She will be a distant dream, if that. And you, Harriet, will be the wife at his side, the mother of his children, the support that he needs, the one he turns to for counsel every day. You.'

'I don't think I want to live my life wondering who he is picking up in nightclubs or taking to hotel rooms. I always expected that I would marry a man who would respect me, love me, cherish me, like Daddy cherishes you.'

Isabel's head dips only a little.

'Please tell me that Daddy has never been like that. That he has never…'

Isabel crosses her ankles and sits a little taller. 'Of course not. Your father is a man of great scruple.'

They sit in silence again. Isabel pats her daughter's hand one last time and stands. She then turns back to regard her from the door.

'Ralph has the potential to become prime minister of this country, Harriet. He might have made a mistake – a foolish and hurtful one – but you have made mistakes, too, don't forget. You have thrown yourself into recklessness when restraint and caution might have been the wiser course. You will learn to forgive Ralph for this, even as he accepts you, with all your faults – and we must hope that he will. Our country needs men like Ralph, and we must overlook their weaknesses and indiscretions sometimes, for the greater good. We have to be strong and virtuous, to show them the way.'

Harriet does not want to be strong or virtuous. She does not know what she wants anymore, and when her mother leaves, despite her own resolution, she buries her head into her pillow and sobs.

43

Thursday afternoon

Maggs talks all the way to the jewellers. Yak, yak, yak. Ruby does not listen. She has heard Maggs's lecture many times before. She can recite it almost as easily as she can recite the alphabet. Always the same: don't linger about, do what you've gone to do, don't run unless you're certain someone is chasing you, don't look guilty.

This is a solo job, though, and Ruby will be on her own in the shop. Maggs will wait outside again, ready to block the path of anyone who might be chasing her down the street.

Ruby knows what she is doing. Maggs needs to bloody shut up so she can concentrate.

Maggs has stopped lecturing and is talking about Daisy. Even here, far away from the Borough and the Forties, Maggs drops her voice.

'She's really struggling, Ruby.'

'I know. I've seen her, remember? I've not cut her off.'

'Annie's torn. She wants to help her out, but she can't let her brothers know – or Freddy Moss.'

'Annie should make up her mind.'

'You're right. I said as much to Annie. The Forties are the Forties, whatever the Elephants say.'

And Daisy will be back on her feet soon without their help; Ruby has made sure of that.

The shop is in sight.

'Shut up now, Maggs. I need to focus.' Ruby feels inside her pocket for the velvet purse. It is within easy reach. If she pokes her fingers into the bag, she can subtly ease out the pieces one by one. She can decide, just by touch, which is which and replace the real gems with them. She will take her time, remain calm, be deliberate. It is the first time she has been sent to do this, but it's hardly her first job.

Maggs halts outside a shop selling clocks. 'I'll wait here,' she says. 'Looks more interesting than the florist.'

There are at least two dozen clocks, of all kinds, in the window. Ruby might spend hours peering at them, if she didn't have work to do. The intricacies of the mechanisms, the painted faces, the different number styles… But she needs to go.

'Alright. I shouldn't be too long, but I can't rush this. It's not smash and grab.'

'Be careful.'

Ruby rolls her eyes at Maggs and grins. She is always careful.

She waits at the jewellery shop door and dips a hand into her coat pocket one final time, as if touching the velvet pouch will bring her luck, like a rabbit's foot.

The unsmiling doorman opens it to her. It is a different man this time, even though he has the same blank expression as the last. The assistant behind the counter is also most certainly not the bird-like jeweller she met on Monday. Everything is as it should be. Annie Richmond has, of course, done her research.

Ruby is the only customer in the shop. In the warm glow of the early evening light, she stands ready to inspect the items she already knows well.

She had been unnerved, on her last visit, to discover that the older man behind the counter shared an acquaintance with the Littlemores. She had considered adopting a different story to avoid raising suspicion, but today's assistant is younger, less authoritative, not so sharp-eyed, so she talks again of a forthcoming birthday and wealthy parents wishing to buy her a gift, confident that the two pairs of ears hearing it will not know it already. She adopts the same manner, the same tone, the same phrases as before – why change what worked so perfectly?

This assistant is more obsequious than the previous man. He does not ask the name of her supposed parents, but instead sets about trying to show off his knowledge. She listens with patient interest as he tells her about the stones, even though he cannot match her own expertise. She nods and smiles prettily, knowing that if she flatters him with her attention, he will be unlikely to notice anything else.

She removes her gloves in order to try on one or two rings,

holding her hand to the light, better to inspect the gleam of the diamonds. She passes a comment that makes the assistant smile warmly, even as he turns to find another tray for her.

It is so easily done. A sleight of hand. He does not see her nestle Solly's paste affair in the velvet slot. And then another two rings.

The doorman is unconcerned, gazing out of the window, probably waiting for his day to end.

Ruby is bent over another tray – brooches this time – when she hears the door open behind her. The assistant looks up and smiles at a new customer, a gentleman in a dark overcoat. The man is looking for a gift for his wife. He sounds uncertain, like a man unused to fripperies but trying his best. An anniversary, she hears him say. Twenty years.

She strokes the brooch she is about to swap and asks if she may look at it in the mirror, hold it to her coat. The assistant nods, comfortable with her presence in the store and keen to help the gentleman in his deliberation. A man who does not know what he is looking for, after all, is a man who might be persuaded to spend more money than he intends.

Ruby picks the brooch from the tray and carries it carefully to a small oval mirror at the end of the counter. It is extremely fine – better even than the crescent moon she swiped from Enderby's. Two concentric circles of platinum set with diamonds and a translucent emerald in the centre. It is nearly two inches in diameter. She imagines wearing this one on the satin gown of her dreams; how it will gleam at her shoulder when she enters the room. She sees a grand staircase, film stars gathered, and all eyes on her as she sweeps, slowly, languidly, down white marble steps.

In the mirror, she can see that the gentleman in the dark overcoat is watching her. She half-recognises him but cannot quite place his face. Someone she has danced with at the Angel, perhaps.

She puts down the mirror and smiles at the assistant. 'It's lovely,' she says. 'I think I'll ask my father for this one.'

She replaces Solly's brooch in the tray.

The gentleman in the coat frowns at it. He appears puzzled.

Something about him makes her anxious. Something in his face, the way his head turns, the way he looks at her.

Inspector MacKenzie.

She is unable to stop the gasp of recognition, but quickly turns it into a cough, as she lurches for the door.

'Bolt the door, man!' MacKenzie shouts. 'It's Ruby Mills.'

But he is too slow. The doorman has opened the door to admit new customers and Ruby slips between them like an eel.

She hears MacKenzie shouting, furious, apologising to the couple he has crashed into, yelling to the doorman to catch her.

'Maggs!'

She has enough breath to call to her friend as she passes at speed, her hand clutching her skirt and lifting it to her knees.

The doorman will not catch her. She is young, quick on her heels and filled with the thrill of escape. And he, as she already knows, will clatter into Maggs, who will innocently lumber into his path as he tries to pass. Maggs won't be hurt. She's nearly as broad-shouldered as he is. And she will be prepared.

Ruby starts to laugh as she bobs and weaves her way through the people on the pavement. This is what she lives for. She had forgotten the joy of running away. She hasn't had to do it for a while.

She has run along three streets, turning twice, before she drops her skirt and slows her pace to a steady trot. No longer a thief, but simply a young woman in a hurry. She begins to take more careful note of her surroundings and assesses where she is.

Slowing her breathing, she recognises the edge of Soho. She might go to the flat, she thinks, rather than straight back to Solly's. Maggs will be furious, as will Annie, but she can live with their rebukes. She wants to see the jewels – her jewels – in her own place. She wants to hold them next to her better clothes. Her skin. And besides, MacKenzie will expect her to return to the Borough.

Only later will she make her way back over the river, once the sky is dark, and hand over the goods to Solly. When the coppers have been and gone.

The party at the Crown tonight will be a good one. She will be feted.

She is looking forward to standing tall again among the Forties.

After weeks of being ostracised, spoken of only with disdain, tonight she will be welcomed back as one of the family. No, she will be more than that. She will be the centre of attention, the star of the show.

The anticipation fills her with more joy than she has known for a long time.

44

Saturday morning

The hangover has only now subsided. Ruby has never in her whole life been so floored with gin. She did not have to buy a drink for herself all night and, as a consequence, she drank a lot. Drunk as a wheelbarrow. She spent all of Friday in bed, groaning.

Everyone cheered her. Everyone heard the story of what happened – how Inspector MacKenzie nearly caught her with several hundred pounds worth of diamonds, but how she slipped away and ran like hell. Everyone has heard Maggs tell of how she got her black eye, and how it was worth it for the money it will bring in for the Forties. Maggs is even planning to *buy* some new jewellery with her share, to commemorate the occasion, she says.

They will tell the story over and over, Ruby knows. Part of the famous history of the Forty Thieves. Even Billy Walsh was impressed, and, under the watchful eye of Edith Lennox, he told her so. She was as gracious to him as she thought fit but pushed him away when he started to try it on. She was having too much fun being congratulated by everyone else.

Riding her luck, she had dragged Daisy Gould out for a drink. Sitting next to Ruby, Daisy was untouchable, whatever Freddy Moss might have thought about it. As the evening wore on, even Annie Richmond had forgotten that she was supposed to be shunning her and threw an arm over her shoulder. Daisy laughed and sang until she grew hoarse. They were all hoarse by the next morning. And thick-headed.

This morning, Saturday, Ruby climbs gingerly out of bed and discovers, to her surprise, that she is well again.

And hungry. She could eat a horse.

She staggers into the kitchen and picks up the kettle from the range. When she shakes it, as she always does, she finds enough water inside so sets it to boil. Solly has been in already – although only recently. There is a fire burning in the grate, recently laid and lit, but the kitchen is still chilly. She pokes the coals and rubs her hands against the young flames, trying to warm herself and rouse herself to a more cheerful mood. She no longer feels as though someone is pounding her temples with a mallet, but she is oddly flat.

'Morning, Magpie. How's the head this morning?' Solly ambles in.

'Couldn't be better.' She scoops tea into the pot. 'Tea?'

The kettle begins to whistle. She pulls it from the fire and the screeching stutters and dies.

'The coppers were around again yesterday.'

'I thought I could hear something going on downstairs.'

'I didn't want to disturb you. Didn't tell them you were here. Said I didn't know where you were.'

'Did they find anything?'

'Of course not. Everything's gone to Grace Bartlett's for now. Annie's orders. We'll keep it all tucked away at the warehouse until the fuss has died down. I'll have a better look before we move it on. There's no hurry.'

Ruby stirs the tea and finds cups. 'No, I suppose not.'

'Cheer up, Magpie,' Solly says, hearing the dull tone and guessing the reason for it. 'You had a good day on Thursday – and a good night, too. There'll be plenty more to come, just you see.'

'Yeah, I'm sure you're right.' Ruby, rummaging for bread and eggs, does not turn around.

'Anyway, there's trouble at the Crown right now. You'd better lie low for a while.'

'Trouble? What trouble?' She faces him now, an egg in her hand.

'All I know is that some of the Elephant boys have been arrested. Billy Walsh is among them.'

'What?'

'Coppers went to the Crown after they'd been here. Clara was furious about it. They arrested Billy. He ran away from them – stupid boy – and got a few bruises for his troubles when they caught up with him.'

'Did the police say why? Did Clara know?'

He shakes his head. 'He's been doing some work over the river – like you. The same man running the operations, I think. That nightclub owner. Apparently, there were raids in Soho yesterday. Clara didn't know much about it, but Billy was involved. And Moss.'

'Peter Lazenby. He runs it all.' Peter could have been arrested as well. 'I need to go out.'

'You need to eat first,' Solly says. 'You won't be any good to anyone with an empty stomach. Go and dress, and I'll fry you an egg.'

He is right. Her stomach aches for food. And if Peter has been arrested, there will be little she can do about it.

'Oh, and Maggs wants you on a job later. This afternoon. She left the details, but I know you're to meet her at three o'clock on the corner of Marylebone Lane and Wigmore Street.'

She groans.

'You're back in the Forties, Ruby. If Maggs says jump, you ask how high. You might have been the toast of the Crown on Thursday, but you're only one of the girls by Saturday. You know how it works.'

45

Saturday morning

The story is in the newspaper. Not the *Kensington Gazette*, but the *Daily Express*.

The *Express* has pursued the story with all of its famed crusading zeal. It has a perfect narrative at its heart: corrupt politicians mixing with rich men and notorious criminals. But the *Express* has made more of it even than that. Already, the reports have told of the aristocratic nightclub owner, and the drug dealers and the prostitutes that haunt his club. Peter Lazenby has been named, linked with criminal gangs from Southwark, Clerkenwell and Birmingham. Deals have been made with politicians that protect the interests of these gangs selling untaxed goods, and so blind eyes have been turned to criminal activity. The details are lurid even as the reality is squalid.

The police have acted swiftly. Men have been arrested. Mr Mortimer, the proprietor of a letting agency next door to the Angel, is among them. Bags of cocaine and crates of whisky were found in his cellar. A surprise raid by the police led to other arrests: men found in possession of stolen goods and women dealing in cocaine are now in the cells.

Ralph, too, has been mentioned by name. Unlike some newspapers, the *Express* favours putting news on the front cover, rather than cluttering it with advertisements. Ralph's name is prominent and visible from every newsstand. 'The golden boy with feet of clay', they have christened him. Everyone knows that mud, like clay, sticks. His name will always be associated with the scandal. With criminality and prostitution. There are others – Charles Haversham and Alexander Somers among them. Haversham is the one who controls the operations, who organises from the shadows, but it is Ralph Christie, the rising star, the bright hope of the party, whose name stands out to the public. Other newspapers are following the lead and making their own inquiries.

Isabel retired to bed yesterday, after she'd seen what the *Express* had published, and has not yet emerged from her room. Harriet's father has spent most of the last twenty-four hours at his club, speaking with associates, members of the party, friends in the police.

There was mention of women in the newspaper – unnamed girls working from the Angel nightclub. Ruby had not been specifically identified. But she might have been arrested.

Harriet shoves her hands deep into her coat pockets and trudges, head down, along the street. She needs to leave the house. Be somewhere else.

She heads to the offices of the *Kensington Gazette*. She has not been very often in recent days, but no one here will associate her with Ralph Christie. No one but Jimmy knows that she is – or was – engaged to him.

And she wants to find Jimmy. Wants to know how it is that the *Daily Express* has published the story he was investigating.

As luck would have it, he is leaving the building just as she arrives, carrying his typewriter, with his satchel over his shoulder.

'Harriet, hello.'

'Your story. The *Express*... How...?' She cannot now form the questions she wants to ask.

'I sold it to them.' He hitches the typewriter in his arms. 'I thought the story needed a newspaper with a larger circulation. They offered me a job on the strength of it – which is a good thing because Pickford has just fired me. Said I should have taken the story to him first.'

'Oh.'

'Look, I'm sorry, Harriet. I didn't know about you – about you and Ralph Christie – until the other day. It was too late by then. I'd already spoken with Blumenfeld, the editor at the *Express*. He wanted to run the story.'

The day they had both arrived late. Wednesday. He had been with Mr Blumenfeld that morning, had given him the story and taken a new job. Blumenfeld's regular reporters had worked on Jimmy's investigations, speedily made their own enquiries, and the story had gone to print on Friday.

'Of course, you didn't know. I never told anyone.' She stares up at the windows. 'I didn't want them to think that I wasn't serious about the job. That I would simply skip off one day to be married...' Her shoulders droop.

'You're still marrying him, then? Christie?' He looks at her hand. She is not wearing the diamond ring.

'It's in my pocket,' she says, flexing her fingers. 'The diamond the size of an egg. I don't know whether I'm marrying him or not. But at least I have my job here.'

'Well, with any luck, Pickford'll give you something more than the women's page to work on.'

'I doubt that. He doesn't think much of my work.'

Jimmy does not contradict her but grapples with the typewriter again. 'I should go. I have a new office to find my way around. And this thing is bloody heavy.'

'Will there be more of it, do you think? More about Ralph?'

'I don't know. I think the *Express* is done with it, but others will likely follow.' He gives her a sympathetic smile. 'I'm sorry, really. Not about Christie. Just sorry that you're caught up in it. You're a nice girl – and not a bad reporter. I hope everything works out well for you.'

'Thank you. You, too. It's what you've wanted, isn't it? A job at a national newspaper? I hope that it really is all you've worked for.'

He nods. 'So do I.'

'Mr Pickford was asking for you.' One of the younger reporters – Harriet has yet to learn his name – passes her on the stairs to the main hall.

'Thank you.' It is as Jimmy told her. Pickford will offer her more work, better work. This *is* what she wanted. She knows it now. Her stomach tenses as she climbs. Hang Ralph and the wedding.

She crosses the floor of the reporters' hall, oblivious to the noise and the fog of smoke. Mr Pickford's door is open. He sits at his desk, reading and smoking, and waves her in. The *Daily Express* lies, tossed in front of him, on top of all the nationals. Ralph's name jumps out at her. She stands, clutching her handbag, trying to ignore it.

He rests the half-smoked cigarette on the edge of his ashtray and gestures to a chair opposite him. 'Why don't you sit down? You look as though you need to.'

'Thank you.'

He sits watching her for a moment, before reaching again for the cigarette. 'I've decided,' he says, 'that your place is at home with your family.'

'At home?'

'You have matters to attend to. This' – he waves a hand over the *Express* – 'will need your time. Mr Christie. I understand that you are engaged to be married to the man.'

She does not know what to say.

He clears his throat. 'I'm letting you go, Miss Littlemore. Asking you to leave the *Gazette*.'

'But I like it here.' She hugs her handbag to her stomach. 'I like my job. I *need* my job. Especially now.'

'I don't doubt that.' He sighs. 'But I'm sorry. Your father has asked me to send you home.'

'My father did what?'

'Your father has written to me asking me to let you go.'

'But my job here is nothing to do with my father.' Her voice rises a little.

He rubs his temple, cigarette still between his fingers. 'It's everything to do with your father. I was only obliged to give you work in the first place because Mr Littlemore is a friend of the proprietor.'

'What?'

'Your father. He spoke to the owner of this newspaper, and you came to see me, and I offered you some work. You didn't know?'

He might as well have punched her. She slumps in the chair, winded.

'You assumed that you were hired on your own merit and ability? You think that I put up with your erratic timekeeping, your late arrivals and your early departures, because I like what you write?'

She stares at him, still uncomprehending. Her father spoke to the proprietor. That is how she came to have this job. All the time she has been here, Mr Pickford has been indulging her – and indulging her father. And now her father wants her to leave. Gerald will say, to anyone who asks, that she is leaving to be free to marry Ralph, to support him while the whirl of scandal surrounds him. But she knows that this is the quiet, devastating consequence of what happened in Selfridges. So, she must leave. All the time she has hidden her engagement in this office, for fear that Mr Pickford would think her flighty or fickle, the sort of woman who would take on a job and leave after a few months, and yet he never took her seriously at all. He had been saddled with her.

'You should go home, Harriet,' he says, not unkindly. 'Regardless of your father's orders, your family needs you.'

She does not wish to go home.

He taps ash into the tray. 'The *Express* and other newspapers will be watching to see how Mr Christie behaves. What he does, who he associates with. This story will blow over – stories always do – but scandal never quite disappears. People, readers, will want to be *reassured* that Mr Christie is, as he would like to appear, an honourable and upstanding member of society. A wife – or at least a fiancée – will help them to see that.'

'And what if he isn't an honourable man? What if he is exactly as the report describes him?'

Pickford stares at her, sucking the inside of his lower lip, before responding. 'Then I wish you all the luck in the world.'

There is nothing she can say or do that will change his mind. It is her father who has decided the matter. She might be the most brilliant writer in the world, a Shakespeare or Milton, and it would count for nothing. She neither gained the job nor lost it by anything that she did herself.

She stands and gives him a curt nod, unable to say anything more, not even a goodbye, for fear of screaming or sobbing.

She walks to her desk – to James Curran's desk – and collects her spare pencils and notebooks into her handbag.

She does not say a word to anyone as she leaves, fixing her lips so tightly together that she imagines her jaw will set.

46

Saturday morning, later

Harriet cannot return home. She is furious with her father – humiliated by him as much as by Ralph. She stamps away from Kensington. She travels east, not looking where she is going, only turning over and over in her mind the wrongs that have been done to her. She passes through Hyde Park, not noticing the crocuses that are now springing up under the trees in vibrant dabs of colour, so dark is her mood. The charming streets of Mayfair, where she had planned her future only days ago, are now oppressive. Behind every doorway of every elegant mansion, she imagines secrets, affairs, corruption and scandal. Who can tell, from the polished façade, what lurks inside?

Only when she discovers that she is in Soho does she slow her pace. It looks different, somehow, from how it had appeared to her before. There is a griminess and depravity about it. A man falls from the doorway of a public house, nearly crashing into her, oblivious of her in his drunkenness. The streets that were brightly coloured by electrical lights in the nighttime and full of fresh possibility in the daytime, now seem grey and miserable in their degeneracy. How curious that she didn't notice until now.

It is in this world that Ruby makes her existence. A wretched life.

She had tried not to think about Ruby over these last two days. She quickly failed in this, and so took to railing at her, in her own imagination, for stealing Ralph – for throwing herself, with all her obvious charms, at her fiancé. She has rehearsed feelings of resentment and jealousy because this is what she supposes she ought to feel.

But what she feels is sadness – grief, rather than betrayal. And, even now, she wants to know what has happened to Ruby. Wants to know that she is well. Safe. That is why she has come here. She is looking for Ruby.

She reaches the Angel and finds it closed. More than closed. It is chained and padlocked. A sign has been pinned to the door, saying that the club is closed until further notice. No other information is given. There is no Ruby. There is no one here at all.

She stands, staring, for several minutes, as people pass around her on the pavement.

Mr Mortimer's letting agency next door is also closed, and a similar notice hangs in the window.

She turns to go. She does not know where to, or what she will do.

Ruby. Ruby Mills is walking towards her, in that slow, sultry, hip-swinging way. This is what attracted Ralph, of course. Harriet can see it. She can understand it.

Ruby has not been arrested.

She pauses, briefly, seeing Harriet, and then continues forward until she reaches her.

'I understand the Angel is closed for a time,' is all that Harriet says.

'It is.'

'What a shame. You'll be returning to Southwark, then? Or are you still stealing from the jewellery shops this side of the river and making use of my name?'

Ruby smiles at that. 'I thought I'd go to Debenham and Freebody later. Always my favourite. How about you?'

Ruby had seemed to Harriet like a soaring bird – free, wild and exciting. She had seen a face, outside Mr Enderby's jewellery shop, so full of life and vigour. She had sat in a café, worshipping. Now, in the dreary daylight, she sees the tiredness, the heavy lids, the slight stoop of the shoulders. She sees a grubby, fast-living woman. Underneath the fashionable coat, red lips and bobbed hair, Ruby is dirty, unwashed, unremarkable.

And yet, here she stands, smirking as though she owns the street, holding Harriet in place.

Those lips had touched her cheek.

But that same mouth has kissed Ralph's. The thought of it makes her ache in her belly for something she cannot describe.

'I believe I shall go home,' Harriet declares.

Ruby stares at her own feet for moment before straightening herself and looking Harriet square in the face. She takes in the pinched expression. There is unhappiness in Harriet's eyes, and a puffiness to her cheeks suggests she has been crying. No wonder. Ruby has seen the newspapers.

Harriet Littlemore had no idea until recently what her fiancé was up to. And now the whole of London knows. The whole of England, even.

For all the money, the pearls, the honey-coloured coat and the smart family, Harriet is lost.

Ruby might almost feel pity.

But she is back with the Forties now. She was carried to her table at the Crown. They chanted her name. *Ruby, Ruby.*

She does not need this woman's name, nor manner, anymore.

She is Ruby Mills of the Borough. And she reigns supreme.

'Home to Ralph?' Harriet is not wearing her diamond ring, so perhaps not.

Harriet, on instinct, touches the pocket of her coat, frowning at the mention of his name.

'No. To my parents' house. My home.'

'Onslow Square. I remember. I'll let you be on your way.' Ruby steps aside to allow her to pass, sweeping her arm in a graceful arc and beaming at Harriet. 'This is no place for a lady, after all.'

No one had seen it happen, and Harriet was too flustered by the encounter to notice, but the carefully folded handkerchief was no longer in her pocket when she came to search for it later.

Ruby turns the key in the door of her apartment. She will gather up her clothes and take them back to the Borough. Some of her clothes. Now that she is with the Forties again, she needs her ordinary daytime coats and hats to be at Solly's. She'll leave the nightclub gowns here. Even with Peter gone, she might still come this way sometimes, take a bath, wander out to a club or restaurant with someone… The rent is paid for a couple of months, and the apartment is useful.

She breathes deeply as she enters. There is a light, fresh aroma in the air. She can smell his cologne.

He is in the bedroom, stretched out on the bed, waiting for her, a picture of ease and contentment.

'What are you doing here?'

'I have a key, remember?'

'I thought you'd be on the run,' she says. She pulls open the drawer of her bedside table and drops in a gold pocket watch and, next to it, a diamond ring, marquise cut, recently acquired. She pushes Harriet's handkerchief back into her coat pocket.

'I am, after a fashion,' he says, pulling her onto the bed. 'I need to leave London. Not for long. Just a few months. I'll be back when the dust settles.'

'You think you'll avoid the coppers?'

He laughs. 'I don't need to avoid them, sweetheart. I've been speaking with them all morning – the ones I know. We've agreed that I'll lie low for a while. As I told you, I have friends I can call on when I'm in trouble.'

'Where will you go?'

'Paris, I thought.'

'What about me?' She slips a hand under his shirt and traces her fingers over his stomach. 'Take me with you. I'd like to go to Paris.'

'Not this time.' He reaches for her hand and clasps her fingers. 'I'm travelling alone. Besides, I hear you're back with Diamond Annie.'

'I am. But I'd still prefer to be in Paris. What happens if I'm in trouble? Who do I call on?'

'Annie will look after you. The Forties.' He begins to unbutton her dress. 'Annie knows what she's doing. I only called to see you before I go.'

Annie is upset that Freddy is in a police cell. Annie Richmond, who never cries, has not left the house for a day. She's sobbing. That's what Solly told her over breakfast. Freddy Moss and Billy Walsh have been arrested. Their rich friend has abandoned them – only looking out for himself – Ruby is certain of that now. They would have been better off sticking with Billy Kimber after all.

'No,' she says, pushing his hand away. 'I ain't got time for this. You're not the only one who needs to be somewhere else. Maggs is waiting for me on Oxford Street. Like you said, the Forties look out for me, and I look out for them. I have a job to do – especially if the Angel won't be paying me now.'

She swings herself from the bed and checks her reflection in the mirror.

He watches her, arms folded behind his head, chuckling.

'Alright. I can wait. How about you come back when you've finished your job in town and I'll take you out for dinner? We'll go somewhere new. Go dancing in a place where I'm not responsible for the staff.'

Ruby fixes her make-up and paints on a fresh slick of lipstick. She will make him spend a lot of money. 'I won't be long.'

47

Harriet stiffens as soon as she enters the hallway. Voices. Men's voices.

Ralph.

She treads quietly across the hallway, towards the stairs. She will go upstairs without them knowing she has arrived.

The loose block on the parquet floor makes a *clack clack* sound as she steps on it.

Hanson, lurking in the doorway of the drawing room, pokes his head around the frame, as though he has been waiting for her.

'Miss Littlemore, I believe your father would like to speak with you.' His voice is clear, precise and loud.

'Thank you, Hanson, but I should like to go to my room.'

Hanson's greeting has brought her father out from his study.

'Harriet, we were just speaking of you. Come…' He waves an arm, as if gathering her into a soirée. There is no doubt in his mind that she will follow.

She does, compliant from years of training and finds herself standing, still in her coat and hat, in his study.

She rarely enters her father's sanctuary. It is a gloomy room, even in the daytime, lined with bookshelves and set with dark furniture. His vast mahogany desk sits in the bay window, enjoying most of the light, but the rest of the room is always shadowy.

Although the air is thick with tobacco smoke, she can make out not only Ralph, but Arthur MacKenzie present in the room. Both men rise from their seats to greet her. Inspector MacKenzie, stony-faced, gives her only a stern nod. Ralph steps forward, both hands extended as if to catch hold of hers.

She folds her arms and frowns. 'Ralph.'

'Harriet, darling, I've been trying to see you for these past days. You look…'

'I look, what, Ralph? Insulted? Confused? Foolish?'

He takes a step back.

'Clearly, the two of you will have matters to discuss.' Gerald takes control of the situation, in a smooth voice. 'But for now, Harriet, you should sit down.'

He leads her to a seat and lowers her into it. She looks out – and up – at the men in the room. For the first time in her life, she wishes her mother were present.

Ralph reaches into his jacket and finds his cigarettes.

She wonders where her mother is. Out. Or still in bed.

Gerald clears his throat as if preparing to address a meeting. 'We have experienced a difficult forty-eight hours. Certain matters have come to light that would have been better kept hidden from public scrutiny. The important thing is that we stand together, and we stand firm.'

'Peter Lazenby's nightclub has closed – temporarily, probably – which will take some of the heat away,' MacKenzie says. 'Lazenby himself has gone to ground for now and will stay quiet. I've spoken with him myself earlier today and he's given assurances. We have arrested a number of drug dealers, along with several women who worked out of the club, and some of the notorious Elephant gang who were carrying stolen goods to various locations around London.'

'I see,' Harriet says tightly. 'And what of the others? The connected and titled men mentioned by the newspapers who have supported and made money off the back of such illegal business practices?' She doesn't look at Ralph.

MacKenzie straightens his back. 'There is very little to connect the criminal activity taking place in the club with anyone of significance. You should be glad of that.'

Little to connect. The police are not investigating further, he means.

'Indeed, we shall probably find that Mr Lazenby himself is only partially aware of what has been happening under his nose. Gentlemen like him can be very naïve, trusting.'

Harriet cannot believe what she is hearing. 'Peter Lazenby is at the centre of it, inspector. You know that as well as I do. Along with Ralph and Charles Haversham.'

'It's not a matter of knowing, Miss Littlemore. It is a matter of evidence. If there is no evidence of wrongdoing, then, whatever the newspapers might insinuate, no court will convict them.'

'But it will convict the drug dealers, the prostitutes and the Elephant Boys who have been doing his bidding? How very convenient.'

'But the good news, Harriet,' Gerald interjects, 'is that if a passing wartime friendship with Peter Lazenby is all that connects Ralph to the nightclub, and Lazenby himself is relatively unscathed, then Ralph's reputation is intact. A little tittle-tattle in the newspapers can easily be dismissed.'

'As long as the mud doesn't stick,' Ralph says, somewhat ruefully, playing with his cigarette case.

'It won't,' Gerald says confidently. 'There is plenty of other news to occupy the journalists. The world will move on and forget about this episode. And by the time an election is called, your star will be on the rise once more. I have it on the best authority.'

And that is that, Harriet thinks. The deals will continue, men like Lazenby will befriend politicians like Charles Haversham and Ralph and operate unhindered – protected – in return for money. Like army generals, they will send their troops to do the dirty work – troops who will risk capture and prison for cash, glory and thrill – while they remain unconnected and unseen. Fine words about honour, courage, duty will be tossed about in high-blown political rhetoric, but away in darkened rooms and nightclubs, the grubby deals will still be done. Somehow this will be of benefit to the country, perhaps. It will keep the world in balance. Everyone will be better off.

Men like Jimmy Cartwright will keep digging away, trying to discover the truth. How long before even he is corrupted, bought, encouraged to keep silent?

Parasites feeding on parasites. She feels sick. She does not know which is worse: that it happens at all or that she has only now come to know of it.

The men are talking amongst themselves, ignoring her. The sound of their conversation echoes, sombre but mildly congratulatory, inside her head.

'Thank you,' she says, standing up, interrupting. 'Thank you for enlightening me.'

'I knew you'd understand, Harrio.' Her father rises to be with her, catching her hands in an affectionate gesture, reminding her of when she was a child. 'We can salvage this together.'

She shakes her hands loose. She is not a child anymore.

'And I have asked the inspector to redouble his efforts regarding that girl you wrote about, the one using your name when she was stealing jewellery. We wouldn't want *your* name connected with jewellery thefts now, after all, would we?' Gerald smiles at his daughter, but there is a sharpness to his voice, and she catches the insinuation.

'Yes, I've already had a brush with Ruby Mills.' Arthur MacKenzie says, standing.

'What's that?' Ralph looks over.

'Ruby Mills,' MacKenzie says, turning to address him. 'The thief Harriet wrote about. She raided another jewellery shop on Thursday.'

'Did you catch her?' Ralph asks casually enough, but his eyes are bright with interest.

'No,' Harriet says. 'No, he did not catch her.'

'No,' MacKenzie admits. 'She slipped away. Managed to swap several expensive rings and brooches with paste imitations, and the shop assistant didn't even notice until she'd gone. But I had her so nearly in my grasp.'

'Next time, then, let's hope.' Ralph shakes his head, the hint of a smile on his lips. 'She's audacious, that's for certain.'

'I've increased the patrols in her favourite stores,' MacKenzie says, standing taller, as if he imagines that Ruby will see him and be intimidated. He turns back to Harriet. 'I've circulated a description of her around her old haunts.'

'She will be in Debenham and Freebody this afternoon.' Harriet flourishes this knowledge before she can stop herself.

'How do you know this?' MacKenzie gives her one of his fatherly smiles. 'Did she tell you?'

'Yes,' she says, still bridling at his manner towards her. 'As it happens, she told me not two hours ago.'

MacKenzie blinks at her. 'She told you?'

'Yes.'

Ralph is staring at her, incredulous.

'Then I had better leave you, Gerald,' MacKenzie says. 'If Harriet's information is correct, then I need to be near Oxford Street.'

Gerald calls for Hanson.

Harriet feels sick. Ruby will be caught now. It will end, and it will be her fault. She puts a hand on the back of the armchair.

'Well done, Harrio!' Gerald beams at his daughter, not seeing the dismay on her face. 'Looks as though you might have helped the inspector find your thief. My clever girl.'

'Who is not clever enough to have a job, apparently,' Harriet says, fighting to contain a storm of emotions. 'A job I rather enjoyed. Mr Pickford has dispensed with my services, thanks to you, Daddy. He said that you wrote to him and asked that I should be relieved of my duties.'

Gerald grasps her shoulders and squeezes her. 'Well, your place is here, Harriet. You can see that now, I think. Ralph and I are agreed that you should be married sooner rather than later. I appraised him of your own situation, that business in Selfridges, and he has – very chivalrously, I must say – already made the arrangements for next month. And the dear boy will need you more than ever now – yes? This will work out well for him, too. A solid family man, respectable wife, and all that. His career depends on you.'

'And mine, it appears, is unimportant.' She twists away from him, stands for a moment, surveying the two men who have decided her future between them, and then turns to leave, desperate to escape.

'I need to take off my hat.'

She stumbles into the hallway, pushing past Hanson.

Ralph runs after her and grasps her hand.

'Harriet, we should talk.'

'I'm not sure that I wish to talk with you, Ralph. At least, not now. You'll appreciate that discovering my fiancé is embroiled in drug dealing, prostitution, and everything else, has been quite a thing.'

'Harriet –'

'And discovering that he enjoys the company of prostitutes for his personal pleasure is quite another.'

'No, that's too far. Don't be ridiculous.'

'Ridiculous? You didn't leave the club with Ruby Mills the other night? Take her home? To what is supposed to be *our* home?'

'What? How could you know about that?'

She closes her eyes for a moment. He has not even tried to deny it. She shakes her head and says nothing.

'I still want to marry you, Harriet,' he says in subdued tones. 'It will be for the best – for both of us.'

She opens her eyes. 'I don't know. I don't know that I can bear it.'

'I love you. You must know that.'

It is the first time he has said this to her. What he loves, has always loved, is the prospect of being Gerald Littlemore's son-in-law.

'I'm tired, Ralph. In the last twenty-four hours, I have lost my job and discovered that the world does not work in the way I had always assumed. I think I need to rest.'

'Of course. You're tired. I'll return later, if you like.' He reaches, instinctively, into his pocket for his watch, to suggest a time. He frowns. His watch is still missing. 'Never mind. Perhaps I should go now, as you say. Leave you in peace.' He ends this stuttering speech with a small bow. A kiss, even on the cheek, would be too much – he appears to recognise this.

Harriet turns away, unable to face him. 'Very well. Perhaps you may visit later. Tomorrow.'

48

Saturday afternoon

They are waiting for her on Wigmore Street. She can see Maggs and Florrie. Edith is ahead, on her own, pretending to be separate. She won't want to work with Ruby. She's still sore that Billy was so friendly the other day, when everyone was singing her name in the Crown. She's probably sore about that, too.

Ruby nods to Maggs.

'I'm sending Florrie in with Edith,' Maggs says. 'I'm not coming in – not with my face like this.' She is still sporting a shiner from her altercation with the doorman from Carrington's, a bruise on her cheek turning from purple to yellow and sludge brown. 'I'm going to wait outside.'

'Alright. That means I'm on my own?'

'Yeah. You'll be good. We're after gloves and scarves. Second floor. Best you can find and fur-lined, if you can. Straight in and out, no messing about.'

Ruby rolls her eyes. 'I don't mess about.'

'No daydreaming, then.'

Ruby laughs. 'I lifted several hundred pounds worth of diamonds the other day and you're fretting about gloves. I know what I'm doing.'

'I know. I always worry.'

'Mother hen,' Ruby laughs back.

'I'll take you out later, little chick. Let's go to the pictures, eh?'

She is tempted. Tempted to leave Peter Lazenby waiting for her all night while she loses herself in the moving pictures for hours.

Ruby leaves Maggs on the street and takes a deep breath in the great hall of Debenham and Freebody. The light scent of fragrance is welcome. She wanders to the glass counter and asks, in her most charming voice, for a dab of perfume. Lily of the Valley. It is a simple smell, and not her usual, but it is innocent. She can walk around the second floor smelling like an English summer's day, like a perfect, fragrant lady. No one will pay her any attention.

She drifts up the grand staircase, admiring the chandeliers, as she always does. The light catches them, and she imagines that each glass droplet is a diamond. The second floor is dull. Maggs has given her the gloves to remind her that she is just an ordinary thief, hoisting with the others. By Maggs's reckoning, Ruby will get above herself, if she's only ever lifting jewels. Gloves will keep her in her place.

Ruby sighs. Perhaps she'll go to Soho later, after all. She can't decide. Peter will treat her, he has said. She could have champagne and dancing and whatever else he decides, or she could share a quarter of aniseed balls and Rudolph Valentino with Maggs.

She picks up a buttoned glove to examine it. Maggs wanted fur. She puts it back down and circles the table, where they are all laid out for inspection. She lifts a blue pair, trimmed with rabbit fur. The fur is soft. Briefly, she remembers Harriet. She drops them into her inside coat pocket and moves further around the table to examine a second pair.

She might wear the red dress again. He liked that one. It is the most sensual of her outfits, and she loves the feel of the silk on her skin. But she also has the emerald-green one that will enhance her eyes. Or she could look for a new outfit later.

She drops the second pair of gloves into her pocket and shoves three further pairs deep into the lining as she muses. What else was she supposed to lift?

The scarves are located over on the other side of the floor. She flicks through them, taking off her own gloves and running a hand over the silk. She glances around to make sure that no one is looking and twists one quickly into a ball, and then a second, and a third, pushing them into her sleeve.

That should do. Maggs won't mind that she's only picked up a few items. She'll be out with the Forties again in a day or two.

She trots down the stairs to the ground floor, to the main hall.

A display catches her eye. Pretty paste jewellery, laid out in circles. Brooches, necklaces, rings. It's nothing like the jewellery she took from that smart jeweller, but the way the shop assistants have laid it out makes it all shimmer brightly. They have set the pieces out on a table covered in dark blue velvet cloth under one of the vast chandeliers. They glint up at her as she passes, like bright stars against the night's sky.

Clever.

She picks up a brooch, a crescent moon, like the one she so admired from Gloucester Road, the one Solly took from her and broke into pieces. She had wanted that brooch so much.

She slips the moon into her pocket and turns towards the exit.

Maggs will be waiting.

A hand clamps down on her shoulder, hard.

She twists to escape from whoever is behind her, but the hand holds her tightly and her arm is thrust up her back.

A man comes running. A woman is shouting from behind her. Another man speeds to assist.

She wrestles free, only to find herself grabbed again.

She struggles like an animal, cursing, shrieking murder, and at the edge of her blurring vision, she sees Florrie and Edith heading for the door.

She is pushed, without warning, against a counter, and more hands, men's hands, invade her coat, under her skirts, feeling for the pockets and secret linings they know will be in there. They pull out scarves like magicians, along with the gloves and the single, crescent-shaped paste brooch, and lay them all on the counter next to her.

'Hello, Ruby.' A familiar voice at her back. She is permitted to turn and face him.

Inspector MacKenzie smiles brightly. 'Fancy finding you here.'

'Ah, shit.'

49

Four months later

Ruby stands outside the door of her apartment. She touches her hair, freshly cut.

She used to dream about this place – the whiteness of the walls, the softness of the bed – when she was lying in her stinking cell.

She licks her lips. Best not to think of it. Three months of her life given over to picking coir. She examines her nails for the coarse fibres from the ropes even now. She did this each evening in Holloway, meticulously, before the lights were turned out. It will be weeks before her hands recover. She clenches her fists to hide the battered tips of her fingers. She'll need a new pair of gloves.

She has been out of prison for a week. The girls – and Solly – welcomed her back as they always welcome back Forties, like a war hero, a film star. She wears her imprisonment with honour, like the boys wear their medals, knowing that she has served the Forties well. She was, at least, lifting for them when she was caught, and not for herself.

For a week, she has sat in the Crown every night, regaining her old life.

She has endured Annie Richmond's Woodbine breath, and Maggs cuffing her on the shoulder every time she sees her, just to 'make sure she's there and awake and not daydreaming again'. Daisy is growing stronger, too – and no longer taking in men. Annie has her out hoisting, now that Freddy Moss is inside Pentonville and unable to criticise.

She has listened to Edith Lennox whining about how Billy will be away for months. He's left her unmarried and with a baby in her belly, so she'll have even more to whine about soon enough. She won't be out on raids once the baby appears, but, for now, a pregnant woman is useful to the Forties. Untouchable in the shops. Edith is lifting more than she has ever done before. It's almost as though the baby is giving her new enthusiasm and energy, a fearlessness.

By day, Ruby has tidied up Solly's shop – swept the floor without a murmur, arranged the jewellery and written up his accounts. Solly has been cooking as though he's feeding an army. She needs feeding, he tells her. He's not wrong. Her coat is still hanging off her shoulders and her cheeks are hollow. Prison food did not agree with her any more than prison life, and she has grown scrawny. She smiles less these days, he says.

But now, she's ready to be rid of them all and back in her own place – at least for a time. She craves the silence and the solitude after prison. And, truth be told, she is drawn once again to the possibilities of the Soho lights, the dancefloor and the champagne.

She told Solly she was going over the river to collect her clothes.

Soho is different in the summer, she decides. Cleaner and somehow less exuberant in the morning sunshine. She will grow used to it.

She stands in the hallway, fingering the key in her pocket. They had taken her coat from her in prison, and the rest of her clothes, and she had worried that the key might have been lost. But it had been safe, tucked into the lining.

Still, she cannot bring herself to try the lock. The rent was overdue some weeks ago.

Eventually, she pulls the key from her pocket, turns it in the lock and pushes the door. It opens. For a moment, she stands on the threshold breathing deeply, closing her eyes, anticipating the loveliness. Not wanting to take any of it for granted.

She catches the scent.

It is this that brings the grin to her lips.

Mrs Ralph Christie sits in front of her dressing table mirror, examining her new haircut in the afternoon light. The man in Chelsea with the French accent really does know how best to style it.

Ralph will be home shortly. He left for Westminster this morning as usual but promised to be home by five.

Her parents are dining with them this evening, and everything will be perfect. Her servants, her beautiful porcelain crockery and her choice of menu will all stand up to her mother's scrutiny.

She has spent the day, as she spends most of her days now, planning dinner with the cook in the morning after breakfast, encouraging the maid to tidy the rooms with a little more effort and choosing flowers for the vases in the drawing room. Delphiniums today, cut from the garden. She did make a brief excursion to Hartleys to find some handkerchiefs for Ralph. She also took a look at the display of summer shoes but decided that she did not like any of them enough to buy.

She read the *Daily Express* this afternoon. Jimmy Cartwright had written a report on some trades' union meeting in Glasgow. She read it several times over, remembering the last time she saw Jimmy, clutching his typewriter, but paying little attention to the piece itself, which did not interest her at all.

There have been no more disagreeable insinuations about Ralph in the newspapers since the spring. The fuss surrounding his connections with a Soho nightclub has, as her father predicted, long since died away.

Her own pretensions to a career have also died. The notebooks and pencils that she had collected from her desk at the *Kensington Gazette* lie untouched in the bureau in Ralph's study. Occasionally, she imagines she might pick up a pen and write something and send it to a magazine or a newspaper, to see whether it might be published. But she knows this is a fanciful notion – and besides, there is so much else to do, now she is married. She wonders how she ever had time for a job. Her old schoolfriend, Charlotte Gibbs, is trying to encourage her to sit on a charity committee, which will also occupy her enormously. And she will travel to the constituency with Ralph next week.

She pulls open a drawer, hunting for a pot of lipstick in a particular shade. A short hairstyle seems to require a touch more make-up – and she no longer has to listen to her mother's disapproval about painting herself like a harlot if she doesn't wish to. She is a married woman now, not a child at home.

They married quickly. At Easter, on a squally April morning, soon after that terrible business with the Angel. And Selfridges. There was no point in waiting, her father had said, once she had decided that marrying Ralph would be alright after all.

It is alright, being married. She is quite content. *Quite* content. She reminds herself of this every evening just before Ralph returns so that she is sure to greet him with a smile.

The sun is warm. Real June weather, and a glorious day. Perhaps they will have cocktails in the garden before dinner. People do that sort of thing in Mayfair.

Her fingers find a small manicure case in the drawer. She knew it would be there, next to the lipstick. She plucks it out, as she does often, allowing it to rest on the palm of her hand. She strokes the cool tortoiseshell with her thumb, marvelling, as she always does, at the smoothness of it. It might be made from silk.

Ruby should be out of Holloway prison by now. Harriet has been counting the days since she saw an account of the trial in the newspaper. She might bump into her on the street, should she ever wish to visit Soho or Southwark. It is unlikely that she will.

In Debenham and Freebody or Hartleys, perhaps. Not Selfridges, of course. She never goes there now.

She puts the case back in the drawer and paints her lips, staring at her reflection, wondering whether anyone would say, these days, that she looked *alive*.

She reaches for a glass bottle and dabs herself with perfume. Her favourite. She has worn it every evening since marrying Ralph.

She tells herself that she wears it to keep him faithful – a subtle reminder that she remembers his infidelity.

She breathes in the scent of jasmine and fastens her earrings into her earlobes. The emeralds catch the light and sparkle.

Historical Note

The Dazzle of the Light is set in a very particular period. 1920 is not 'the 1920s', and the images of flappers, gin palaces, Bright Young Things and hedonism that we might associate with the 20s had not yet come into focus. Instead, Britain and other parts of Europe were grappling with the catastrophic aftermath of the Great War and the Influenza Pandemic. Many were scrapping to make a living. Men returned from war bewildered and altered – physically and mentally. Women were in the very early stages of enfranchisement and professional employment. The Representation of the People Act, enabling women to vote, was passed in 1918, but only for women over thirty who held property.

The Forty Thieves were a real, all-female crime syndicate who had been in existence since at least the nineteenth century, in some form or another. They were in their heyday around 1920, when department stores like Selfridges and Debenham and Freebody offered opportunities for shoplifting and were only beginning to realise that they needed eagle-eyed store detectives to tackle this issue.

The Forties were glamorous and ruthless, and caught the attention of reporters whenever they appeared in court, dressed up to the nines. The gang was always led by a 'queen', and the most famous of these leaders was Alice Diamond, who provided the inspiration for my Queen of the Thieves, Annie Richmond. Many of the crimes and schemes in this novel are based on the Forties's real-life activities. Later in the 1920s, they became known as the Forty Elephants – possibly a hint at their association with the south London Elephant and Castle gang, or maybe a reference to how they looked when they padded the insides of their clothes with stolen goods.

If you want to learn more about the Forty Thieves/Elephants, then a good place to start is Brian McDonald's *Alice Diamond and the Forty Elephants: Britain's First Female Crime Syndicate.*

Debenham and Freebody sadly no longer exists (Debenhams was liquidated in May 2021, as I was submitting this novel). Whiteleys was a store in Bayswater. Selfridges still rules Oxford Street. Hartleys, the store on Kensington High Street where Ruby first makes her appearance, is entirely my own creation.

If you would like to know more about early twentieth-century department stores, then look at *Shopping, Seduction & Mr Selfridge* by Lindy Woodhead.

The *Kensington Gazette* also emerged from my imagination, but in this period, there were many small-scale local newspapers offering regular – even daily – news. You can find out more in Kevin Williams's *Read All About It!: A History of the British Newspaper.*

The Angel nightclub is loosely inspired by the 43 Club on Gerrard Street, run by the infamous Kate Meyrick. In 1920, Meyrick was running Dalton's, in Leicester Square, mentioned in this novel by some of Ruby's colleagues. Later that same year, the 43 opened. See Judith R. Walkowitz's *Nights Out: Life in Cosmopolitan London.*

The cocktail Harriet drinks in the novel – the White Lady – was allegedly invented by real-life Savoy bartender Harry Craddock in 1920 when he joined the hotel. When the American Bar was refurbished in 1927, he buried the ingredients in a cocktail shaker in the walls: 2 parts gin, 1 part Cointreau, 1 part lemon juice, shaken over ice and strained. Enjoy.

Acknowledgements

I would like to thank my editor, Jenna Gordon, and the whole team at VERVE Books, not only for loving this novel from the start, but for working with such care and attention to bring it to publication. It has been a joy to work with an editor who understood the characters as well as I did, and a team so committed to making the novel come alive.

Thank you to Elsa Mathern for capturing the essence of the book so beautifully and dynamically with this cover.

As always, I am grateful to my agent, Laura Macdougall at United Agents, who juggled my writerly hopes and dreams alongside a new baby – hello, Thea! – and to Olivia Davies, also of United Agents, whose initial prompt led to this book.

As I researched this novel, I made contact with writers whose knowledge of the history and culture of the period immediately after the First World War helped me immensely. Among them were Lucy Jane Santos, who gave me tips about early-twentieth-century make-up and shopping – and sent me down some delightful fashion website rabbit holes – and Jonathan Holmes, who shared his awesome knowledge of the music of that period.

The life of this book began exactly a hundred years after the date it is set, in March 2020. Writing it was my solace during the first Covid lockdown, undertaken mostly in the early hours of the morning, when, like many others, I was restless and awake. In the daytime, I was (again, like many others) trying to do my job via Zoom and simultaneously teaching a reluctant nine-year-old how to calculate percentages and use adjectives. So, I salute, in passing, my son's teachers at King's St Alban's and my former colleagues at Worcester Cathedral.

I spent a lot of time during lockdown with my son, Sebastian, and my husband, Tim. I am always happy to be in their company, even though I was forced to watch far too many Marvel films in 2020. Tim, at least, was happy to engage in cocktail research during lockdown – which we decided was crucial to the novel.

This book is, in part, about female friendship. I am blessed with many wonderful friends whose laughter and good sense keep me going. In particular, I'm shouting out to Yvonne Pollitt, Sarah Henderson, Jenny Floyd, Elaine Wilmore, Hannah Persaud, Kay Garlick, Nikki Groarke and my cousin, Meriel Comley-Bull.

But this book is dedicated to two dear friends who know me almost more than I know myself, whose opinions matter greatly and with whom I have laughed and cried for many years: Faith Claringbull and Jane Tillier.

Book Club Questions for *The Dazzle of the Light*

1) How sympathetic do you find Ruby and Harriet's personal plights? Do you think Harriet's opportunities are as limited as Ruby's? Could either of them ever hope to fulfil their ambitions?

2) How do you view the Forty Thieves and the crimes they commit? Are they amoral and dangerous, or do you think their actions are justified and deserving of compassion?

3) Ruby Mills is preoccupied by glamour – why do you think this is, and where do you think her ideas about glamour come from?

4) What do you think of Harriet's desire to help Ruby, and her notions of how to do so? Does Ruby need to be helped?

5) Discuss Harriet's parents' reactions to Ralph's scandal. What would you do if you were in Harriet's position? Is Harriet's relationship with her father better or worse than the one she has with her mother?

6) What role do men play in the novel? How do they treat and relate to Ruby and Harriet? And how do Ruby and Harriet view them?

7) There are strong currents of desire within the novel, but is there any love – romantic or otherwise?

8) Do you think Ruby's future lies with the Forties? If not, what might her life look like?

**If you enjoyed *The Dazzle of the Light*, look out for *The Lost Girls*
by Heather Young, available now from VERVE Books!**

In 1935, six-year-old Emily Evans vanishes from her family's summer house
on a remote Minnesota lake. Her disappearance destroys the family – her
father takes his own life, and her mother and two older sisters spend the rest
of their lives at the lake house, keeping a decades-long vigil for the lost child.

Sixty years later, Lucy, the quiet and watchful middle sister, lives in the lake
house alone. Before her death, she writes the story of that devastating
summer in a notebook that she leaves, along with the house, to the only
person who might care: her grandniece, Justine. For Justine, the lake house
offers freedom and stability – a way to escape her manipulative boyfriend
and give her daughters the home she never had. But the long Minnesota
winter is just beginning. The house is cold and dilapidated. The dark, silent
lake is isolated and eerie. Her only neighbour is a strange old man who seems
to know more about the summer of 1935 than he's telling…

'Haunting'
***Sunday Times* (Crime Book of the Month)**

'An absorbing neo-gothic novel'
***Times & Sunday Times Crime Club* (Pick of the Week)**

VERVEBOOKS.CO.UK/THE-LOST-GIRLS

VERVE BOOKS

Launched in 2018, VERVE Books is an independent
publisher of page-turning, diverse and original
fiction from new and exciting voices.

Our books are connected by rich, story-driven
narratives, vividly atmospheric settings and memorable
characters. The list is tightly curated by a small team of
passionate booklovers whose hope is that, if you love
one VERVE book, you'll love them all!

VERVE Books is a separate entity but run in parallel
with Oldcastle Books, whose imprints include the iconic,
award-winning crime fiction list No Exit Press.

**WANT TO JOIN THE CONVERSATION AND FIND OUT
MORE ABOUT WHAT WE DO?**

Catch us on social media or sign up to our newsletter
for all the latest news from VERVE HQ.

vervebooks.co.uk/signup

📷 f 𝕏 ♪ **@VERVE_Books**